KNIGHT OF FLAMES

INHERITANCE, BOOK TWO

AK FAULKNER

KNIGHT of FLAMES

A.K. FAULKNER

Knight of Flames © AK Faulkner 2019.
Cover design by Dominic Forbes.

All rights reserved. No part of this story may be used, reproduced or transmitted in any form or by any means without written permission of the copyright holder, except in the case of brief quotations embodied within critical reviews and articles.

This book is a work of fiction. The names, characters, places, and incidents are products of the writer's imagination or have been used fictitiously and are not to be construed as real. Any resemblance to persons, living or dead, actual events, locale or organizations is entirely coincidental.

The right of AK Faulkner to be identified as author of this work has been asserted by them in accordance with the Copyright, Designs and Patents Act, 1988.

First electronic publication: August 2016.
Third edition: September 2019.

discoverinheritance.com

Jack of Thorns is set in the USA, and as such uses American English throughout.

CONTENTS

Prologue	1
1. Quentin	7
2. Quentin	14
3. Laurence	20
4. Quentin	26
5. Quentin	33
6. Laurence	39
7. Quentin	45
8. Laurence	51
9. Quentin	57
10. Laurence	63
11. Quentin	69
12. Quentin	77
13. Quentin	84
14. Quentin	93
15. Laurence	98
16. Laurence	104
17. Quentin	109
18. Quentin	117
19. Quentin	124
20. Quentin	131
21. Laurence	137
22. Laurence	143
23. Quentin	149
24. Quentin	155
25. Laurence	162
26. Laurence	168
27. Quentin	174
28. Quentin	181
29. Laurence	189
30. Quentin	195

31. Quentin	201
32. Laurence	207
33. Quentin	212
34. Laurence	218
35. Quentin	223
36. Quentin	230
37. Laurence	237
38. Quentin	244
39. Laurence	250
40. Quentin	256
41. Laurence	264
42. Quentin	270
43. Laurence	274
44. Laurence	278
45. Quentin	283
46. Laurence	291
47. Quentin	297
48. Laurence	303
49. Quentin	311
50. Laurence	317
51. Quentin	324
52. Laurence	328
53. Quentin	336
54. Laurence	342
55. Quentin	348
56. Laurence	356
57. Quentin	362
Epilogue	373
Acknowledgments	377
About the author	379
Inheritance	381

PROLOGUE

SIX YEARS AGO

It was only the second-worst day of Quentin's life.

The first was last week, when he found the body. Now he sat in furious silence, eyes forward, the killer to his left and the innocents on his right, while a stream of well-wishers and onlookers passed her coffin to pay their respects.

The coffin was absurd, almost repugnant. It seemed preposterous that she could be in there at all. It was mahogany with brass rails along each side for the pallbearers to lift it by, but most of the casket was covered by cloth which bore her crest as the Duchess of Oxford, bright and colorful on such a dismal day.

His thighs hurt. The black wool of his suit's trousers was not enough to keep his fingers from digging into his flesh.

"Do not disappoint, Quentin." His father remained motionless, and his voice was a low rumble. "Your mother would not wish for you to disrupt her service."

He felt his fury ratchet up another notch. It burned deep in his core, hot and cold all at once, sucking the energy from his body, his thoughts, and his patience.

We would not be here if you had not killed her.

He daren't say it, though. No. If those words spilled out of him, he would lose his self-control, and his mother deserved better. As much as he despised his father, the fact was that this was Mama's funeral, and anything which had to be said could wait until she was peacefully interred in the family mausoleum.

The thought of that once-vibrant woman rotting away in catacombs turned the dial another notch.

"Icky," Freddy whispered.

Quentin managed to swivel his eyes to the right and met his twin brother's gaze. Frederick was only hours younger than himself, but where Quentin had inherited dark hair from their father, Freddy had lucked out with Mother's blonde. They both had Father's eyes, though: colorless, almost uncanny.

"Just get through this," Freddy continued. "For Nicky's sake."

Quentin's focus shifted. Beyond Freddy was Nicholas, their younger brother. Quentin and Freddy were nineteen, but poor Nicholas was six years behind them.

God, what an age to lose a mother.

The poor boy was struggling to maintain his composure, but he hadn't the practice Quentin and Freddy held under their belts. The funeral was enough to fray the edges of Quentin's nerves, but Nicholas was teetering on the edge, his eyes red-rimmed and bright and his cheeks pale in contrast.

Quentin looked to Freddy again, desperate to pull some strength from him. How could he be so damn calm, so collected?

Freddy inclined his head faintly. "Just one more hour, Icky," he whispered. "That's all I ask."

Quentin gave the slightest of nods and returned his gaze to the coffin. The rage failed to subside, but at least—for now—it had stopped growing.

He had found her in her rose garden.

The weather was glorious, not a cloud in the sky, and he was home early from a day in London visiting with friends. Freddy was off at university on the first year of his studies, but Quentin was too thick for university and so hadn't even applied.

She loved her roses. She tended them every day, even if only to pluck away the occasional dead leaf. Father often argued that it was a task for the gardeners, but she wouldn't allow them near her garden. It was her space.

He found her on the ground, and at first he thought perhaps she had just fallen. But she was so pale. So ashen.

He knew that she was dead.

It was a ball of ice in his gut, that knowledge. For all that he ran to her and tried to wake her, he knew that she was cold and empty. The pallor of her skin was like nothing he had ever seen on a living person.

Living people weren't gray.

He had no real grasp of what occurred after that. Father claimed one of the staff heard him scream and sent for an ambulance, but Father was a liar. All Quentin knew was that he didn't sleep that night.

The priest was talking.

Quentin blinked and struggled to pay attention. The stream of people going past had ended, and now some religious figurehead was making long-winded statements about how beloved the Duchess was. Quentin wasn't at all sure whether the man were a priest, a vicar, or what. Were there distinctions? Did they matter? He'd always found religion frightfully tedious, but that left him somewhat bereft of information at this juncture. All that seemed to matter was that a man Quentin didn't know was making sweeping statements about a woman *he* probably didn't know, regardless of how often they may have met.

The rage had not abated. Through the droning speech and infrequent sniffs from Nicky, it burned white hot. Now and then Freddy squeezed his wrist and it dragged him into the present, but more often than not his mind wandered away to happier times. Times filled with laughter and smiles.

Father stood and approached the podium, and Quentin gasped as that darkness left his side. It sharpened his senses, nailed them to the here and now, as the one thing in this world he could truly say that he despised stood before them all and presented the façade of a man grieving for the loss of his beloved wife.

"Icky," Freddy whispered. "Hold."

The world began to blacken at the edges, blotting out as though a vast emptiness consumed it. Radiant in the center of his vision stood the Duke of Oxford, tall and flawless, his hair peppery at the temples and his forehead deeply lined with sincerity.

This man was their father, and that knowledge sickened Quentin.

"I have to go," he breathed, so faint that he doubted Freddy heard him.

"Ten minutes," Freddy hissed. "Ten bloody minutes."

A stiff breeze whipped at his hair. It ruffled the edges of the banner draped across the coffin and tugged on the priest's robes.

Now was a rotten time for the weather to be turning.

"Margaret was a dreamer." His father's voice was sonorous, and his gray eyes were fixed at some midpoint in the crowd. "The eldest of three sisters, heir to the Dovecote family's legacy, and the most beautiful woman that I ever had the good fortune to meet. Mother to three sons of whom we could never have been more proud." His gaze shifted to Quentin before it passed on to Freddy and Nicky.

The blackness encroached toward the podium. All other sound became muted, muffled, until there was nothing left of it. Just the abyss and Father's award-worthy performance at the center.

Cold seeped through his clothes and caressed his skin. He felt as though he stood at the heart of a hurricane, gale forces ripping at his body.

Whatever Father said, it didn't matter. It was a hum of nonsense now.

"You killed her," Quentin said.

The hum ceased.

"Quentin."

He knew that tone. The soft way in which it heralded his father's disappointment.

It twisted the dial one final notch.

Wind rushed from Quentin's lungs as the rage surged loose. "You *killed* her!" he screamed. "You liar! You killed her!"

"Quentin!"

Something took his arm, and he wrenched free, but it came

back. He heard muted screams and wailing cries. They came from some distance away, reaching from the blackness.

"You're a murderer!" His throat was raw from the yelling, but he couldn't hear his own words over the howling of winds.

Then the abyss swallowed him whole.

1

QUENTIN

IN THE DYING DAYS OF APRIL, THE WEATHER IN SAN DIEGO HINTED that it would soon reach the end of Quentin's ability to tolerate. It was warm and sunny, not yet unbearable, but growing hotter week after week and only likely to continue doing so. If this was April, he all but dreaded August. Thank goodness the Americans were ardent supporters of air-conditioning.

He regarded the outside world from the back of his taxi. Gone were the days when the local cab drivers would try to take him downtown by the most scenic and expensive routes available. He had chivvying them along down to a fine art and would usually reach the Jack in the Green within half an hour. The route this driver had taken was the same as most chose: a highway that was five lanes in either direction, with scrubland and half-dead-seeming palm trees on both sides. It held an almost desert-like beauty, although his own preference was for greener lands. The only thing to pay attention to for most of the ride were other cars.

Quentin disliked this part of his situation the most. The tedious trips to and fro. He could be a patient man, but perhaps it was time to consider moving to a more central location. One in which he could be closer to Laurence.

Was that foolish? He had only met the fellow in January. They had been what Laurence called *dating* for a handful of weeks. And that dating was a pleasant experience, certainly.

Especially the kissing part.

He bit his lip and silently counted down from ten. It would not do to be anything but calm and collected in a taxi.

Laurence insisted that Quentin was free to kiss him whenever he wished, but he was still not sure that it wasn't an imposition of some sort. Even though Laurence swore that it wasn't, and even though if Quentin didn't get around to it Laurence would give up waiting and ask permission instead.

Was he a coward? Did he refrain from asking often because he knew that, sooner or later, Laurence would take the initiative?

Now and then he harbored the suspicion—despite protestations to the contrary—that Laurence was on some level frustrated with him. Perhaps Quentin *should* lead more often. It wouldn't be so bad, would it? He *did* enjoy Laurence's company, the man's vibrancy and ease, his warm laughter and tender embraces. While Laurence may have insisted Quentin be the one to court him, Quentin had not disagreed.

Any frustration, then, wholly made sense within that context. Laurence was waiting to be courted, and Quentin had stalled at the first step. They went to lunches and to dinners. They spent time together attending live music events and shopping. Quentin took him anywhere that Laurence wished to go, and then left him at home alone every evening with nothing but a soft kiss and a smile.

He knew that Laurence wanted more. But what that more could be, Quentin wasn't sure. He saw it in the longing in the florist's gaze and in the occasional invitations to stay the night. Laurence had even cut down on his smoking so much that he went days without reeking of it. This was unlike any form of courtship he had been exposed to. Everyone he had ever known courted women, for a start.

What did one do to seek the attentions of another man? Buy flowers? Laurence worked in a flower shop, surrounded by the city's most breathtaking blooms every day. Gift him with jewelry? Laurence wore none except the occasional leather thong coiled around either wrist. Offer his accounts to Myriam for her to study? That seemed so incredibly formal, and Laurence was anything but.

Quentin was adrift. He had no one to ask for advice, and everything to lose should he err.

The taxi switched onto the city's streets. It passed hotels and parking lots, banks and offices. This was the faceless part of San Diego, and though it looked entirely different, it reminded him of the City of London with its glass towers and empty heart. The only benefit of being here was that it meant they were only five minutes from the shop now.

Five minutes to seeing Laurence today.

It was a peculiar way to measure time, but he felt as though he had lost all other means of measurement. How long until he saw Laurence? How much time before they were together again? The ache which only ever abated in the younger man's presence was still with him, and it would begin anew the moment he stepped into a taxi this evening.

He had his card in hand ready to pay the instant they pulled up outside the shop, and with thanks to his driver he eased out, passing immediately from the cool of the car and into the oven of the city.

Quentin strode across the pavement swiftly and entered into the shelter of the shop's recessed doorway.

He was here.

A deep breath, and he pushed the door open. Cool enveloped him once more, bearing with it the sweet scent of peonies and freesias. He heard Laurence's laughter beyond the tinkle of the shop's bell.

Quentin raised a hand to ease his sunglasses off. With a flick of his fingers the earpieces were folded, and he tucked them into the breast pocket of his jacket.

"Anyway," said a woman at the counter. Not one that he recognized. "Do you get off work any time soon?"

The woman was hardly a day over twenty, and she leaned across the counter in a way which he found quite distasteful. Her top had the thinnest of shoulder straps and ended before her shorts began. Blonde hair was piled up on top of her head in a loose bun, and her sunglasses were pushed up into the mess. She was toying with a receipt between her fingers.

He was not the best judge on such matters, but he was reasonably convinced that the young lady was flirting with Laurence.

Quentin narrowed his eyes.

"Soon," Laurence chuckled with ease. "But I'll be heading out with my boyfriend." He cast a bright smile and easy wave toward Quentin. "Hey, baby!"

"Darling." The word was, even as it left him, quashed flat with the calm he used to tamp down on the sudden spark which flared in his heart.

He didn't want this woman anywhere near Laurence.

Goodness, that was awful of him, was it not? The poor girl wasn't to know. All she had done was ask when Laurence might be available to…

To what?

He drew a deep breath and halted awkwardly halfway to the counter.

She straightened up and took a pot of flowers into her arms, then turned a friendly smile on Quentin. "Well, don't ask, don't get. No chance of a threesome? I've got a thing for really hot guys."

Quentin blinked. "A what?"

"Uh, no." Laurence's cheeks were unmistakably red now, and he hurried out from the counter to walk the customer toward the door. "Sorry. I totally would, but it's not his jam. Take care, huh?"

"Sure. You too." She dropped her sunglasses down to her nose and headed on out with her purchase in her arms.

The bell jangled in her wake, and Laurence bolted the door then flipped the sign to *Closed* and came closer.

"You're looking hot."

Quentin raised his chin. That strange burn in his chest hadn't diminished with the young lady's departure. It felt like shame and anger, fear, and helplessness all jammed together into one tight ball, and he had no idea what he was supposed to do with it. He knew what he *wanted* to do with it, but he wasn't at all sure it was correct.

He wanted to kiss Laurence. To lay hands on him and hold him tight. He wanted to do everything in his power to make Laurence understand that the florist was *his*.

"Quen?"

His breath hitched, and he focused on Laurence's deep, dark eyes. They were inches away. When had Laurence gotten so close?

"Who was she?"

Laurence's head tilted to one side and he laughed. "Just a customer. They come in here all the time, wanting to buy stuff. Flowers, mostly. You might almost think this was some kinda flower shop."

"Has she been here before?"

Laurence's gaze clouded briefly, then he shrugged. "Don't think so. Anyway." He raised his head and grinned. "She thought you were sexy. And she's right. Where are you taking me this evening, sexy?"

He had a reservation, but the name of the restaurant eluded him, disappearing into that tightness inside him as though it had been swallowed whole. "Um," he said.

"Quen?" Laurence stepped closer. "Is something wrong?"

Quentin's heart gave a heavy *thud*.

Yes! Everything is wrong! Didn't you see the way she looked at you?

Laurence's gaze flickered back and forth, then his lips curved into a slow smile. "Baby," he cooed. "Are you jealous?"

He had no immediate answer, and yet Laurence seemed to expect one, so he shifted his weight faintly and said the only words which his brain was willing to provide.

"You are mine."

Laurence's cheeks flushed red again, and his eyes widened. "Goddess," he whispered. "You have no idea how hot that is." He leaned forward, then ground to a halt a hair's breadth from Quentin's lips. "Can I?"

"You may."

Laurence's lips were on his before the words had fully left him. His hands gripped Quentin's waist and their chests touched.

Quentin leaned in and grasped the edges of Laurence's apron. He was, he thought, growing used to this business. Lips came together. They lingered. And then they moved apart. It was pleasant, gentle, and tender.

But this kiss was not. It was beyond his limited experience and expertise. Laurence's breathing was hard, and his lips parted. It drew Quentin's own lips back, and then Laurence's breath was in his mouth and his was in Laurence's in turn, and his heart began to pound like he'd run a mile to get here.

It didn't seem to end, and he couldn't tell whether that was a good thing.

He craved more.

When Laurence's tongue touched his own it was like going from sober to drunk with nothing in between. His limbs trembled, and his grip on Laurence's apron was all that held him on his feet. Dizziness swirled around him, and nothing existed but Laurence's hands on his hips and the obscene thing between them which masqueraded as a kiss but felt like so much more.

Nobody would take this from him. Absolutely no one. Whatever he had to do to make sure that Laurence never left him, he would do it. Good God, this had to be witchcraft. Nothing else could explain why this felt dangerous and terrifying and exciting at the same time. His muscles were tense, ready to run, yet here he remained.

Laurence's touch faded from his waist and returned at his shoulders. It spread from there up his neck and over his ears until it settled in his hair, fingers warm against his scalp. He gasped quickly as Laurence took hold and tugged.

Quentin didn't know what this was. He didn't know what he was supposed to do with it. It wasn't a kiss. It was something more. Something which seared at him, threatened to consume him, and laid waste to all his doubts. It reduced the whole world down to a single act, one without a name, and the best that he could do was cling to Laurence as a drowning man to driftwood as he relied on the other for breath.

It was beautiful and frightening and he was half-convinced that it would never end.

He didn't think that he wanted it to.

2

QUENTIN

LAURENCE PULLED AWAY, LEAVING A VACUUM WHICH MADE Quentin sway on the spot.

"Quen." Laurence rasped his name. "I really don't wanna say this, but I think you need to calm down."

His thoughts were a mess, but those words cut through them into a response he had been training himself for these past few weeks. He closed his eyes and drew a breath, then began counting down from ten. He didn't need to understand what was happening. If Laurence said he needed to calm himself, that took precedence.

Three. Two. One.

When his eyes fluttered open there was little sign of any mess. A few of the lighter flowers had been tossed from their pots and lay strewn across those below them, but other than that there had been no damage.

He licked his lips and swallowed, then forced his fingers to release Laurence's apron.

Laurence's fingers eased free of his hair and came to rest on his shoulders.

Quentin gazed up into Laurence's features and found them etched with hunger. Those deep eyes were alight and his lips were pink and moist.

"I..." His throat strangled his voice, and he coughed to clear it. "I apologize."

"For what?" Laurence took his own lip between his teeth and bit down on it.

"For the, um." He waved his fingers vaguely, but couldn't even pin down what he wanted to gesture toward. He was inexplicably drawn to the sight of Laurence's lip, trapped between teeth, and he had the most absurd thought.

Could *he* do that? Was that acceptable? Pleasurable?

Was Laurence hinting at something? The man was infuriatingly subtle sometimes, and his suggestions would fly far above Quentin's head.

Laurence glanced around the shop, then back to Quentin. "Are you saying sorry for a kiss?"

"You call that a kiss?" He almost laughed at the notion of *that* being remotely conflated for what he knew a kiss to be.

"Uh-huh." Laurence's eyes grew narrower and his teeth showed. "Wanna see what else I call one?"

"Yes." He said it without a thought. A single word, and yet it carried all the power in the world: power that Laurence gave him willingly. The power to say no if he ever needed to.

That mattered. It mattered more than he could squeeze into words. It seemed like such a simple thing, so obvious, and yet Laurence always checked, always made sure that Quentin was safe. He wasn't such a fool as to believe that anyone else would do this for him. This was Laurence's gift alone.

Laurence licked his lips. He gave a slow nod. Then he ran his thumbs tenderly along Quentin's jaw as he leaned forward and tipped his head. His tongue slid slowly along Quentin's lower lip.

Quentin's breathing sped up in an instant. He felt for Laurence's apron, but rested hands around his waist instead. As the florist's tongue invaded his mouth more slowly, more patiently, he couldn't help but close his eyes and reach for it with his own.

Laurence's fingers began to trace unhurried lines up the back of his neck and toy with his hairline, and it sent a shiver through his whole body. His head wanted to sag forward. His limbs became boneless.

His teeth found Laurence's lip and snagged it a moment.

Laurence groaned and pressed against him. Nails scraped along his skin. There was a notable hardness against his hip.

He let go and forced his eyes to open in time to catch Laurence's expression: lips apart, cheeks ruddy, eyes lidded.

Had Quentin *done* this to him?

"Goddess," Laurence whimpered. He rubbed his curls and limped away to put flowers back in their pots. He moved stiffly, as though he'd been injured.

Doubt worried at him now. "Did I hurt you?"

"No." Laurence coughed into a fist. "Oh shit no, Quen. You really didn't, baby, trust me. Man, you're…" He waggled a yellow rose. "You learn fast, you know. Gotta hand it to you."

He would be lying to himself if he tried to believe that Laurence's words didn't fan his ego a touch, and he squared his shoulders.

Laurence cleared away what little mess there was, then hurried over to bring down the shop's security shutters. The motor whirred and the links in the barrier clanked until the whole shutter was in place, and then all was quiet once more. "I'm gonna need to, uh, shower before we go. Have we got time for that?"

"We do." Quentin looked toward the beaded curtain which led to the back of the shop. "No Myriam?"

"Naw. She's away this weekend for Beltane. She does a lot of community stuff, and she's doing workshops and a couple of talks at the local festival."

"Ah." Quentin nodded a little.

Laurence and Myriam were Pagans. Quentin's grasp of religions was poor at the best of times, but he at least had some vague understanding of a few Pagan terms, whether through Laurence and Myriam's patience or from some vague recollections from childhood. Beltane, so far as he recalled, marked the beginning of summer, just as Imbolc had launched spring. He was reasonably sure fire would be involved, but then that seemed to be a common thread among Pagan festivities. If the local celebrations were at all like those back in England there may well be a maypole, too.

Laurence chuckled as he led the way to the stairs. "Don't worry. I won't drag you into our crazy Pagan ways, hon. Besides, I've gotta keep the shop running, and Rodger's out on deliveries almost all day every day now. We're gonna have to hire more staff."

"I don't know that I would use the word 'crazy,'" Quentin said softly as he followed. "I may not share your beliefs, darling, but that does not make them irrational."

Laurence paused with his keys in hand and glanced down at him. The darkness of the stairwell made it difficult to make out his expression.

"We did encounter a god," Quentin added. "One might think that actually validates your stance."

"I—" Laurence exhaled, then unlocked the door to his apartment. "Thanks, Quen. You don't know what that means to me."

He inclined his head and tailed Laurence inside.

Quentin had grown accustomed to the cramped living conditions within this space. It no longer affronted his sensibilities. He wasn't convinced that he himself could live in such a small area, but he had at least learned that, to Laurence, this was enough. He moved to the dining table and settled into a chair as he waited for Laurence to shower.

"So, uh." Laurence dropped his keys into the bowl beside the door, then ran a hand through his curls. "You're sneaky, you know that?"

Quentin's eyebrows lifted. "I am?"

"Yeah. You just swept the whole birthday thing under the rug, didn't you?" Laurence unfastened his apron and pulled it off over his head. He folded it as he watched Quentin from the doorway. "You came here every day when my rib was healing and you didn't say a word about it."

Quentin leaned back in his seat and crossed his legs, then rested his hands in his lap. "It did not seem relevant."

"Uh-huh. So that makes you twenty-five now, right?"

"Mm." He preferred not to think about it.

"Yeah." Laurence stalked closer and leaned past him to set the apron on the dining table. "And then after I was all healed up you kinda forgot to mention it, am I right?"

"Just so." Quentin gazed fixedly at Laurence's ear.

"You don't get away with it that easily, man." Laurence grinned at him. "You're a great nurse, believe me, but you're a terrible liar."

Quentin pursed his lips and shifted his focus to Laurence's eyes. They were crinkled in amusement, which only served to embarrass him further. "Well. At least I am a tremendous nurse."

"Nuh-uh. You don't get to deflect this." Laurence crossed his arms and leaned his hip against the table. "Anyway, you're used to missing birthdays, right?"

"Correct."

"Then you're okay with this one being a couple of months late."

"Really," he protested, "there's no need for—"

"There's every need," Laurence cut in. "I think it's about time you started having decent birthdays, Quen. So we're late this year. We won't be next year, okay?"

Quentin blinked at him.

Laurence's eyes flitted away a moment, and his posture shifted. His limbs loosened up, and he turned aside to rest his backside on the table, half-sitting on it. "I mean," he murmured, "if you're still around next year. You know, like... you don't have to stay here if you don't want to."

"Where else would we go?"

Laurence puffed out his cheeks and turned to face his own feet.

Quentin frowned up at him. "The shop is here, darling. We can hardly pack it up and take it with us."

"I meant, like..." Laurence shrugged. "I meant if you left or something."

"Not without you, Laurence." Quentin fussed with the crease of his trousers to straighten it as it passed over his knee. "Really, you do have some funny ideas. What would I do without you? Go home?" He snorted at that. "Out of the question."

"Okay." Laurence rubbed his own arms briefly, then stepped away from the table. "So, yeah. Your birthday. I know I let it slide a while 'cause of the rib and then the increase in business from all your rich friends and stuff, but I really wanna do something special for you."

"Now?" Quentin watched him.

"Nah. We've got plans tonight." Laurence chuckled and ran his palm over his stubble. "But this weekend. I'll make sure Rodger can take the shop Saturday afternoon then we'll go do the thing."

"Which thing in particular?"

Laurence just smirked at him. "You'll like it, I promise."

"Mm."

"Anyway. I'm gonna go shower, then you can take me out. The wooing's still your job, baby. Gotta make you work for it."

Laurence disappeared through to the bathroom with a brief laugh, and Quentin rapped his fingers slowly on the dining table as he tried to work out what Laurence might have up his sleeve.

"You don't have to stay here if you don't want to."

Quentin snorted. What a preposterous suggestion. Where on Earth else could he possibly want to be?

3

LAURENCE

LAURENCE SHUT HIMSELF IN THE BATHROOM AND LEANED AGAINST the door with a sigh. All the blood from his brain was obviously in his cock right now. That was his only excuse for getting maudlin during such a lighthearted conversation.

He'd never given any thought to the idea that Quentin might leave him. Not really. Hell, he was too busy dedicating his thoughts to figuring out how to get past first base with a guy who was terrified of exactly that. But the simple fact was that he'd once had a vision of Quentin in his arms, both of them about to be consumed by fire, and the only future he'd seen beyond that was of himself without Quentin.

Was Quentin going to die in that fire? Did Laurence make it out alone?

Would he leave Quentin in there to save his own ass?

The idea made him hate himself for even thinking that he could be capable of doing that, but then he'd spent years injecting himself with heroin and making his mom clean up the mess. If that wasn't the definition of selfish, what was?

He groaned as he dragged his work clothes off and tossed them into the laundry basket. He didn't want to think about heroin. Not now. Not when he'd had a month without any cravings.

One tiny moment of doubt and it was right back there, wasn't it? Clamoring for his attention. Whispering promises it could only keep for a few short hours.

Think about Quentin.

The earl had an air about him which gave Laurence something to latch on to. He was caring and kind. Goddess, a cab from La Jolla was over fifty bucks each way, yet Quentin took that journey every day to be by his side during his recovery, and now that Laurence was working again Quentin still came down on the days Laurence didn't drive up to visit him.

In two months that worked out to something like six thousand dollars in cab fares.

Just to see Laurence.

A quarter of Laurence's annual salary spent on cab fares, and that was only to and from the shop. It didn't include all the times Quentin insisted they take a taxi so that Laurence could have an evening off from driving them everywhere, or all the times he had taken Laurence shopping. And by the Goddess that man could shop. If fashion were a national sport, Quentin could represent his country in the Olympics.

Sometimes it felt as though Quentin were marking him, making Laurence his through deciding what he wore or where they ate, and it was an undercurrent Laurence wasn't averse to. It felt safe, like Quentin was protecting him, taking charge, ensuring the world knew that Laurence belonged to him and that he would tolerate no interference on the matter. And earlier, downstairs, the look on Quentin's face when he found a customer flirting with Laurence was seriously hot. That was pure territorial jealousy right there, but not Dan's kind. Not the kind where Laurence was made to feel small, where he was belittled and abused for daring to speak to another human being. Quentin's possessiveness wasn't something which led somewhere Laurence didn't want to go. Hell no.

It led somewhere Laurence *needed* to go. That kiss! Goddess, his body tingled at the memory of it, and then—

And then they'd done it again, and Quentin had bitten his lip, and Laurence quivered as a part of him struggled not to beg for more.

His groin pulsed in time with his heart, his erection stirring back to life while his mind replayed those heavy, deep kisses, unlike any he'd gotten out of Quentin before.

He'd have to take care of that before he could go out, or his entire evening would be blue balls. Again.

Laurence hurried into the shower and turned the water on so that he could go through the latest in a growing line of unsatisfactory but necessary solo outings.

His mind was much clearer once he'd taken care of business. Laurence could focus now, but his thoughts just circled back to Quentin's mixed signals. One moment the guy was all confidence and domineering attitude, and the next he was distant and closed off. If being descended from Herne the Hunter gave Laurence any abilities to see into that obtuse skull, he hadn't discovered them yet.

He gazed at his reflection while he brushed his teeth and saw Herne's eyes looking back at him.

"Wait until you've had the dream," he mumbled around the toothbrush. He spat saliva and mint into the sink. "Everything will become clear."

Like hell it had.

Whenever he tried to talk to his mom about it, she seemed to think that the dream held all the answers to any questions he might come up with, but the only question he really had was *what does it mean?*

He didn't dare tell Quentin about it. How could he? They'd just defeated Jack. Their lives were god-free right now and they could get on with normal, everyday living, so how could he possibly say to the man he yearned for every waking moment, "Oh by the way, I'm actually descended from another god. No, not Jack. Herne. Yeah, you know. Wyld Hunt Herne"?

He couldn't. Quentin would have questions, and Laurence didn't have the answers.

He rinsed his mouth out and went through to the bedroom to change into fresh clothes.

Quentin had picked out almost everything he owned now. T-shirts, shorts, shirts, pants, even down to shoes and socks, Quentin's eye for fit and color dominated his wardrobe. The man had seeped into his life, his thoughts, his dreams, and Laurence hadn't even tasted his tongue before today. He felt like a teenager mooning over some crush, and Quentin was almost as unobtainable as one.

He could turn on the charm. Laurence was sexy and he knew how to use it, and now he knew he had a god in his genetic makeup, he should be unstoppable. Jack may have been half full of lies, but he'd also half-spread truth. The god said things which only made sense in the context offered by Laurence's newfound knowledge.

Prince of the Forest. Heir to the kingdom. You are life. You are the hunter. They seek to control you because they fear you.

That wasn't too nice a thought. If that was what drove Quentin's little possessive streaks then it was suddenly a whole lot less sexy.

Was it the underlying cause behind everything else, too? Herne hadn't wasted any time bedding Sara, Laurence's ancestor, and Jack had called him *the satyr who isn't fucking*. Was horny supposed to be his natural state?

He grabbed pants and a loose shirt and dragged them on without paying any attention to what color they were or whether they fit his mood. His brain was too busy veering back toward Dan—toward Laurence's thoughts of hunting the man down and tearing out his guts for daring to threaten Quentin in any way.

That was a hunter's instinct. Goddess, the things Laurence had wanted to do, the images which had surged into his mind, were inhuman. Jack said he was a killer, and Laurence didn't want to believe it, yet he drove home from Quentin's apartment one day fantasizing about plunging his hands into Dan's intestines and ripping them from his lifeless body.

His lip curled as he buttoned his shirt. A low snarl rumbled in his throat.

Dan was gone. Whether Jack killed him the moment he took Dan's body, or whether Laurence had killed Dan the same time as he'd destroyed Jack didn't really matter to him. The man who had been gaslighting him for months had gone away, and couldn't hurt him anymore. Better still he couldn't hurt Quentin either. That the price of this freedom was Dan's death didn't bother him as much as he thought it should. So maybe he was a killer. Maybe it was in his heart, his blood.

Maybe he was okay with that.

Which brought him full circle. To Quentin. To whether or not the earl was trying to control him because that was *his* nature, or because Laurence frightened him on some level other than sexual. The sex thing he could take; that was Quentin's fear and always had been. Laurence was no good at patience, but he'd have to learn or he'd scare away the only person who had ever been good to him. The only one Laurence wanted to stick around for more than a few weeks.

The one he loved.

But if Laurence scared Quentin because of this Herne thing, because Quentin on some instinctual level sensed that Laurence was a hunter, then maybe that would be insurmountable. He didn't know, and didn't want to think about what would become of them if that were true.

He had to get inside the earl's head somehow. Figure out what he was thinking. Try to tease out of him hints and suggestions and deflections which together formed some kind of picture of what exactly was going on between Quentin's ears.

All without losing him.

Laurence tucked his shirt into his pants and gazed at the mirror. He'd apparently picked out brown slacks and a green shirt, which played well with his blond curls and light stubble. He looked like an Adonis, if Adonis had been less ripped and more otter. He took a deep breath and released it slowly, pushing the tension away and forcing his shoulders to unwind. He pushed damp curls back from his forehead just enough to give himself a slight windswept look, then fixed a lazy smile in place.

He would get to the bottom of this, and if it took all his charms to do so then that's what he'd have to use.

4

QUENTIN

Quentin had to check the note he'd made on his phone to remember which restaurant it was. He'd had the niggling suspicion that it was Mexican, and was thankfully correct.

Laurence protested too much whenever Quentin attempted to take him to places which the American deemed "fancy" or "expensive," and Quentin had begun to develop a feel for which price range Laurence considered acceptable. Twelve dollars for a main course appeared to suit him best, fifteen at most. Anything beyond that earned a squint and some small complaint that Quentin was spending too much.

Laurence drove them. Now that the man had cut back on smoking weed the van smelled considerably less like a sweaty armpit, which was a tremendous relief.

Their table was on a wooden veranda which overlooked the ocean, and Quentin couldn't help but smile to himself. Laurence was a wild thing, and the setting fit him in every way that it did not suit Quentin. The ocean breeze played through Laurence's curls and allowed the evening sun to filter through them, bathing them in gold.

He was breathtakingly beautiful.

The longer days and brighter sun had begun to lighten

Laurence's hair, turning it from blond-brown to the color of honey, lighter at the tips than the roots. More often than not he had a fuzz of stubble outlining his jaw and it served to emphasize his cheekbones. Despite the physical strength which enabled him to ferry stock from his mother's truck into the shop each morning, he was not bulky.

The man was perfect in every way, and he was here, sparing Quentin every available moment he could.

It was an unfathomable gift. The opportunity to gain new memories, *happy* memories was one Quentin wasn't sure he would ever have again. Not since the funeral. Yet here they were.

He took a deep breath and held it, tasting the salt spray on the air. Every detail he could etch into his mind, every wash of the tide and every dip of Laurence's head, had to be captured.

He couldn't bear the idea that he might forget something so precious.

"You should eat a bit more than that, Quen," Laurence chuckled.

Quentin released the sea air and glanced to his plate. He had made what he considered a good dent in the oversized meal, with over a quarter of it devoured already, but Laurence was always capable of clearing his plate.

"It's quite spicy," he offered.

Laurence snorted with the scorn that deserved. "You eat curry, baby. Don't think I've forgotten."

The waiter came by to refill their glasses of ice water, then whooshed away like a ballerina. Quentin relented and neatly skewered another piece of chicken with his fork, then duly chewed it under Laurence's watchful eye.

"Are you happy?" Laurence gestured between them with his knife. "With us, I mean. Like…" He shifted in his seat and leaned his elbows on the table edge. "You. Me."

"Of course." He set his cutlery down and reached for his water to take a slow sip. "Are you?"

"Yeah." Laurence chuckled. "Don't get me wrong. You know there's places I wanna go. But not until you're ready."

Quentin took another sip and feigned ignorance. If Laurence was about to suggest that they take their clothes off at some point, he most certainly was *not* ready. But if what Laurence proposed was more of the sort of kissing they had done at the shop earlier, then he had to admit that it had its appeal.

"I know," he finally said as he returned his glass to the table, careful to set it precisely in the ring of condensation it had left on the napkin it rested on.

Laurence fiddled with his knife, and leaned back. His face turned toward the sea a while as the hilt of the knife tapped lightly against the tabletop.

Quentin took the opportunity to force another small mouthful down.

"You don't really talk about your family much," Laurence murmured.

"Correct."

"Do you think they'd mind us together?" Laurence looked across to him and cut into his enchilada.

"I don't care what they would or would not mind." Quentin set his cutlery aside and nudged his plate away.

"Okay." Laurence's eyes flitted to the plate as though he were checking if Quentin had eaten enough. "But do they know you're gay?"

"I am not gay, Laurence." Now it was his turn to watch the water.

"But you're dating a guy—"

"I am dating *you*." He snapped his attention to Laurence and straightened in his seat. "You are not 'a guy,' Laurence. You are—" He scrambled for the words, all of which fled him in that instant. "You are *you*."

"But what if there was another me out there? I mean, obviously not as sexy as me, but someone's gotta be close, right?" Laurence's grin was lazy, almost disarming.

Quentin stared at him. Whatever the other man was trying to imply, Quentin could not fathom it.

"Do you..." He hesitated and swallowed as fear washed through him. "Do you wish for me to find someone other than you?"

"No!" Laurence shook his head so hard that his curls bounced. "Goddess, Quen, no! I'm just..." He rapped his knuckles against the table. "I'm just trying to work a few things out, okay? You keep saying you're not gay, but you're obviously not straight, so maybe you're bi, or maybe you're..." He trailed off.

"Does it matter?"

"I don't know. It mattered to me, when I was younger." Laurence sighed and swigged his water. "I used to think there was something wrong with me. I liked girls, but I had a thing for guys, too. It wasn't until I learned the word 'bisexual' that it finally clicked, and I kinda wondered if we could work out what word fit you, and then you might feel... I dunno. Less alone."

Quentin pressed his lips together as he mulled over Laurence's words. He could see that it made a certain sort of sense, to know what you were and to gain the confidence that there was nothing wrong in it, but Quentin did not feel as though there was anything *wrong* in his interest in Laurence. It was out of the ordinary among his peers, yes, but nothing about it felt incorrect.

They fit together. In all the ways that they should not, somewhere in the chasm caused by their differences was the key to this match. For Quentin's lack of knowledge and experience, there was Laurence. For all that Laurence was confident and sexually forward, he had a core of self-doubt which Quentin's own fortitude shored up. They were pieces of a puzzle which, individually, showed little and yet when nestled together revealed a complete picture.

He needed Laurence on the most fundamental level he could conceive of, and so perhaps Laurence's search for a word was not for Quentin's benefit, but his own.

"Then it matters," he concluded with a soft smile. "Laurence, I want nobody but you. I have neither interest nor inclination toward anyone who is not you, let alone an entire gender. If I should ever—" He broke off to take a breath and steady his nerves. "If I should ever lose you, I want no other. Ever."

Laurence's mouth opened. His eyes were wide. There was a delicate flush of pink in his cheeks and along his neck. It set off nicely against the green shirt that he wore.

"If there is a word for that, then I do not know it." Quentin rested his hands over the arms of his chair.

"Flattering is what I call it," Laurence mumbled. He coughed and rolled his shoulders, then sank back. "Thanks, Quen. You, uh. You kinda wear your heart on your sleeve, don't you? It's nice." He chuckled briefly. "So would they be okay with you dating another man? Your family, I mean?"

"It is irrelevant." His fingers tightened on the chair a little.

"What I'm trying to ask is whether they'd make you leave me if they found out about us, hon."

Quentin quirked an eyebrow. "I would fight until my last breath against it, darling."

"Man, you're intense." Laurence wet his lip with the tip of his tongue. "How about you courting a commoner then? Is *that* okay?"

"I do as I wish, dear boy." Quentin rocked his jaw a moment and watched Laurence squirm in his seat. "Is something troubling you?"

"Naw." Laurence hesitated, then laughed it off with a shrug. "I just wanna be sure you're not, like, scared of me or anything."

At that, Quentin couldn't help but lift his eyebrows. "Of you?" he echoed. "Absolute nonsense!"

"Well, I mean, the thing with the plants—" Laurence spoke carefully in public places. "It could be scary, right?"

"As could—" Quentin waved his fingers through the air to indicate his own ability. The one which Laurence was aware of, at least.

He lowered his hand and reached for his water, hiding in it as he feigned a long drink. The fire had only occurred once. An accident. Nothing more. A coincidence. Whisky was highly flammable, after all, and detonating it telekinetically had obviously triggered some sort of reaction. There was little use in taking it as anything but a reminder to retain control over his emotions at all times.

"No, *your* gift is dirrrty," Laurence purred.

Quentin chuckled. "How so?"

"Oh, come on. You have total control over everything around

you." Laurence leaned in and lowered his voice. "You could overpower a pro wrestler, hon. You can sure as hell put *me* wherever you wanted to, you know." He bit his lip. "Goddess, Quen, you could do anything to me and I couldn't lift a finger to stop you."

"And that isn't in the least bit frightening?" Quentin leaned in, drawn forward by the return of Laurence's hunger.

"No. No it isn't." Laurence adjusted his position and laid his arms across the table, reaching for Quentin's hands.

"Then allow me to assure you," he murmured as he slid his fingers around Laurence's, "that I am not at all afraid of your gifts either."

Laurence searched his gaze, then nodded and squeezed his fingers. "Okay. Thanks, Quen. I'm sorry for being weird."

"If that were worth apologizing for," Quentin said dryly, "we would be at it all night."

Laurence turned bright red, which suggested he'd taken Quentin's words to mean something lewd. It was a frequent habit, and Quentin had long given up attempting to work out which words in particular were the ones Laurence found especially evocative. There was little rhyme or reason to it.

And besides, it was not unbecoming.

"Now, what is this birthday idea you had?"

Laurence's eyelids drooped a moment, and then he blinked and leaned back with a laugh. "Oh, man. You *are* sneaky!"

"Absolute rot." Quentin did his best not to smile as he looked for and made eye contact with their waiter. Only then did he allow the smile to show.

"Uh-huh. Lure me in, then bait and switch on me." Laurence gave a soft snort. "Don't think I'm not watching you, Banbury."

"I wouldn't dream of such a thing." His smile widened as the waiter approached, and he added, "May I have the check, please?"

Laurence waited until the waiter had gone again. "Uh-huh. You want a ride home, or are you walking from here?"

"You are an unholy terror, darling." Quentin brought out his wallet in readiness. "Not to worry. I shall simply attempt to tease it out of you later this evening."

Those words appeared to have a more profound effect, and Laurence remained silent as Quentin paid the bill.

Silent, and red as a lobster.

It was adorable.

5

QUENTIN

Laurence squeezed the button on a key fob which hung from the ignition and waited for the eight-foot-tall gates to Quentin's driveway to slide open.

Quentin had attempted to fish for clues as to this birthday surprise on the way home, but Laurence smiled his way through it all and pretended that he didn't have a clue what Quentin was even talking about, so once the truck was parked Quentin unbuckled his seatbelt and hopped from the cab.

Gravel crunched underfoot, and he took his own key from his pocket as he approached the front door.

Laurence hurried after him and leaned against the door frame while Quentin slid his key into the lock. "So are you gonna invite me in for tea?"

"Obviously." He glanced up to Laurence, then allowed his lips to twitch into a faint smirk. "Although I'm afraid that it may cost you."

"Uh-huh. And what's the price?"

"A hint. Just one." He opened the door and led the way past his neighbor's door and to the stairs, which he hopped up with ease. "And then I promise I will leave you be."

"But then it's not a surprise." Laurence followed close behind and kicked his shoes off once inside. "And I think it'd be better if it was."

"Hmm." Quentin eyed him as he removed his own shoes and hung his jacket.

"And if you don't stop poking your nose in," Laurence added with a low rumble in his chest, "there's gonna be consequences."

"Consequences?" Quentin straightened and held his head high, though he couldn't quite match Laurence's height. "One does not bow to threats."

Laurence's grin turned sly. "Oh it ain't a threat, baby. It's just a fact."

"You wouldn't dare!"

What Laurence wouldn't dare, Quentin had no idea. But he trusted the man implicitly. If the worst Laurence could threaten him with was a kiss, he was hardly about to object to that.

"I wouldn't, huh?" Laurence's teeth flashed in the dim evening light from the full-height windows, and he trailed fingers down Quentin's chest until they reached his waist. They rested there.

Quentin gazed up at him. There was something electric in the air: the anticipation of a cat choosing the right moment to pounce on its prey. He had a sudden moment of empathy for field mice, and the challenge he had been ready to issue stuck in his throat.

Laurence tugged. In a second he'd pulled Quentin's shirt free from his waistband and slid his fingers beneath the material. They brushed against skin.

Quentin gasped at the touch, unexpected and warm. A flicker of worry flashed across his thoughts.

Scars. He'll feel the scars—

"See, I happen to know," Laurence rumbled close to his ear, "that you're ticklish."

Quentin grasped at air. He twisted and stepped back, but Laurence moved with him as though they were glued together. And then those fingers moved.

His touch was light. Not the brutish thing that Freddy used to call "tickling," but a gentle twitch of his hands which brought his palms into contact with Quentin's sides. Quentin bucked involuntarily and wrenched back, laughing without meaning to.

KNIGHT OF FLAMES

Laurence withdrew his hands and held them up, palms toward Quentin in surrender. "You okay, hon?"

He panted and coiled arms across his stomach. His skin still twitched and spasmed, settling like ripples in a lake after a stone had been tossed in.

Was there an answer to Laurence's question? There was far more than *no* or *yes* could convey. His skin's nerve endings were scattered and torn. He knew were Laurence's hands had begun, but the sensations came from nonsense locations: his stomach, his chest, as well as his waist. Sometimes the displacement was less than an inch, other times it felt like a mile. He knew this, knew his own body lied to him, and when he bathed himself it was a situation he was well used to. But when touched by another, his response was uncontrollable.

Freddy used to delight in this. Once he had learned Quentin was ticklish he'd taken great pleasure in jabbing him in the side or inflicting tickle-torture the moment Mother's back was turned. Thankfully Freddy was in a different dormitory at school, so incidents were few and far between, but they had hardly been Quentin's favorite childhood moments.

Laurence's touch was unlike any other. Light and gentle, and it stopped almost as soon as it had started. There was that watchful look on his face, that care for Quentin's comfort as he waited for an answer.

Quentin tugged his shirt straight and huffed.

There is nothing to fear here.

Other than the touch reminding Laurence of the horrid mess which lay just beneath his clothing. He knew. He'd seen it before. But then Quentin hid it, buried his shame, and retreated behind his armor and Laurence wasn't supposed to get past that. He wasn't supposed to know that Quentin was flawed.

That he was broken.

Laurence was still there. Waiting. Not pushing.

Quentin closed his eyes. Just for a moment, to try and understand what was so confusing about such a simple question. He needed a second to process, to try and line everything up neatly until it made sense.

"Quen?"

"I think so," he said. "Are you?"

When he opened his eyes, Laurence seemed confused. His brows were drawn together, and a faint smile lingered which hadn't reached his eyes. "Me? Sure. Why wouldn't I be?"

"Well, you—" Quentin gestured weakly to his stomach.

You touched me.

Laurence looked down between them, then his smile took hold properly. "I know what's under there, baby. Nothing scary. Nothing bad. Just you. All you."

He swallowed. "Then... Yes. Thank you."

"Oh, don't thank me." Laurence strolled toward the sofa and sank onto it. His knees spread, and he beckoned. "I might do it again. You never know, man. Depends whether you're gonna keep asking questions about your birthday present."

"Ah." He smiled dryly. "Consequences."

"Told you."

"Mm." He approached the sofa and settled by Laurence's side, turning to face him with one arm resting along the back of the furniture.

The ball was in his court. With a few words Laurence had handed everything to him. All the power, all the control over what may or may not come next. Endlessly considerate, always letting Quentin set the pace even in such seemingly harmless interactions.

Laurence turned to face him and laid his arm alongside Quentin's, fingers resting against his shoulder. "You know, traditionally in this country if you've invited a guest into your home for tea, you then make the tea."

Quentin snorted a short laugh. "That is the tradition in England also. Forgive me. I was... distracted. What would you like? Assam? Orange Pekoe?"

"Got any of that Ceylon?"

"I do." He hesitated. "I will trade it for a hint."

"But hints come with consequences."

"That would be the purpose of a trade: to circumvent such consequences."

Laurence laughed and leaned in toward him. "Man, you're a glutton for punishment, aren't you?"

He laughed softly and watched as Laurence came closer.

If you wished to lead more, here is your opportunity.

And most likely that was Laurence's offer, too. He always handed Quentin the reins, and perhaps that was more than the kindness it seemed. It was possible that Laurence was giving Quentin the chance to do as he had asked: to woo him. Not with flowers or gifts, but in a language that Laurence understood and had been teaching him these past weeks.

I am not a coward.

He trailed his palm over Laurence's sleeve and up toward his neck, where his fingers eased into the curls behind Laurence's ear. They were soft and dense, slightly damp with sweat, and warmed by his body.

Laurence watched him as he leaned closer. Before Quentin could open his mouth to ask, he whispered, "Yes."

He dipped in and brushed his lips to Laurence's and found that Laurence opened his mouth slowly without any prompting. Quentin tilted to the side as he pressed harder, and then he took the plunge and eased his tongue tentatively toward Laurence's.

Laurence sagged against him. His hands fumbled at the hem of Quentin's shirt. At first he pulled at it, but then his palms found Quentin's skin and rested either side of his torso.

Quentin's breath caught. His fingers tensed and gripped locks of hair.

Laurence moaned into his mouth. They shared breath as though they relied on one another to stay alive, and each of Laurence's exhalations came with a soft, keening sound that vibrated against Quentin's tongue and seemed to flow beyond, into his own chest.

Quentin leaned back. His other hand felt for and clutched at Laurence's shirt. He was drowning, but he wasn't yet ready to reach for the surface.

They were one. Connected, dependent, mindless, and heated. He surprised himself when he let out a faint moan and for a second he'd thought Laurence had made the sound, but it was him. It had to be him, because Laurence responded with a deeper sound, almost a growl, and then Quentin was on his back and Laurence was over him, hands moving up to his ribs, weight pressing down, heat washing over him.

Quentin's breath came quickly. His brain seemed to have shut itself down. Everything was Laurence: the strength of his musk, the residual spice in his mouth, the warmth of his hands, the weight of his body. There was a slow pressure building inside him, and his trousers began to feel too tight.

Laurence's hips pressed against his own, but didn't quite meet. There was hardness there instead, keeping them apart, yet stabbing pleasure into him as the weight squeezed them together.

His heart jammed against his ribs. He was desperate to breathe. He heard his pulse—throbbing and uneven—in his own ears. There was a sickness in his stomach which made it cramp, and the pain from it shot down his legs and into his arms.

Fear chased the pain. He felt trapped, pinned, and smothered. Laurence's body was crushing him.

He was so dizzy that he wasn't sure which way was up anymore. His head swam. He tried to push Laurence away, but his arms were leaden and unresponsive. He'd lost control of everything from the situation to his own body, and that realization pushed him further toward total panic.

He couldn't breathe anymore. His heart couldn't last.

He was going to die.

6

LAURENCE

THERE WAS SOME COMFORT IN FEELING QUENTIN'S AROUSAL through his pants. Laurence had been curious whether Quentin might be fully asexual, but there was a pretty damn clear signal down below that demanded an equal response from his own cock. Hell, it urged more. It made him buck and moan like a stag in rut. For all that he'd had to take care of himself lately, Quentin's body hard and writhing under him reached into his lizard brain and primed him for sex.

Wind whipped around them. It came from nowhere. It didn't start as a breeze, but rather as a full-formed gale that dried the sweat from his scalp in seconds. Well, that wasn't wholly unexpected: Quentin lost control when he was afraid as well as upset, but he was damn excited so far as Laurence could tell.

You should check.

He tried to quash the tiny voice of doubt. *Go away. We're getting somewhere at last!*

Yeah but you really ought to check.

He groaned in frustration and raised his head. "Quen?"

Quentin's gray eyes were wide with terror, irises almost swallowed whole by his pupils. His skin was pale as milk, and he was hyperventilating.

Laurence's gut tightened.

He'd done this.

He pushed too hard, and now Quentin was in a full-blown panic attack as if Laurence had tried to assault him or something.

Goddess, that hurt. No, it more than hurt. It was a body blow to everything he'd worked hard at ever since he'd laid eyes on Quentin. All the baby steps, all the care, all the patience and self-control rent asunder by his own stupid, *stupid* prick.

He eased back slowly until he was free of Quentin, then curled against the back of the couch. "Quen?" His voice shook. "Quentin? Baby? Can you hear me? You need to calm down."

He heard a crack. He didn't dare raise his head in case he got hit by a chair from the dining table or anything else that might have broken free from gravity.

Quentin was afraid of him.

Laurence choked back a sob and curled his arms around his knees. "Baby? Please, come back to me? You're gonna lose your security deposit if you keep going."

There was a lot of glass in those windows. Enough to cut him to ribbons if Quentin didn't regain control.

"Quentin!"

He sat and waited as Quentin screwed his eyes shut and held his breath.

He waited.

Quentin counted down from ten, didn't he? That was how he clawed himself back whenever he went overboard? Laurence tried it himself, but he reached zero twice before the winds finally died down.

He gnawed at his thumb and fought the urge to say anything.

Goddess, it was the longest thirty seconds of his life, and he had nothing to occupy his time with but the haunting memory of the fear written in Quentin's gaze. Each unit of time that dragged past him heaped more shame and loathing in its wake, because Laurence wouldn't ever do a damn thing to hurt Quentin—not in a million years—and yet the man he loved was scared witless of him.

Laurence hiccupped and rubbed his eyes with the palms of his hands to try and take away the sting.

They were too different. Too opposed. Even if Quentin was demisexual it wasn't going to be enough. Laurence was horny every single day. He'd been hanging on, holding back, waiting, but it wasn't going to work. Not if Quentin was going to treat him like a rapist after *he* initiated something.

Laurence scowled and pushed himself to his feet, then strode around the apartment like a caged tiger. He righted fallen chairs and found a towel to soak up the water from a spilled vase of flowers. He gathered the blooms together and almost tossed them in the trash, but couldn't bring himself to do it, and returned them to the vase which he refilled from the kitchen sink.

It helped his helpless anger subside enough for him to risk a glance toward the couch.

Quentin was back at last. Upright, watching Laurence with confusion and worry.

Laurence sucked his teeth and set the vase back on the dining table. "What do you remember?"

"You were here." Quentin tapped the couch. Laurence heard the soft pat of his hand against the leather cushion.

"And that's all?"

Quentin's head bobbed faintly. "Are you all right?"

Nervous, ridiculous laughter bubbled out of him like gas escaping from soda. "Me? Am I all right? You're the one who went off like a bomb, Quen."

"Why?"

His laughter escalated to near hysteria, and he stalked back to the kitchen to toss the towel into the washer. "You were kissing me. Making out like you meant it. You were all over me, Quentin, then you just—" *Got an erection.*

You got hard, and panicked.

He sagged against the kitchen countertop and sighed. "You noped out, baby. You just flipped the switch and went to your happy place, and it took a while for you to recover."

"Did I hurt you?"

Only in every way it matters.

"No." The word was thick in Laurence's mouth. "I think you broke a window, but only in one corner."

"You look wounded," Quentin said quietly.

Laurence laughed again. It wasn't funny. Nothing was funny about any of this. He laughed so hard that tears spilled down his cheeks and he had to lean against the counter for support. "Wounded?" The word sounded strangled and distant. "Fuck, Quentin, you looked at me like I'd tried to—" He hiccupped. He couldn't say it, didn't dare say that word in Quentin's presence. That was a seed that he mustn't ever plant. If it found fertile soil it'd take root and that would be the end of them.

His stomach churned. Bile burned its way up to the back of his throat and he coughed, then shifted to the sink so that he could spit it out and wash it away. It left his mouth tasting like a trash can.

Black tar was better than this, and that was a shitty grade to shoot up on.

The craving slammed him out of nowhere. It clawed at his throat and made his skin itch. He began a litany of requirements, a list of everything he was going to need.

Lighter. Spoon. Water. Needle.

He coughed and spat into the sink. There was a weight between his shoulders. His vision blurred with tears, and as he wiped them with the back of his hand a glass of water came into view and he grabbed at it. Downed half of it. Swilled out his mouth and spat it into the sink. Poured the rest away as he worked out that it was Quentin's hand on his back.

"I'm sorry." Quentin spoke quietly.

Laurence shook his head. He gripped the edge of the sink and fought to drag his mind off the needle. Weed. He needed a joint.

His tobacco tin was in the glove box.

It wasn't much, but it was a thin thread of salvation. If he could get to the truck he could light up. If he could get stoned, he might stay away from trying to score some heroin. If he could make it through to morning he'd be too busy at work to find a dealer. If he made it to the afternoon he'd be too busy with Quentin to score a hit.

If Quentin ever wanted to see him again.

"Laurence?"

"I can't—" He fought to stand up straight, and Quentin's hand dropped away. He missed the touch immediately. "You didn't mean anything by it, baby," he whispered, his throat dry and hoarse. "It's not your fault."

Quentin didn't answer. Laurence turned from the sink to find him standing so close, yet so far away, his shoulders hunched and head hanging like a chastised child's.

He wanted to reach out, to draw Quentin into his arms, to tell him that nothing was his fault and that everything would be okay. He couldn't. Couldn't touch Quentin in case the man reacted to it. Couldn't comfort him because he needed to comfort himself first.

He couldn't stay.

"Look, I, uh." Laurence cleared his throat. "I've gotta get home. I'm opening the shop in the morning. What with Mom being gone. You, uh." He sighed. "You promise you'll come by in the afternoon?" He swallowed and added in a small voice, "Please?"

"Of course," Quentin breathed. "I promise."

He nodded. It made him dizzy, so he had to stop. "Promise me something else?"

"Anything." Quentin gazed up at him.

"No alcohol."

Quentin searched his gaze, then nodded. "No heroin," he said quietly.

"Deal." He patted his curls awkwardly, and set off toward the door. "I gotta go. See you tomorrow, baby. I'm gonna get some sleep, and eveything'll be okay."

"All right."

Laurence rushed from the apartment. Quentin could shut the door behind him, he didn't care. He couldn't stay there a moment longer, not with Quentin looking at him like he had cooties. He rattled down the stairs and out into evening air so warm that it brought his sweat back by the time he reached the cab of the truck.

He searched the glove box for the tin, jammed a joint into his mouth, and sucked on it as he lit it. He sat there, drawing deeply, pulling it into his lungs as fast as he could until the buzz took hold.

Only then did he trust himself to start the engine, and by the time he hit the I-5 he was onto the second joint.

He'd made a deal. No heroin.

He clung to that brittle bulwark, because if he didn't there was nothing to keep Quentin from drink anymore. That was the deal. A life for a life.

Just one more night. That's all he had to hold on for.

Just one.

7

QUENTIN

He slept poorly. How could he do otherwise? He had blacked out, and when he came to Laurence was hurt. Oh, not physically, no, but that didn't make it any less a disaster.

Quentin had hurt the one person in the world he cared for.

He showered and meticulously cared for his scars after. He shaved while glowering at the dark circles beneath his eyes in the mirror. He had to get away, find some space, room in which to breathe. While those feelings usually precipitated a move to a new city, this time it would mean leaving something precious, and he couldn't bear the thought of it.

He would have to run on a far less metaphorical level.

Coward.

Quentin grimaced at his reflection and turned out the light.

His route had become routine now. He would jog from the apartment to the southernmost point of Windansea Beach, by which time he would have warmed up enough to traverse the rocky beach at speed. From there the terrain became actual rock and required a great deal of precision to traverse safely. Onward, hugging the shoreline, he would pass through the Marine Street beach, alongside Cuvier Park and then onward to La Jolla Cove, finally reaching the Shore where he could really cut loose and hit full speed. The return journey took the same pathways.

The run always made him sweat almost to the point of dehydration, and that would only grow worse with the summer heat. He could not jog in anything less than full-length jogging bottoms or tops lest prying eyes catch a glimpse of his skin, and the bottle of water he took with him was empty by the time he reached the cove today.

It hardly seemed to matter. Not in comparison to what had occurred last night.

What the hell was wrong with him? There had to be a problem —a serious one—if Laurence's reaction was anything to go by. The poor man had shrunk in on himself as though Quentin had caused him serious injury.

And what if, one day, Quentin *did* do him physical harm? He blacked out during his episodes, and lost all control over his telekinetic gifts. His power switched into some sort of defensive panic which hurled any and every object nearby around as though they were child's toys. By all accounts he had done serious harm to Dan during such an encounter, and then to Jack during the same sort of situation.

If he were to hurt Laurence during one of his blackouts, that would be utterly unconscionable.

His footing faltered, and he stumbled on smooth sand.

Where was he?

Quentin looked up and used a sleeve to wipe sweat from his eyes as he assessed the view ahead. Creamy cliffs jutted from the white sands, so similar to those of Dover and yet a world away from them.

This was the northernmost end of the beach. Bloody hell, how had he come this far without realizing it? He'd even passed the pier, which was there when he turned on the spot to search for it.

You could do worse than hurt him.

You could kill him.

Sand at his feet began to jitter and bounce as though heralding an earthquake.

He could kill Laurence, without even being aware of it. He was a danger to every living thing.

How often had this happened? Had he harmed his way from one city to the next without knowing it? He'd thought that being shunned by society was down to his behavior at Mother's funeral and his father's condemnation of Quentin's actions, but what if it ran deeper?

Had he hurt those who initially gave him shelter?

He tried to run, but the fear clawed at the back of his throat and brought whorls of sand cascading around him as he moved. He couldn't afford to let panic take hold. Not here.

Not anywhere.

He stumbled from the beach and up to a bench nestled among flowering shrubs, where he collapsed against the solid seat and screwed his eyes shut.

Ten. Nine.

Every breath was a struggle. He had to regain control. He *must*.

For Laurence's sake.

Six. Five.

You will compose yourself, Quentin. You are Heir Apparent to the Duchy of Oxford. You will behave as such.

His father's words were unwelcome, although perhaps the man had a point. Everything was about control with him and Quentin had hated it, but what if driving the old stiff upper lip into his son had been less about traditional socially acceptable behavior and more about handing Quentin the keys to reining in this amount of power?

He gasped and gripped the bench seat.

Did his father *know*?

Did the Duke somehow comprehend Quentin's gifts?

He shook his head and gripped harder. He'd lost count. He had to start over.

Laurence had taught him some meditation techniques. Simple counting and breathing were not enough now, so Quentin tried to still his mind. He listened to the crash of the ocean. He focused on the twist of ozone in the air and the cries of seabirds. With each breath he tamped down on just one tip of the wildfire raging in his heart until he felt able to open his eyes.

The only wind now was that from the ocean. The shrubs around him waved gently in it.

The world was safe from him once more.

Quentin took his hands from the bench and rested them in his lap as he leaned back and watched the sea. He didn't dare try to pick over any of his thoughts from the past few minutes, so instead he watched the water and allowed the combination of sight and sound to dominate his senses. He watched as water broke into surf, white blooming from the blue like a flower bursting into blossom. Birds waded in the shallow tide and picked at anything remotely tasty. There were small puffs of white clouds in the sky. People had begun to populate the beach: some jogged or ran, others were walking their dogs.

He needed water. His mouth was dry, and the morning would only grow hotter as time passed.

"Hey. Is this seat taken?"

Quentin turned toward the voice and found a man roughly his own age standing at the end of the bench, one hand outstretched toward the space at Quentin's side.

"No, not at all," he murmured.

"Thanks." The fellow sat.

Quentin glanced over him, his attention momentarily snared by the American's demeanor, and he looked perhaps a second or two more than was polite while he tried to work out what had caught his eye.

The man wasn't especially interesting to look at from an aesthetic perspective. He took no particular care over his grooming other than to maintain cleanliness, and as such his brown hair was ill-cut and lacked shine. He had at least shaved recently, but likely with a blunted razor if the dulling red rash at his throat was anything to go by. His clothing fit him well, but not so much that it had been tailored to him.

No, there was something in the cant of his head, the tilt of his shoulders. He held himself with such confidence that Quentin suspected that the mediocre grooming was some sort of feint.

KNIGHT OF FLAMES

He readied himself to stand, satisfied that he had identified the trait which had tugged on his attention.

"Oh, hey. There's no need to leave on my account."

Quentin offered one of his polite, practiced smiles. "It's quite all right. I was merely resting a moment. One has quite the run to continue on with."

"'One,' huh?" The American nodded to himself. "What are you, like, out of Downton Abbey or something?" He leaned forward. "You're probably loaded, right?"

"Probably." Quentin stood and tugged on the cuffs of his hooded sweatshirt to ensure that they were neatly aligned.

"How about you just hand over anything valuable, huh?"

Quentin blinked at that and turned to gaze down at the stranger. "I beg your pardon?"

To his credit, the American looked every bit as baffled as Quentin felt. The man cleared his throat and stood, although he didn't come any closer. He spoke slowly and clearly, as though addressing an infant. "Are you carrying anything of value? Cellphone? A watch? Your wallet?" Then he reached out with his right hand. "If so, give them to me."

Quentin regarded him in disbelief. Was the poor fellow bonkers, or was this actually some surreal attempt at mugging?

"Why would I do such a thing?" he murmured. He maintained an even tone lest the stranger turn out to be violent.

Or armed.

But the other man seemed, if anything, completely confused himself. His eyebrows were drawing themselves together, and his gaze had begun to sweep up and down Quentin as though some answer could be found hidden on his person. "Uh." He shook his head. "Because I told you to?"

"Dear boy, if I always did as I was told I would not be here to begin with." Quentin tilted his head a little. "Are you quite all right?"

Confidence bled from the stranger. His shoulders hunched. His eyes turned furtive. He wrung his hands together and then stuffed them into the pockets of his trousers. "Sorry. I'm sorry. I, uh. I have no idea what just came over me." He blinked and shook his head again. "You, uh. You have a nice day, okay?"

"Thank you. You also." Quentin nodded faintly and stepped away from the bench. The more distance he put between himself and this seemingly unwell fellow the better. He was crazy enough himself without having another flavor of insanity on hand to upset the balance he'd managed to achieve here.

He set off at a light pace to warm up, and didn't look back. It was best not to, lest the poor chap decide to have another go at it —whatever *it* was supposed to be.

8

LAURENCE

LAURENCE'S MORNING WAS TOTALLY MISERABLE. HE HAD TO WORK his ass off before he opened the store to get orders ready for delivery, and then Rodger had showed up an hour late making some lame excuse which basically boiled down to *Myriam's away so I slept in*. The idea which had seemed so awesome for Quentin's birthday yesterday started to look like a whole different ball game after the freakout last night, but if he tried to tell Quentin not to come over this afternoon where would that leave them?

He scratched at the inside of his elbow while serving a customer, and only noticed the gesture once the middle-aged lady had paid and left.

He had to get the situation with Quentin fixed or he'd be up shit creek.

Laurence plastered his best customer service face on when the doorbell jangled, then ditched it with relief when he saw who had entered. "Hey, man."

Ethan came to the counter and hopped up onto it, sitting with his back to Laurence. "'Sup, dude? You still alive?"

Laurence snorted at him. "Yeah. You don't get rid of me that easy."

They'd been buddies for a few years now. After Laurence left rehab the first time he met Ethan in a bar and the guy steadfastly refused to sleep with him, but it turned out to be because Ethan was head over heels for some dude who owned his own taco stand. When that fell through, he was crazy in love with one that worked at the zoo, handling bugs in front of kids all day.

Whenever Laurence was free, Ethan wasn't, and vice versa. For four years Laurence had failed to get into Ethan's pants, not for lack of trying, but maybe it was for the best. Ethan found "the one" every other week, and that'd sour their friendship if Laurence ditched him after they'd banged.

"I don't?" Ethan cast a crooked grin down at him. "I see you hanging with some megastars all over Twitter, dude. Rich ones, famous ones, good lookin' ones... Rumor is you're boning some hot British guy now?"

Laurence shrugged.

"Haven't seen you in ages is all," Ethan admitted. "So I figured I'd stop by and see if you and me were okay."

"Yeah. I'm sorry, man. I've been really busy." He brushed his curls back from his forehead and puffed out his cheeks, then let the air out in a rush. "Want some tea?"

"Naw, but I'll take coffee. And weed, if you've got any?"

"I'm all out." Laurence headed through the curtain to the back room. "The greenhouse got wrecked and I haven't grown more yet."

"Too bad." The beads clattered as Ethan joined him. "You managed to ditch Dan at last, right?"

Laurence shrugged as he grabbed a mug and filled it with coffee from the machine. "He hung on a while, but yeah. Gone now. How 'bout you? Who are you in love with this week?"

"Fuck you." Ethan laughed and took the mug as he perched by the table. "Just because you haven't found him yet doesn't mean I won't."

Laurence eyed him and pulled a faint smile out of his ass before he turned to make himself a mug of tea.

"So if you aren't growing..." Ethan slurped, then sighed. "Wait. You're not back on the hard stuff, are you, dude?"

Laurence swiveled on the balls of his feet and offered both arms to Ethan. "Check if you want."

"Like I don't know you can inject anywhere?" Ethan looked up to him and puffed a wisp of his long mousy hair out of his eyes. "If you're not using, Laur, that's all I care about. But no weed either? Don't take this the wrong way, but that doesn't sound like you."

Laurence sighed and finished making his tea, then sat by Ethan's side. "Been cutting back on it."

Ethan's stare burned a hole in his ear.

"Quentin doesn't like it." He blew on the tea. "He's not a smoker."

"Quentin's the new guy, right? The hot royalty?"

"He's not royalty. He's an aristocrat. Don't ask me to explain the difference," he added after taking a mouthful of tea. "Weird British stuff."

Ethan chuckled. "That's kinda overbearing, isn't it? Telling you whether or not you can light up?"

Laurence shrugged and swallowed more tea. The drink was too hot, but it beat waiting for his head to straighten itself out enough to give Ethan a decent answer.

Maybe Ethan had a point. From his perspective, Laurence had dropped his friends like a hot potato the moment Quentin entered his life, and the guy had already got him to cut back on most of the things he enjoyed in life: sleeping around, smoking pot, staying out late to get wasted. It had to look to Ethan like Quentin had swooped in out of nowhere and completely taken over, especially as all Ethan had to go on was Twitter gossip.

It wasn't like Quentin was another Dan, though. Goddess, no. It was different. Not just because Quentin was gifted, not just because he'd nursed Laurence back to health after the fight with Jack, not just because he was richer than Croesus. Quentin just… liked to be in charge.

How is that different?

"Maybe," he sighed.

"I just want you to be happy, dude." Ethan clapped a hand on his shoulder and squeezed it. "Is the sex good at least?"

Laurence was too tired to hide the side-eye he gave Ethan.

Ethan's eyes grew and his pupils dilated. "You're shitting me!"

"Ethan!"

"You're not even getting any?"

"He's got—" Laurence hesitated. "Issues."

"Fuck." Ethan let go of his shoulder and drained his coffee. "When was the last time you saw a new movie?"

"Uh..."

"Went out without him?"

"Um..."

"Do you even get any time to yourself?"

"Sometimes!" Laurence's irritation grew at the rapid barrage of questions.

"Getting a little co-dependent, huh?" Ethan moved to the sink and placed his mug in it. "I just want you to be happy, dude, especially after that asshole Dan. You can't go letting him ruin you for life."

"It's not—"

The bell above the front door jingled, and Laurence grimaced.

"Saved by the bell," Ethan muttered.

"Maybe." He rubbed his face and adopted his more customer-friendly expression as he headed through the bead curtain.

Quentin was there.

Laurence's heart leaped. He felt dizzy. He'd half-expected Quentin not to show, and half-forgotten that he was even supposed to arrive. Did this mean Quentin was okay with last night? Had he come to tell Laurence it was all over?

Goddess, Laurence hadn't even had time to sort through his own feelings about what had happened. He'd shoved it all in a box and tossed the key somewhere out of reach so that he could get on with the day and not call Mikey.

Quentin's lips parted a touch, then his eyes flitted aside to look behind Laurence.

"Hey. You must be Quentin." Ethan stepped forward and offered his hand. "I'm Ethan. Laur and I go way back."

Quentin took the hand and held it briefly. "I see."

The temperature seemed to be falling sharply in the confines of the shop. Quentin's gaze was assessing Ethan like the man was an invader in his personal space, with his chin raised and his posture stiff.

Laurence eyed them both a second before it clicked.

Quentin was *jealous* again.

A little squeak sounded from the back of his throat, and he swallowed in case anyone but him heard it. *Fuck*, Quentin jealous was so goddamn hot. Everything possessive and controlling in the Brit came out in that look, that stiff posture, and Laurence had to hold himself steady before he threw himself at the guy's feet. It was ridiculous. All Quentin had done was *look* at Ethan and Laurence was pushed toward the edge.

He drew a breath, and a small voice intruded.

How dare he?

How dare Quentin be remotely jealous after the way he'd responded last night! He'd treated Laurence like a potential rapist for fuck's sake, and here Laurence stood wriggling in anticipation of something that looked more and more like it wasn't ever going to come.

"I sense a disturbance in the Force," Ethan chuckled. "I should get going. Oh, hey! Laur!"

"Huh?" Laurence rubbed his eyes.

"Why don't you and Quentin come over one night? You can meet Aiden. We can do a double date, get a few beers, watch a movie, play some games?"

That caught Laurence off guard, and he snorted. "Who the hell is Aiden? Wait, don't tell me—"

"He's the one!" Ethan crowed with delight.

Laurence groaned. "Oh, man."

"C'mon. You bring yours, I'll bring mine, we can all get to know each other!"

"We'll think about it, okay?"

"All right! Catch you later, Quentin!" Ethan patted Quentin's shoulder as he headed for the door, and Laurence had to stifle a laugh at the look on Quentin's face.

The bell jangled, and Laurence sipped his tea as he eyed Quentin.

Was Ethan right? *Were* they co-dependent?

That wasn't really fair, though. There was a whole lot Ethan didn't know. Laurence had never mentioned his gifts, not even to his best friend, and he sure as hell wasn't going to tell him about Quentin's. Ethan didn't know Quentin was an alcoholic or that he blacked out if he got scared.

Quentin eased his hands behind his back. "Ethan?" he asked.

"Just a friend," Laurence said. "Never anything more."

Quentin nodded.

And just like that, it was all right. It was like sunlight breaking through clouds.

He believes me.

Dan would have cajoled. He would have wheedled. He would have harped on about seeing Laurence with another human being for days on end, then thrown it in his face during an argument a month later. He'd always been a biphobic little shit, but it really came out in force during a fight.

But Quentin took Laurence at his word. Laurence said that there was nothing there, and Quentin was content with that.

He trusts me.

Laurence smiled slowly and put his mug on the counter. There was a glimmer of hope there, hidden in all the upset and hurt.

Maybe, just maybe, if Quentin trusted him, they could recover from last night.

"I'm glad you came," he breathed.

9

QUENTIN

QUENTIN HAD TO ADMIT TO HIMSELF THAT, IF ONLY FOR A SECOND, he would not have blamed Laurence in the slightest if he'd decided to flirt with another. Not after the abominable way Quentin had treated him last night. Good God, the man deserved far, far better.

If he wished to be worthy of this beautiful, kind creature, he would have to work to improve himself.

"How could I not?" he murmured, stepping toward the florist. "I owe you more than a mere apology."

Laurence remained in place and rubbed his arm. It was a defensive gesture, one likely intended to comfort himself as well as erect some small barrier between them as Laurence's arms came together in front of his stomach. "You don't owe me anything, Quen."

Quentin stopped. The urge to raise a hand, to touch Laurence's arm, was strong, but if he'd scared the poor boy witless last night then that may not be the best move to take. He pursed his lips and glanced toward the nearest display of roses, then offered up, "Ethan seemed nice."

"He's a decent guy," Laurence mumbled. "Just falls in love way too easy, too often. It's hard for him. Every new guy he meets is the one, you know?"

Quentin shook his head softly. "I do not," he murmured. "That must be difficult for him."

"Yeah." Laurence shifted his feet, then slowly lowered his arms and reached for Quentin's hands. "Are you okay?"

"Of course." He furled his fingers around Laurence's and allowed a small smile. "Although I had quite the peculiar morning, I must confess."

He recounted his strange encounter at the beach. There wasn't really much to tell. It had only stuck with him due to the sheer absurdity of it all, but if he were to be honest he would rather speak of that than discuss last night. Yes, he owed Laurence more than an apology. He would have to improve his composure, and that required practice and patience, neither of which could be rushed. For now the distraction of talking about an unrelated event at least meant that they were communicating again. The rest would come in time.

Laurence's hands squeezed his own. "Are you okay?"

"Always, darling."

"I'm serious." Laurence scowled and let go so that he could move his hands to Quentin's hips. "What if he'd tried to hurt you?"

"To what end?"

"To mug you!"

Quentin couldn't help but chuckle at that.

"It's not funny, Quen!"

"If the fellow really wished to take anything from me, he likely would have." He dared rest his hands on Laurence's biceps at last, and was relieved that the other man didn't flinch away. "Items can always be replaced. People cannot."

Laurence huffed. "But what if he'd been armed?"

"I think you and I both know that I should be able to defend myself in such an eventuality."

"I don't know." Laurence leaned forward until his chin came to rest on Quentin's shoulder, his cheek to Quentin's ear. "I'm sorry, baby. I don't want you to get hurt, that's all."

Quentin shifted his chin to Laurence's shoulder and allowed his eyes to drift closed. "I understand."

Laurence's scent mingled wonderfully with that of the shop itself. A myriad of different blooms whose perfumes interleaved in the background were overlaid by the warmth of Laurence's own, his unique musk which came from hours of hard work and very little else. The man wasn't one to load himself down with conflicting odors from colognes, aftershaves, or hair products. He had said once that he could smell the chemicals in most of the toiletries available and tended to choose organic or natural products. The only time there was any lingering fragrance about him was after he'd washed his hands with Myriam's foaming hand soap in the back room, which usually smelled of lemons or verbena.

His aroma was earthy and strong, and it reassured Quentin on some intrinsic level he could not explain. Being enveloped in the familiarity of it was like finding his way home after years at sea.

Quentin sighed gently and shifted his arms to wrap around Laurence's torso. "Thank you," he whispered.

"For what, hon?"

"For being you." He turned faintly so that he could press a light kiss to Laurence's jaw, and then he leaned back and opened his eyes. "Now. You requested that I stop by. Am I too early?"

"I just gotta wait for Rodger to get back. He was late this morning, so he's an hour behind on everything else."

Quentin quirked his eyebrows. "The cat is away, hmm?"

"Yeah." Laurence's lips twitched. "You're gonna love this, though. I hope. I mean, if you don't like it just say so, but I really think you're gonna like it."

"Ah, am I allowed a hint at last?" Quentin laughed warmly.

Laurence's eyes gleamed and he stepped away. "No. It's still a surprise. We're gonna need the truck, too."

"Hmm." He watched Laurence retreat. "Very well. I shall wait."

ONCE IN THE TRUCK, Quentin began to suspect that they may be on their way to the farm. The route was initially the same, but once they overshot the turn Laurence usually took he was beyond his knowledge of the area north of the city.

Laurence chuckled. "Nope."

He huffed and tore his attention from the turning and lounged back in his seat as though unfazed. "Am I being kidnapped?"

"Nope. You get to go home at the end of the day." Laurence's grin grew, and he lounged one arm out of his window, fingers waving in the air as though he were grasping at it.

"Then where are we headed?"

"You really wanna know?"

Quentin didn't answer immediately. It was a more interesting question than he supposed Laurence recognized. He was not at all fond of surprises, but then few surprises were pleasant, and he doubted that Laurence would intentionally plan anything that Quentin would not enjoy.

That meant it boiled down to trust. Did he trust Laurence to furnish him with a pleasant surprise? And such a question ran far deeper, did it not? Because if he could not trust Laurence on this, then where was that lack of trust to end?

This man had never harmed him, and never would. Therefore Quentin's trust had to be absolute.

"If you wish to tell me," he conceded, "I would like to know. But it is not necessary." He looked to Laurence, and then reached out to touch his thigh lightly. "I leave it in your hands, darling."

Laurence brought his hand back inside the truck to take the wheel so he could lay his other over Quentin's on his thigh, and he spared a moment's eye contact. "Okay." Eyes forward, his attention returned to the road. "There's a pet store in Carmel Mountain that runs adoption events every weekend." He grinned. "I thought we could go see if there were any dogs you liked."

Quentin blinked slowly.

"You, uh." Laurence's voice faltered. "You do like dogs, right? I thought I remembered you said once you had loads as a kid—"

Quentin nodded. "I do. I do! My God, Laurence, are you serious?"

Laurence's laughter was tinged with relief. "Yeah. I am."

Excitement rippled through Quentin. It began in his gut and then it was everywhere at once.

A dog!

He hadn't been around animals for what seemed a lifetime now. When he chose to leave home he lost access to the kennels and stables alike. Most of the friends he used to have didn't own pets in their London homes, and since then the constant restlessness had made animals untenable. It would have been most unfair for them to be on the move all the time.

The thrill grew. A dog! His *own* dog!

He made a sound alien to his own ears, like the squeal of a small child, and his fingers tightened on Laurence's thigh. "Oh my goodness! Are we allowed to bring one home today? Do we have to wait? Is there paperwork to fill out? How much does it cost? I have no dog food! Oh, but you said it's a pet shop, so they should have plenty, yes? And bedding? Toys! What about toys? Do you know what dogs they will have? Are they neutered already? Wormed? They must have had their vaccinations or they wouldn't be all together, yes?"

"Holy shit, Quen!" Laurence gripped the wheel and all but punched the turn signal. His head whipped to the mirrors and then he veered the truck toward the shoulder until they came to a halt half off the road.

"What? What's wrong?" He whipped his head around to look outside. Had they narrowly avoided an accident? Quentin hadn't been paying attention in the slightest.

The gravel outside the car was bouncing away from them.

He took a breath and turned to Laurence.

Now that they had stopped he could hear it. Fixtures in the truck rattling and straining. Items in the back throwing themselves against the sides of the van. A candy bar wrapper sweeping along the dashboard.

Laurence was wide-eyed, his stare fixed on Quentin. "I thought you *loved* dogs, man!"

"I do!" Quentin protested.

"Then what the fuck's going on?" Laurence grabbed the wrapper and thrust it into the ashtray.

"I don't know!"

Laurence rolled his window up, then squeezed Quentin's hand. "You gotta calm down."

Quentin looked down at their hands, then stared at Laurence. "This is—"

This is because I'm happy?

His mood crashed. It was one thing to lose control due to fear or upset, but to deny himself happiness felt cruel.

"Baby," Laurence said. Urgency strained the word.

Quentin gave a grim nod and closed his eyes, then began the countdown.

10

LAURENCE

Laurence kept one hand on the wheel and the other on Quentin's fingers as he waited, all the while praying that the van would still be drivable once Quentin got a lid on things.

He'd seen the look on Quentin's face before the man realized what was going on. That wasn't fear. It wasn't alarm. Goddess, he'd been full of all the glee of a kid in a candy store. Laurence had never seen him so excited, and now he was left wondering how the fuck things had started to tear themselves apart.

The rearview mirror cracked, and he cursed under his breath.

The concentration on Quentin's face was intense, and nothing Laurence could do would hurry him along. All he could do was be there.

All this time he'd thought it was some kind of defense mechanism. Quentin's gift triggered and he'd go to his happy place while whatever threatened him either got torn to shit or ran away screaming. But this wasn't terror, and Quentin wasn't protecting himself.

Could it be that last night wasn't because Quentin was afraid? He'd been aroused, and if the guy lost control at the thought of getting a dog he didn't stand a chance with being turned on.

Laurence peeled his fingers away from the wheel and flexed them before they got stiff.

If they ever got to have sex, was that going to set Quentin off? Would they have to make sure the room was totally empty before they even got to the heavy petting? Laurence wasn't down with being hit in the back of the head by a flying chair in the middle of things.

The rattling ceased, and Laurence looked toward the back to make sure everything was settled in there, too. It all looked pretty much done. There wasn't a whole lot there to get wrecked, but Quentin had broken what few empty vases and pots had been neatly stacked in a corner.

Dating this guy was pretty expensive.

Quentin released a breath and carefully opened his eyes.

"You got it," Laurence assured him. He offered a small smile. "You okay?"

"I am." Quentin licked his lips cautiously. "I apologize. I did not anticipate such an occurrence."

"It's okay, man." Laurence rolled his window down again and rested his elbow on the edge. "We'll get it figured out one day. You can use your gift without being upset, right? It works best when you're calm?"

Quentin's gaze remained even, and he inclined his head. "Correct."

"Then it doesn't rely on your emotional state. They're separate. You'll get better at it, and you'll be able to cut loose once you've had more practice, okay?"

He didn't know whether it was true, but he knew what he'd want to hear if he were in Quentin's shoes right now. He'd want to know that he'd be free to laugh and love and be excited. Goddess, the poor guy was staring down the barrel of a lifetime spent being on top of every single thought in case everything went to shit. Laurence couldn't let him believe that life was nothing but a prison from here on out.

Quentin turned toward him and squared his shoulders as best as he could in the passenger seat. "I have been somewhat lax in exercising this particular skill," he murmured. "I will do better."

"All right." Laurence leaned over. "Kiss?"

"Yes."

Laurence gave Quentin a light peck on the cheek, then patted his leg. "C'mon. Let's get off the shoulder before the cops come ask what we're doing here. Just… try to keep a lid on it, okay? We can figure out the rest later."

"I concur," Quentin said softly.

Laurence looked him over a moment to be sure he was okay, then pulled back out onto the interstate.

THE MOMENT they were out of the truck, Laurence could hear excited barking from inside the store, and he took Quentin's hand.

"Just take it easy," he said. "Okay?"

Quentin closed his eyes a few moments, then nodded as he opened them again.

"So here's how it works." Laurence walked him toward the store. Hopefully giving Quentin something to focus on would keep him calm once they went inside. "We check out the dogs they have here, and if you like one we show them ID and fill out the forms. There's a fee, but I've got that covered, okay? And if there aren't any here that you want we can come back next week, so don't feel like you have to pick one you don't like."

Quentin dipped his head as he listened, but as they went from the heat of a Saturday afternoon to the cool, air-conditioned interior, his eyes gleamed with delight and his features lit up.

It hurt to even think about telling him to calm down. Laurence didn't want to be that guy: the one who kept taking the fun away, the bad cop. But he couldn't let Quentin go off in here.

"Baby," he whispered. "Focus."

Quentin swallowed, and exhaled slowly.

"All right. Let's see what they've got, huh?" He grinned and released Quentin's hand, then followed him further into the store.

What they had was a whole lot of dogs. The store had a huge space in the center where a pen had been rigged up, barriers slotted together in a huge circle with the craziest mix of dogs he'd seen in one place before. There were people wearing polo shirts with the rescue organization's logo on them who were chatting with customers while the dogs barked or wagged or lay fast asleep disinterested in the whole process. There had to be twenty dogs here, at least. Everything from the tiniest Chihuahua to some kind of massive shaggy bear-dog that looked like a cross between a German shepherd and a grizzly.

Quentin cast him a questioning quirk of his eyebrows, and Laurence gestured to the pen. "I don't think you can go in, but you can walk around the outside and see if any of them like you."

"All right." Quentin smiled a moment and then peeled away from Laurence's side.

Laurence hung back, out of the way. There were other customers, not only to coo at the dogs but also just here to pick up supplies, and he tried to find a place to stand which was out of their way yet allowed him to keep an eye on Quentin. He ended up lounging against the barrier itself, and smiled as he watched the other man circle the pen.

Quentin wasn't at all the way he was with Ellie. With Myriam's dog, Quentin's playful side showed itself, but here he was more composed, even distant, and Laurence at first thought Quentin was doing his best to stay calm. The more he watched, the less sure he was that was the case.

He knew Quentin had a way with animals. Ellie had fallen in love with him like he was long-lost family. Wild birds didn't flee his presence. Big cats in the zoo didn't find him nearly as offensive as they did most tourists. But watching him now Laurence was struck by just how *good* he was with the dogs here.

Quentin moved slowly and crouched often. He offered his hand to be sniffed, and he would murmur so softly that even Laurence's keen hearing couldn't make out the words. Dogs sniffed him, licked his hand, and allowed him to reach through the barrier to fuss their flank or under their chin. When he stood he did so without sudden movement, and whatever dog he'd just made contact with began to follow him until, by the time he was most of the way around the pen almost all the dogs in it were tailing him. It seemed beyond just "good with animals" and risked veering well into the realm of Disney princess.

Laurence blinked and rested his elbows on the barrier.

Did Quentin have more than one gift?

Jack had stressed that neither of them were what he called "run-of-the-mill psychics." Laurence held more than one gift—and seemingly unrelated ones at that—because it transpired that he was descended from Herne the Hunter, but if Quentin were at all descended from a god then shouldn't Jack have picked up on it? He'd made it clear that he knew what Laurence was way before Laurence found out for himself, but more than once he'd stated that he had no idea what gave Quentin such power.

But this wasn't telekinesis. No way. These dogs weren't being dragged around against their will. They were like kids tailing the Pied Piper, their tails up and their tongues hanging out, relaxed. It was one of the weirdest things Laurence had seen while sober, and if *he* thought it was weird...

He straightened and checked out the rescue center staff, only to find that most of them had also noticed. Those not with other customers were watching the dogs, and one middle-aged lady with a clipboard had started talking to Quentin.

"Shit," Laurence muttered. He pushed away from the barrier and hurried around the pen, affecting his best lazy smile on his approach. He looped an arm around one of Quentin's and leaned against his side. "Hey baby," he cooed. "Found any you like?"

Quentin broke into a restrained smile and squeezed Laurence's arm. "Two," he breathed.

That lone word snapped Laurence right back to the here and now. "Two?"

"Please?"

Oh *Goddess*, how could he resist those eyes?

Laurence cleared his throat and offered the clipboard-wielding woman a polite smile. "Hey," he greeted her. Then he looked to Quentin.

The eyes were still there, big and adorable.

"Fine," he sighed. "Which ones?"

Quentin gestured to a nearby Border collie who seemed surprisingly calm for her breed, and then on to...

Laurence groaned.

Quentin had chosen the gigantic bear of a dog.

"Are you sure you need *both* of them, baby?" he grumbled. "That one's two dogs all on its own!"

"I know the offer was for one," Quentin breathed. "I will cover the fees of the other."

"Naw. There's no need for that." Laurence gnawed on his thumb, then let out a sigh of defeat. "Okay, okay. If you want them both, let's do it." He smiled to the lady and reached for her clipboard. "I'll do the paperwork."

She stepped over the barrier and led him to a counter they could lean on, and he had to wonder whether this was as good an idea as it had seemed when it burst into his head the day before. What if Quentin's landlord didn't allow pets? What if his maid was allergic to dogs?

He bit his tongue. It was way too late to think this through. That was all stuff he should have figured out before he'd told Quentin where they were going today. He cursed himself silently for being a total damn idiot and filled out the forms in silence.

This plan had better damn well work.

11

QUENTIN

Quentin watched in awe as Laurence carried a huge bag of dog food through to the kitchen, slung over one shoulder the same way that he ferried soil or fertilizer into his mother's shop. He made it look so effortless, when in fact Quentin knew it to be far too heavy to lift himself without the use of his abilities.

Laurence landed the bag heavily and leaned it back against the wall, then wiped his forehead with the back of his hand. "I think that's everything up from the truck now."

"Thank you." Quentin had removed the dogs' collars and allowed them to investigate the apartment, although the collie was less interested than the other, which so far as he could tell was a mixture of German shepherd and Rottweiler. Entirely understandable. The poor girl had been in foster care for well over a year. This was a wholly new environment for her. Quentin and Laurence were both strangers.

And she was blind.

"No worries." Laurence came over and fussed the larger of the two dogs on the head, and her tail thudded briefly. "You sure about these two, baby? They seem kinda... I dunno. Withdrawn."

"They are perfect." He moved to Laurence's side and eased an arm around his waist. "As are you."

"Uh-huh." Laurence looked him dead in the eye, then smirked. "What aren't you telling me?"

"I've no idea what you mean."

"We go in for one dog and come out with two. What aren't you telling me?"

Quentin pursed his lips. Laurence was rather astute at times, and it seemed that this was one of those moments. "According to their paperwork, the collie is named Grace, and the bitsa is called Pepper."

Laurence opened his mouth, then shut it again. "Bitsa?"

He laughed and stepped away. "Bits-a-this, bits-a-that."

"Oh!" Laurence peeled his shoes off. "Grace and Pepper, huh. I like 'em. But you don't get away so easy, baby."

Quentin inclined his head, then gently ushered both dogs toward the bathroom. There was an odd odor to Grace in particular, as though she had rolled in something unsavory on her way to the shop, which he wouldn't at all put past a dog of her breed. "Grace is blind," he tossed over his shoulder.

Laurence padded after him. "She *what?*"

He stripped his waistcoat off and laid it over the back of a chair in the bedroom as he passed by. "That's why they've been unable to rehome her," he murmured. "She can't see a thing, Laurence. Blind as a bat, aren't you, sweetheart?" He crouched to let her sniff his hand before he ran it alongside her shoulder so that she knew who was touching her. "The only reason they haven't yet put her down is because her foster careperson refused to allow it. I couldn't leave her there with such an uncertain future. Could I?" he asked Grace. "No, I could not. Shh. You're quite safe." He hooked his arms under her and, with the aid of his gift, gently lifted her into the bathtub.

Laurence sighed softly. "You're such a softie. It's pretty adorable. But how does that mean *two* dogs?"

"Ah." Quentin switched to Pepper and heaved her into the tub alongside Grace. "Pepper, on the other hand, is bored. She's a mixture of at least two highly intelligent working breeds and she does very little all day. She needs a job to do or she will be a handful." He rolled up his sleeves and reached for the shower head.

Laurence was quiet as Quentin fiddled with the water until he was satisfied with the temperature and gently introduced it to Grace's coat. "You're not seriously telling me," he said at last, "that you're gonna train Pepper to be Grace's guide dog?"

"It should come reasonably easily to her," he offered. "She's very empathetic."

"You got that in, what, twenty minutes?"

"No." Quentin laughed softly as Pepper tried to drink from the shower head. "Five."

"Like, what? Dr. Dolittle? He's a fictional character," Laurence added. "Talks to animals."

"That one I do actually know," he admitted. "Mother used to read a variety of stories to us. *The Voyages of Doctor Dolittle* was one she was very fond of." He shook his head. "But no. Not like that. Dogs express themselves through their facial expressions, their body language, as well as their vocalizations. Their ears, tail, the eyes, it all comes together to form quite readable communication." He paused and glanced over his shoulder to find Laurence leaning against the door frame. "Just as with humans, although rather easier to understand."

Laurence was giving him the most speculative of looks, then came over and perched on the edge of the tub. "It just seemed kinda more than that, you know? All those dogs following you around the store."

He had no idea what Laurence could be implying, and so he simply responded with, "Mm." He gently ran water over Grace's coat and chased it with his palm to smooth it and any dirt off her. "Now it is you who is dancing around the subject matter."

"I dunno." Laurence reached out and ran his fingers through Quentin's hair, brushing it out of his eyes for him. "Has it always been like that with animals? When you were a kid?"

"I suppose." He flinched and turned away as Grace shook herself and sprayed water everywhere, and snorted at her. "I think that's as clean as we're going to get you, isn't it, sweetie?" He turned the water on Pepper instead, who started trying to bite it. "Ah, no. None of that, Pepper."

"You're getting wet." Laurence's chuckle was low. Sly. Presumably he inferred something crude by his comment.

It seemed to be the case that Laurence's crudeness was usually intended as flirtatious. Although Quentin was hardly experienced in such things, he could try to reciprocate.

He smiled wryly and flicked the shower head toward Laurence for a second. "And now so are you," he observed.

"Ah!" Laurence leaped from the tub, but it was too late. "Man, I shoulda seen that coming."

"You really should have."

"It doesn't work that way."

"So it would seem." Quentin continued bathing Pepper and closed his eyes whenever either dog decided to shake themselves to try and dry off.

Laurence grumbled as he sat. "Oh, Goddess, now my ass is wet." He huffed and rested his hands on one thigh. "Baby, can I ask you something?"

"Of course."

"Do you remember your mom's funeral?"

Quentin's mouth dried. He felt queasy. His hands shook as they tried to direct the water, so he reached over and turned it off. Only then did he realize that if he wished to get the dogs out of the bath he would get considerably wetter, but there was nothing he could do about it. He took a towel from the rack and wrapped it around Grace before he lifted her out and placed her on the mat.

"Like, there's a rumor online," Laurence said with care. "About the weather."

Quentin shook his head. He really had no wish to talk about this today, and he concentrated on rubbing Grace until she was tolerably damp.

"I wondered if maybe it could have been your telekinesis. You were pretty upset, right?"

He closed his eyes briefly.

Pretty upset.

There was no way to answer that. Not without giving voice to every little ounce of vitriol stored in his memories, and letting any of that out risked frightening the dogs.

"Sorry," Laurence mumbled. "I just…" He sighed and fetched another towel, then heaved Pepper out of the tub and began to dry her off. "I figured if the weather was your doing, then it proves your gift was active long before you ever learned it existed. And if it was, then maybe you've got other things going on too. Were any of your friends there? Did they see it happen?"

"We didn't really speak of it." He sighed and rose to his feet. The towel went into the laundry basket, and he gently steered Grace out into the living room.

The discussion wasn't ended so readily. He knew that. Laurence was persistent. A dog with a bone. He had scant moments to gather his inner peace before the quizzing continued, so he moved to the windows and gazed out at the ocean. The rhythmic to and fro of waves in the distance was moderately calming, and he began to breathe in time with it.

"That had to be hard," Laurence eventually said. His voice wasn't too close.

Quentin shifted his focus until he saw Laurence's reflection in the glass, seated on the couch, facing away from him.

He looked back to the sea. "I have been cut off in every conceivable way. Apparently I was ill-behaved at the funeral. The atmosphere at home afterward was quite…" He trailed off.

Hostile. Intolerable. Toxic. Terrifying. There were so many words to choose from and none of them encompassed the visceral horror of remaining in that house without her. She had always been there. Every time he stumbled and fell she raised him up. Whenever he had an accident she was by his side when he woke. Every single time his father's disapproval reared its head his mother was there to turn it aside, and with her gone so were the walls which she had erected to protect him.

What she protected him *from* he could not quantify. Sometimes it seemed as though her calling was to be the angel who guarded her children from the very world itself. Mostly it was not until she was gone that he truly grasped how much he feared his father, and he could not even put a name to the dread which filled him whenever the man was in the same room as he was. It was insidious and sickening. It filled him with shame and loathing all at once, with no grasp of where those feelings came from.

And yet Quentin knew without a doubt that his father had been the one to kill Mother. He did not know how or why. There was no blood, no sign of injury. The coroner ruled it a cardiac arrest due to a previously unknown weakness in the heart. Whether Father had leveraged his money and influence to bring about that verdict or had used some unknown means to genuinely trigger a heart attack he didn't know, but the certainty persisted.

He pressed his lips together as he looked to the sea. Was it a gift his father had? Quentin lacked the knowledge all those years ago that such things existed, but now? It would answer so many questions if his father had been able to kill her from afar. Had he seen her in her garden from his office and used some sort of psychic ability on her?

Had he watched her die?

His hands balled into fists. Nails dug into his palms.

He had no choice but to count down from ten.

All the while, Laurence remained patiently silent.

"I could not stay," Quentin breathed. "I couldn't bear it. I left. I ran." *Like a coward, I ran.* "I had no property at that time, and so I visited with a friend in London while I had my wealth manager gather my assets together, but in the midst of all that Bertie tossed me out on my ear. Said that I was an embarrassment and that I shouldn't visit again. I managed to sponge off of Podge for a few days, but that ended much the same way. Ended up in a hotel for a month until I could purchase a place on the Thames, but it became apparent that I'd been cut off completely. No one would have me at a social event, they wouldn't acknowledge me if they saw me in town."

"Goddess," Laurence whispered. In the window, his reflection turned to face Quentin, arm stretching across the back of the sofa. "That's horrible!"

Quentin shrugged faintly. "Ultimately I could not tolerate it. I sold up and moved to New York."

"So what made you leave New York?"

"Too close to home." He rested his forehead against the glass and allowed the cold to seep in and distract him from the memories. "Too many people I knew who would take transatlantic flights for a week or two of shopping. Too easy for Father to find me and demand that I return home, and too easy for him to turn everyone against me when I refused to go."

"So you bounced again," Laurence said.

"Correct. I do my best to avoid paparazzi and old money. The longer I can go undiscovered, the longer I am able to remain within a single location." He sighed softly and withdrew from the glass. "He has done his best to make it so that I cannot run forever. He has ended my allowance. I am forced to live on what little my wealth manager allows. Hence—" He waved helplessly at the apartment around them. "I rent," he said simply, knowing that Laurence saw nothing unusual in that. "I keep it as simple as I can while also retaining some degree of privacy. I exist on a small subsidy gleaned from the interest on my investments which, in the current economic climate, is quite minuscule."

He didn't want to watch Laurence's reaction to that news. Hell, he'd never wanted to deliver it. It wasn't the sort of thing one discussed, but Laurence deserved to know. It wasn't fair. Of all the illusions Quentin wrapped around himself this was the least shameful, and Laurence had already seen through the others.

"You're broke?" The sofa creaked faintly as Laurence stood. His footfalls were soft against carpet, coming closer.

"Not the word I would choose." Quentin sucked his teeth and looked to Laurence's reflection. "I would say... limited."

"But you spend a fortune!" Laurence placed a hand on his shoulder and tugged. "Look at me, baby."

Quentin turned, but he couldn't meet Laurence's eyes.

Laurence cupped his chin and raised it with a gentle touch. "You can't keep throwing money away on cab fares, Quen. You must've spent enough to buy half a damn car already just coming down to the shop." He frowned and traced his thumb along Quentin's cheek. "Do you even know how much everything's costing you?"

"It doesn't matter."

"Of course it matters!"

Quentin shook his head faintly. "I can't be without you, darling. I need you. I can't bear to be apart. Whatever that costs, I will spend it gladly, because I love you." He leaned into Laurence's touch and rested his hands against the taller man's chest. "I love you," he whispered.

Laurence groaned and wrapped his arm around Quentin, drawing him tight against his chest. "I love you too, baby. I'm sorry." He sighed. "Why don't I look over your accounts for you sometime? I get the feeling you're not used to the concept of false economy."

Quentin laughed weakly. "I have no idea what that is."

"Yeah, I guessed as much. Let's have dinner, then you can play for me after."

Quentin glanced past Laurence to the piano. The last gift his mother had given him. The only thing he had now to remember her by.

The gift which had brought him and Laurence together.

He raised his head and met Laurence's gaze at last. "I think," he whispered, "that is a fine plan."

12

QUENTIN

COME THE MORNING, QUENTIN TOOK THE DOGS OUT ON HIS regular route. He couldn't jog with them: this was a wholly new place for them both, and he was all but a stranger. In time, with care, he had no doubt that Grace would learn to follow Pepper's lead and that they could both pick up the pace, but for now a gentle walk was plenty, and he restricted them to Windansea Beach once they arrived.

He had a variety of items with him, packed into a courier bag slung across his chest. A squeaky toy, some treats, a bottle of water and a collapsible bowl for the girls. The trick was to find out which motivated them more: the toy or the food. Pepper, it soon became clear, vastly preferred the toy, whereas Grace was much more interested in treats.

He had two hours until the dogs would no longer be allowed on the beach, so he worked with them patiently, figuring out which commands they already understood and rewarding them for their efforts. It was mostly time spent bonding so that they would begin to see him—and one another—as part of their new pack.

"You're good girls," he cooed. "Very good! Shall we walk a little farther? Pepper, heel. Good girl!"

He strolled along with Pepper at his heel, and Grace fell into step behind her, following her scent. Quentin talked to them both, nonsense mostly, just so that they heard his voice and knew that they had his attention, and their tails slowly drifted upward into reasonably relaxed, trusting positions.

It was Grace who began to flag first, which was not unexpected, so he led them up steps so that he could sit at a bench. He filled the water bowl for her and watched the world go by as she drank.

He was trapped here.

Quentin frowned as the stray doubt invaded his peace and quiet. He wasn't *trapped*. He was simply... unable to leave.

They're the same thing, dimwit.

It didn't matter, surely. He didn't want to leave. Laurence was here, and an entire shop was hardly a portable thing.

He grimaced and turned his attention outward, allowing his gaze to pass over beach users below. Joggers. Dog-walkers. The peculiar fellow from a few days ago.

Quentin blinked and leaned forward, peering down at the beach from his vantage point.

The fellow wandered, flanked by two others: an older man, and a woman his own age. As a trio they were quite mismatched, with the two lagging a step behind and dressed formally for what seemed to be a stroll along the beach. They were alert, too, both checking their surroundings while the one in the lead simply wandered.

Quentin had seen that sort of positioning and attentiveness before.

They were bodyguards.

The woman looked his way and locked eyes on him, then pointed, and the others turned.

Quentin leaned back in his seat and crossed his legs. This did not bode well. If there was to be a second attempt at mugging, why bring bodyguards? If the encounter had been only that, why search for him as they were so clearly doing?

They were approaching rather lackadaisically to intend harm, but Quentin was not about to rule anything out. He urged Pepper and Grace to sit, and idly packed away the water bowl as the trio ascended the white-painted wooden steps.

"We meet again," the fellow up front said as he crested the top of the steps.

"Such a coincidence," Quentin replied with all the distance he could inflect.

"Naw. I came looking." He stopped only inches from Quentin's knees and offered his hand. "The name's Kane. Kane Wilson."

Quentin rose to his feet and disregarded the hand. "Banbury," he responded. He made a point to look to each of the bodyguards, and then back to Wilson. "How may one be of service, Mr. Wilson?"

"Mr. Banbury, huh?"

Quentin did his level best to refrain from flinching.

"Look," Wilson said. "I think we might've gotten off on the wrong foot the other day."

"That tends to happen when you tell people to hand over their valuables," Quentin murmured.

"No, not really." Wilson gestured to the bench. "Mind if we sit?"

"Yes."

"Sit down."

Quentin arched an eyebrow at him. "This conversation will go very poorly if you speak to me that way again."

The woman at Wilson's shoulder whistled to herself. "Did he just—"

"Yeah," Wilson said. "See what I mean? Look, Banbury. I'm sorry. That was a demonstration for the guys. I didn't mean to cause any offense." He thumbed toward the woman. "This is Mia. Or Miss Torres, I guess you're gonna want to call her."

"Hey," she said.

"And this here is Sebastian Wagner."

The older man eyed Quentin a moment, then looked away.

"And what was this demonstration intended to show?" Quentin returned his attention to Wilson.

"Let's just say you probably wouldn't believe me if I told you." Wilson slid his hands into his pockets and regarded Quentin as though he were attempting to solve a jigsaw puzzle. "I'd like to get to know you better, if you have the time."

Quentin looked between the three of them. None were on edge, and he saw no evidence that any of them were armed, although he suspected that they most likely were. Wagner carried himself like a man who held some military training, with that peculiar bearing which enabled him to stand rock-still without wavering in the heat. Torres was more relaxed. A fidgeter. She shifted her center of balance often, and sometimes turned her back on them all to scan the horizon, but she was calm and collected. Wilson had the confidence of a man who had two bodyguards at his back.

"And if one lacks the time?" Quentin addressed Wilson.

"What is it with this 'one' thing all the time?" Wilson narrowed his eyes. "Okay. You want me to get down to business. I get it. This looks weird to you. I totally get that, too. I'm just some random dude who keeps telling you to do weird shit and you're like 'who the hell is this guy,' am I right? Of course I am." He smacked his lips. "You see, here's the killer, Mr. Banbury." He paused. "I'm psychic."

Quentin blinked slowly.

Wilson's satisfied grin and broadened shoulders suggested that he expected Quentin to be impressed or, at the very least, surprised. An expectant man would not wait long for a reaction, and so Quentin said nothing and allowed the silence to stretch until it became awkward.

Wilson's features began the slow crumple of dissatisfaction, and then curved downward into an unhappy frown. "Don't you wanna know more?"

"Dear boy," Quentin breezed, "psychics are—as I believe the phrase goes—a dime a dozen. One can hardly move for people who claim to communicate with the dead or—" he waved his hand vaguely and left his sentence hanging because he frankly had no idea what it was that stage psychics claimed they were able to do.

"Oh, shit no!" Wilson guffawed and almost doubled over in doing so, and Quentin stepped aside to avoid coming into accidental contact with him. "No, okay, I see! No, those are performers. They're cold-readers and bullshitters of the highest order." He slapped his own thigh as he straightened himself up. "No way. I'm the real deal."

"Are you." He didn't intend it as a question.

"Here's the thing, Mr. Banbury. I say what I want people to do, and they do it. I control minds." He hesitated. "Except not yours for some reason. For all your pretense I already know you're not part of the herd, so how about you drop it and we talk like adults?"

Quentin pursed his lips, and then retook his seat, reaching to fuss both dogs. "You may sit," he murmured.

There seemed little point refuting Wilson's claim. His words made a certain amount of logical sense. Wilson had evidently expected Quentin to simply hand over his valuables on command, and was most put out when Quentin refused to do so. And Quentin's refusal to sit on command had seemed to surprise Torres. If it had been of interest to Wagner the man hadn't shown it, but then were Quentin correct about his supposition that Wagner was former military personnel, then he would expect the man to keep a lid on his reactions.

If Wilson were telling the truth, however, then what kind of man used his gift to rob strangers?

Wilson sat so as to leave plenty of personal space between them. "Nice dogs. You didn't have them the other day."

"Correct." He held their leads loosely and sat back against the bench. "If you are able to control people, why on earth would you do so to relieve them of their property?"

"Ah, that's not really the kind of thing I like to discuss in public." Wilson chuckled and rested an elbow on the back of the bench. "Like I say, we got off on the wrong foot. I'd like to start over."

"And you brought bodyguards because...?"

Torres barked a short laugh.

"Because as much as you don't know me from Adam, I don't know dick about you either." Wilson shrugged. "And whoever or whatever you are, I've already found that I can't protect myself against you. If you were in my shoes would *you* come here without a safety net?"

Quentin idly neatened the seam of his sweatpants. Wilson's perspective was not unreasonable. With no idea of what Quentin may be capable of and the sure knowledge that his gift could not protect him, it did make a certain amount of sense to not go into the situation undefended. Especially as their first meeting had been an attempt to mug Quentin. Anyone could anticipate a less than favorable response to a second encounter.

"Why *did* you come here?" Quentin murmured, turning his focus to Wilson. "This is not where we first met, but even if it were why would you risk exposure this way?"

Wilson shrugged again. "Skinny thing like you, dressed like that? You get a lot of exercise. A mile-long beach ain't gonna cut it, so odds are you daisy-chain your way along as much of the coast as you need to, and you exercise regularly. Someone that neat and tidy is usually pretty predictable and returns to the same spots over and over, but you weren't at La Jolla Shores, so we cast the net wider. And the exposure?" Wilson shrugged. "Like I say. I'm curious. I've never met anyone who can bounce me the way you did. You're different, and I'd like us to talk. But not here. Here's too open. Anyone can listen in."

Quentin raised an eyebrow and glanced around. There were very few people around, and those nearby were walking with a purpose rather than lingering.

"It's complicated. And I promise you I'm not a petty thief or a crazed murderer or whatever else you might be thinking. There's a bigger picture." Wilson hesitated, then leaned in and lowered his voice. "I'd really like to talk it over with you. We can ask each other all the questions we could ever want to, and then when all's said and done at least you know why I go around trying to rob rich people around here, huh?"

He regarded Wilson a while and watched the man's expression waver between hopeful and desperate. "Where, then, do you propose is safe to speak?"

Wilson's features creased in a triumphant grin and he clapped Quentin on the shoulder. "I have a place in Lower Hermosa." He gestured behind himself. "Just south of here, on the Camino de la Costa, up in the six thousands. Come by later. We can talk, you can see what we're doing there, and maybe then you'll find the answers you're looking for."

Quentin's glance flitted to Wilson's hand, and the man removed it quickly. "Very well," he murmured. "The address?"

"6208," Wilson answered. "Little white gate. Can't miss it."

Quentin inclined his head and eased to his feet. "After lunch, then."

"You're on!"

He gently ushered the dogs forward and cast a polite nod to Torres and Wagner as he passed them, and then continued on along Neptune Place until he could take the first available street away from the beach. Only then, as he ascended a hill whose sidewalks were awkwardly lined with palms which cut into the space at regular intervals, did he allow his features to relax.

If Wilson were up to anything underhanded, he'd offered Quentin the ideal opportunity to work out what that might be, and it would certainly pass the time until he could see Laurence again.

He felt a slight, small smile break out. This was progress, was it not? He was interacting with common people, and much more importantly, perhaps he had found others like himself. Laurence and Myriam were the only other psychics he knew of, but Wilson not only spoke of such matters in front of Torres and Wagner, he anticipated that both could defend him.

The odds were high that Wilson's bodyguards not only knew what he was, but were also psychic, and the opportunity to learn more was too great to pass up.

Whatever happened, at least he would find some answers.

13

QUENTIN

ALTHOUGH THE CAMINO DE LA COSTA WAS NOT BEYOND WALKING distance, Quentin chose to arrive by taxi rather than allow himself to be baked by the early-afternoon sun. That sort of exposure caused premature aging, and he was dead set against it.

He approached the white gate. It was set a little way back from the sidewalk, and the wall it was embedded in was shrouded in well-manicured trees. Behind him, on the far side of the road, the steep hill meant that houses closer inland were far higher than those closer to the sea, which offered an additional degree of privacy to the property from the curbside: Quentin stood no chance whatsoever of seeing anything of interest beyond all this greenery.

The property was certainly private, which Quentin almost resented.

He tried the gate and found it to be locked, but there was a small intercom box to the right of it, so he thumbed the button, and soon the gate clicked without anyone's answer. He eased it open and slipped past, then nudged it closed.

Beyond was a small, neat courtyard in Spanish red brick, with a few small steps down to the level of the block paving. Potted plants were dotted around the trunks of trees, and past them were the white-painted brick walls of a reasonably modern building. With its shuttered windows and arched doorway it echoed Spanish Colonial architecture, although he wouldn't imagine the building to be pre-twentieth century.

The front doors opened and Wagner emerged onto the doorstep, where he waited with his hands clasped in front of him. "Mr. Banbury."

Quentin headed toward him and evaluated the older man every bit as closely as the American was looking him over.

Wagner was close to Quentin's own height, though thick-soled boots gave him a boost. His skin was tanned and lined, and he didn't even wear sunglasses to protect the delicate skin around his eyes from damage, but at least there was some length to his hair on top to protect his scalp. He wore loose, casual, off-brand clothing and could readily pass for a thousand other men on the street if it weren't for his rock-solid bearing.

"Just Banbury will suffice," Quentin answered as he joined Wagner on the doorstep. "Mister is incorrect."

That elicited a blink, but little else. "Sure. Banbury. Follow me."

The building was, it soon became readily apparent, far larger than the discreet frontage hinted at. The hallways were wide enough to contain their own furniture, from tables and chairs to works of art. It felt like an uncomfortable echo of home. Wagner led him from one hallway to another, through white-lined corridors and down white-painted stairs until after a couple of minutes they passed out the other side entirely and Quentin was confronted with a pleasant vista.

A swimming pool glittered blue in the sunlight, but beyond it was a low wall, and after the wall was the sea itself. Perspective suggested that the wall was only low on this side, and that the other continued the steep decline of the hill the house was embedded into.

He turned and glanced back up at the building and found his supposition about the privacy offered by said hill to be well-founded. What appeared from the street to be a little gate and some trees was, from where he now stood, revealed to be a three-story mansion easily large enough to house seven or eight bedrooms, as well as assorted other features. He couldn't even make out the properties farther uphill.

"This way."

Quentin turned to tail Wagner down pretty red-stone steps toward the pool, where another layer of privacy in the form of a hedgerow easily eight feet tall separated pool from mansion. They passed beyond it and into an area of patio which surrounded the pool, with outdoor furniture dotted around: tables and chairs, and umbrellas large enough to shade several people at once.

Wilson sat beneath one such umbrella, a bright expanse of material which cast a shadow ten feet wide. He didn't rise, but he did at least gesture to a chair by his side which was also protected by the cover.

"Thank you," Quentin murmured to Wagner, whose only response was to take up a standing position behind the chairs.

He eased down into one of the wooden seats. It was painted white, as was the table it faced. Quentin drew the chair back from the table rather than tuck himself in, and he rested his elbows on the armrests.

Wilson had shucked his average-fitting street clothes for a more casual look, now sporting board shorts and a brightly-colored T-shirt. He reached for a pitcher of lemonade on the table and poured a drink. Chunks of ice clattered against the glass, which Wilson then offered to Quentin. "Olive branch?"

Quentin considered, and then accepted the lemonade. "Thank you."

"I'm not gonna waste your time here." Wilson took a swig from his own tumbler, which had been there long enough to form condensation. "But for that I'd ask you don't waste mine either. Is that fair?"

"I think so." Quentin took a sip. The drink was wonderfully chilled, and had surprisingly little sugar compared to most so that the acidity of the lemons cut through and made his mouth water.

"I'm psychic. Gifted. Talented. Touched. Whatever word you wanna use for it, I've got it. But so does everyone else who lives in this house." Wilson used his drink to indicate the mansion. "Me,

Wagner, Torres, the others. Everyone's ability is different, but we all have one. I can control people. Wagner can create and manipulate fire. Torres is electrokinetic."

Quentin feigned another sip from his glass as he assimilated this stream of information. If Wilson spoke the truth, then he had gathered quite an eclectic team together under his wing.

"To what end?" He set the glass down.

"Protection," Wilson said simply. "We're not normal. Not you, not me, not anyone here. There are over seven billion people in the world. Half of them want to kill the other half for the weakest of reasons. Ideology, color, resources, whatever. I'm not so dumb as to think they wouldn't want to kill us for what we can do, and nor are you or you wouldn't have pulled your clueless routine this morning."

Quentin wasn't sure whether he should feel flattered that Wilson considered it a routine. "And how does coming together here offer that protection?"

"We have privacy. Peace. We can practice our talents away from prying eyes. We can talk to one another without having to hide who or what we are. This is a safe space for us." Wilson looked to the pool. "A place to live and work, but also to relax and find some sanctuary. We all do our bit to contribute to our continued safety." He tapped the table with the palm of his hand, then turned to face Quentin. "I'm a thief. You know that. Running this place isn't cheap. We have to eat, drink, pay the bills. We're all human, even if we're a little more than everyone else. So I steal. I take from the rich, and I pay for the groceries. I pick targets who can afford to lose some trinkets. Nobody gets hurt, and I make no apology for what I do."

"But it cannot be terribly cheap, a property such as this?" Quentin's gaze flickered toward the mansion. "Would it not be better to find something less well situated?"

"The great thing about wealthy neighborhoods is they have a nice low crime rate. Cops come when they're called. Home invasions are minimal. Neighbors are discreet. People around here, they all drive to and from their houses and they never say hi to the people who live right next door to them." Wilson smiled, but not with any real pleasure. "Anyone we offer shelter to can come and go whenever they want and they aren't gonna get questioned or assaulted. They're a mile from stores and amenities but don't have to walk down a single dark alleyway or through any deserted parking lots. If they want to go downtown we're close to a whole bunch of bus stops. This is the safest place in San Diego County, and that's all I want for all of us."

"It is an interesting dilemma," Quentin conceded.

"You're telling me. Look, why don't we head inside and I'll introduce you to some of our kids? Then you can tell me what you think from there." Wilson stood and stepped out into the light.

"Children?" Quentin frowned. He stood quickly and moved around the table.

"Most people's powers manifest in their teens, right when kids are still trying to figure out who they are and whether they wanna be an astronaut when they grow up. We do what we can to find 'em before they decide showing off to their friends is a really great idea. C'mon. Let's go see who's home."

Quentin allowed Wilson to lead him back up the stairs to the mansion. He didn't need to look back to know that Wagner followed them both.

HE WAS LED past two doors of empty rooms before they came to one which was occupied.

Wilson peeked in, then pushed the door open fully and gestured for Quentin to follow. "Here we are," he announced. "I thought for a minute there everyone had left home."

Quentin stepped into the room and paused just over the threshold.

The room was larger than his entire apartment, but crammed with furniture which took away much of that space. There was an overabundance of chintzy sofas and armchairs, footstools and tables and side-tables and occasional tables and frankly far too many tables altogether, most of which were home to a single ornament or lamp. And, oh, so many lamps. He could only suppose that there had been a sale on at some point. The glorious ocean view was almost ruined by the amount of poor taste between him and it.

Some of the remaining room was occupied by a trio of youngsters, not one of whom looked to be a day over twenty.

Quentin stood still as Wilson approached the teens. There were greetings exchanged, though mostly the youngsters were eyeing Quentin as they spoke quickly and quietly to Wilson. In turn, Quentin observed their postures, their expressions, the way they moved their hands and their eyes. The three of them, all young girls, were wary of him to differing degrees. One had retreated slightly into the comfort of her armchair. Another sat forward on a sofa as if ready to fight him with her bare hands if necessary. The third remained hidden in her book and only peeked over the top.

He lowered his head slightly. Here he was, a stranger in their safe space, an adult who had been trusted not to do them harm. No wonder they were frightened. They knew less about him than he did them, although he presumed that Wilson was informing them of the situation while he waited.

The idea that anyone might do harm to children was abhorrent. That they had to hide here away from their families for being born different made his heart ache.

"Mr. Banbury?"

Quentin blinked as his reverie was interrupted.

Wilson waved him over. "This is Estelita, Soraya, and Kimberly." He nodded to each girl in turn.

Quentin approached and offered his hand first to Estelita, a Hispanic girl whose long, dark curls spiraled over her shoulders. She couldn't have been old enough to drive a bloody car, let alone face anyone who might wish to harm her, and he had to center himself a moment before he could speak.

"Estelita?" He crouched to be below her eye level when she took his hand. "My name is Quentin. It's a pleasure to meet you."

She gave his fingers a brief squeeze. "I like your accent."

He smiled to her. "Thank you. I like your hair."

"It's okay," she mumbled, flicking it over her shoulder.

He chuckled, then moved so that he could offer his hand to Soraya. "Quentin," he said again. "And you are Soraya, yes?"

Soraya was a slip of a girl, though older than Estelita, with deep blue-black skin and short, textured hair. She carried herself with confidence, her head high and a challenge in her eye. "Yeah." She looked down to his hand before she took and held it only briefly. "You're British?"

"I am." He nodded.

"Huh." She took her hand back.

He smiled to her, then moved to the last of the three, a heavily-freckled white girl with ginger hair and pale blue eyes.

She held a book like a shield, and regarded him across the top of it. "Kim," she said.

"Quentin," he answered.

She said nothing more, and so he moved to another armchair to sit rather than loom over them, from where he could see that Wagner had entered the room and was watching him closely.

"So why's he here, Kane?" Soraya looked up to Wilson as she pulled her legs up onto the couch and crossed them.

"Because he's different, too."

"How?"

"I don't know." Wilson shrugged.

"But if you don't know, how do you know it's safe for him to even be here?" Kim's eyes widened, and her book drew closer to her chest.

"Because if he tries anything, Sebastian will drop him where he stands." Wilson dragged a wooden chair over and sat on it. "But I don't think he will."

"I don't think he will, either." Estelita fidgeted with the hem of her T-shirt.

Soraya faced Quentin and propped her elbows on her knees. "Okay then. You first. What's your talent?"

He sat back and rested his hands in his lap as he looked to her. She was smart, of that there was no doubt, but she also appeared to see herself as the protector in this group. He couldn't help but wonder whether that was a natural instinct or a developed one.

Had she faced off against people who had tried—or, heaven forfend, succeeded—to hurt her? Regardless, the sort of child who was this direct appreciated directness in return, and any attempt to deflect or sidestep her questions would lead to lasting mistrust.

"Telekinesis," he said.

He thought he saw a brief flicker of curiosity in her eyes, but then she pursed her lips. "Okay. Show us."

Quentin tilted his head, but looked to Wilson first.

"Sure. Why not?" Wilson said.

"Very well." He spared a glance to Wagner to ensure the man wasn't about to set him alight, then he reached for each and every item of furniture in the room which didn't have someone sitting on it, and eased them from the floor.

Estelita and Kim squealed, and Kim clung more tightly to her book. Wagner's eyes narrowed, but Wilson's widened. Soraya let out a quick gasp.

Quentin's grip on every table, every lamp, every footstool was firm and steady, and he raised each a few feet from the carpet and then held them there while Estelita, Soraya, and Wilson went to go examine different items, to poke and prod, testing the strength of Quentin's hold.

"You can lift all this stuff," Wilson said slowly, "at once."

Quentin eased the collection back to the floor and waited until he was certain nothing would fall over before he released them. "Correct."

"It's pretty cool," Soraya said, affecting a disinterested tone.

"It's *awesome!*" Estelita breathed.

Wilson flexed his hands as he sat down. "Yeah, it's... impressive." He tapped his palm on the arm of his chair and took a deep breath. "So, Quentin. Can I call you Quentin?"

Quentin thought a moment, then dipped his head. "You may."

"You know, if you're not doing anything with your life, I would really appreciate it if you'd consider visiting once in a while. You've got a degree of control I've never seen before. If you can find a way to teach that, we've got a lot of kids here who could really benefit from it."

His eyebrows rose slowly, and he took a quick breath. "I have... no experience as a teacher," he said carefully.

I'm not especially bright. I have only known about this ability for three months. I am no suitable example for anything!

"But you've got experience in mastering an incredibly complex gift." Wilson spread his hands. "I know I've got no right to ask for any favors, but if you *can* help, it can only benefit."

"Please?" Estelita turned wide, hazel eyes on him.

Quentin laced his fingers together, but whatever reluctance he had was already breaking down.

Children, for God's sake.

"I shall consider it," he murmured.

"That's all I ask," said Wilson.

14

QUENTIN

QUENTIN LET HIMSELF INTO HIS APARTMENT AND CROUCHED DOWN to greet the dogs. They were a little perkier now, but he reckoned that it would be a day or two before they were fully themselves.

"Have you been good girls? Hmm? I bet you have. Shall we see?" He ruffled their shoulders fondly and set off to examine the living room for any signs of accidents or destruction, but the worst he could find was a selection of dog hairs all over the sofa. "Very good!"

His afternoon had been unusual to say the least. He could not quantify it as either good or bad, but it was certainly informative.

There were more psychics in San Diego than even Laurence knew of. Was that because Wilson had gathered them all beneath his wing, or did Laurence simply move in different circles? Regardless, it would be knowledge that Laurence would be keen to hear of once he was done with work for the day.

Quentin crossed to the kitchen to refill the girls' water bowls, and then he fetched a glass for himself.

Wilson's young psychics had spoken of their abilities. Soraya was a clairvoyant, able to witness events up to a mile away from her own location if she chose. Estelita had remarkably enhanced senses and could make out fine details on birds far out to sea. Kimberly's gift was something Wilson termed "stealth," which appeared to be some facility to pass relatively unnoticed when she wished to. As these had not been especially demonstrable talents, Wagner had made a display of his facility with fire, conjuring a small flame in the palm of his hand.

It was, Quentin admitted, remarkable. The flame was present without any wick or wax, no detectable source of fuel, and yet it had hovered above Wagner's hand until the man willed it out of existence, all without doing him any harm.

He sipped his water as he lingered in the kitchen, lost in thought.

They had each spoken of their gifts. Some with pride, others with indifference, but each of them had something in common: they had one ability apiece.

But Laurence? Laurence could see the future *and* the past. He could grow plants unnaturally fast and then control them to move in ways they would not otherwise. He could even smell and taste things beyond Quentin's palate, which he considered to be refined.

And Laurence suspected that Quentin's rapport with animals went beyond empathy and body language. He believed that it might be psychic in nature. If that were correct then perhaps Quentin had another feather in his cap which lay as-yet undiscovered.

What if setting whisky on fire had nothing whatsoever to do with his telekinesis?

It was almost too ridiculous to conceive of.

Almost.

But he *had* triggered a fire, albeit a small one, and it had not been voluntary. If this truly lay within his power, then it was grotesquely remiss of him not to gain control over it. It was one thing to have an accident and throw a few items of furniture around the room or break a window, but another entirely to burn down his home and risk the lives of the dogs, his neighbors, himself, and potentially Laurence too.

That was not remotely acceptable.

He tapped the rim of his glass against his lip, and then set it down in the sink and began to search through the kitchen cupboards. There was, he was reasonably sure, a bag of little candles stuffed in one of these corners. He wasn't sure if they were from the landlord or left by a previous occupier, or even whether the maid had supplied them. He had no idea why anyone would keep a bag of little candles in thin tin-like cases either.

He found some spare pots, a roll of aluminum foil, and a disgruntled spider before he eventually discovered the bag tucked away in an otherwise empty drawer. There had to be fifty candles in there. The text printed on the bag declared them to be 'tea lights,' though he'd never made tea with a candle in his life.

While Wagner may be able to set thin air on fire, Quentin thought it best to try with an item at least designed to not only take a flame but also to prevent that flame from rushing off to burn down everything else willy-nilly. He bore the bag through to the dining table and tried to tug it open as he sat, but the bloody thing was built like the Bank of England, so he reached for the knife block in the kitchen and withdrew one of the smaller blades, careful to steer it into his hand across the intervening space without risking the dogs or his own fingers. Once he had it, he sliced the bag open, and the little candles spilled across the table.

He set the knife down, neatened up the tea lights, then drew one closer and stared at it.

How *exactly* was one supposed to start a fire?

Learning to control his telekinesis had been a hurdle, but at least there he had some facility with it to begin with. The fire had been a purely one-off event under circumstances which had already unleashed the full force of his then-new gift. He had been so upset by the thought that Laurence's life might be in danger that things had gone badly awry.

The key, he had learned with the telekinesis, was to pick apart what he had *done* from how he *felt*. Allowing his emotional state to rule when and how his gift manifested was no use to man nor beast. Indeed it had almost led to their total defeat at Jack's hands.

He stared at the little candle wick.

It failed to catch fire.

"Yes, that would be far too useful, wouldn't it?" he groused. Heaven forfend people be able to use their abilities.

It had to be hard to teach children how to control powers they may have only ever manifested during an argument or in the midst of grieving, likely made all the more difficult by the pressures of being a teenager at the same time. While he was not so foolish as to believe that his school life had been at all like those of the teens Wilson had gathered together, some things seemed universal. He had not been alone in railing against adults at that time, demanding the right to be treated as an equal far before he had earned such status. Nor had he been the only one to navigate the tricky classroom and social politics of who one may wish to be friends with or whether one shared a friend's opinion on any given subject.

To develop unpredictable and potentially life-threatening powers in the midst of all that? Dear God, it would be terrifying! As though teens didn't feel isolated enough already, to be handed a "gift" which marked them out as undeniably *other* could be the sort of thing which pushed one closer to the edge.

His fingers spread slowly across the table's glossy surface and he shook his head to focus his will. If he could do this, then he had personal experience of gaining control over more than one talent, and that might be invaluable insight in aiding those younger than himself. It offered a perspective that only Laurence and Myriam shared.

Laurence had shown him how to learn. All he needed do was apply that knowledge.

Quentin allowed himself to relax into his seat, and he waited. He chased away stray thoughts until he was calm and there was little else in the world but himself and the candle.

Burn.

No. That wouldn't do it. He did not look at items around him and think *lift* or *carry*. He simply took action, as though in command of limbs that none could see. Those items became an extension of himself in a sense. If he wished his arm to move, it did so. If he wished the table to move, it did so.

He gazed at the candle until it was no longer external. It was a part of him. He wished it to come closer, and it did so. That was how these things worked.

He wished it to catch fire, and it did so.

He caught his breath and watched the tiny flame flutter into existence and nibble away at the candle wick until it caught hold.

It was as though his will extended beyond the physical confines of his body. He kept his hands firm against the table as he reached for more candles and drew them toward himself, then pushed fire outward into them one at a time. Some sputtered and failed. Others succeeded with gusto.

A little fine-tuning would be required, as was to be expected.

He had made fire.

A myriad of little lights danced in front of his gaze, bright and lively. There were enough that his face and hands were warmed by their proximity. The flames were happy little blobs of light, melting the wax below them until they had tiny reflective puddles to celebrate in.

They were beautiful.

There was an unspeakable fascination with fire lodged soul-deep within the human psyche, and Quentin suspected that it was because it was recognized like no other phenomenon on earth as a thing of incredible transformative power. It could fuse materials together or destroy them utterly. It swept through forests and left fertile lands in its wake. It was a force so wild and free that whether one feared or admired it, the response was utterly primal.

Man could control much, but the ability to harness fire was one of his proudest achievements.

Quentin allowed a slow smile to creep forth. As the flames grew and began to intertwine, a certainty settled into place.

This was power.

15

LAURENCE

Laurence swept the shop floor with a broom to move dirt, stray petals, and fallen leaves toward the back room.

The shutters were already down. He'd closed the store and emptied the register's drawer already. He wasn't used to working weekends any more, but it was no more hectic than a weekday, just in different ways. During the week most of their business came from phone or internet orders, and at the weekend it was walk-ins, but ultimately it seemed to lead to the same amount of overall work.

He pushed the assorted litter into a dustpan and tipped that into the trash just in time to see his mom's truck pull up in the alley.

Ditching dustpan and broom, he washed his hands so that he could start making tea, and waved to her through the window as she exited the truck and headed for the door.

"Bambi!" She swept in and wrapped her arms around him in a tight squeeze. "Blessed be!"

"Bright blessings!" He grinned as he hugged her back.

"Did you have a good weekend?"

"Yeah!" He nodded. "You? How did the gathering go?"

"You would have loved it, dear!" Her features were sun-pink, and her hair was more frizz than curls. "Hopefully by Lammas we'll have a few more hands on deck here so that you can come along. And bring Quentin!" She winked and tweaked his nose between finger and thumb.

"Mom!" He chuckled and moved to pour the tea. "You figure he'll still be here by then?"

"You haven't been tempted to look and find out for yourself?" She bustled to the table and perched on a stool there. For a moment she tried to get her hair under control, then waved her hands as she gave up on it.

Laurence shrugged. "I dunno," he admitted. "What if I don't like what I see?"

"Then you work to bring about a different path, dear. But you've already done that, haven't you?"

He stirred. The spoon clinked against the edges of the mugs. "I don't know what you mean."

"Dogs, Bambi?" She chortled and wagged a finger at him. "Very smart. You are trying to make a free spirit put down roots. Giving him responsibilities. Be careful, though. Too many at once and he will feel trapped."

"Mom!" Laurence's face burned and he felt his gut do a backflip. "How do you *do* that?" He tossed the teabags and added milk, then took the mugs to the table.

She reached for her tea and smiled wryly. "Do you think you're not enough to make him stay yourself?"

Laurence sat heavily. He curled his hands around his mug and held it until the heat became too much and he was forced to shift his grip to the handle. "Well, what if I'm not?"

"Oh, Bambi." She leaned closer until she could nudge him with her shoulder. "We are children of Herne. People are drawn to us. It is on us to choose with whom we share our hearts. You have chosen him."

He ground his teeth together. "But what if he doesn't choose *me*?"

She gave a soft laugh. "Do you see that happening, dear? The poor boy is besotted with you. He worships the ground you walk on."

Laurence sighed out his frustration and fidgeted with his mug.

He had to admit that his mom was right. Quentin treated him like a prince. It wasn't just the shopping or the restaurants. It ran far deeper than that.

Quentin gave Laurence his time. His attention. This willful, powerful man could go anywhere he chose, and he chose Laurence day in and day out. He listened, he offered his thoughts, he held Laurence in his arms and ran fingers through his hair. The guy had stacks of invitations to parties in super A-list locations and he disregarded them to sit in a tiny apartment over a flower shop on the edge of the Gaslamp Quarter.

"Mm-hmm," Myriam said.

"Fine." He blew on the tea and sipped it cautiously, but it was still a bit too hot. "Mom… Do you think there are others out there like us? I mean like you and me?"

"Children of Herne?"

He glanced to her. "Man, I hadn't even thought of that. I just thought, like…" He shrugged. "Other gods."

"I wouldn't doubt it." She raised her own mug. "I haven't ever met one that I know of, but that doesn't mean they aren't out there."

"Yeah," he agreed.

"You think that Quentin could be one?"

"I dunno." He ran the tip of his tongue along his teeth, then bit down on it briefly. "Jack knew what I was before I did. So why didn't he know what Quentin is?"

"Well, perhaps Jack could only home in on lineages close to his own?" Myriam leaned against the table and tilted her head back to gaze at the far wall. "If he was the Green Man then he is connected to Herne if only by proximity to Cernunnos. If Jack and Herne are aspects of Cernunnos then he may even have felt related to you himself."

Laurence grimaced at the thought. Had he really been caught in some kind of esoteric custody battle? Had Jack felt that he owned Laurence? He'd sure behaved like that was his opinion, and if that was how gods responded to encountering their descendants he kinda hoped Herne didn't have any plans to stop by.

Would Herne behave as Jack had? That mental image didn't sit right with him. It didn't mesh with the Herne he'd dreamed of, the hunter who offered his love freely and with respect. There had been power, but also wisdom and kindness.

No. Herne was not Jack, and he wouldn't treat Laurence like a commodity. That wasn't the kind of god Laurence wanted to think he'd come from.

"Or Quentin's not descended from a god at all," Myriam offered.

"And there's no way of knowing," Laurence agreed with a soft sigh. He peered into his tea and swirled it slowly.

"Do you want to talk about what happened?"

He shrugged. "One asshole god took over the body of one asshole ex-boyfriend and I killed them both. Two-for-one. And I'm kinda okay with it, to be honest. I dunno whether I *should* be, but I am. I'm not..." he took a deep breath. "I'm not saying I'm gonna kill anyone or anything that pisses me off. But this one time?" He downed a mouthful of tea. "Yeah. I can live with it."

"I knew that you would destroy Jack," she mused. Her gaze drifted across the wall and to the sink, and finally to her son. "I knew it in my heart, Bambi. But I also know that your path leads to darkness and I can't move you from it."

He sat up slowly and frowned at her. "What do you mean darkness?"

"Ah. That I don't know." She shook her head. "But the darker the night, the brighter the morning when it comes."

Yeah that's super helpful. Thanks, Mom!

He slid from his stool and began to pace between the table and sink, nursing his mug of tea.

"But that's not what I meant anyway." She flashed a warm smile his way. "I meant do you want to talk about what happened between you and Quentin this weekend while I was gone?"

Laurence's eyelids fluttered as he tried to shift gears from vague portents of a terrible future and relationship advice time with Mom. The two didn't mesh together at all and it took him a moment to push his half-formed qualms back down before they could get out of hand. "Uh." He drank the rest of his tea and put the mug in the sink. "Nothing happened?"

Myriam chuckled at him. "When I leave everything is roses. When I return you've bought him dogs and you're afraid he'll leave. Don't think a mother can't tell when her child's upset, dear."

"How do you even know I did that?" Laurence crossed his arms.

She winked at him, then chuckled. "It's a lot less impressive if I tell you my secrets, dear, but all right." She dug around in her pockets and withdrew her cellphone.

Laurence groaned. "Twitter."

"Of course, dear!"

"Mom!"

Goddess, life was *weird* when you dated an earl and had famous customers. His Twitter feed now had over three thousand followers. People snapped pictures of him and Quentin in the weirdest places, then not only posted them online but tagged him in their posts so he could *see* how creepy they were. Like he was supposed to retweet them or say things like, "thanks for intruding on my personal life!" And Quentin wasn't even really famous. He just seemed to attract attention because he hung with rock stars and actors and other people way more famous than himself while also being incredibly photogenic. The general public was obviously okay with some eye candy while they waited for the big names to show up.

And now even his mom was Twitter-stalking him.

"See? Your mom's not really as amazing as she seems to be." Myriam laughed. "I think now's the time, Bambi. You need to know the truth."

"What?" he grumbled.

"There's no Santa Claus. He isn't real."

He huffed and pulled his apron off, and went to hang it beside Rodger's. "I'm gonna go see Quen, Mom. Try not to tweet about it."

"I'll try my best!"

Laurence gave her the stink-eye as he disappeared out the

back door, but all she did was make a display of picking up her cellphone and typing on it.

16

LAURENCE

THE GATE ROLLED OPEN, AND LAURENCE PARKED HIS TRUCK IN THE space set aside for Quentin's apartment. He crunched across the gravel and let himself in, then took the stairs inside two at a time and rapped on Quentin's door loudly in case he was at the piano.

He heard a deep bark. Panting and snuffling near the door. Then footsteps.

He smelled burning.

Laurence frowned and leaned closer just as Quentin opened the door. "Baby? Are you okay?"

Quentin looked startled, and his lips parted a second before he spoke. "Of course. Is something wrong?"

"Sorry. I, uh." He sniffed. The scent was definitely there, but as he stepped past Quentin and into the apartment everything looked fine. He couldn't see any scorch marks, no blackened smoke up the walls or across the ceiling, nothing. "Did you... try to cook something?"

The door clicked closed behind him. "Ah, no?" He cleared his throat. "Why do you ask?"

The Brit was hiding something. It didn't take any in-depth knowledge of the guy to figure that out, but Laurence did know him better than anyone, so it stood out to him like an emergency flare. He turned as he nudged his shoes off and Pepper rubbed her nose all over his thigh. "Quen, you know you can't cook, baby. What if something bad happens and I'm not here? What if the place burns down?"

Quentin waved a hand vaguely. "Really, darling, I'm quite all right."

"I had a vision—"

"I know." Quentin reached for his hand and squeezed it. "But I have something to tell you."

Laurence took hold of the lurch in his gut and drew Quentin closer. "Okay." He gripped Quentin's hand and gazed down into his eyes. "Sorry, hon. What is it?"

He followed as Quentin tugged him to the couch, and settled down beside the earl as he sat. Not once did Quentin release his hand.

It felt wrong. There was a secret here, and Quentin wasn't in any hurry to tell it to him. Like the doctors after his dad's heart attack, who seemed to think that if they just paused a few moments that would somehow make the news easier to swallow, Quentin waited until they were settled before he looked Laurence in the eye.

Out with it! He wanted to scream. *What is it? What's so big you can't just tell me!* There was panic bubbling just beneath the surface of his fake patience, provoked by the faint scent of smoke which permeated the air.

"The odd fellow I told you about on Friday," Quentin finally began. "Do you recall?"

Laurence couldn't help it. His fears began to twist into a knot. "Did he come back? Did he hurt you?"

"Yes, and no." Quentin flashed a bright smile and dropped a hand to Laurence's thigh. "He's psychic."

"What, he just came out and told you this?" Laurence stared at Quentin as if he showed signs of sprouting a second head.

"More or less. Obviously there was some back and forth at first. He was suitably circumspect, but he explained that he does what he can to aid other psychics. He has a property over in Lower Hermosa. It's virtually on the beach. We popped over there—"

"You went to this guy's *house?*" Laurence wanted to tear his own hair out. It was like Quentin was totally blind to the potential for regular, everyday danger even after he'd almost been killed by a god.

"Oh, yes." Quentin nodded. "He's something of a mother hen. He seems to see it as his duty to gather up any psychics in need of aid and provide for them. There are children there with the most extraordinary gifts—"

Laurence swallowed the lump in his throat. Words came out of Quentin's mouth and none of them were "I took care," or "I remained alert." Instead he seemed filled with enthusiasm for the kindness and largesse of a guy who so far as Laurence could tell had tried to rob him.

"—few adults, of course, to protect the children. One of them was able to create fire from nothing!"

Fire.

Laurence sat bolt upright and grabbed Quentin's arm. "He did what?"

"Just that, darling!" Quentin seemed far too enthusiastic about this. "He held out his hand—" he raised his own, palm-up, to demonstrate "—and made fire. No fuel, nor did it burn him. Isn't that astonishing?"

"No!" The word was strangled and barely came out right. "What if it's him, Quen? What if he's the reason for my vision? What if he kills you?"

"He has no cause to do so." Quentin's flawless eyebrows drew together in concern.

"That we know of!" He shook his head quickly.

How was this so hard for Quentin to understand? The guy could be so sharp, so perceptive sometimes, and at others he was denser than hardwood. How could he cut to the heart of Laurence's insecurities one minute, then blithely follow some random dude into a house full of psychics the next?

Quentin just sat there with a slowly fading smile, his eyes upturned like those of a wounded puppy. Goddess, he'd been so excited, hadn't he?

Laurence felt like an asshole.

"I'm sorry," he whispered. "I've had a hectic weekend. And I just kinda worry, you know? I don't want you to get hurt."

"I understand." Quentin smiled a little, fleetingly, then reached out to pet Pepper's head.

"I can't protect you if I'm not there."

"Nor I you," Quentin murmured.

Laurence huffed. "You can't hang out at the shop all day." Then he rolled his eyes and leaned back. "Which I guess is your point, huh?"

Quentin inclined his head.

"Okay. Fine. So Lower Hermosa?"

"Correct."

"Let's go over there."

Quentin blinked and withdrew his hands. "Now?"

"It's only, what, a mile from here at most?" Laurence shrugged and hopped from the couch. "I've got the truck. C'mon, show me."

"Is this appropriate?" Quentin rose more slowly. His frown had returned. "I was invited. They may be unsettled if I were to immediately bring someone else they do not know."

Laurence walked over to his sneakers and pulled them on. He crouched down to tie his laces, and glanced over to Quentin while his fingers worked. "I just wanna check the situation out, okay? If everything's legit, then that's great. If not, then we found out sooner rather than later."

Quentin fidgeted with the lay of his shirt, nimble fingers darting along cuffs and waist in a series of automatic gestures he undertook whenever uncertain. "Perhaps it would be best to visit at a more suitable hour?"

Laurence switched to his other foot and checked the laces, then bounced up to his feet and swept curls back from his face with the palm of one hand. He held them back a moment, tightly scrunched in his fingers, before he let them go. They stayed up a second, but fell forward straight after, and he huffed. "I've got a job, Quen. I can't just turn up places for afternoon tea or whatever it is you do with your time. I have to be there all day, whether I'm in the shop or out on deliveries, and I only get free at six o'clock most evenings. It's either gonna be now or some other late visit." He planted his fists on his hips and regarded the Brit. "Not everyone's got all day to get their shit done."

Quentin finished fussing with his clothes, and sauntered toward the door, fetching shoes on the way and stopping by Laurence's side to slip them on. "You make a certain amount of sense," he admitted. "I can see how it may be difficult to attend at another juncture."

"Yeah." Laurence sighed and drew his keys out. "Just a bit. Look, how about we go do this, then we pick up dinner on the way back, and we can cuddle up after and maybe kiss, huh?" He dipped his head so that he could peek up toward Quentin through lowered lashes.

Quentin raised his head and met Laurence's gaze, and the delicate ivory of his cheeks gave way to a soft flush.

Bingo!

"That sounds ideal," Quentin murmured.

"All right!" Laurence grinned and took him by the arm, and while there was a little whiff of smoke which tailed them, it at least made sense now. Quentin had met a pyrokinetic. He'd been near a fire. That's all it was. They'd go over there, meet the guy, and Laurence would be able to get a sense of whether he was the sort of person who'd burn down a building with Laurence and Quentin trapped inside.

Perfect.

17

QUENTIN

Laurence seemed quite tense as he drove to Wilson's property, and Quentin couldn't help but feel guilty for it. The poor lad must have been worried sick.

Perhaps, even if Quentin were only to admit it to himself, he had cause to be. It simply hadn't occurred to Quentin that heading off to a private location with a total stranger for the flimsiest of reasons could be at all risky. There was no cause to do him ill, but the fact that Laurence perceived there may be one should really be something Quentin took more notice of in the future, should it not? Laurence had proved time and again that he was far more familiar with how the world truly functioned than Quentin was.

In this, then, he was forced to acquiesce. He would introduce Laurence to Wilson, and then trust Laurence's judgment on the situation. Assuming that he accepted the judgment, of course.

Laurence parked the truck a little way down the street and they walked the fifty or so yards to the gate with Laurence slowly adopting a more relaxed demeanor, complete with easy smile and an even easier gait, and Quentin pursed his lips at the transformation before he pressed the intercom.

It took almost a minute this time for the gate to click, during which time Laurence attempted to push the button twice more, and Quentin deflected his hand both times.

"What?"

"I'm sure it was heard," Quentin said softly. "Have a little patience."

The gate finally clicked, and Quentin pushed it inward. He held it long enough for Laurence to pass through, and then closed it after them both.

Laurence let out a low whistle. "Wow. This is pretty sweet!"

Quentin looked around the small courtyard, but couldn't see what had impressed Laurence so much, and before he could answer the front door opened.

Wagner exited and pulled himself upright, blocking entry to the house at his back. His attention was on Laurence. "We weren't expecting anyone, Banbury."

"I have no means of contact other than arriving on your doorstep, alas." Quentin approached with a gentle gesture toward Laurence, a flick of his fingers. "This is Laurence. I trust him unreservedly."

"You do, huh?" Wagner didn't move. "Why's he here?"

"'Cause Quentin ain't the only psychic game in town," Laurence chuckled. "How's it going, man? I'm Laurence Riley." He offered Wilson his hand. "I'm Quentin's boyfriend."

Wagner looked to the hand before he clasped it. "Huh."

"I apologize for the impromptu arrival," Quentin murmured. "If now is not a good time, perhaps we may schedule an appointment?"

"No need for that." Wilson himself appeared in the doorway behind Wagner. "It's okay. Soraya says she knows him."

Quentin blinked and looked to Laurence, who himself looked surprised.

"Soraya Brown? Little girl? Clairvoyant?" Laurence's smile warmed. "Yeah, man, is she here? She's okay? That's awesome!"

"Not so little anymore." Wilson laughed. "She's seventeen."

"Whoa! Seriously?" Laurence passed Wagner like he wasn't even there anymore and grabbed Wilson's hand. He shook it energetically. "Man, time flies, doesn't it?"

Laurence was at it again, and Quentin couldn't stop himself from letting a fond smile slip free. Laurence was a master of social occasions, be they one-on-one meetings or larger gatherings. He had the ability to go on a charm offensive which could win over customers and strangers alike, and it took the most dour of dispositions to keep his warmth at bay. To turn away from Laurence was like turning one's back on the sun itself, and Quentin often envied his effortless way with other people. He himself found it a strain to interact for too long. He could feign extroversion for social occasions, but it was incredibly taxing to do so.

But Laurence? He was already inside the house, chatting with Wilson, and they were hitting it off like they'd known each other forever.

Quentin exchanged a glance with Wagner, then followed them into the pleasantly air-conditioned interior.

With Laurence chatting to Wilson, Quentin found himself able to pay more attention to his surroundings. There was a whole area to the left of the entry hall which he had not visited earlier in the day, and it seemed that they were not about to now. The existence of that corridor suggested that garage doors on the street belonged to this property, so he hardly had a burning desire to go investigate.

The stairs were another matter, though. Broad and ostentatious, they swept on up to the next floor in a fashion which seemed somewhat out of keeping with the rest of the property's pseudo-Spanish style, and beside them was a small door with buttons alongside, indicating an elevator. Installing one was no easy feat in a pre-existing building, which lent further credence to his supposition that this mansion was not terribly old.

The urge to nip off up those stairs and have a poke around was strong. It would be impolite, likely to the extent that they would not be invited to return, but his gaze lingered on the stairs as Wilson led them to the same living space Quentin had been shown before.

"Hey! Soraya! How're you doing? Goddess, you got tall!"

Laurence bounded toward the lanky girl who gave him a warm hug.

"Yeah, I'm good. You? Your mom? Still hippies?"

Laurence laughed as he squeezed her. "Yeah, yeah. Still selling flowers. You haven't been spying on us, have you?"

"Naw. Maybe. Naw." Soraya gave Quentin a smile and raised her chin to him. "You're back."

"I am." Quentin offered his hand. "Laurence wanted to stop by."

"Oh, you guys are together, huh?" She nodded sagely as her narrow fingers squeezed his own. "Talk about unexpected. I gotta get back. Catch you later, okay?"

"Thanks, Soraya," Wilson said as she left. "C'mon, guys, let's talk."

Wilson sat, and Quentin waited for Laurence to do so before he himself settled down.

"Why is it you're here?"

Wilson's question landed between them like something a cat had coughed up. Quentin couldn't help but notice that Wagner had shut the door and was now standing before it in his stoic guard posture.

"We—"

"I wanted to check it out," Laurence cut in. "I'm not gonna bullshit you, man. I just wanted to make sure if you had kids here that everything was above board." He shrugged. "But you've got a good thing here, looks like. Soraya's smart. She wouldn't trust you if you hadn't earned it."

"Yeah." Wilson's shoulders lowered, and he patted his palm against the arm of his seat. "She's a smart girl. How'd you meet?"

"Eh, Mom's pretty active in the local Pagan and Wiccan communities. She's a priestess and does a lot of festivals and celebrations, workshops. Some of those events are open to all, and Soraya was at one a few years back. She and some friends figured they'd go laugh at the crazy witches, but then Mom got talking with her." Laurence gave a lazy one-shouldered shrug. "She came by the shop a few times to talk about what she could do, how she felt, that kind of thing, but I don't think she really felt comfortable with our religion and she stopped coming over."

Quentin rested the back of his hand against Laurence's thigh while he listened.

"That's pretty cool," Wilson said. "Tell me, Laurence. What's your ability?"

"Which one?" Laurence blinked.

"You're psychic?" Wilson prompted. "Why don't you tell me what your psychic ability is?"

"Which one?" Laurence repeated. His eyes narrowed slowly.

The room seemed to still. Quentin glanced between Wilson and Wagner and found that both were equally unmoving. Wilson even seemed to be holding his breath.

Laurence punctured the atmosphere with a laugh. "I mean, I can grow plants real fast, or I can get them to move how I want them to. I've got pretty sharp senses. Not, like, the traditional five. All of them, you know? Balance, direction, temperature, as well as the whole sight, smell, touch, all those." He smiled, his teeth flashing into view a moment. "Probably make me a pretty good hunter, if I was that kinda person. But I'm not. I just sell flowers, man."

"Two gifts?" Wilson leaned forward sharply. "How is that possible?"

"I dunno." Laurence mirrored Wilson's posture, leaning forward himself. "Is it unusual?"

"Yeah. Yeah, it is. I've never met anyone with more than one. Or, like with your plants thing, if they seemed to be more than one at first glance—the deeper you dug the more you realize they're just parts of the same ability. But heightened senses *and* plant control?" He laughed and bounced to his feet. "This is awesome!"

The door burst open, and Wagner was almost knocked aside by a horde of youngsters, Soraya at their head. Quentin picked out Estelita and Kimberly, but there were others, seven in total. They shot across the room and clustered around Laurence, clamoring with questions.

"You control plants?"

"You've got more than one power?"

"You're hot!"

"How do you do it?"

"Can I learn?"

"Whoa!" Laurence put his hands up, then he pointed at Soraya. "Were you eavesdropping?"

"Uh…" She sucked her teeth and shrugged. "Yeah, okay. Maybe. A little."

"All right, all right," Wilson intervened, shooing the teenagers out of the room like they were a flock of seagulls. "Go on, get. You know you're not supposed to nose in on other people like that."

"But—"

"Aww—"

"We only—"

"Go!" He waved them out with a sigh. "I'm sorry about that. Kids. No boundaries, you know?"

"Yeah." Laurence chuckled and took Quentin's hand before he stood, and Quentin drifted automatically to his feet. "I totally get it, don't worry."

Quentin closed his fingers around Laurence's and remained silent. There was an undercurrent here he wasn't quite privy to. Laurence wanted to leave, or he wouldn't have gotten up and drawn Quentin with him, so Quentin adopted his polite smile and waited.

"We should get out of your hair, though," Laurence said smoothly. "You've got a full house, looks like. Thanks for seeing me on, like, zero notice."

"No, no! Thanks for stopping by!" Wilson came over to clasp Laurence's shoulder. "Any time you wanna do so, just come on in. You're welcome whenever, seriously."

"Thanks, man!" Laurence grinned, then leaned over to kiss Quentin's cheek. "C'mon, baby. Let's go get dinner."

Quentin's lips quirked at the touch of those warm lips to his skin, and murmured, "Of course, darling."

"Great!"

Laurence had him bundled up in the truck in almost record speed. They'd whirled through the hallway in a flurry of handshakes and assurances, and once they were out of the gate Laurence hooked an arm around his waist and led him down the street to the waiting vehicle. They were in and the truck was moving before the smile slid from Laurence's features and his gaze hardened.

Quentin watched the transformation with unease. It was further testament to Laurence's urgency in leaving the place. The more distance they gained the less happy Laurence seemed to be.

"What is wrong?" he murmured.

Laurence shook his head and glanced down to his dashboard. "Just a sec, baby, okay?"

"Of course."

The truck headed south a few minutes before Laurence relaxed. "Soraya's only good for a mile," he eventually said. "She can spy on stuff happening next door, but the farther away it gets the harder it is for her." He pressed his lips together. "I don't trust Kane."

Quentin blinked quickly. All the handshakes and back-patting, the smiles and laughter, and he had somehow misread it all? "I don't understand."

"Quen, there's no way in hell I would have told him I had more than one gift. It's not normal. Not that I know of, anyway. If he'd asked, I would've told him about the plant thing. Instead I let him know I had other stuff in the toolbox." He hissed. "He told you he was psychic. Did he tell you what his gift is?"

"He—" A sickening sense of guilt flooded him. "He is able to control people." Quentin sighed. "He tells them what to do and they do it."

"Fucking hell!" Laurence slammed his hand against the steering wheel. "Fucking... Fuck! I'm such a fucking moron!"

"This is not your fault," Quentin murmured.

"Yes, it is! I got so caught up worrying about the damn fire I didn't even *think* to ask you what Wilson does! Is that how he got you to go there with him?"

"No." Quentin shook his head. "His gift does not work on me."

Laurence scowled and gripped the wheel tighter. "Right. The mugging he screwed up. That makes sense. Fuck."

Quentin swallowed and folded his hands together in his lap. "You did not tell him everything," he offered.

"No," Laurence agreed. "I figured the cat was out of the bag, I better give him what he was looking for before he went digging for more."

"And that is why we left so quickly."

"Yeah." Laurence grit his teeth. "Baby, we've gotta talk."

That didn't sound at all ominous.

18

QUENTIN

They reached Quentin's apartment by what seemed an unusually long and complicated route, and Quentin could only suppose that Laurence was attempting to avoid Soraya being able to find them should she try.

He greeted the dogs as they headed inside, and Laurence was busy fiddling with his cellphone as Quentin fed them and fetched plates for the take-out they had collected along the way.

"Okay," Laurence muttered. "Looks like we're a mile and a half as the crow flies. We should be safe." He carried the food over to the dining table and helped Quentin sort it onto their plates. "You, uh. You promise not to, like, flip out or anything?"

"That does not sound at all reassuring," Quentin said. "Would you like tea?"

"Sure. Thanks." Laurence wiped his palms on his chinos, then sat at the table and fiddled with his fork while he waited.

Quentin did not hurry the tea. Laurence was nervous, but so was he. Nobody held onto a secret unless they were afraid that it would forever change their world.

There was, after all, a reason he did not wish to discuss other aspects of his day's discoveries.

Was there anything at all that Laurence could say to him which would be so bad, though? How *could* there be?

He added the milk and ferried cups to the table, then sat and reached for his cutlery. "All right," he said. "Out with it, darling."

Laurence stuffed noodles into his mouth and chewed, but Quentin waited for him.

"I had this dream," Laurence began once he'd swallowed.

"Mm?" Quentin finally speared a piece of chicken. He didn't eat it.

"I dunno. More of a vision, I guess, though I've never tried looking so far on my own. It's gotta be at least a couple thousand years ago. I don't know." Laurence's knee butted against Quentin's below the table, then came to rest there. "It was this woman. I was her, and she was running away from something, and she met—" he gulped a breath. "She met Herne the Hunter, and one thing kinda led to another, and—" Laurence bit his lip and gnawed on it a moment. "They're my ancestors. Sara… and Herne. He looked like me. I mean, I look like him. Goddess, I don't know. It's fucked up."

Quentin racked his brains. Buried in there, the name *Herne* seemed familiar, dancing just out of reach. He laid his fork down, the chicken untouched.

"Herne is… a forest spirit?" he eventually offered.

"He's a god." Laurence reached under the table to squeeze Quentin's leg. "There's a whole bunch of Wild Hunt gods, and the theory is they're all just aspects of one horned god, Cernunnos. Herne's aspect was as a protector, a huntsman. He could see through time, make things grow. He was a master of the hunt." He lifted his gaze and sought Quentin's eye. "It's where my gifts come from," he said weakly. "I think I'm… I think I might not be, like, a hundred percent human."

"Oh."

Quentin couldn't work out what else to say. It seemed so ludicrous that he struggled even to parse Laurence's words, as though the man had spoken a jumbled mishmash of nonsense and now waited for Quentin to say that he had understood. Did it matter, though?

Laurence's brows were creased in worry, and his dark eyes lined with fear. It was ultimately irrelevant whether or not

Quentin understood. What was much more important right now was that Laurence was scared.

Quentin reached for Laurence's hand and settled his own over it. "Darling, you are *you*." He dipped in to meet Laurence's eyes and struggled to corral his own thoughts into words. "I did not believe that you were psychic. I didn't believe that I was. But we are. We exist. The things that we can do are not in our imaginations. So it does not matter where they come from. It changes nothing. Perhaps it allows a little context, yes, but are you less human for it?" He took a deep breath and let it out slowly. "You are Bambi Laurence Riley. You are radiant. Unique. And if your abilities are somehow distilled from a dalliance with a god centuries ago, that does not diminish who *you* are. Not in the slightest."

Laurence blinked quickly, then wiped at his eyes, but not before Quentin saw the redness, the moisture. "You don't mind?"

"Mind?" He raised his free hand to cup Laurence's cheek, and brushed away a light tear with the tip of his thumb. "Darling, if I were to ever hold ancestry against you, I would be throwing stones from within the safety of my glass house."

Laurence groaned a little as he leaned into Quentin's palm. "Is your family really that bad?"

"Mm. Let's not sour the day with such talk."

Laurence closed his eyes briefly and pressed his lips against the heel of Quentin's hand. "Okay."

The kiss tingled. It was such a delicate thing, so light and fleeting, that it seemed to linger past its ending, and Quentin had to pull himself together to stop his brain from blanking.

Laurence's eyes fluttered open and he watched him a moment, and then his lips curved into a slow smile. "Baby? Do you like that?"

"Like?" Quentin echoed. It was too late. His mind was already addled by the touch, and repetition was the best he could do.

Laurence released a throaty chuckle and tilted to kiss Quentin's hand again.

He felt warmth surge to his cheeks.

"Uh-huh." Laurence cupped Quentin's hand in his own and

trailed light kisses down toward his wrist, gazing up at him as he did so.

The touch of lips to his wrist shot those tingles along the length of his arm. He gasped when Laurence's tongue darted out to tease his skin. His breath couldn't come quickly enough, and when it did it made him light-headed. The touch was *almost* a tickle, but not quite, and became something else instead. It was sensual. Pleasurable. It pushed all thought away and left him with nothing but sight and touch.

"Oh, man." Laurence sighed and slowly eased back. He released Quentin's hand, laying it down on the table between them. "Goddess, you're so beautiful, Quen. Especially when you look at me like that."

"How?" The word came thickly. Talking—even one lone syllable—was a struggle.

"Like I'm a god," Laurence breathed.

Quentin smiled weakly. "You are," he murmured. "A little."

The fog in his head began to dissipate. He leaned back, and with great reluctance, reclaimed his hand. He reached for his fork and finally ate the piece of chicken. By the time he finished it, he was reasonably certain that he was not about to break any more glass.

Laurence pushed some noodles around his plate in between mouthfuls. "I had an idea," he said after a while.

Quentin had made it through about as much as he could eat by then, and nudged his plate away. "And that idea is?"

Laurence glanced to the plate, then shrugged. "It's about your... You know. The thing that upsets you."

Quentin reached for his tea and held it. "I see."

"Hear me out. I think..." Laurence licked his lips. "I think there are things we can do without, you know. Doing *that*. Things you might like. Enjoy." He reached for Quentin's hand again. "Like just now. That was nice, right? You liked it?"

"I..." Quentin took a mouthful and swallowed it quickly. "I... Yes..."

"And you didn't break anything." Laurence let go. He gestured around them, to the untouched apartment. "Maybe 'cause I stopped, maybe 'cause you're getting better at controlling it, I dunno. But I was thinking maybe I could stay a night."

"Stay?" Quentin blinked slowly. "Here?"

"Yeah." Laurence nodded so quickly that his hair bounced.

"I don't understand." He looked around the apartment. "Do you mean to sleep?"

"Sure. Yeah."

"But where?"

Laurence's attention flickered toward the door to Quentin's bedroom, and he cleared his throat. "Well, uh…"

Quentin's stomach heaved. His dinner felt heavy, like he'd eaten a pound of stodgy bread, and his body seemed to want to reject it all of a sudden. He swallowed, trying to prevent that from happening, and leaped to his feet to get to the sink just in case he failed.

A stiff breeze followed him.

The bedroom.

Oh, God, he wants…

He wants to…

"Baby, no!" Laurence clambered from his chair so fast that he nearly knocked it over, and had to grab at it to stop it from falling. "Wait, hear me out. I'm not suggesting we do *anything* like that, okay? Whatever it is you're thinking. Calm down. I'd never do anything to hurt you, Quen, you know that!"

He gripped the edge of the sink and stared into it.

Calm down.

How could he? He felt sick. He needed to—

"Quen." Laurence was at his side now. "Baby, listen. You need to calm down."

Quentin screwed his eyes shut and tightened his hold on the sink.

Laurence was right. This was how Jack had defeated him, and if Quentin couldn't reel himself in under the slightest hint at anything sexual then it could be used against him again by anyone who learned his weakness. He wouldn't be able to protect himself *or* Laurence, and that was unacceptable.

Ten. Nine. Eight.

His lungs trembled and shook with every breath he drew. Every exhalation rasped from his throat.

Seven. Six.

He could feel Laurence's presence at his side, even though the American hadn't laid a hand on him.

Five. Four.

The sink was cool beneath his hands. Steady. He tried to focus on it and push everything else aside.

Three. Two. One.

The sickness subsided slightly, and he belched a little. A breeze still swept around him, but he opened his eyes and breathed as evenly as he could, gazing fixedly at the wall until even that gentle stirring of the air settled down.

"Are you okay?" Laurence asked softly.

Quentin waited a few moments until he was sure that he could answer safely. "I apologize. I was... not prepared."

"It's all right, hon. Take your time."

Quentin nodded faintly, and managed to relax his grip on the sink. He reached for the tap and rinsed his hands in cold water, then fetched a towel to pat them dry with. By the time he folded the towel and returned it to its rail on a cabinet door his queasiness had passed. "Very well. I confess to finding this idea somewhat—" He broke off.

Disgusting?

Vile?

Terrifying?

"You're cute when you can't figure out what word you wanna use." Laurence offered up a small, sheepish smile. "Look. Your bed's the size of a small country. You sleep in pajamas. So how about, some time, we just... sleep. I'll wear pajamas too. I'll even sleep on top of the sheets and you can sleep under them so there's no chance anything can touch accidentally. And if you get uncomfortable I can just pick up my pillow and come out here to the couch." He waved toward the sofa. "It's big enough to sleep on. I've done it before. It's no big deal. But we can *try*. And maybe if you can see it's not scary we can, you know, do it again some time?"

Quentin folded his arms across his chest and huffed slightly. "And you wish to do this tonight?"

"Ha. I'd love to. But I'm not prepared. I don't have PJs with me, no toothbrush, no clothes for work tomorrow. But how about I bring some supplies along, leave them here, then whenever you wanna give it a try we're ready?"

"And if I do not wish to try it?" He arched an eyebrow.

Laurence gave him that sly little smile of his and bumped hips against him. "You telling me you don't like having me here in the morning? You wake up, and I'm already around? Don't gotta wait around until I finish work in the evening? 'Cause *I'd* like that. To see you before I go to work. To sit down and have breakfast with you..." Laurence paused and eyed him. "You do eat breakfast, right? You don't just skip it like you try to do with every other bit of food that comes close?"

He scowled at Laurence. "I eat breakfast," he lied.

"Great! Then I'll bring some things, we can stow them away, then any time you feel like letting me see you before you've shaved let me know. Deal?"

Quentin blinked at Laurence and couldn't help but marvel at how the man had turned panic into calm.

"Very well," he sighed. "You have a deal."

19

QUENTIN

It was strange to wake up and immediately regret not allowing Laurence to remain overnight.

What would it be like, to open his eyes and see Laurence by his side? Could he do it, or would it lead to disaster?

Quentin eased himself out of bed and padded through to feed the dogs, but all the while the idea of having Laurence here as he made his tea, had his shower, and dressed to take the dogs for their morning exercise nibbled away at his thoughts. By the time he had the girls in their harnesses and led them down the stairs, it had turned into a feat of analysis, with lists of pros and cons settling into place.

Cons: Scared. Could hurt him. What if I look hideous in the morning? What if he sees something?

Pros: Laurence.

Every single con seemed counterbalanced by the single, glaring pro. At the very least there would be no harm in allowing Laurence to store a few things at his apartment in the eventuality that Quentin agreed to his proposal, surely.

Satisfied that he had managed to come up with a course of action which would suitably delay any actual decision, he took off toward the beach.

AFTER LUNCH, once the dogs were settled for their afternoon nap, he walked to Wilson's mansion and was greeted with open arms.

"Quentin!" Wilson stopped short of actually hugging him, thank goodness. "No Laurence today?"

"Alas he is gainfully employed," Quentin explained as he followed Wilson through the house.

"Eh, someone's gotta do it. You gonna start calling me Kane yet?"

"Potentially."

Kane snorted and continued out to the rear of the property. "What brings you here today?"

"I thought somewhat on your suggestion," Quentin murmured. He made a beeline for the shade of an umbrella. Now that May had arrived, nature seemed to have sensed the change in the calendar month and had ramped up the temperature a couple of degrees, and he'd already gained a sheen of sweat from the sun-beaten walk even though it was only a mile and a half. "I would like to try."

"Try?" Kane looked confused for a second, then his mouth parted in comprehension. "Oh, to see if you can teach the kids?"

"If you are still amenable?"

"Amenable?" Kane clapped his hands together. "Dude, I'm delighted! I can tell them to try harder and they will, but I'm a terrible *teacher*, you know? They're totally different things, and I can't be here holding their hands when there's other shit to be done."

"Oh?" Quentin offered a thin smile. "Such as?"

"You know. The usual. Robbing the rich to give to the poor. Hey, you're British! You know all about Robin Hood, am I right?"

Quentin wasn't sure his vague childhood memories counted as expert knowledge, but he inclined his head. "A little," he admitted.

"Okay. Let me go see who we've got at home. Where do you wanna set up?"

"I thought out here would be rather pleasant," Quentin mused.

He looked toward the ocean. "It's a calming environment, not at all confined, and the risk of damage to the house would be minimized. You have the benefit of privacy in this garden, and no neighbors are able to see into it, so we should be able to work without being spotted."

"Not sure many of our kids can do any damage, to be honest." Kane squinted up to the house.

"Perhaps not. But I was hoping that Mr. Wagner might be available to assist?"

"Sebastian?" Kane turned back to him, hand shielding his eyes so that he could look to Quentin. "How?"

"His perspective is different from mine." He said it smoothly, and startled himself with the sincerity of his words. It was simpler to conceal a motive behind genuine truth than it was to lie altogether, it seemed, though his pulse still picked up a little with guilt over the deception. "Perhaps between our shared experiences we may find some way of communicating to the students."

Kane nodded slowly. "Okay. Sure. I don't know how talkative he'll be, but I'll get him to come down here."

"Thank you."

Quentin settled into a chair to wait, and Kane strolled up the steps to the mansion.

So far, so good.

KANE HAD RUSTLED up seven youngsters in total, including the three young ladies Quentin had previously met. Most of them were nearer twenty than not, thank goodness, but a couple were fifteen years old, including Estelita. Some pulled their chairs out onto the lawn to escape the shade of umbrellas and sunbathe while they listened—or at least feigned an excellent charade of doing so—while others remained around the tables. Sebastian sat to Quentin's right, and loosened from bodyguard to instructor with ease once Quentin explained what was required of him.

Of the seven students here, none of them seemed to have

especially demonstrable gifts, and so the immediate hurdle was in knowing whether or not any of them had succeeded in whatever they attempted to do. Soraya was clairvoyant, but also reasonably confident in her ability. Estelita could eavesdrop on the neighbors, but Quentin thought that to be in poor taste and had her focus on her sense of touch instead. There was a young lad in his late teens called Felipe who claimed that he could see people's auras, but he far preferred to sunbathe than practice. Kimberly was nervous about even attempting to use her ability to hide, lest —ironically, Quentin felt—anyone see her doing it.

He walked them through his own process for differentiating between conscious control and emotional response, and had Sebastian give them a few demonstrations of his pyrokinetic power while discussing with him how their different approaches worked for them.

Sebastian's gift was rather more advanced than a simple little flame in the palm of his hand, Quentin soon learned. The man could engulf an entire arm in flames a foot high and then project them outward to consume a target.

That certainly impressed the teenagers, once Sebastian had immolated a chair.

It impressed Quentin.

He had to shelve that for the time being, though. The children took absolute priority.

The oldest lad present was easily old enough to be Laurence's age. Clifton was lanky and white, and hid under the shade in what Quentin considered a splendid display of common sense. He purported to have a talent which intrigued Quentin almost as much as Sebastian's: he was able to reach out to an animal's mind and have it follow his commands without saying a word to them.

It was something the lad seemed to enjoy entertaining himself with. Now and then he would gaze up into the sky and a seagull began to turn in lazy circles before Clifton released it to continue on with its day, but as the afternoon drew on he seemed to grow more lethargic.

Initially Quentin had supposed it could be the heat, but the others were starting to flag, too.

"Shall we call it there?" He offered. "Everyone seems a little worn out."

Soraya chuckled at him and stretched her arms over her head. "'Course we are. We've been working our asses off for like two hours."

There were murmurs of agreement from the students, except Kim, who looked fresh as a daisy. But she hadn't practiced at all.

Were they worn out so readily by the practice? When Quentin had first begun to learn to master his telekinesis, Laurence had taken him to Myriam's farm and he had worked with heavy machinery for hours before any fatigue had begun to take hold, but these youngsters were ready for a nap.

"Then now seems as good a time as any to rest," he agreed. "If you found this helpful, I would gladly make it a regular event."

"Great!"

"Awesome!"

"Whatever."

The last was from Soraya, but she at least gave him a dry smile before she led the charge back toward the house. Almost all the youngsters followed, except Felipe, who promptly shed his shoes and T-shirt then dived into the pool.

Quentin turned to Sebastian and smiled to him. "Thank you for your assistance. I'm not sure they would have been so willing to listen had you not been here."

"Don't be so hard on yourself." Sebastian crinkled his nose as he watched Felipe do laps. "Goddammit, I keep telling them not to go in the pool without a buddy around."

"Perhaps he is counting on you?"

Sebastian snorted. "Probably. Bodyguard, lifeguard, it's all the same thing, right?" He looked to Quentin at that. "You're good with kids."

"You think so?" He straightened up in his seat. It was a near-automatic response to praise.

"I know so. Too many people talk down to teenagers, treat them like they're kindergartners or trainee criminals or something. You treat 'em with respect, and teens crave that above pretty much everything else." Sebastian checked on Felipe a second before he continued. "And you push hard. They're gonna sleep like babies." He smiled briefly.

"Ah, well." Quentin laced his fingers together. "Ultimately it is a commingling of practice and exercise, is it not? One cannot improve without finding one's own limits and then pushing beyond them."

"True, true." Sebastian turned toward him and leaned in a few inches. "How much practice have you done?"

Quentin tilted his head in a question. "What do you mean?"

"I dunno. I've just never met anyone as young as you with such precision and ability under their belt." Sebastian leaned back as he shrugged. "You lifted half the living room yesterday. Today you're doing demonstrations for two hours and not even flagging. Did you manifest young or something?"

"Ah." Quentin tapped his thumbs together a moment. "It's rather complicated. But no, I did not."

"Then how'd you learn so fast? Because I've been with my talent for twenty years, you know? It's taken every one of those years to get where I am today."

Twenty years?

Quentin blinked slowly and tried not to look surprised. He had no idea whether or not he achieved it. "I have been trained as a classical pianist from the age of five. I learned the self-discipline required to practice daily and to push my own limits. All I have done is apply that rigor to my gift once I discovered its existence."

"Damn." Sebastian nodded to himself. "Yeah. I learned all the same things in the Army, but you don't sign on with the Army when you're five. Guess I should have learned the piano, huh?" He chuckled and shook his head. "A *pianist*," he repeated.

"I don't think I would be terribly good as a soldier," Quentin laughed softly.

"And I'd make a shitty pianist." Sebastian smirked.

"Then we have both, I would say, developed along the path which best suited us as individuals."

"Yeah." Sebastian sobered a little as he checked on Felipe. "What are you, twenty-five?" At Quentin's nod, he continued. "How'd you get to be so smart?"

"Oh, don't mistake this for intelligence." Quentin chuckled. "I get it all from Laurence's mother, I assure you."

"Smarts ain't always the same as grades." Sebastian regarded him with an oddly neutral gaze. "If you're bright enough to listen to her, then you're doing okay."

"That's..." Quentin hesitated, then swallowed.

A lie.

His immediate instinct was to rebuff Sebastian's claim that he might have a brain between his ears somewhere. After a disastrous set of results at each wave of school exams he was under no illusion that he could pass for bright, and it was so much worse in comparison to Freddy's academic career, as though one twin had been born with all the intellect that the other lacked. But there was something in the way Sebastian said it, the way his expression was even and his voice steady, that gave him pause.

It was empathy.

Sebastian understood.

Quentin drew a breath and offered a grateful smile.

"Thank you."

20

QUENTIN

HE TRIED TO TURN, BUT THERE WAS A WEIGHT ACROSS HIS CHEST. It held him down against the sheets and trapped him like a fly in amber.

Quentin gasped for air and woke in an instant. His sight blurred and he blinked quickly to clear it. The weight remained. He hadn't dreamed it.

In the dark, he could hear breathing. Not just his own. Someone or something was in here with him.

Calm. Stay calm.

He swallowed and swiveled his eyes, trying to make out shapes in the dimness of his bedroom. A body lay to his right, and he became aware of its breath against his shoulder, warm air penetrating his pajamas.

It was snoring.

Ever so faintly, the mass of curls which lay on his shoulder snored.

There was a word for this creature, this invader he shared a bed with. A name.

Laurence, his brain helpfully offered, completely unapologetic about not having done it sooner.

What the hell is he doing here?

"Man, I can't believe you've taught them so much in one week! They're doing great!"

Quentin swelled with pride. Daily training and exercise had led to two very well-behaved, friendly, lovable dogs. Grace had learned to trust his lead, so they were now able to jog for short distances, and Pepper had a protective streak which meant that she was never far from Grace's side even during play.

"I did what I could," he said with false humility.

"Maybe you should be a dog trainer." Laurence chuckled. "How's it going with Kane's kids, anyway?"

"Reasonably well." Quentin petted Grace's head as she settled by his feet. "Some are more eager than others, but who can blame them? It's hard work."

"I guess." Laurence leaned against his side and eased an arm around him. "You know, baby, I'm so proud of you. You're making so much progress."

"Thank you." He settled his arm around Laurence's shoulders and began to run fingers through his hair.

"Mm." Laurence sighed softly and relaxed against him. "I was thinking maybe I could stay tonight."

Quentin's fingers stilled.

Laurence waited quietly.

"Tonight?"

"Bite the bullet, Quen. I won't hurt you. I won't do anything without your permission. Let me prove it to you."

Quentin gnawed on the inside of his cheek as he forced his fingers to move once more. It took him several minutes of deliberation before he could answer.

"Very well."

Laurence's snoring faded into subdued, slow breaths.

Now that he was fully awake, Quentin could make out finer details. Laurence's arm was slung across his chest, and the man was laid out alongside him, dead to the world. Laurence's cheek was on his shoulder, and his lips were faintly parted.

Quentin eased an arm out from beneath the sheets and then laid it to rest above Laurence's.

The florist had done as promised. The bedsheets remained between them, a barrier which was—now that Quentin thought about it—more symbolic than genuinely protective. He had worn pajamas throughout, although Quentin questioned whether or not a matching set of shorts and T-shirt constituted "pajamas." Most importantly, nobody had been harmed.

Laurence's breathing was subtle and steady. His curls were a tousled, unruly mess. Those lips were relaxed, and looked so soft.

Quentin took a deep breath and shifted his hand to Laurence's shoulder. It was warm through the soft cotton top, and not nearly as hard and thin as his own. Where Quentin was built like a greyhound, Laurence was more of a Doberman with sleek musculature and hidden strength, and those muscles provided a little padding over his bones.

Laurence's eyes flickered behind the lids, and then slowly eased open halfway.

Like a boy caught with his hand in the cookie jar, Quentin froze. There was absolutely no way to claim that he hadn't put his hand on Laurence, that he wasn't lying here watching him sleep.

"Mmm. Morning." Laurence wriggled a hand up to rub his eyes. "You sleep okay?"

"Yes." The answer surprised him because it was true. He had anticipated that he would lie awake for hours, fretting over his situation, but it had taken him at most an hour to fall asleep once he had grown accustomed to Laurence's alien presence. "Did you?"

"Oh, man." Laurence yawned into the back of his hand and rolled onto his back to stretch. "Like a fucking baby. Your bed is amazing. How do you ever get up in the morning? I'd just lie here all day!"

Quentin's hand, freed from the shoulder beneath it, instead clutched at the sheets. He shuffled onto his side and risked a slight smile.

Laurence glanced to him, then grinned and raised his arms out of the way. "C'mere. I won't bite."

It took a few seconds to comprehend what it was that Laurence was hinting at, but then the lightbulb came on. Quentin eased himself closer, wriggled until he was alongside Laurence, and Laurence's arms wrapped around him.

"Goddess, this is great." Laurence set his lips to Quentin's forehead and kissed tenderly. "What time is it?"

"I have no idea." He could feel Laurence's heartbeat through his chest, see the rise and fall of every breath.

This was a memory to retain.

"Urgh. Maybe I can call Mom and tell her I'm sick."

"She would not believe you." Quentin chuckled.

"And I guess you've gotta get up and take the girls for a walk, huh?"

"Mm." He listened for them, but couldn't hear the dogs stir, which meant that it couldn't be six o'clock yet. They were both incredibly accurate with their breakfast demands.

"Fast asleep," Laurence confirmed. "You need a shower before you go?"

"I see little point," Quentin admitted. "We shall be out for quite a run, and I shower once we are home again."

Laurence laughed. "Baby, that was an invitation. To join me? In the shower?"

Quentin blinked, and then sat up abruptly. He had to fight the sheets to do so, but managed to pull himself free of them. "Laurence!"

"Hey." Laurence rose more slowly, stuffing hands through his hair to push it out of his eyes. "It was an offer, nothing more. And it's not like you've got anything I've never seen before."

His embarrassment was so complete that he felt the tips of his ears burn, and he drew sheets into his lap. There was a stark difference between knowing on an unspoken level that Laurence had removed his clothes and dressed his wounds after Jack attacked him, and having that knowledge presented to him so bluntly.

"I didn't mean it like that." Laurence's tone softened. He swung his feet off the bed and stood, then stretched and yawned. The action exposed inches of his midriff as it tugged his T-shirt up.

Quentin found himself looking at taut, warm-toned skin with a light dusting of dark blond hair below his belly button.

"Nuh-uh. No eyeing the goods when you've got no intention of making a purchase." Laurence smacked his lips and tugged his shirt down. "Perv," he grinned. "You need the bathroom, or can I go get ready for work?"

"Feel free." He nodded toward the bathroom door in case Laurence had somehow forgotten where it was.

Laurence grinned and loped his arms over his shoulders to grab his shirt, then he pulled it forward over his head as he turned away. "Okay, hon. Your loss."

Quentin only had a moment's glimpse of Laurence's back, rippled like an athlete's, before the other man disappeared into the bathroom and shut the door.

He released a breath and waited for the sound of the shower before he slipped from the bed and dressed himself in record time. He only wore running clothes to take the girls for their morning exercise, so it wasn't too difficult to be ready so quickly. Except he had no access to the bathroom now. Even if Laurence hadn't locked the door, it would be most improper to go in there while Laurence was using it.

And that meant that Quentin couldn't shave. He couldn't brush his teeth. Good God, he couldn't even wash before he left the house.

He fidgeted with his cuffs and headed out of the bedroom to feed the dogs. Perhaps if he dithered enough Laurence would emerge from the bathroom and Quentin could pop in there to make himself less of a shambles.

But then Laurence would want breakfast.

Bloody hell!

He hadn't gotten anything in for breakfast. There had been no warning. Laurence had only suggested he remain last night, a Sunday night, and now Quentin would be caught with bugger all edible in the apartment. Laurence was sure to insist that a cup of tea did not constitute a meal.

The best option all-round was to take the girls for their exercise right now and not be here when Laurence left the bathroom. Yes, that seemed the most sensible plan, so he fetched their harnesses and refilled their water bottles, then all but ran out the front door.

It wasn't until they had reached the beach that it occurred to him what a spectacular mess he'd made of the entire affair.

21

LAURENCE

He couldn't really blame Quentin for bailing on him by the time Laurence got out of the shower. Once he realized there wasn't any food in the apartment it became pretty damn obvious why the earl had left without even saying goodbye. That didn't mean it hadn't stung for a few minutes, but Laurence didn't have time to hang on to his ego here. Something important had gone down.

A breakthrough.

Laurence stayed the night, and Quentin was *okay*. No fight, no calamity, no panic. That was a huge leap, and Laurence was willing to take it.

But that didn't mean he wasn't going to bring groceries over the next time.

With June only a week away, staying the night at Quentin's happened every two or three days now. Always with pajamas, always with the sheets between them, but Laurence was okay with that. He was even okay with the drive into San Diego every morning, despite the rush hour traffic. They got up, shared breakfast, then Quentin took the girls and Laurence hopped into the truck. It worked like a charm, and the more it happened the more Quentin grew used to it.

Baby steps.

Laurence whistled to himself as he sorted through the week's orders, making sure they were organized by delivery date. He leaned against the counter so that he could man the shop at the same time, while his mom worked in the back room preparing the afternoon deliveries.

They'd taken on a new member of staff to help with the uptick in business. Maria knew very little about flowers, but she was warm and friendly, and more than happy to drive around delivering orders for five hours a day while her children were at school. It meant that they could handle almost twice as many orders, but now the choke point was the lack of greenhouse on the roof. They'd have to wait until the books recovered from the cost of hiring Maria before they could sink a lump sum into replacing what had been destroyed in the fight with Jack.

The bell above the shop door jangled and he tore his attention from all the slips of paper, then grinned when he saw Ethan. "Hey, man. You looking for some flowers?"

"Ha ha. I thought we were gonna hang out some time, dude?" Ethan came over to slap Laurence on the back, then fiddled with the order forms. "Your mom's got you working at last, huh?"

"Hey, don't mess with those." Laurence grabbed bulldog clips and quickly snapped them into place around each pile to keep Ethan from shuffling them all together.

"He works very hard," Myriam called from the back. "Hello, Ethan!"

"Hey, Mrs. R!" Ethan called out. "So, how about it? You, me, Aiden, Quentin, this weekend?"

Laurence snorted in surprise. "You're still with Aiden?"

"What's that supposed to mean?"

"Just, uh." Laurence blinked, then shoved Ethan's arm. "Asshole. Oh, hey. Do you want a job? We can use another pair of hands around here, give me more time to help Mom with arrangements…"

"No way, dude. I like my job." Ethan shrugged. "Okay, I like the tips. Do people tip florists?"

"No."

"Then you're on your own, dude. How's it going with your hot British sex god?"

"Well, he's hot and British, but ixnay on the exsay." Laurence sighed softly and headed out from behind the counter to fiddle with the flowers on display.

"Still no dice?" Ethan hopped up and sat on the counter. "Any more ideas on those issues of his?"

Laurence shook his head and kept his voice low, nodding toward the bead curtain to let Ethan know his mom was back there. "I dunno. It's so weird. He's not afraid of intimacy. Like, he'll cuddle, kiss, he'll be so thoughtful and kind, and then—" He sucked air between his teeth. "Then it's DEFCON 2 the moment anything gets hot and heavy."

"So what're we looking at?" Ethan frowned and kicked his heels against the counter stand. "You think someone hurt him?"

Laurence swallowed and his hands stilled against the flower pots. He didn't like to think too much about what might have gone on, but for all Quentin's insistence that his scars came from accidents, most of them ran in lines. Some crossed over other, older injuries, which meant the previous one had healed before the new one came along. The only thing that made sense was too horrible to even think about.

"Yeah," he rasped. "Yeah, someone hurt him. Bad."

Ethan hissed. "Fuck. You think he was raped?"

"I don't know." His head was swimming. He felt sick. Goddess, he'd been so caught up in helping Quentin get over his fears, but what if all he'd done was push past his wounds?

"Have you asked?"

Laurence nodded weakly. "Yeah, I have, but he insists nothing like that's ever happened."

"You think he could be lying?" Ethan hopped off the counter and came closer until he could rest his hand on Laurence's back.

"No. No, he's a really shitty liar." Laurence laughed weakly.

"Like, comically bad. Little kids lie better than he does. But—" He hesitated.

Did he have the right to discuss this with Ethan? This was Quentin's personal business, and he might not appreciate it being aired between friends like gossip. But then Laurence wasn't capable of working this all out alone. He'd tried. It didn't work.

"Promise you won't say a word," he muttered.

"Cross my heart, dude."

Laurence glanced toward the bead curtain again. "He, uh. He kinda..." He bit his lip. "Fuck, man. He has blackouts, okay? If he gets scared, if he's threatened, he just shuts down, and he's forgotten all about it the next day."

Ethan gave a low whistle. "You wanna get the hell away from that, Laur. Don't get caught up in crazy!"

"Shut the fuck up, asshole!" He shoved Ethan square in the chest and pushed him away, and his hands balled into fists the moment there was space between them.

"Whoa, hey! Chill out!" Ethan raised his hands and eyed Laurence's fists.

Laurence huffed as he lowered his arms, and wrapped them around himself. "Prick," he muttered.

"I deserved that." Ethan dropped his own hands and stuffed them into his pockets. "How'd you know? Like, have you seen it?"

"Yeah." Laurence sucked his teeth while he quickly assembled a half-truth. "He got into a fight with Dan. Dan threatened him, like sexually, and Quentin just went." He snapped his fingers. "Next day he was like it never happened. Totally forgot the whole thing."

"And you think he's done this before and so whatever's happened to him he's blacked out on then erased, right?"

"I think so, yeah." Laurence shook his head. "Fuck. I swear if I ever find out who it was I'll nail their dick to a table then tear their fucking heart out through their ass."

"Jesus," Ethan breathed. "That's... one hell of an image. Thanks for that."

"Yeah," Laurence agreed. "You're welcome."

"Well. Think it over. About coming over for some beers, I

mean." Ethan sighed. "Maybe do you both some good to get out and socialize, you know? He doesn't get weird if other people are doing PDAs, right?"

"Fuck, are you and Aiden gonna be playing tonsil-hockey all damn night?" Laurence moved back behind the counter and fidgeted with the stacks of orders, sorting them into one big pile and then separating them out again when all the bulldog clips stopped them from sitting neatly. "No, he's okay with that. I haven't seen him flip out about people kissing nearby. I mean, I think it makes him a little uncomfortable, but not to the point where he has a blackout."

"I think we can tone it down a little. Or at least I promise we'll try to. Just kick my ankle if we're getting too into each other."

Laurence nodded briefly. "Sure. Okay. I'll talk to Quentin about it, I promise."

"Awesome. We can do a cookout or something."

Laurence smiled, but his agreement was drowned out by the sound of the bell, and he straightened up to look professional. He quickly tugged his apron in case it had gotten creased, and he placed his hands against the countertop. "Hey, welcome to the Jack in the Green. If there's anything I can help you with, just ask."

The man who entered seemed vaguely familiar, and Laurence maintained an easy, friendly smile while he tried to work out whether he was supposed to know the guy's name. Had they met at a bar, maybe? Was he a minor celebrity? With the amount of Neil Storm's buddies who kept stopping by it could be anyone.

"I believe there may be, yes." His voice was smooth, deep, and bore a British accent.

Goddess, was it raining Brits in San Diego lately?

"Sure thing! Are you looking for anything specific?"

The Brit meandered around the shop, eyeing the flowers on display. He was tall and fit, somewhere in his twenties, and he wore cream slacks and a crisp white shirt which he'd rolled up to the elbows. His blond hair was trimmed and neat, and he had sunglasses which he'd pushed up into it.

"Mm. Answers, really." He turned from the flowers and sauntered toward the counter, and rested a hand on it once he got there. He raised his chin and met Laurence's gaze.

Laurence was about to answer, and then he caught sight of the man's pale, colorless eyes and everything clicked into place.

Frederick.

Quentin's brother, Freddy.

Freddy was here in the shop, which was either an incredible coincidence, or it meant that Freddy knew where Quentin was.

Laurence licked his lips and regarded Freddy, then raised his head.

"Only if I get some from you, too."

22

LAURENCE

"This seems like one of those private talks I keep being around for," Ethan chuckled. "Catch you later, Laur."

Laurence blinked and tore his gaze from Freddy just in time to wave as Ethan hurried out of the shop. "Sure, man. I'll call you."

The bell jangled, and then they were alone, though Laurence could still hear his mom working in the back room.

Freddy was maybe equal to Laurence for height. His hair was lighter, more yellow, but he was broader than Laurence. There was none of Quentin's skinny frame present with his twin, and if Laurence hadn't seen pictures of Freddy online he might not have guessed they were related. There was some slight resemblance in the jawline, and those eyes of course, but everything else was different.

Freddy was looking him over every bit as Laurence was checking him out, and then the man broke into a cheerful smile. "Frederick," he said as he offered his hand. "Although I would presume that you know who I am."

Laurence shook it slowly. "Yeah," he admitted. "Enough to recognize, anyway."

"Wonderful! That saves some time." Freddy withdrew his hand. "No, Icky doesn't know I'm here. Yes, I found you through Twitter. No, neither Father nor Nicky know you exist. Father would never lower himself to using the internet, and Nicky spends far too much time on Tinder."

Laurence stared at him.

Freddy couldn't be more different from Quentin. He knew what Twitter and Tinder were. He used *I* instead of *one* with strangers. His posture was loose and relaxed. He looked as though he ate reasonably portioned meals and didn't pick at them like a bird.

"Why'd you call him Icky?"

"Because his middle name's Ichabod." Freddy winked. "Were those most of the answers you wanted?"

"I guess?" Laurence rubbed his jaw with his palm and eyed the man. "Why're you here?"

"That's an easy one. You're the first whiff of a relationship I've ever caught Icky within a hundred miles of. Up until now, not even a rumor. Frankly I thought his cock might have dropped off, but now here you are, and it's already been going on a few months." Freddy smiled idly. "And since the poor boy hasn't a clue how to look out for himself, I'm here to do it for him lest you turn out to be some remarkably successful gold-digger. No offense intended," he added. "But he's my brother. I want to make sure he's safe."

"Man, you must think I'm some kinda cockroach." Laurence crossed his arms.

"I don't know what to think, dear boy. But Icky is heir apparent. We wouldn't want some yobbo to run off with the family jewels, would we?" Freddy chuckled.

Laurence wasn't wholly sure what a *yobbo* was, but it didn't take a rocket scientist to work out that it wasn't a term of endearment. "Okay. I'm not after his money." Not that Quentin was anywhere near as wealthy as the earl presented himself to be. "Is it nice going out with a guy who's richer than me? Sure." He shrugged. "But it's awful at times, too. He drops the kind of money it takes me months to earn, on things I could never afford, and sometimes that sucks, you know?" He looked Freddy over. "No, you probably don't know. But I work hard for what I've got, and it's difficult to be in love with someone who's got way more than I'll ever have and hasn't worked a day in his life to earn it. He does everything in his power to make me feel like a million dollars, and I can't even afford to take him to a fancy restaurant or have the time off work so we can spend a few days on the beach together. You might think he deserves better than me. You could even be right. But I love him, and he loves me, and that's just the way it is."

Freddy nodded as he listened. He remained quiet a moment after Laurence stopped speaking, and then murmured, "I can empathize with that situation. It doesn't take shared circumstances to have an understanding of what it must be like to see someone else receive—for free—all the things which you yourself could not possibly attain no matter how much effort you put in."

Laurence blinked at him. Freddy's stance was open, leaning toward Laurence a little. He was making eye contact and speaking to Laurence as an equal, not as a commoner. But most importantly, Freddy didn't offer him an ounce of pity, only his acceptance of Laurence's words as truth.

"Thanks, man." Laurence dipped his head.

"No, thank you. You have no reason to be so honest with a stranger." Freddy flickered a brief smile. "I have answers. Your turn."

Laurence bit the tip of his tongue. He had questions. A lot of questions. But he couldn't go barging in and alienate the man before they'd spent more than ten minutes in the same room together. He had to at least try to tackle the subject without letting his anger reach the surface.

"Quentin says that he was accident-prone as a kid." He lifted his chin and met Freddy's eye. "Do you remember any of the accidents?"

"Ah." Freddy idly tapped his fingers against the countertop. He glanced toward the door. "If you are asking whether I was present, then yes. For a few. But we did not really play together as friends when we were children. Quentin is not, ah..." He winced. "Academically accomplished," he said with care, "and so we had very little to talk about together as we grew up."

"You're saying you're smart and he's dumb." Laurence felt a surge of irritation.

"Oddly, no." Freddy looked to Laurence as he shook his head. "It's a common misconception. He's simply a kinesthetic learner, whereas I am more suited to memorizing data. Academia rewards those who can file away facts and recite them in examinations. Icky's a bright fellow, but he likes to get his hands involved. He's also an introvert, and people do so like to mistake withdrawn for unintelligent." He waved a hand in a gesture which reminded Laurence of Quentin's motions. "But where he enjoys music, horse riding, and climbing trees, I vastly prefer to settle down with a book, discuss philosophy, or head off to lectures. It makes for very stilted conversation."

"Oh." A ripple of sheepish embarrassment washed Laurence's annoyance away. "Sorry."

"It's quite all right." Freddy chuckled softly. "We are both here to protect him. It no doubt puts us both a little on edge, wouldn't you say?"

"Yeah." Laurence rubbed his jaw. "Okay so you do remember some of the accidents though? Like, he says one time you hit him with a car or something?"

Freddy groaned. "Honestly, he's never going to let me forget that. I had only been behind the wheel for half an hour. Have you ever driven a manual?"

"A manual... Oh, you mean a stick shift?"

"Ah, yes. One of those. Manual transmission." Freddy clicked his tongue. "Not bloody easy when you've never done it before, and Icky comes charging out of the house while I'm trying to reverse the thing. Only dinged him a little. My God, the fuss though! Almost cost the chauffeur his job!"

Laurence stared at him.

"I was fifteen." Freddy coughed into his hand. "Although it was private property, so there was nothing illegal about it, but it did make it rather tricky to see another fifteen-year-old darting across the back of a Rolls. Anyway, just some gravel rash. Nothing broken. Didn't learn a bloody thing, though. Managed to get himself run over on his eighteenth birthday."

Laurence shifted his weight as he listened. So far as Quentin had recounted, his last accident had been on his eighteenth birthday, and he had been run over by a car, but he couldn't recall whether it was Freddy driving or someone else. Could it be that Quentin had conflated two similar accidents? That didn't seem impossible, especially with Quentin's difficulty in remembering traumatic events.

"But not by you?"

"Oh, no." Freddy shook his head. "We're a day apart, and by then I was well and truly away at college, getting rat-arsed all week in celebration, as you do when you're away from home and turning eighteen." Freddy laughed briefly. "Alas I only heard about it after, when Mother called to tell me the news." He sighed a little at that and glanced away again. "Rather more serious than when I bumped him over, too. Broke something. An arm, I think. Or ribs. God, I don't know. Isn't that horrible?" He pinched at the bridge of his nose. "He's had so many bumps and scrapes that it's all sort of jumbled together."

"Yeah, I can imagine." Laurence grimaced at him. "I gotta admit it looks kinda weird from the outside. You know that, right?"

"Oh, I wouldn't deny it in the slightest," Freddy agreed.

He eyed Freddy, then nodded. "Have you come here to take him home?"

"He's a grown man. He has responsibilities." Freddy paused. "And it is *my* responsibility to see if I cannot persuade him to face his future with some bloody spine in him. But I am not going to take him anywhere. I would simply like to see him stand still for five minutes rather than sprint off at the hint of anything he deems troublesome." His cool, gray eyes gazed at Laurence, almost in a challenge. "I do hope that you aren't about to tell me that Icky doesn't do any such thing."

Laurence rocked his jaw. He wanted to say exactly that. He wanted to leap in to Quentin's defense and tell Freddy that he'd got it all wrong.

But it was true. Quentin ran from his problems, whether literally or metaphorically. He stuck his head in the sand and waited for the storm to pass him by, or he'd pack his bags—and his piano—and move to another city or country. He stood up to Jack and refused to be cowed by a god, and then stammered at mention of his own father.

"No," Laurence sighed. "I'm not gonna say that."

Freddy nodded. "As to why I am here, in this shop, speaking with you?" He shook his head a little. "Because I imagine that he would not take kindly to seeing me without warning. He would likely assume that Father has sent me to fetch him, and then he'd run off again. Please, Mr. Riley, if you would do me the kindness of asking him if he will speak with me, I shall be in your debt."

"You want a meeting?"

Freddy inclined his head. "Yes."

"When?"

"At his earliest convenience. I have a suite at the Hotel Palomar. It isn't terribly far from here, on Fifth Avenue."

Laurence nodded. "Yeah, I know it."

Freddy smiled and offered his hand. "I am there all evening. If you cannot persuade him to stop by I shall be disappointed, but I will understand completely."

Laurence took Freddy's hand and shook it. It was warm, soft like Quentin's, but broader. "I'll ask him. You don't mind if I come with him, right?"

"No." Freddy smiled. "I was rather hoping that you would, actually. It might be the difference between him coming or staying away altogether."

"Okay." Laurence returned the smile. "I'll see what I can do."

"That's all I ask."

23

QUENTIN

"Laurence does know he's welcome here, doesn't he?"

Quentin sipped his lemonade and watched the ocean. The laughter of people playing in the pool provided a tolerable level of background noise, and it was entirely possible to forget that they were all here to protect themselves from the world beyond the mansion's walls.

"He does," he finally said. He cast a smile toward Kane. "But he doesn't have a great deal of spare time. That and he isn't terribly comfortable with your particular gift."

"Eh." Kane shrugged. "That's fair enough." He put his glass down on the table, empty, still wet with condensation. "I've really gotta thank you, you know."

"Mm?" Quentin tore his gaze from the sea and peered at the psychic. "For what?"

"For coming here so much. For spending time with the kids. They're really bonding together. You're helping them with more than just their powers."

"Oh, really, it's nothing." Quentin smiled and turned his attention to the pool, where Sebastian was perched overlooking it in case of trouble. "I only wish there were more that I could do."

"You're doing plenty, believe me." Kane chuckled. "Hell, I've even seen Sebastian smile." He looked toward the house with a pensive look in his eye, and then faced Quentin. "I've been thinking."

"Uh-oh."

Kane snorted at him. "I don't want this to be a short-term thing. The house, the kids. I want this to last. Not in the legacy sense—I don't wanna be remembered for anything, but I want us to be here whenever we're needed. Whenever a kid gets thrown out on the street for being a freak, whenever they get bullied for doing stuff nobody else can." He tipped his head back and stared blankly up at the umbrella which shielded them from the harsh afternoon sun. "I got it pretty bad in high school."

Quentin frowned gently and placed his own glass down beside Kane's. "Bullied?"

"Yeah. I mean, sure, everyone's got a high school bullying story, am I right? But it goes horribly wrong when one person is psychic."

Quentin waited. He watched the ocean again so as not to make Kane feel uncomfortable or pressured to continue. Instead he simply gave the man some time.

Kane patted his hand against the table. "I'm not a big guy. Never was. But I was one weedy little motherfucker at school. Wasn't into sports; I preferred playing games with all the other nerds. Same old story." He closed his eyes. "Got roughed up a lot, called names, stuffed into my own locker, you know, the usual. Got pushed down some stairs once, broke my arm. The other guy never got punished 'cause he was on the football team. Headed for a scholarship. Gonna be a big name. Everything's gotta be pushed aside so we can turn these meatheads into superstars." His Adam's apple bobbed as he swallowed. "One day I just... snapped. He and his pals were shoving me around. They'd already given me a swirly and they were going in for another, and I just—"

Kane broke off and pushed himself out of his chair to pace around the table.

"What is a swirly?" Quentin asked quietly.

"Shit. It's where they hold your head down the toilet bowl and flush. You drown for all of like thirty seconds. It's the high school version of waterboarding. Which is a torture technique you probably also haven't ever heard of."

His breath caught in his throat, and he coughed into the back of his hand. "My God," he croaked. "Children do this?"

"Oh yeah." Kane's nose crinkled. He thrust his hands into his pockets and came to a standstill overlooking the pool. "I screamed at him to go fucking kill himself."

Quentin winced at first, and then the understanding crawled up into his brain like a spider, settling in and making itself at home. "Oh, God," he breathed. "And that's when your gift manifested."

"You got it in one." Kane rubbed his face with his hands and turned his back to the swimming teenagers. "He just walked right out of there, went up to the roof, and threw himself off it. First they all thought he was messing around, but then they all left me to go follow him, and I could hear him begging them for help. I didn't go after them. I ran to the Principal's office to tell them what he'd just done to me. I figure he was already dead by the time I made it to the office. They fought him, they said. Once he got near the edge of the roof he was crying, begging them to stop him, and they tried, so he beat the shit out of them until he could break free and jump."

Kane returned to his seat. As he moved his hands to the armrests, Quentin could see that they were shaking.

"Motherfucker dived off like a champion swimmer, too. Made sure he went head-first. Jesus fuck, man." He shook his head quickly. "Head fucking first!"

Quentin blinked. Now would be a poor time to allow his horror at such an event to come to the fore. Kane had endured enough from his own guilt already, it seemed. He took a deep breath and exhaled slowly, and then reached out to rest his hand against Kane's arm.

"I am so sorry," he said.

"You know, when you're a kid, words like death and hate are just these abstract concepts. You've been told they're bad, so you wish them on your enemies because you want bad things to happen to them. But then you find out what death really is, and..."

Kane shook his head. "And I did that. I killed him with my *voice*. How do you even begin to deal with that?"

"I don't know," Quentin admitted.

He certainly couldn't imagine carrying that guilt with him. To have killed another, and to have done it with a gift he wasn't even aware he possessed? It had to have been utterly miserable when Kane eventually realized that it had truly been his words which had sent a boy to his death.

"That's why you do this, isn't it?" Quentin leaned back as he withdrew his hand.

"If I can save even one of them from having to live with this for the rest of their lives?" Kane shook his head. "I can be a thief if that's all it takes. Steal from the rich, give to the needy, that kinda thing. I don't want anyone to get hurt."

Quentin nodded. He could understand that sentiment completely. "How much does it take?" he murmured.

"What?"

Quentin nodded toward the house. "All of this. How much does it cost?"

"Oh, shit, now you're asking." Kane squinted for a few seconds. "Close to fifteen thousand dollars a month."

Quentin blinked at him. That was, by his reckoning, over ten thousand pounds, which seemed rather affordable for such a sizable property. "You steal that much every month?"

"Yeah." Kane reached for the pitcher and refilled both their glasses. Ice clinked as it fell from the jug. "Now you know why I'm usually busy."

"Where does the money go?"

"Well, it's around four thousand a month just on groceries." Kane chuckled. "Some of our older friends don't live on site but they still swing by now and then, and others do live here but they have jobs and eat out a lot, so the numbers fluctuate, but on average there's eighteen mouths to feed any given month. That's including the adults who are here full-time like Sebastian and Mia. Then you've got all the utilities. Electricity, water, internet. That's another couple thousand. Social activities are another thousand: movies, hanging out with normal kids, joining clubs, whatever they wanna do to stretch their wings. Clothes. Gas for the SUVs. Public transportation. Pool maintenance. Equipment. It's lots of little things and they all accumulate, and we don't even pay rent. God, the mortgage on this place is like ninety thousand dollars a month." He shook his head at that. "I can't cover that sort of cost."

Quentin raised his eyebrows. Ninety thousand sounded far more in line with what he had anticipated a property like this one to cost. "Then who does?"

"The owner's one of these overseas investor types." Kane sipped his lemonade. "Buys up property then lets it sit there empty for years on end while there are people homeless who can't find a place to stay. Isn't that obscene? They take property off the market, which pushes up the price of the remaining homes and puts them out of the reach of your average American family, and then they just sit here growing in value and one day they'll be sold for a sickening profit, none of which benefits the people around here at all. None of that money will touch the local economy. It's disgusting."

"You're squatters," Quentin realized with a slowly-growing sense of horror.

"Hey, we pay all the bills. We're not costing the owner a single cent. We're keeping the place well-maintained where they'd just leave it to rot. Everyone's a winner."

"But what if the owner chooses to sell it out from under you?"

"Then it'll probably be to another overseas investor who never even looks at the place. Have you seen the furniture? We're talking pure 1990's kitsch in there. This house ain't been visited by an owner in years."

Quentin shook his head slowly and reached for his newly-filled glass. He held it while he tried to fathom what possible course of action there could be to at least secure a future for this group of youngsters, if not those to come in the future. Condensation dripped onto his thigh, and the cold penetrated his trousers.

A mortgage of a hundred thousand dollars a month was likely beyond his means. He would have to ask Laurence to go over his accounts. But he had assets tied up in long-term investments which he should be able to liquidate. It would take time, but it was feasible. The question was merely one of whether or not it would be enough.

Of course, if Father hadn't cut him off this wouldn't even be an issue. Quentin would step in without a second thought. He may have to shed a property or two to afford it, but it would be worth it. Kane had a good purpose here, and Quentin had—over the past few weeks—grown to share that purpose.

He enjoyed teaching. He wasn't necessarily any good at academic subjects, but encouraging children to gain more strength and finesse with their psychic abilities had proved incredibly rewarding. The thought that any of them could be rendered homeless, defenseless, by the whims of a faceless property magnate sifting through their portfolio gave him serious cause for concern.

He took a breath to speak, but was interrupted by a buzz from his pocket.

"Oh, do excuse me," he murmured. He set the glass aside and withdrew his phone to find a text message from Laurence.

I'm outside. Can you come meet me?

By the time he'd replied and pocketed the phone, Sebastian was on approach to their table.

"Sorry to interrupt," Sebastian announced. "Mr. Riley's out front for you, Quentin. Says it's urgent."

"I do apologize. It would appear that something has come up." Quentin eased from his chair and straightened his cuffs. The motion helped him keep his nerves settled.

What on Earth could be so urgent that Laurence had come to collect him?

"Hey, no problem. We were just shooting the breeze anyway." Kane stood and shook Quentin's hand. "I gotta get back to work. This money ain't gonna materialize itself outta nowhere."

Quentin grimaced as he returned the handshake. "Best of luck."

"Don't need it." Kane smirked.

24

QUENTIN

Laurence remained taciturn until they reached Quentin's apartment. Quentin was well used to this now: Laurence would quieten down anywhere within a mile's radius of Kane's mansion lest Soraya spy on them. Quentin had insisted that she would do no such thing, but Laurence wouldn't be swayed on the matter, so he had to sit and wait until Laurence was willing to reveal the nature of the emergency.

Once they were inside, Laurence seemed intent on remaining silent.

Quentin greeted the dogs and checked their water bowl, then sighed softly. "Come on, darling. Spit it out."

Laurence huffed. He paced over to the windows. He stalked to the couch and sat down. Only then did he speak. "Your brother Freddy's in town. He came to the shop. He's looking for you."

His gut lurched. The floor seemed to fall away from beneath his feet. His vision grew dark at the edges. He felt his heart fight to get out of his chest while his lungs ached for air. It was all he could do to grab for the back of the couch as his knees threatened to give way.

How quickly could he pack? Would it mean leaving everything behind again? Clothes could be replaced, but scheduling movers to get the piano took time, and they would require a destination address, which meant the priority was making a decision on where to go and then sourcing an apartment there. In which case, all he had to pack for was a short trip. A few days' change of clothing and so on. He could ask Laurence to drop him off at the airport, and then it would be a simple matter to purchase a ticket for the next available outbound flight and go wherever it took him, and then Laurence could look after the dogs in the interim. That meant he would need his passport.

Passport. Wallet. Small carry-on bag. That was all he would need.

He felt more in control once he had a plan of action, and he made his way toward the bedroom to pack.

"Whoa! Quen!" Laurence sprang into his path. "What're you doing?"

"Packing."

Laurence's dark eyes grew wide, and he grabbed Quentin by the arms. "Baby, wait. He just wants to talk to you. He isn't gonna tell your dad where you are. He's not here to take you home. He just asked me if I could see if you were willing to meet with him, that's all. If you don't want to we won't go, okay? But that's *all*."

"I will not go home." His voice seemed distant, as though it came out of someone else.

"Then stay. Stay here." Laurence took a deep breath. "With me. Goddess, Quen, don't leave me over this, please!"

"Leave... you?" Quentin blinked, and when his eyes opened the darkness had receded some. "I'm not leaving you, darling!"

"You were all set to pack your bags and just go!"

"But—"

But *what* exactly? His plan hadn't gone that far. Find a new home, send for his belongings, and then what? Did he expect Laurence to walk away from his job, his mother, and settle with him in a completely random location?

You bloody idiot.

He let out a soft sigh and settled his hands on Laurence's hips. "I apologize," he whispered. "I was not thinking. I'm not leaving you, Laurence. I cannot ever leave you."

"Don't you dare," Laurence muttered. "I'm not letting go of

you, Quen. You've got a life here now. Do you understand? Me, Mom, the dogs, these kids you're looking after, we all *need* you. Don't you dare turn your back on all of us!"

He shook his head, and the last of the fog cleared. "How did he—"

"Fucking Twitter again." Laurence grimaced. "I feel like I've got stalkers. It's weird as shit. Freddy found you on Twitter, found me, found the shop. He doesn't know where you live so he came to talk to me instead. But I don't think your dad knows. Freddy's acting alone." He paused for breath. "So maybe we should just go see what it is he wants before you go running away."

Quentin licked his lips before he stepped in closer. His hands eased around Laurence's waist, and he drew the taller man into a close embrace.

"You are right," he admitted. "Let's see what he's after."

And if what Freddy wanted was for Quentin to go home, well. He still had Plan B to fall back on.

THE HOTEL PALOMAR seemed from the street to have been constructed out of two entirely differing buildings. The lower half was an angled frontage, all glass and points, but the top floors looked more like a modern apartment complex, square and shiny. It squatted opposite a parking garage, of all things.

It would not have been Quentin's first choice, that was certain.

Laurence led the way, poking at the button in the elevator and then checking door numbers until he stopped outside one and glanced to Quentin. "This is it," he said softly. "Ready?"

"About as ready as I can be," Quentin muttered.

"Well we're high enough up you can throw him out the window if it comes down to it." Laurence squeezed his hand, then rang the doorbell.

The door opened within seconds, and Quentin was confronted by a face he hadn't seen in years.

Freddy had aged. It seemed so obvious that he would have, but to be confronted by it was jarring. The man was forever twenty in Quentin's memory, and the differences were stark. He was broader, more mature now. His forehead bore faint lines which weren't there five years ago. His fashion sense was still rather bland, it seemed, with his adherence to pale colors and casual dress, but Quentin had to admit that it did suit him.

"Icky," Freddy said.

"Freddy." Quentin frowned awkwardly.

"Come on in." Freddy ushered them into the suite.

Laurence let him go first, and Quentin wandered through to an airy, open living room with floor-to-ceiling windows and a set of stairs leading up to a second floor. The double height of the suite allowed for the room's windows to continue up to the ceiling of the upper level. It gave the living room an incredible sense of space, emphasized by its placement on a corner of the building, allowing for two of the four walls to be windowed. The view was incredible, with the city spread out below them, and even a glimmer of the bay visible between other skyscrapers.

It was all very much to Freddy's taste, with the modern, sparse decor and contemporary fixtures.

"Something to drink?"

He turned and found Freddy already pouring whiskey from a decanter.

It looked bloody tempting.

"No. Thank you."

Freddy lifted an eyebrow and then offered the drink to Laurence, who shook his head.

"No, thanks. We don't drink anymore."

"Who are you, and what have you done with my brother?" Freddy stoppered the decanter and carried the glass with him to a vast, gray couch, where he settled and took a sip himself.

Quentin snorted softly and sat within arm's reach. He waited for Laurence to sit by his side, and then regarded Freddy.

It was odd, to say the least. The last time he'd seen his brother was in London around a year after Mother's death. Quentin had been ostracized by his handful of friends, and Freddy had sneaked off into town to catch up over dinner. Really, though, all he'd done was try to persuade Quentin to come back home, and in the end the meeting had been the last nail in the coffin of Quentin's desire to stay in England.

That wasn't Freddy's fault. It wasn't Quentin's either.

It was Father's.

"I presume," Quentin murmured, "that this will be another attempt to have me go home?"

"Ouch." Freddy placed the glass on a small occasional table by the end of the sofa. "Honestly, Icky, you're twenty-five years old. You have duties. You are heir apparent. You've left us in the bloody lurch, and you don't give a toss about anyone other than yourself. So, yes, I would quite like for you to go home. But at least hear me out as to *why* I would ask that of you."

"Why?" Quentin reached for Laurence's hand and took it. It helped to keep him calm and grounded. "What is there to say that you didn't say in London?"

"An awful lot, as it happens." Freddy leaned forward and rested his elbows on his knees. "It's a complete shambles there, you know. Father refuses to allow me to assist with running the estate. He insists that it must be you. If the old boy drops dead there will be no one who knows what the hell to do with the place, how it's managed, who does what around there. We'll probably end up forced to sell it to the damn National Trust, and you know how much they do love to get their hands on our homes. We'll lose the pile just to cover the damn inheritance taxes. Do you know how to avoid this?"

Freddy huffed and continued. "You. I don't know why he's so bloody insistent, but it has to be you. Once you're able to run the place properly he'll transfer everything into your name. That skirts the tax issues and keeps it all in the family for another generation. But I can't help you in this. I don't know why." He sat back and threw his hands up in frustration. "He refuses to let me sit in on meetings, to even let me get a whiff of the books. He won't introduce me to the staff on the business side, only the household side. I haven't a clue who schedules all these county fairs and fetes on the grounds, I don't know who sets up the antiques fairs or how much we charge for stalls. I haven't any idea who manages the petting zoo or liaises with schools to organize their day trips. If you wait until after he pops his clogs we won't have any of the information we'd need, and I cannot help you figure it all out."

Quentin huffed at him. "I will not go back there, Fred. I'm not doing it."

"Nicky's joining the RAF, you know."

That was like a punch to the kidney, and Quentin gasped. "No!"

"He's eighteen, Icky. *Eighteen!* Do you even care? He was a child when you walked out, and now he's going to go and get himself shot out of the bloody sky!"

Laurence's fingers tightened around his hand, and he glanced toward the drink on the table.

Nicky was thirteen when Quentin swanned off to London. Fourteen when he left the country, but they hadn't seen one another for a year by then, yet they'd been so close before Mother died. And Quentin had run away and left him under Father's roof.

Jesus, he'd been so selfish.

"You lost track of time. It happens." Freddy snorted. "Well, I've spent all these years reading Law, since I'm clearly going to be homeless and destitute unless I get off my arse and take care of myself. And you? What have you done to earn an income once it all goes to hell?"

"I—" His voice stuck. It wouldn't come.

"Fuck all, just as expected. My God, Icky, when are you going to grow up?"

Heat rose to Quentin's cheeks.

"No, don't answer." Freddy jabbed a finger toward Laurence. "And this?"

"Hey!" Laurence scowled. "I'm a person!"

"You are," Freddy agreed. "And Father won't see things that way. He will utterly lose his rag if he finds out about the two of you. Where do you think this is going, Icky? You can't ever marry the lad, that's for certain. By all means keep him on the side, but your primary duty is to find a suitable match and produce some heirs of your own, and Father will—"

"I don't *care* about Father!" Quentin launched to his feet, releasing Laurence's hand on the way. "And I certainly don't care for what he wants!"

"You bloody fool!" Freddy stood more languidly. "Stop and think for one minute, will you? If you are so utterly certain that he killed Mother, what the hell makes you think he won't bump your delectable little florist off to make you do what he wants you to?"

Father.

Kill.

Laurence.

The world blackened. It grew cold. The wind whipped his hair and seeped through his shirt.

He thought he heard a scream. It sounded like rage and thunder.

His throat was raw.

25

LAURENCE

Laurence didn't have time to process what Freddy had just said. They were over twenty stories up, surrounded by massive sheets of glass, and Quentin was going to wreck the place if Laurence couldn't stop him. Furniture had already started to bump across the carpet. Freddy's whisky glass shattered against the stairs and splattered liquid over the pristine white paint.

Quentin's screaming was inhuman.

"Baby?" He leaped to his feet and took Quentin's hand as he stepped in front of the earl. He tried to make eye contact, and reached up to cup his cheek. "Quen, you have to calm down. I'm right here. Nobody's gonna hurt me, baby."

Quentin sucked in another breath.

"Quentin!"

He didn't seem to be getting through, and Quentin didn't look like he'd shut down the way he usually did, so Laurence took a gamble.

He leaned in and kissed Quentin before another scream could come.

It wasn't elegant. It was sloppy, uncomfortable, and Laurence's lip got trapped as their teeth bumped together.

The air rushed out of Quentin's lungs, and he gripped Laurence's arms so tightly that it felt like they might bruise.

Laurence pulled back. "Calm down," he said urgently. "Or it'll be you who kills us."

"If he—"

"Calm down."

Quentin's eyelids fluttered. Rage still whitened his skin.

"Goddess, Quen, your dad isn't even *here*," Laurence hissed. "Get a grip."

Quentin licked his lips, then closed his eyes and began to regain some rhythm in his breathing.

Laurence took a deep breath himself. If he'd ever suspected that Quentin hated his father, this had thoroughly proved it. But it showed Quentin's fear, too—his terror that someone would hurt or even kill Laurence. And the storm that fear had launched was such a raw, powerful thing that Laurence couldn't help but be flattered.

Shit, Quentin would tear the world apart for him, wouldn't he?

He swallowed and glanced toward Freddy, and found the man standing exactly where he was before Quentin had gone nuclear. His hair was in a mess, but otherwise he looked completely unruffled.

Freddy met his gaze. "Well," he said thoughtfully. "This explains a few things. What is it, exactly? A haunting? Possession? A curse?"

Laurence swallowed. There wasn't any way of getting out of this. The penthouse was a mess, and Freddy would probably have to pick up the bill for any damage. The least the guy deserved was the truth.

"No. None of those." He glanced to Quentin, who was still pulling himself together. "He's telekinetic."

"I see." Freddy turned toward the sofa as it finally settled a few feet or so away from where it had been. He idly smoothed his hair back as he regarded Quentin. "And when he gets angry it goes off?"

"Yeah." Laurence bit his lip. "You seem to be taking this all pretty calmly."

Freddy tutted faintly. "I was at the funeral, Laurence. It was near-identical. He went bonkers, started screaming, and impossible things happened. I am neither blind nor stupid."

Laurence felt the tension ebb from Quentin's body, and he turned back to face him. "Baby?"

"I am all right." Quentin's voice was hoarse. He took his hands from Laurence's arms and rubbed his eyes lightly. "I can't... I'm sorry. I couldn't stop myself."

"Well you're going to have to learn," Freddy said.

"He's been trying!" Laurence felt a rush of protective anger flood through him. Freddy had no idea what they'd been through, or how hard Quentin had already worked to come this far.

"Then he shall have to try harder." Freddy gestured around himself. "How much of this can you fix, Icky?"

Quentin looked to the room around them and, one by one, furniture dragged itself back into place. He settled sofas down in the grooves their weight had dug into the carpet. Tables and chairs returned to their former locations. Shards of glass cut themselves loose from the pile and came to rest on the largest table in the room, along with shattered pieces of table lamp and a decorative vase.

Laurence watched it all in a commingling of amazement and pride. Quentin's control—when he *was* in control—had come in leaps and bounds. He could move everything from heavy couches to tiny shards of glass and do it all with the finesse of an artist, when four months ago he wasn't even aware he had this power.

Goddess, it made Laurence want to find out what that level of control could do to *him*.

He coughed into his hand and sat on the couch. His hands rested loosely in his lap, and he crossed his legs to hide his erection. Thank the Goddess he'd chosen loose pants today.

Freddy nodded to himself. "Good. Well then. It seems obvious to me that you had better bloody learn to keep a lid on that temper of yours. We cannot risk the media discovering any of this." He checked the sofa with a sweep of his hand before he sat.

Quentin blinked quickly. "The media?" He sank slowly into his seat.

"Of course. The media control mass belief." Freddy shrugged.

"If the media start to believe in this nonsense, then the public will. We were fortunate with the funeral. Everyone present wrote it off as a confluence of weather and a child throwing a tantrum. The more frequently it occurs the less of a coincidence it is."

Laurence took Quentin's hand and stroked it slowly with his thumb. "I'm all for keeping it secret," he said. "But what's your motive?"

"Likely the same as yours." Freddy raised his head. "What will happen once the vast majority of the eight billion people on this planet realize that some of them have impossible superpowers? Icky cannot be the only one, so his is not the only safety at stake here. Worse, we all know what humanity is like once it detects a threat within itself. The few who have such talents will not be the only targets. History does so love to repeat itself. Think of the sheer number of innocents murdered in the name of witch-hunting, or the Japanese Americans sequestered away in concentration camps for the crime of having ethnic ties to an enemy. Human beings are, *en masse*, violent and petty creatures who will rush out to murder anyone who is remotely unlike themselves." Freddy crinkled his nose. "Imagine how they will respond to those who are indistinguishable from themselves, yet who differ in such a terrifying way. They will murder innocents over small coincidences. Thunder cracked while he spoke, so he was clearly a freak and I shot him! A wind came out of nowhere, so I shot him! Clouds appeared, so I shot him! Bloody hell, if this gets out, mankind will tear itself apart on an unprecedented scale! There is nothing people covet so much as power, and when others have it and they do not it turns from desire to fear."

"Man, that's bleak." Laurence shifted uncomfortably in his seat. Freddy's speech had, at least, taken care of his erection, but left an aching depression in its wake.

Freddy shrugged. "And this is before we even take into account the fact that Icky is aristocracy. We have been eroded for a century and the only way that we survive is by keeping out of the way and remaining generally inoffensive. It has become fashionable to scream 'privilege' at families who have dedicated *centuries* to gathering such might. Hundreds of years spent in loveless marriages, serving our people, unable to simply retire once we pass a certain age. We are slaves to our inheritances, and all the commoner sees is a big house or a flashy suit and they make erroneous assumptions about our lives while lauding forgettable celebrities and actors who make millions every year entertaining the masses. Now imagine what might occur if these people get it into their heads that the aristocracy is filled with *Übermensch*. It would be the French Revolution all over again. Beheadings in the bloody streets." He shook his head. "And that is before we even consider the personal risk to Quentin from others like himself. There is clearly a will to remain hidden. I do not believe that in the entirety of the world's population he is the only one, yet we have not heard of any. Why? Because they're not idiots either. They know on a deep, intrinsic level that the world will eradicate them if they reveal themselves. They don't exist. They haven't had their Stonewall and they don't *want* it. So how long do you think Icky will survive once they see him as the source of the leak?"

Quentin's fingers tightened around Laurence's, and he sighed softly. "That's a rather negative outlook, isn't it?"

"He's right though, Quen." Laurence shook his head. "Man, I wish he wasn't, but he is. I got bullied all the way through school just for being bisexual. Imagine what kids would do to each other over psychic powers. That's what this guy Kane's all about isn't it? Protecting these kids from the world. And that's what you're helping him with. You go over there and you teach them because you know he's right. You know they need a safe space."

Quentin pursed his lips.

"Keeping this a secret is for the best," Freddy said quietly. "I'm sorry, but it is. You must learn better self-control, Icky. You cannot indulge yourself with these little outbursts of yours. I do not care what causes them. Until you are able to comport yourself properly you are a danger to yourself and to others, and not merely to those who are physically nearby when you go off, but to those halfway around the world who have never even heard of you." He pressed his lips together into a thin line, and his gray eyes were soft with sadness. "That is simply how it must be."

"I am trying," Quentin insisted.

"Try harder." Freddy glanced to the whisky stain on the wall. "It would be unwise for you to return home at this juncture," he concluded. "If Father is at all capable of the things that you believe him to be, then you cannot face him with such poor restraint. The man's will is inviolate, and he will break you."

Laurence saw the frustration in Quentin's narrowed eyes, his tightening cheeks, and the press of his lips.

"I think he's right, hon." He raised Quentin's hand and kissed it lightly. "You've made so much progress, but you've got a ways to go yet."

Quentin eyed him, but his features slowly relaxed, and Laurence gave a slight smile in return.

Laurence turned to Freddy and got up from the couch. "Thanks, man. It's been… interesting. But I think maybe we should get going. Quen likes some time to digest information, and I think this is a pretty huge thing to chew on."

"I understand." Freddy stood and offered his hand, and Laurence shook it. Then he offered it to Quentin.

Quentin rose slowly and regarded the hand. He took it, as though unsure whether it might bite.

"Thanks for coming, Icky. I mean it."

"Thank you for…" Quentin trailed off. "Being here."

Laurence smiled and hooked his arm through Quentin's. "Yeah. Seriously. Thanks a bunch."

Freddy inclined his head. "Icky's my brother. I won't have him killed by an angry mob."

"Yeah." Laurence looked to Quentin and squeezed his arm. "C'mon, baby. Let's go."

He escorted Quentin to the door and spared a look to Freddy, who followed them with a solemn expression which was only briefly marred by a glimmer of wonder when he passed the stack of fragments on the table.

The poor guy had just had his world turned upside down and his brother revealed to have gifts beyond anything he had imagined, yet his immediate concern was for the safety of others.

Yeah. Freddy was all right.

26

LAURENCE

He drove all the way up to Quentin's apartment without saying a word. He was used to this now; Quentin's need to process events at his own pace, to work through them until he reached a conclusion. Nothing Laurence did could hurry him up, and so he paid attention to the road and kept his mouth shut.

The difference in the twins was striking. Dark and fair, stiff and relaxed, jittery and confident. They were cut from wholly different cloths, that was for sure. And where Quentin took ages to work through new information, Freddy hadn't batted an eyelid. He was quick. Astute, too. Laurence doubted that anything ruffled the guy.

He'd make a great lawyer.

Laurence opened the gate and parked the truck. He followed Quentin upstairs. And once Quentin had fed the dogs, Laurence decided that enough was enough.

"So," he said, as casually as he could. "Wanna talk?"

Quentin pursed his lips and poured water into the kettle, then huffed. "Kane goes through fifteen thousand dollars a month!"

Laurence blinked at him. The statement was so unexpected that it took him a couple of seconds to remember who the hell Kane even was, and another couple to confirm to himself that

Kane had nothing whatsoever to do with the meeting they'd just come from with Freddy.

"Uh." Laurence peeled his sneakers off and lined them up by the door. "I meant about..." He squinted at Quentin. "Fifteen grand?"

"Mm." Quentin gave a quick nod.

"What's he doing with it? Eating it?"

"Well, he has around twenty mouths to feed, all told." Quentin fished out teabags from the only slightly-less-bare cupboards and dropped them into cups. "Utilities, transportation, all sorts of bits and bobs. Apparently it all adds up."

"Yeah. That happens." Laurence grimaced. "He ask you for any?"

"No." Quentin shook his head. "No, not at all. It simply came out in conversation. He didn't ask, nor did I offer." His lips pursed faintly, though, and he focused his attention on pouring the tea.

Laurence scowled a little and headed for the kitchen. "But you were thinking about it, right?"

Now Quentin looked plain shifty.

"You haven't *got* that kind of money, baby." Laurence sighed and settled his hands on Quentin's hips. He rested his chin on the slightly shorter man's shoulder. "I know you wanna help, but you're already doing everything you can."

Quentin leaned back against Laurence's chest briefly. "If I went home, I could afford it."

"Yeah. But Freddy's right, isn't he? You're not ready for that." He eased his hands carefully around until they settled over Quentin's flat stomach. "You're used to rebuffing gold-diggers, right?"

Quentin snorted. "Good God, yes."

"Can you tell me with a hundred percent certainty that Kane isn't playing a long con?"

"A what?" Quentin dug the teabags out and added the milk and sugar. The teaspoon clinked as he stirred.

"A confidence trick. You know, where someone weasels their way into your heart then makes off with all your money. A long con can take months to pull off." Laurence pressed his lips briefly to the side of Quentin's neck. "Sometimes it needs a whole team to pull it off."

Quentin tutted softly. "I very much doubt it, darling." He turned, and Laurence released him so that he could move freely. "Although he is most certainly squatting in the property without paying a penny for it. That part may well be a con."

Laurence took the cup Quentin offered him. "Huh? How's he getting away with it?"

"Apparently the owner is an overseas investor who is unaware of Kane's use of the building."

"Risky." Laurence winced and meandered toward the couch with his tea. "Unless he's using that mind-control thing on the owner to prevent him from selling the place."

"That is not an option which had occurred to me," Quentin murmured as he settled beside Laurence.

"And we're totally sure his gift doesn't work on you?" Laurence eyed Quentin cautiously.

"He appears to have long given up on even trying it."

"Man." Laurence puffed onto the surface of his tea and coiled his legs up on the couch by his side. "If you could control people with a few words, what'd you use it for?"

"I..." Quentin blinked at him. "I have absolutely no idea."

He laughed at that and leaned against Quentin's side. "You've been hanging out with the guy for ages and you haven't even thought about it, have you?"

"It hadn't occurred to me, no." Quentin sipped a little of his tea.

"Goddess, you're adorable." Laurence grinned and patted his thigh.

"What would *you* use it for?"

"Uhhh." Laurence coughed and gulped down a mouthful of tea that was too hot, then gasped as it scalded the roof of his mouth. "Fuck. Uh, I, uh."

It was easy to think offhandedly that he'd use that kind of power to sleep with whomever he wanted, but would he *really*? He'd never gone to bed with anyone without their permission, no matter what sleazy thoughts had crept into his head here and there. Shit, he thought about bending Quentin over and fucking him at least once a day, but he hadn't *done* it. There was a world of difference between being horny and being a total slimeball.

Had Kane ever used it that way?

Laurence winced at the thought. The temptation had to be multiplied a hundredfold if it was you who held that kind of power; if you knew without a shadow of a doubt that you and only you had the means to make anyone and everyone do whatever you wanted them to.

What would that kind of knowledge to do a person? That was a gift that could screw you up, surely? Very few people really had to deal with that level of temptation in their lives. The most strenuous moral dilemma they ever faced was finding a twenty on the sidewalk and feeling a twinge of guilt as they stuffed it into their pocket.

"I guess I don't know," he finally admitted. "Maybe you don't ever know until you've actually got that kind of power. We don't know what a totally different person would do with your gifts, or with mine." He trapped the tip of his tongue between his teeth and let his gaze drop to Quentin's chest. "Though I totally know what I'd do with yours."

"You do?" Quentin raised one of those flawless eyebrows.

"Ohhh yeahhh." Laurence chuckled into his tea. "You don't wanna ask, baby."

"Ah." Quentin sniffed. "Something lewd, no doubt."

"Oh yeah." He sipped, bit his drink was still too hot, and it made his mouth burn all over again, so he leaned forward to put it on the table. "You, uh. You mind if I ask something?"

"Not at all."

Laurence probed the roof of his mouth with his tongue. It felt soft. Probably already blistered.

"You seem to kinda like this Kane guy," he mumbled.

"Well." Quentin eased an arm around Laurence's shoulders. "I think what he is doing is admirable. He wishes to use his power to help others."

Laurence glanced up to him. "You don't, you know, *like* him?"

Quentin's eyebrows came together, and his lips quirked in confusion. "Did I not just answer that question?"

"No, I mean—" Laurence huffed. "You're spending a lot of time together. Do you—" He paused and licked his lips. "Do you find him attractive?"

Quentin reared back, his eyes wide. "My God, Laurence, no! Absolutely not!" He pulled a face like Laurence had just dropped his pants and taken a dump on the couch. "Good Heavens, why would you even ask such a thing?"

Laurence dropped his feet to the carpet and shrugged. "Hey, if you're allowed to get jealous, so am I, okay?"

Quentin blinked at him in such confusion that Laurence couldn't help but feel slightly foolish. "But... I couldn't possibly... No, Laurence. Just no. Heavens!"

"Urgh." Laurence stood and stepped carefully around the dogs, who had draped themselves up against the edge of the couch. "Sorry, baby. I trust you. I'm just being weird."

"I don't know," Quentin relented, leaning back against the sofa and watching Laurence pace. "You have a point. I behaved quite unreasonably the other week."

"Eh." Laurence shrugged. "Whatever. Water under the bridge. Anyway, it's hot when you get jealous. I like it. Shows you want me. I know, I know you do anyway, but it's..." He shrugged. "It's nice to be wanted like that, you know? It's nice to have someone want you all to themselves. And it's kinda amazing that someone like you feels that way about me. I have to pinch myself all the time to make sure it's not a dream." He paused and turned toward Quentin. "Would you mind if I stayed the night?"

Quentin rose slowly and approached. He offered his hands, and took Laurence's gently. "Of course you may. Is something troubling you?"

Laurence stepped in until he could lean against Quentin's chest, and sighed. "I think I just need some contact, you know? I need you."

Quentin nodded and leaned in to kiss Laurence's cheek. "Then stay," he said quietly. "And let me hold you."

Laurence groaned against his shoulder. "Please."

He closed his eyes, and Quentin's arms wrapped around him. They stood together, the only sound their breaths, and Laurence felt safe.

But more than safe, he felt loved.

27

QUENTIN

How could Laurence possibly think Quentin found anyone but him *attractive?*

Quentin held the florist in his arms. He felt the warm breath against his neck, and the rise and fall of his back beneath his hands. Poor Laurence seemed to be at his wits' end of late, and he usually required some physical contact to improve his mood.

This hug could not last all evening. Certainly not standing in the middle of the living room the way that they were. But even if it could, would it be enough?

For either of them?

Freddy was absolutely right. Quentin had to get better at facing his fears. Oh, that wasn't what his brother had *said*, but in the end they were one and the same: Quentin's composure cracked the most when he was afraid, and running away all the time would not improve that situation in the slightest.

An idea began to form, and he frowned at it.

He *couldn't*.

It was too much. Too soon.

But Laurence...

He glanced to the blond curls an inch from his nose, lightened by the sun and cramped by the hat he often wore at work. From here he couldn't see Laurence's face, but did he need to? No. The man was saying all that he could already: the tension in his shoulders, the shallow breaths, the way he clung to Quentin and held him tight. Something had unnerved him, shaken him, and it didn't take a genius to work out what. Not after seeing the mess Quentin had caused in Freddy's hotel suite.

He had been frightened. Perhaps by Quentin, possibly by the thought that Quentin could at all find another person attractive, maybe even by the thought of Quentin's father doing him harm. The cause did not matter. All that mattered was Laurence.

And Laurence did respond best to touch.

So perhaps this idea was not a bad one. He would have to face some troublesome qualms head-on, but if it benefited Laurence then the net result was positive.

He cleared his throat a little. "I, um. I don't... *quite* know how to say this, but..." He swallowed.

Laurence drew back far enough to peer at him, brows drawn quizzically over his dark eyes. "Sorry. Do you wanna go sit down?"

"No, I, um." He took a deep breath and pulled himself upright.

Say it!

"I find that, um, after a strenuous day, it can be quite relaxing to, um."

Laurence's head tilted slowly. "To what?"

"Have a nice long soak. Er. In the bath. You know? Warm water, head back, and just... relax?"

"Oh." Laurence smiled in understanding. "Yeah. Same. I don't often get the time, though."

"Well, um." Quentin squared his shoulders. His gaze drifted to the far wall. "Would you like to, um. To do that. To have a soak? In the bath?"

"Sure, I..." Laurence's eyes grew wide. "Wait. Quen. Do you mean, like..." He licked his lips. "The same time as you? Like, together?"

"Mm." Quentin nodded quickly.

"Goddess, I'd love to!" Laurence caught his breath. "I mean, uh. If you want to. If that's okay with you." He hesitated. "Like, do you want me to keep my briefs on, or..?"

Quentin coughed and stepped away, circled the table, and snatched up his tea to gulp swiftly.

Ten. Nine. Eight.

He swallowed until the mug was empty, then he took it to the sink and placed it in there.

Three. Two. One.

"I confess to not really having thought that part through," he answered, once he was sure his voice would be steady.

Once there was space between them.

"Okay, well." Laurence cleared his throat. "Could be an awesome new way to wash our underwear, I guess."

Quentin blinked. He turned to regard Laurence, only to find the florist with a broad grin on his face.

"What? We could keep our socks on, too. Get 'em all nice and clean!"

The bright amusement in Laurence's eyes was infectious, and soon Quentin allowed himself a small smile. "You are terrible," he murmured fondly.

"Me? You're the one who suggested we get our clothes off and share a bath together. I'm shocked!" Laurence faked a gasp and raised the back of his hand to his forehead. "Shocked, sir!"

Quentin bit the inside of his cheek and approached the sofa. He sat on it slowly, easing down to Laurence's side, one leg folded beneath himself so that he could face Laurence.

"Thank you," he said.

"For what?" Laurence smiled his way.

"For..." Quentin waved his fingers. "Defusing things."

Laurence's smile faded and he reached for Quentin's thigh to squeeze it. "Baby, this is amazing. I'm really proud of you. If you really want to do this, though, I think it's a good idea to work out ahead of time how exactly it's gonna happen."

"I—" He broke off.

"I know. You haven't thought that through." Laurence's eyes creased gently in warm amusement. "So let's think it through now. Your tub's not wide enough for us to be side by side, so one of us is gonna have to be in front, and sit between the other's legs. Would you rather be in the back, or at the front?"

"Um." Quentin glanced down toward Laurence's lap.

Beyond his clothes, Laurence had... Well. There was no real way to avoid the truth of the matter.

Laurence had a penis.

And...

And it would be there, and present, and behind him, and—

Quentin closed his eyes and calmed himself as he counted down, until he could speak.

"I feel perhaps it would be best if I were to go to the back," he breathed.

"Okay. Good. That's good, baby." Laurence took his hand away, and Quentin had to open his eyes to see where it went—back to Laurence's own lap. "In the back's good, okay? I think that's a great idea. You can get yourself settled, and then you just let me know when you're ready."

He bobbed his head faintly.

God, what was he getting into here?

"Then I'll come in and I'll get in in front of you, but if you want me to stop at any time just say and I'll leave again, okay?"

He nodded again, more firmly.

"You'll have to part your knees so I can get in, then once I'm sitting you can get comfortable again, and you won't be able to see anything under the suds and stuff, will you? So it'll be just you and me and we can relax."

"Ha." Quentin swallowed, then bit his lip. "Right. I can bloody well do this. It shouldn't be at all difficult. And... and if we change our minds we can just... stop."

"Bingo." Laurence leaned back. "You're really okay with this?"

"Um." He cricked his neck and squared his shoulders. "I need to get better. And that means... It means confronting things, not running away from them."

"I totally agree. But I want to make sure you are ready for me to see you." Laurence dropped his gaze to Quentin's chest, then glanced up to him again. "Because I *am* ready, but I don't want you to freak out when you realize."

It took Quentin a moment to work out what Laurence meant.

My scars.

Christ, he hadn't thought this through at all! Even if Laurence only looked for a moment, to guide himself into the bath, he would still *see*.

Again.

He was struck with a deep, vertiginous sense of vulnerability. Laurence would see him without his armor, without his gloss and grooming, his layers of distraction and obfuscation. Raw and unadulterated. And, yes, Laurence knew that the scars were there. He had removed Quentin's clothes when he was unconscious, he had redressed the wound Jack had inflicted, but...

No. No *but*.

He would do this.

Quentin rose and crossed to the bedroom swiftly.

"Quen?"

"I shall fill the bath," he answered.

He didn't look back.

HE DANGLED his fingers into the water as he sat on the edge of the bathtub. He supposed that he would need to add less water to begin with, although he didn't know how to work out how much less, and in the end it seemed to be roughly the same amount before he washed suds from his hand and turned off the tap.

It was warm enough. For him, at least. Would Laurence prefer the water to be hotter? God, so many considerations to make.

This really was the most poorly thought-out idea he'd ever had.

You could call it off.

He grimaced at himself.

"Coward," he muttered.

Quentin closed the bathroom door and peeled off his clothes. He took no joy in it, nor did he spend a great deal of time on the task. It was perfunctory and swift. Best to get it done with.

Could turn the light off.

He ground his teeth and set the clothes into the laundry basket, and without dithering any longer he eased himself into the bath until the water surrounded him and the foam hid him from the chest down.

The water was a little too high, wasn't it? Or not?

He drew some of the foam toward himself to be certain that his lower half was thoroughly hidden, and then cleared his throat.

"You may come in," he called.

He distracted himself with attempts to sculpt the foam into peaks as Laurence entered the bathroom, and only glanced up when he heard the door click shut.

Laurence was fully clothed.

"Hey." Laurence lowered the toilet seat so that he could sit on it at a nice, safe distance. "You okay?"

Quentin nodded briefly and fussed with the foam.

"Okay. I'm gonna just start with the easy stuff. Socks. T-shirt. Let me know if you need me to stop."

"All right."

There was no need to look away as Laurence peeled his socks off, although he found that his eyes tried to do so nonetheless. It took effort to watch.

As Laurence pulled his T-shirt off over his head, it ruffled his hair and made the curls stand up at the back. He didn't look at Quentin. Instead he stood and dropped the material onto the floor, where it covered his discarded socks, and turned to face the bathroom door.

His thumbs hooked into the waistband of his chinos, and eased them down.

Quentin sank into the water slowly, and tried his best not to look away.

It wasn't terribly difficult.

Laurence's body was sculpted and toned. His legs were muscled like an athlete's.

And really, if you think about it, I am seeing no more of him than I might a swimmer on the beach.

Never mind that the setting was private, or that there was something captivatingly sensual about Laurence's method of undressing: slow and patient, revealing inches at a time as he bent forward to ease the chinos down over his shins. No. If he were to focus on the fact that sunbathers frequently wore less he would be absolutely fine.

That worked up until the point where Laurence began to tug his briefs down.

Quentin couldn't look. It was rude. Beyond rude. It was an invasion, a violation. He stared blankly at the wall inches from his nose.

You've seen the Parthenon sculptures. The Greeks and Romans put all manner of bottoms and other parts in their art. This is nothing new to you.

It wasn't enough to convince him. Flesh was considerably different from a two-thousand-year-old artwork. He simply could *not* look.

Absolutely not.

"Could you move your legs, baby?"

Laurence's voice was close, and it startled Quentin. He parted his knees and turned his head in time to see Laurence's backside swing inches from his nose as Laurence's toes broke through the foam and into the water.

Laurence said something or other.

"Mm-hmm," Quentin responded.

It was, he had to confess, fascinating. This intensely personal part of Laurence's body, something Quentin should never see, was close enough to touch. He could make out pale hairs which were feathered sparsely across his bum and grew more dense toward the dip between his cheeks.

The water rippled, and Laurence sank down until his rear was beyond Quentin's ability to see.

He let go of the breath he had held on to for so long. He had no grasp of when he'd stopped breathing.

Laurence leaned back against his chest, and his forearms lay along the bathtub's sides. The water was up to Quentin's collarbone now.

"Oh man," Laurence groaned. "This is great."

Given a few moments to think it over, Quentin was inclined to agree.

28

QUENTIN

If he were to steadfastly ignore the fact that Laurence's backside was nestled snug against his own privates, the experience was pleasant. Quentin eased his arms around Laurence's waist and held him in his arms, and so long as they remained still he could almost pretend that it wasn't bare skin beneath his hands.

Laurence's head tipped back against his collarbone, and the man closed his eyes.

Quentin slowly allowed his legs to relax, and the sensation of Laurence's body between them was, while not unexpected, still an unusual feeling. It gave him a strange sense of power, to be coiled around this wild creature without it doing him any harm, as though he had tamed it.

Laurence was naked as the day he was born. So was Quentin. But Freddy was absolutely right: Quentin did not have the luxury of losing his cool at every single provocation. He had to face his... what had Laurence called them? His *triggers*. Quentin had to learn to identify those triggers and to handle them appropriately before another Jack came into their lives and used those triggers to defeat him. And look at him now, with no clothes, with another naked man in his arms, with their bodies touching, and their—

Ten. Nine. Eight. Seven!

He counted all the way down to *one* as he stared at a fixed point on the far wall, and it seemed to work. Thus far nothing had broken, nor even so much as fallen to the floor.

Laurence's lips twitched into a slow smile. "Do you want to touch anything?"

Quentin blinked at him. "I, er. I... Such as?"

"Anything." Laurence cracked open an eye and tilted his head to peer up at him. "Arms, legs, tummy, whatever. It might be good for you. Like..." he licked his lips. "I dunno. It's up to you, baby. You can touch me wherever you want. Explore whatever you want. If you think it might help."

"I don't know," he mused.

"The way I see it, if you touch things while you can't see them, that's like half the battle, right?" Laurence's smile widened. "Then maybe some time you can look without touching, then put the two together. Baby steps."

It sounded logical, Quentin had to admit. "You do not mind?"

"You have my total permission to put your hands on me, Quen."

He couldn't work out how to begin. Should he take his hands from Laurence's stomach and start from the top, or could he simply use the current location and move on from there?

"Hold on." Laurence sat up, which caused the water to slosh between them as it filled the vacuum. "Why don't we get the soap and you can wash me? Does that work?"

"Oh!" He smiled at the sheer brilliance of Laurence's suggestion. "Of course."

Quentin twisted to reach for the bar by his shoulder. He dipped it into the water and lathered it between his hands, then slid it back into the little ceramic tray before he laid his hands to Laurence's shoulders.

"You're doing great," Laurence said.

"Well of course. I have hardly done anything."

Laurence snorted at him. "Shh. Just take a compliment, will you?"

Quentin gave an overdramatic sigh. "Very well."

His hands spread the lather across Laurence's shoulders,

where it mingled with sparse clouds of foam to create a creamy, silken layer of tiny bubbles. The muscles and skin beneath his touch were firm and smooth, and the fine dusting of blond hairs there would occasionally pop free of the bubble layer after a few moments.

What must it be like to have skin like this? To not have to care for it, to know from a touch where exactly that touch had taken place, and to know that beneath your clothing you were whole? Attractive, even?

He had some inkling of what that could be like. His own hands and forearms were unmarked, and below the knee he was unscathed also. His neck, scalp and face were without scarring either, and so were he to touch his fingers to any of those areas, they behaved in a manner he considered to be normal. They felt unsullied, and they didn't pretend that the touch had landed elsewhere or make his body spasm to escape the sensation.

Laurence's entire body was this way, so far as Quentin knew thus far. No twisted nerve endings, no peaks or troughs, no random discoloration. He even had a smattering of body hair where Quentin had long since lost his own, or it had never even grown there, or he simply shaved it away because little patches here or there were unsightly.

Not that the rest of it isn't unsightly.

He pursed his lips and focused on gently bathing Laurence's back, scooping handfuls of water to wash the suds away and smoothing his hands over the cleaned skin once they were gone.

Laurence obligingly raised one arm, and then the other, so that Quentin could wash beneath them. There was a moment of giggling from Laurence as Quentin soaped his armpits, and Quentin smirked faintly.

"Are you ticklish?"

"Maybe," Laurence drawled with a laugh, and laced his fingers together behind his head.

"Mm." He chuckled and washed the suds away, taking care not to tickle Laurence in the process. When he was done, Laurence began to lower his arms, so Quentin added, "Oh, no. Keep them up."

"Huh?" Laurence paused, then raised his arms again. His movement was slow and unsure. "You're not gonna tickle me here, are you? We'll get water all over your fancy floor."

"No." Quentin fetched the soap. "But I do quite like seeing them there."

Laurence fell silent as his fingers interlocked over his hair.

Quentin swallowed. Had he done something wrong? Said something offensive?

"Goddess, you've got no idea how hot you are," Laurence finally croaked.

The muscles of his shoulders flexed, and the sheen of water made them glisten in the light as they did so. But Quentin wouldn't be able to reach Laurence's chest with him seated forward as he was at present.

"Lean back."

Laurence let out a slight groan as he did as he was told, and Quentin supported him with his chest as his arms took the soap to Laurence's front. He could see enough through the triangle formed by Laurence's elbow to guide his hands, and began to rub lather over the skin he could see.

The chest was as firm and yet as supple as the back had been. There was a little more hair, which prickled playfully at his palms as he smoothed his hands across it, and there were soft bumps under his touch which grew harder with each pass of his touch.

Laurence's breath quickened.

"I'm sorry," Quentin murmured.

"What for?"

"Um." He hadn't the faintest idea, so he continued to wash until his hands dipped below the water and ran the soap over Laurence's stomach.

"You can keep going," Laurence whimpered. "If you want."

Quentin huffed at him. "Darling, if I go any lower, I'm going to —" He broke off.

Touch you.

Something hard bumped against the back of his hand, but Laurence's arms were still raised.

He recoiled, and then caught himself before he could fling water across the room.

"You can do it." Laurence's voice was strained. His arms trembled. Water dripped down him and fell into the bath.

There was very little foam left. Quentin had mingled most of it with soap as he'd cleaned Laurence.

"Please?"

His own breath caught at that. Not necessarily the word, not by itself, but the keening desperation with which Laurence uttered it and the sight of him so helpless with his hands behind his head and his skin glistening and his body with nothing but Quentin for support.

He bit his lip and returned his hand to Laurence's stomach.

"It's the same," Laurence whispered. "That's all it is. You've…" He swallowed, and it made his throat bob hypnotically. "You've touched yourself, right? I mean, you have to, to go to the bathroom? To bathe?"

"I, er." He frowned. "It is hardly the same."

"It's not gonna hurt you, baby."

Quentin huffed. "And what if it hurts *you*? Have you considered that at all?"

Laurence squirmed. His rear bumped against Quentin's groin, which sent all kinds of warm sensations rippling through him.

"How could it hurt me?" Laurence said.

"Because it…" Quentin tutted at him and placed his hands against Laurence's hips to hold him still, but that only elicited another groan from the florist. "Because it will."

"Do you trust me?"

"Of course!"

"It won't hurt me, Quen." Laurence arched his back slowly. "Please. Just do it. Just for a second. Just do this. Get it over with. Then at least you'll know. *Please!*"

His irritation mounted.

Coward!

He gritted his teeth and eased one hand forward. He followed the curve of Laurence's thigh, the crease between leg and groin, until his fingers found a thick thatch of hair.

Laurence's chest rose and fell with every passing second. His body quivered.

Quentin focused on what he could see of Laurence's features: the tightness in his cheeks, the wide open eyes, the parted lips. His fingers continued after some pause, adhering to the dip until the hair grew thicker still and the flesh beneath curved away from his leg.

The outer edge of his thumb bumped against something firm, and the reaction from Laurence was immediate, who gasped and leaned fully back against Quentin's chest.

"Quen," Laurence whispered.

"Shh."

Not now. It took every shred of his concentration, his control, to remain still and to tamp down on the panic which bubbled away in his gut. If he had to relax any of that to talk, goodness knew what might happen. No, he could do without any intrusion right now.

It did not help that he was certain his own prick had grown hard. There certainly seemed to be much less space between Laurence and himself than there had been earlier.

He pressed his teeth against Laurence's shoulder as he counted down, and then through sheer force of will alone managed to turn his hand and close his fingers around a thoroughly alien shaft.

Laurence whimpered. He squirmed.

But his arms stayed up.

Quentin coiled his free arm across Laurence's stomach to hold him still. He didn't have the words to tell him to stop, couldn't spare the second it would take to tell him to quiet down.

The... the *thing* in his hand was hard and soft all at once. With the side of his hand against Laurence's body, it passed over his palm and between finger and thumb. He had no idea of the size of it beyond his hand.

Jesus Christ you're holding it, you're holding it, you're—

His jaw flexed. He pressed himself against Laurence's body, stifling his panic against the other man's flesh, biting down on his shoulder to keep himself from tipping over the edge. He could count all the way from ten to zero but it wasn't going to make these sensations, this knowledge, this *everything* stop.

"Fuck," Laurence gasped. "Goddess, *yes*, Quen! Shit, yes!"

Christ, he wanted... *something*. It ate away at his insides, burned in his thoughts, made every inch of him rigid with need, but he couldn't work out *what* it was he ached for.

His thumb moved, and Laurence groaned. He raised his head and pulled free of the skin he'd trapped, only for Laurence to whimper. Every sound, every motion, it all sang to him.

He did this.

He had reduced Laurence to putty.

A twitch pulled at the corner of his mouth.

"Let me show you," Laurence begged.

Quentin gazed to the redness on Laurence's shoulder where his teeth had been, and a voice fell from his lips which he felt distant from.

"All right."

Laurence's arms shook as he lowered them. They sent ripples across the water's surface as they disappeared. Then one hand closed around Quentin's and tugged.

Quentin remained frozen. He was going to hurt Laurence, he was going to break something, surely this couldn't—

His hand moved, and bumps passed against his palm, yet the skin seemed to stay with him as though he had hold of a cloth and were wiping down another surface with it. He couldn't work out what he might have expected, but this wasn't it. It was as though there were a solid core over which skin were only loosely attached, able to move around.

He felt almost as if this were happening elsewhere, or to other people. He was fixed in place, gazing over the arch of Laurence's chest, watching every quiver of his ribcage and every flutter of his eyelashes. The sounds which escaped Laurence's throat were intoxicating; the way he bucked and twitched under Quentin's hand was irresistible.

There was a thrum between his fingers and palm. A pulse which wasn't there a moment ago. Before his attention could turn to it fully, Laurence cried out. His back arched. His hips lifted, and water sloshed over the rim of the bath. Before Quentin could even fathom whether or not Laurence was hurt, the man sank back down against him, and his hold on Quentin's hand relaxed. He gasped for air and fell against Quentin's shoulder, his mouth wide and his eyes shut.

Everything which had been taut in his arms grew slack. From tip to toe, Laurence turned from unyielding to subdued, and suddenly it seemed as though all the vulnerability in the room had pivoted upon an invisible axis.

Laurence was weak. He was helpless and exhausted, a veritable babe in Quentin's arms.

The need which had reared itself within him seemed inexplicably satisfied with this outcome.

29

LAURENCE

Laurence whistled as he worked. He couldn't stop himself. He'd hummed through making breakfast. He'd sung loudly to Nineties power ballads on his morning commute to the shop. Now that he was here assembling arrangements he was dancing and whistling his way back and forth between the shop and the back room to select blooms and sprays for each arrangement on the orders list. All his mom did was chuckle at him whenever he sailed through the bead curtain.

Everything was so alive today. The colors of their flowers were vibrant, and their scents smelled divine. He could almost taste the perfumes in the air as he bustled around like a worker bee.

Are you really going to tell me you haven't realized your powers are stronger when you're fucking someone?

Jack's words rang in his ears, and he gasped.

Could that be why his mom's gift mostly came in hints and instinct? Because Dad was dead?

He shook his head to himself. No. She'd said when she tried to teach him that it came to her more subtly anyway. She didn't always get visions, and she sure couldn't transform bamboo into a fully-grown tree or make vines move under her command.

His senses did feel sharper today, though. It could be his imagination, or maybe that he was high on life, but there sure was an improvement.

His head rose as the bell above the shop door rang.

"Hey, Mrs. R! Is Laur in?"

Ethan's voice, cheerful and bright.

"He is, dear. Go on through."

"Thanks!"

By the time Ethan made it to the curtain, Laurence had washed his hands and was patting them dry with the hem of his apron.

"Hey, Ethan!"

"Laur! Good to see you, dude!" He paused, then a sly smile crept across his tanned face. "Oh, man, do you look like the cat who got the cream! You dirty dawg!"

"Shit, man, is it that obvious?"

"Oh hell yeah." Ethan smirked and hopped up onto the table. "You score at last, huh?"

"Shut up!" Laurence laughed and filled the kettle.

"No way, dude." Ethan swung his feet and narrowly avoided knocking over a stool. "So? Come on, you can't hold out on me. Details!"

"I totally can."

"C'mooooon! At least tell me what it was like!"

Laurence sighed as he gathered mugs out of the cupboard and lined them up in front of the electric kettle. "He's so amazing," he breathed. "Goddess, he's... I'm so proud of him, and—" He felt his face grow hot at the memory of Quentin's teeth on his skin. "I dunno. He's kinda toppy."

Ethan feigned a shocked gasp. "You didn't!"

"Don't even go there." He dropped teabags into the mugs as he poked his tongue out.

"Laurence 'I bottom for no one' Riley!" Ethan crowed.

"No, asshole!" He huffed at the other man. "I didn't mean like that. We didn't fuck."

"Then what do you...ohhh!" Ethan's feet stopped swinging and he leaned forward. "He's a kinky one, huh?"

"I dunno." He shook his head. "Man, I really don't know. He seems to like taking charge, but he could just be bossy."

"Well, he's like royalty or something, right?" Ethan affected a British accent which sounded jarring to Laurence's ear. "Jeeves, suck one's cock this instant, and don't spill any on my pants!"

"It's trousers," Laurence snorted as he struggled not to laugh. "That is the worst British accent since Dick Van Dyke!"

"Fuck you, dude, that's the best British accent ever." Ethan laughed and his feet began their pendulum swing again. "You jelly."

"Totally am not."

"Okay, so come on. Tell me more! I've met the guy all of once and even then he gave me the cold shoulder. Now *there* was a guy who's jelly." Ethan paused, then added, "What's with all the hot British guys you're drowning in lately, anyway?"

"Oh, yeah." The kettle clicked, so Laurence poured the steaming water into each mug. "That was Freddy. He's Quentin's brother. He just wanted to chat. Why'd you bail on that so fast, anyway?"

"Eh. I dunno. I felt like it was gonna be one of those private talks." He hopped from the table. "Was it?"

"Yeah. It was, as it turned out." Laurence stirred until the tea had infused. He tossed each bag into the trash, then added milk from the fridge. "Quentin's kinda estranged from his family. Freddy just wanted to touch base and found him thanks to damn Twitter." He offered Ethan's tea to him, then picked up the one he'd made for his mom. "But it was pretty good in the end, you know? We got some stuff aired, talked about things…"

"Oh, stuff and things, huh? So specific."

Laurence snorted at him and headed out front with Myriam's tea. He set it down on the counter by the checkout for her and they exchanged smiles before he returned to the back room.

Ethan had relocated to a stool and was waiting for him, expectation etched across his face.

Laurence sighed as he sat. "If you could have any superpower, what'd it be?"

"Like if I got to choose one from the superpowers store? Huh.

Invisibility?" He grinned. "It's always invisibility or flight, isn't it? And if you're invisible you can perv on people in the showers and if you fly you can, well, fly. So that's the choice, isn't it? Perving or free transportation. Unless you can only fly at walking speed. And it uses as much effort. But then I guess there aren't so many people flying as there are walking so it's peaceful. Unless some asshole shoots at you. But they could do that when you're on the ground, so—"

"Bloody hell, it was just a simple question!"

"'Bloody hell'?" Ethan laughed. "You spend too much time with your boyfriend. Get out more."

Laurence coddled his mug between his hands and frowned. "Do you really think people would shoot at you if you were flying?"

"Obviously." Ethan rolled his eyes. "Dude, can you imagine how crazy the preppers will get if they find out people have superpowers? It'd be confirmation of the coming zombie apocalypse or whatever it is they're so scared of. In fact, yeah, maybe I'd want teleportation so I can get away from them. Unless superpowers are the majority, in which case I'm going with flight again 'cause then I'm not gonna get made illegal just for being different."

Laurence grimaced into his tea and took slow sips. He hadn't expected Ethan's worldview to be as bleak as his own.

Laurence knew damn well that Freddy was right. He didn't want to believe it, but it was an inescapable truth of human nature that once people gathered in numbers they began to form groups, and didn't hesitate to bully or ostracize anyone who didn't fit in. Black, gay, Jewish, transgender, disabled, it didn't matter. One by one the stragglers got pushed aside with horrifying fear and anger.

Bisexuals.

Addicts.

Yeah, he didn't need to be reminded what it was like. Whenever he dated a guy people were all, "Oh so you've realized you're gay at last?" and when he dated a woman the response was, "The gay thing was just a phase, huh?" Almost anyone who accepted that he was bisexual assumed it meant he'd cheat on his partner at the drop of a hat, and this was attitude from *adults*. Kids had been way worse.

Most kids thought high school was hell. But most kids didn't know what hell was really like.

Hell was the constant, everyday background hum of being *other*. Of enduring joke after joke. Of being told he was a slut like it was undeniable fact. Of seeing posts on social media which declared people like him were "amoral" and "disgusting" and deserved to be killed.

Of finding the only thing that didn't care was heroin.

He'd been beaten. It wasn't all erasure and verbal abuse. He'd undergone everything from attacks in the bathroom to a punch in the face at lunch. Did he doubt someone would shoot him for his ability to see the future, or if they knew that he could urge plants to do his bidding?

No. The seeds of Freddy's words had found fertile ground, and all Ethan had done was add water.

"What if," he said slowly, "it wasn't you?"

"What, with the cool powers?" Ethan eyed him.

Laurence nodded. "Like, say you find someone's got the power to fly, and it's not you. You don't have any powers. Nobody has. But you find this one person, and maybe you catch them at it, but you find out somehow they're not like you. What do you do then?"

"What I do, personally?" Ethan put his mug down and squinted at the window a while. "I tell them their secret's safe with me," he murmured.

"Seriously?"

"Yeah." Ethan shrugged. "I would guard that secret with my fucking life, dude. It ain't none of my business to out anyone. If they want someone to know, they'll tell when they're ready."

Laurence scowled at him.

"What?"

"Fine." Laurence swallowed the rest of his tea.

He was either about to make the biggest mistake of his life, or... Well, no. Who was he trying to kid? He'd already made the biggest mistake of his life. This was damn tame by comparison.

"But I swear to the Goddess that if you fucking shoot me, I'm gonna be pissed."

30

QUENTIN

Despite the blistering heat, Quentin far preferred to teach the teens out in the garden. There was plenty of shade, and the allure of a dip in the pool once their work was done seemed to have a positive effect on the will of the youngsters to put in the effort.

The faces changed, of course. Some days were more popular than others, but that meant when it was less busy he was able to focus his attention on individuals. Soraya and Kimberly had yet to miss a single lesson and their efforts seemed to bear fruit. That or Quentin was deluding himself, but even Kane agreed that the teens tired less readily, that they had more focus and control over their gifts. Soraya was sure that she could see farther than a mile now, though not by much. Felipe muttered that he was "pretty sure" auras were clearer to him than they had been a few months ago.

It was hardly the strides he had made with his own gifts, but perhaps there truly was something to be said for the discipline which came from two decades as a pianist. Many of these young people were not only disused to applying themselves, but their confidence was so low that many saw little point in the attempt.

That, he felt, was the most upsetting thing of all. The adults in their lives had failed them so awfully that they didn't have it in them to believe in themselves. Some had been forced to early maturity, while others retreated inward to the safety of their own thoughts.

Kimberly was one of those to retreat, and that temptation was more alluring to her thanks to her gift, a sort of pseudo-invisibility which allowed her to pass unnoticed even among friends.

So when she failed to attend today's practice, he at first suspected that she may be playing a prank, and that would be tremendous progress: not only had she achieved a level of finesse with her ability that even he could not spot her, but also she had gained the courage to try a practical joke. And then when the joke drew on too long, he wondered whether it was he who was too distracted by thoughts of last night's events to be able to see her.

But she simply wasn't there.

He continued with the others, of course. Perhaps Kimberly was poorly today, but when he idly asked about her during one-on-one conversations he found that none of the others had seen her all afternoon.

Ultimately, once youngsters began to take themselves off to the pool, he sat by Soraya.

She eyed him. "What'd I do?"

"Nothing untoward." He paused, then smiled gently. "That I know of. I wondered whether we might put your gift to some use, if that's all right?"

"You wanna spy on someone!" She raised her chin at him and peered along the length of her nose. "I kinda thought better of you, you know?"

Quentin spread his hands slowly. "I hope it's nothing like that. I am concerned for Kimberly's absence. I thought that, were she close enough, you might be able to find her and ensure that she is at least safe?"

She eyed him before her head lowered. "Okay. But if she's out of range there's nothing I can do."

"I understand."

Soraya drew a deep breath and closed her eyes as she exhaled.

Quentin crossed his legs as he waited. It was difficult to keep his mind from wandering, and yet it felt disturbing to allow it to go freely where it wished to, because what it seemed intent on dwelling on was last night.

He should be proud. He had not only done something which frightened him immensely, he had done so without ruining the bathroom. And he remembered the event, which was both a blessing and a curse he supposed. A blessing, of course, because retaining memories of events seemed something other people took for granted, and yet for him it was never a given. And a curse because it raised far too many questions.

What on earth had possessed him to bite Laurence, for goodness' sake? Laurence insisted that it had not hurt, and indeed the mark had entirely disappeared by morning, but the fact remained that he had done it. Then there was his own body's reaction to the whole affair, which took so long to subside that Laurence had casually offered to "take care of it" for him, which was wholly out of the question.

Did he want to see Laurence in that wild, abandoned state again? God, yes. It seemed such a ridiculous thing to crave, but he knew with certainty that what he felt went beyond *want*.

It bordered on *need*.

How could that possibly be? It made no sense at all for him to need something he had never before required.

"Hey. Are you even listening to me?"

"I am sorry," he blurted automatically. He blinked and looked to Soraya. "I wasn't paying attention. I apologize."

Her eyelids showed the movement of her eyes beneath them as she turned her head back toward the ocean. "I've got her. She was real hard to find, though. She's getting good. I thought at first she was out of range."

He exhaled with relief. "She's all right?"

"Eh. She's not hurt, if that's what you mean?" There was a note of doubt in the young woman's voice, and her nose scrunched up.

"That's a good start, certainly." Quentin tilted his head toward her. "But you seem unconvinced."

"She's being weird, okay? She's—" Soraya huffed. "She's stealing stuff."

His eyebrows climbed. "Kimberly?"

"I know, right?"

"What is she stealing?"

"I dunno. It's kinda like a vest. Like, uh…" She leaned forward and her eyebrows pulled down, though her eyes remained closed. "Like a tactical vest? It's got all these pockets and Velcro and shit. Black, no sleeves. And there's others like them on a rack. She's indoors. She just, like, put it on and then walked away wearing it without paying."

"A tactical vest?" He frowned faintly. "Do you mean body armor?"

"I dunno. I guess? It's way too big for her." She paused. "Now she's taking it off again. She's putting it in a truck. Just tossing it right on in the back there."

Quentin watched her as she continued to watch Kimberly. "Do you know where she is?"

"Some kinda fair. Like, a gun show, maybe? It's hard to look around—" She gasped, then grimaced. "Okay, yeah, that's a gun show. She just passed some totally sketchy-looking dude with a whole stall of pistols or whatever."

Quentin unfurled his legs and stood. "Thank you."

Soraya's eyelids fluttered open, and she squinted up at him, shading her eyes with her hand. "What're you gonna do?"

"Have a word with Kane," he admitted. "Kimberly shouldn't be at such an event. If she feels the need, then we need to know why."

"You mean chew her out for stealing, right?" She sniffed at him.

Quentin pursed his lips. "She's a sensible young lady," he answered. "She knows better. So if she *is* stealing, she has good reason to."

Soraya nodded slowly at him, and her eyes relaxed a little. "You're okay, Quentin."

"I shall be more 'okay' once I'm sure Kimberly is safe," he murmured.

HE FOUND Kane in the room the American used as his office. Quentin had long suspected the original architect intended for this to be a sitting room. It looked out onto the garden, but the view was partly obscured by the hedge which bordered garden and house.

"Hey." Kane looked up from his laptop as Quentin knocked on the open door. "Come in. What's up?"

Quentin blinked as he stepped into the office. "Is it just you today?"

"Adulting, you mean? Yeah. I figured with you here Mia and Sebastian had time to go do some chores. Nothing's gonna hurt the kids with you around." He chuckled and closed the computer's lid down. "Were you looking for one of them?"

"No, no." Quentin wandered to the windows and observed the teens splashing about in the pool. "Although I should point out that I cannot swim, so I make a poor choice in lifeguards."

"Seriously? What're you doing in San Diego if you can't swim, huh?" Kane grabbed his cellphone off the desk and tapped away at it. "I'll get Sebastian back here. Thanks for letting me know. You mind sticking around until he gets back? I mean, even if you can't go in, you can at least drag them out if they get into trouble, right? Your telekinesis works underwater?"

"I haven't tested it," Quentin admitted.

"I guess that's worth trying before we rely on you to save anyone from drowning then." Kane put his phone down. "You really can't swim? Why not give it a try here? Sebastian can probably teach you."

Quentin grimaced. Allowing Laurence to see his skin was as far as he was willing to go. Other people? No. Absolutely not.

"It's quite all right," he murmured. "Regardless, I have a more pressing issue."

"And that is?"

"Kimberly seems to be at a gun show, stealing items."

Kane stared at him. "This is a joke, right? I never really get the British sense of humor. It's pretty dry."

"It is not a joke." Quentin pressed his lips together. "She failed to attend today's lesson, which is most unlike her, and so I asked Soraya if she could locate Kimberly, which she did."

"Stealing stuff at a gun show," Kane said slowly. "What kind of stuff? Are we talking guns, or stallholders' money, or what?"

"Soraya said tactical vests, which I presume are what Americans call body armor?"

"No, not the same thing." Kane's phone buzzed and he checked it. "Okay, Sebastian's on his way." He looked up at Quentin. "A tactical vest's got pockets for spare magazines, some of them have concealed compartments for your holster, or belts you can clip other stuff onto. They're not armored, though."

Quentin felt some small sense of relief. Vests with pockets seemed rather less worrisome than vests designed to halt bullets.

"Tell you what. Rather than keep you hanging until Sebastian gets here, why don't I go keep watch on the kids?" Kane pocketed his phone as he stood. "Then when Kim gets back I'll talk to her, and see why she's stealing shit."

"Are you absolutely certain?" Quentin adjusted his cuffs. "I do not mind the wait."

"Naw, I'm sure you wanna rush off to see that man of yours. I know if I was that way inclined I'd be all over him." Kane grinned and squeezed Quentin's shoulder. "See you Thursday?"

"Mm." He gave a faint nod. "Thank you."

"Hey, it's what we're here for. Gotta look out for the kids, am I right?"

Quentin inclined his head and excused himself. While he wasn't exactly looking forward to a walk in this stifling heat, at least he should be able to find a taxi relatively swiftly, and those were blessedly air-conditioned.

And the sooner he departed, the sooner he would see Laurence.

31

QUENTIN

HE SMILED TO MYRIAM AS HE ENTERED THE SHOP.

"Ah, Quentin!" She bustled out from behind the counter, her arms cast wide. "You missed the tea by minutes. The kettle's probably still warm, dear, if you would like a cup?"

Her arms were around him before he could answer, and she squeezed him tight.

"Oh, no, thank you. It's quite all right." He tried to move his arms enough to at least hug her around the waist, but then she was gone again, whisked away to the counter by legs which seemed to almost move at a blur. "Is Laurence here?"

"He is!" She grabbed her empty mug and passed it to him with a smile. "Would you be a sweetheart and take this to him?"

"Of course." He smiled as he took it.

"Thank you so much."

By the time he made it through the bead curtain, mug in hand, Laurence and his friend Ethan were quiet where he suspected they had not been mere moments ago. Had Myriam's greeting been an alarm of sorts?

Laurence smiled sweetly and plucked the mug from his grasp, then took it to the sink. Rather conveniently that enabled the florist to turn his back on Quentin. "Thanks, baby!"

"You are welcome." He looked to Ethan and nodded politely. "Good afternoon. Ethan, isn't it?"

"Sure is, dude!" Ethan sounded far too enthusiastic. "Great meeting you. Do you mind if I call you Quentin? Like, it's not Prince Quentin or anything, is it?"

"Er." Quentin blinked slowly. "No, no. Not at all. Quentin is fine."

"Great! So, uh. Oh! I was just telling Laur he needs to bring you over on like a double date with me and Aiden some time. Go out for a meal, or come over and we can order pizza and watch a movie. It'll be great!"

"Aiden is… your boyfriend?" Quentin surmised.

"Yeah!" Ethan's gaze became dreamlike.

Quentin couldn't help but thaw at the expression. Ethan was clearly extremely fond of this Aiden fellow. "Well, then perhaps we should," he agreed.

"Awesome!" Ethan crowed.

Laurence washed the cup out and set it on the drainer, then smiled as he turned back toward Quentin. "So what's up? Everything okay with your day?"

"Oh." Quentin pursed his lips and wondered exactly how to broach the subject without at all mentioning that a young clairvoyant lady caught an invisible girl stealing equipment. He considered a few seconds, and then spoke with care. "Is there a gun show in the area today?"

"I dunno." Laurence grimaced as he tugged on his earlobe. "I don't like guns. It's why California's so awesome." He clearly read Quentin's questioning expression, because he added, "We've got pretty tight gun control laws here. Some people are trying to stop that, but for the moment it's way harder to buy guns here than in other states. We've even got zones were guns are totally illegal, like around schools, on public streets, state parks, that kind of thing."

"Yeah," Ethan cut in. "But there's always that show up at Del Mar, right?"

Laurence blinked at him. "There is?"

"Dude, you live under a fucking rock. They do this gun show

like three or four times a year. The residents up there are pissed about it, because it's all out-of-town business that comes in, sells guns in their backyard, then leaves again."

"And is there one today?" Quentin persisted.

"Let's see." Ethan whipped out his cellphone and tapped at it with the speed of practice. "Yeah, there is. Why?"

"Where exactly is Del Mar?"

"Like twenty miles up the coast. Maybe twenty-five." Ethan pocketed his phone.

"Yeah, I think it's around ten miles north of La Jolla," Laurence added.

Quentin blinked. "That can't be—"

He stopped himself.

That can't be possible, Ethan, because Soraya can barely see more than a mile away at best.

Yes, that wouldn't sound bonkers in the slightest.

Laurence and Ethan were both staring at him, so he cleared his throat. "Would they sell tactical vests or body armor, do you think?"

Laurence looked to Ethan, who shrugged and said, "I dunno, dude. Maybe. Easier to order online though. I think you can get actual armor at uniform stores, but you need ID. I mean, you've actually gotta be a cop or an EMS or something to be able to buy it. Civilians can only get the vests." He grinned. "Afraid of Americans?"

Quentin raised an eyebrow. "That makes no sense." He frowned at Ethan. "How is it that you are able to purchase weapons but not armor?"

"'Cause there ain't an armor lobby," Ethan snorted.

That made no sense either, but Quentin saw little point in digging any deeper.

"Anyway, I better head out. I've gotta go get ready for work." Ethan jumped off his stool and offered Quentin his hand. "Good meeting you properly at last."

He took the hand and smiled. "You also."

"Catch you on the flip side, Laur." Ethan waved and hurried out through the bead curtain at a suspiciously quick pace.

After the door bell had jangled, Quentin blinked to Laurence. "What on Earth was all that about?"

Laurence circled the table and slipped his arms around Quentin's waist. He leaned in and offered his lips, so Quentin tipped up to meet them for a light kiss.

"Nothing?" Laurence offered once their lips parted.

Quentin gazed up at him.

"Fine!" Laurence sighed and his shoulders sank. "I kinda maybe told Ethan about my gifts."

A spark of anger sputtered to life, and Quentin quashed it with deliberate care. For all Freddy's lecturing—and Laurence's agreement—about keeping these things a secret it would be hasty to assume that Laurence did not have good cause for what he had done.

A *bloody* good cause.

He tilted his head faintly and waited until he was sure he was in control of himself before he spoke. "Might I ask why?"

"I trust him. We've been BFFs for years. And I haven't told him about yours. Only mine."

He searched Laurence's gaze and found some apology there, mingled with worry.

"I don't understand," he said with care. "After such a song and dance about the dangers of people learning that these things exist."

"I just..." Laurence sighed and rested his cheek against Quentin's shoulder. "I needed to know that not all people would be like that. I guess I had to prove to myself that not everyone would be a total bigot. I need to know there are allies out there, somewhere."

Quentin raised his hands to rub slowly over Laurence's back while he tried to process the news. It was easier to digest the unpalatable when it was broken down into bite-sized pieces, and so he did what he could to reduce this large problem into smaller fragments.

He knew that Laurence was a social creature, that the man was far more at ease in a crowd than Quentin himself. Laurence also had friends where Quentin did not, and he supposed that one thing people did with friends was share secrets. And perhaps in Laurence's experience fewer friends had turned against him than had betrayed Quentin's trust over the years. Their situations, then, differed.

Laurence *had* been betrayed, though. His friends sold him drugs. His friends left him to die in an alley after an overdose. So when Laurence spoke of need, it was possible that he meant it was more than a desire to know that he was accepted. Perhaps he also needed to test Ethan, to know that the man wouldn't stab him in the back.

He was testing Ethan.

Quentin blinked, and then tightened his hold.

"Anyway." Laurence squeezed him. "What's all this about gun shows?"

Quentin pursed his lips. "Kimberly was absent from today's practice. I asked Soraya to locate her, and she found Kimberly stealing tactical vests from what she thought to be a gun show. But if the nearest of those is ten miles from Kane's property..."

"Then Soraya's better with her gift than she's letting on," Laurence concluded with a grimace. "Ten miles? Shit, that's way over what she told me."

"No." Quentin shook his head. "She has been improving, but not to that extent. We've measured her reach to little under a mile and a half now."

"She could be faking it."

"I..." Quentin blinked. "To what end? And why would she then give herself away like this rather than merely claim not to have found Kimberly?"

"I dunno, man. Kids lie about weird shit." He shrugged. "But if you want, I can try to pin it down."

"What do you mean?"

"Well. I'm supposed to be able to look through time in all kinds of directions, not just see the future." Laurence smiled faintly. "Can't hurt to try it, right? Then I should be able to figure out where she was, when she was there, and what she was doing at the time. If she was really at Del Mar this afternoon stealing vests off a stall, that might be enough information for me to work from."

Quentin leaned in to kiss him again. "If you could, darling, that would be wonderful."

"For you, baby?" Laurence grinned. "Anything."

32

LAURENCE

HE HAD TO WAIT UNTIL HE WAS DONE WITH WORK, WHICH MADE Quentin adorably restless and gave Laurence far too much opportunity to eyeball the Englishman's ass as he paced around the back room. Laurence plowed through the list of orders, creating arrangements as fast as he could, but it still took him until after five o'clock to finish.

He led Quentin upstairs and deposited him in front of the TV with the remote in his hand, then he crossed to his altar and settled down cross-legged on the floor before it.

He needed to clear his mind before he could work. Holding Quentin, kissing him, stirred memories of the night before, and his thoughts were invaded by the way Quentin held him, bit him, touched him, pressed his erection against Laurence's back...

Laurence sucked in air and adjusted himself. He wriggled on the spot, then sighed with some relief.

The sound from the TV stuttered and cut from conversation to music to shouting as Quentin began to channel-surf. That should occupy him a while; Quentin rarely found anything he wished to watch for very long. Not unless it was kittens. He always stopped for kittens.

Laurence rested his arms over his thighs and allowed his eyes to drift closed. While he wasn't working with the altar in any way and so didn't need to cleanse the space before he began, he still vastly preferred to be near it for any attempt to see through time. The presence of his tools and his connection to the spiritual world provided him a grounding beacon, a sense of place and time to return to once he pulled his hand from the stream.

Damn Jack for that analogy. He'd suggested that time was a river from which Laurence should pluck visions as a hunter might catch fish, waiting patiently on the banks until the opportunity presented itself. He hated a lot about Jack, but the god had taught him well, and now he waited for the right fish to swim within reach.

Del Mar. This afternoon. A gun show. A girl called Kimberly.

Time rushed by, in no mood to wait for him. Half-formed glimpses of yesterday and tomorrow bobbed to the surface, and he almost reached for yesterday just to see Quentin's face in the bathtub, but he managed to hold back. It wasn't what he was here for, and if his gifts came from Herne it felt disrespectful just to use them to watch his own orgasms.

A bubble swirled by his hand, and in it he saw Kane. It wasn't what he had come to see, but it drifted tantalizingly close, and his instincts screamed at him to act.

He dove for it and snatched it from the stream, immersing himself within the vision.

"What took you so long?" Kane rose from his desk as Sebastian entered the room.

Sebastian closed the office door. "We were unloading the truck." He narrowed his eyes and added, "You didn't say it was an emergency. What's the problem?"

"Quentin noticed Kim was gone. He got Soraya to look for her."

"So?" Sebastian shrugged. "Soraya has limits."

"No, apparently today was the day she had a fucking breakthrough." Kane kept his voice low. "She found Kim right in the middle of stealing some vests."

Sebastian moved to the window and peered out of it. "We know people's powers can be affected by their emotions," he mused.

"You think she found Kim because she's got a crush on her?"

"I've heard worse ideas." Sebastian ran his fingers around the edges

of the windows as though searching for something. "She's more protective of Kimberly than all the others combined. She'll be pissed you sent her to a gun show."

"Yeah, well, now I got a problem."

Sebastian glanced to Kane, then sighed. "Soraya told Quentin what she found, and he brought it to you?"

"Hole in one." Kane patted the palm of his hand against his desk.

"Is he on board yet?"

"Shit, I don't know." Kane's scowl grew deeper. "I've got no idea what motivates him. I don't trust him."

Sebastian snorted a faint laugh at him. "You can't control him," he countered.

"Same difference."

"You're an asshole." Sebastian shrugged and turned his attention to the nearest wall. "Only trusting what you can control."

"I trust you."

"Same difference."

There was an undercurrent of hostility to both men. It shot between them like lightning and left a bitter taste in its wake.

Kane controlled Sebastian, and Sebastian resented him for it.

The epiphany jolted Laurence out of his vision, and he gasped for air.

He heard the tiny yips of puppies, and for a split second he tried to work out whether he'd sunk into another vision, but a look toward the sound made him snort in amusement. Quentin hadn't found kittens on TV. Instead he'd found some program showing a clutch of chocolate Labrador puppies, and he had even leaned forward to watch it.

Laurence laughed. "You're so cute," he explained as Quentin turned to face him.

"Me?" Quentin looked innocent.

"Uh-huh." Laurence stretched before he stood, and he sauntered over to plop beside Quentin on the couch. He leaned across the Englishman to grab the remote and turn the TV off, or Quentin would get sucked back into it again.

Quentin's lips pursed as the puppies were taken away.

"I didn't see it," Laurence said. He wasn't about to apologize. Or to stop leaning against Quentin's chest.

"Ah. Well. Never mind. You did your best."

"I saw something else, though. I figure it was after you left Kane earlier."

Quentin met his gaze, and his dark eyebrows slowly climbed his forehead in an unspoken question.

"Sebastian came to Kane and they were talking." He outlined the conversation he'd witnessed while it was still fresh in his thoughts, and then he sighed faintly. "I got the impression Sebastian's not there of his own free will."

"And Kane is uncomfortable that I am," Quentin mused.

"Yeah."

Quentin frowned at him. "Do you think he is in control of the children, too?"

"I dunno. But if he doesn't trust what he can't control, it makes sense he's done it at least once, just to make sure. And why *would* this kid go to a gun show to steal things unless he made her do it?"

He knew it was the wrong thing to say the moment it came out of his mouth. He leaned back out of the way as Quentin launched to his feet, his features set in a sudden determination.

"I shall have to find out what he's up to," Quentin stated.

Laurence groaned inwardly, and struggled not to let it show. Instead he gave a calculated shrug and leaned back against the couch. "Or we could just walk away."

Quentin blinked. "What would that achieve?"

"Well, the guy's up to something. Do we really wanna risk getting involved?" He bit the inside of his cheek. "I don't wanna see you get hurt again, baby."

He wasn't all that keen on getting himself hurt again, either.

"He has children under his roof. We cannot walk away, Laurence."

Laurence swallowed at the vehemence in Quentin's statement, the fire in his eyes. There'd be no discussion on this, no argument. Quentin had made his mind up.

Goddess, he was so fucking hot when he was like this: his will absolute, his decision made, his confidence unshakable. Laurence dug his fingers into the cushions beside him to keep from throwing himself at the guy's feet. What the hell *was* it with Quentin?

"You're right," Laurence groaned. He hated it, but there it was. There were children involved.

"Fine," he sighed. "But not now."

"Laurence—"

"No. Baby, let it rest. Sleep on it. We'll go there tomorrow and talk to Kane, and we'll figure out what he's doing, okay?"

That made Quentin pause, and he blinked down at Laurence. "We?"

"Yeah." Laurence sighed. "I'm not letting you go in there alone. But promise me if he starts making me do or say anything I wouldn't, you'll throw him out the nearest window, okay?"

"I will certainly oppose any attempts to make you act against your will." Quentin nodded curtly. "And if he does not cease, then defenestration may become an option."

Laurence grimaced and rose from the couch. "Just watch out for Sebastian. Whether he wants to or not it's his job to protect Kane." *And he uses fire.*

He swallowed tightly.

"Sebastian is unlikely to prove troublesome," Quentin murmured.

"What? Isn't he, like, ex-Army or something? What if he just plain shoots you?"

"Disabling a gun is hardly problematic, nor is removing it from his hand."

"Do you even know how guns work?"

"Altogether too well."

Laurence blinked at him, but Quentin was dead set on a confrontation now. Maybe he was just talking the talk to make Laurence feel more confident.

Yeah, right.

"Fine. Tomorrow. Tonight we go to your place and cuddle."

Quentin's hard features thawed slowly, and then his shoulders relaxed. "Very well."

33

QUENTIN

True to his word, Laurence had done nothing more than cuddle all evening. Quentin wasn't able to work out whether that was a disappointment, but there was little use worrying at it like an open wound. If he wished it to be more he would have to be the one to request more, it seemed, and for that to irritate him was incredibly unfair when Laurence worked so hard to ensure Quentin's comfort and safety.

He ran with the dogs in the morning as Laurence left for work with the assurance that he would return after lunch, and true to his word he arrived a little past two in the afternoon.

They made it to Kane's property before half past two and were greeted at the door by Sebastian, who led them to Kane's office with hardly a word spoken the entire time.

"Quentin?" Kane blinked at his phone, then looked up again and smiled more broadly. "Laurence! Hey! Long time, no see!"

"I feel it incumbent at this juncture, before we begin, to make something abundantly clear." Quentin stopped several feet from Kane's desk and crossed his arms. "Any attempt to control what Laurence does or says will be met with hostility, and you will not be given a second chance on the matter."

He caught a glimpse of the briefest of smirks from Sebastian to his left.

Kane rose from his chair with slow caution and set his phone down on the desk. He looked between Laurence and Quentin, then said, "What's this about?"

"You sent Kimberly to steal from the gun show," Quentin answered.

Kane opened his mouth a second before words came out. "What makes you think that?"

"Oh come on, man," Laurence interjected. He hooked his thumbs into the pockets of his shorts. "It doesn't take a rocket scientist to figure out. Soraya saw her load the gear into a truck. I'm guessing a girl Kim's age doesn't own a truck, right? In fact..." He paused and jerked his chin toward Sebastian. "I bet you sent a designated driver with her, and that's why Sebastian wasn't here yesterday either. C'mon, guys, it's one thing to steal money for food, but getting kids to do it is low."

Quentin kept his mouth shut. Laurence was extraordinary, and didn't need Quentin fracturing the excellent lie he'd just told.

Kane's jaw worked as he drew a deep breath, and Quentin narrowed his eyes to make it clear that he meant what he had said.

"Fine," Kane said as his breath collapsed out of him. "Jesus. This wasn't how I wanted it to go."

"Kane—" Sebastian grunted.

"No. It's okay. If they're gonna be around here they should know." Kane patted his hand against his thigh, then strode to the door. "Let me show you guys something."

Quentin glanced to Sebastian and lifted an eyebrow, but the man only gave him a faint nod in return.

Sebastian had to operate under his own free will most of the time, surely? Kane had to give an order for it to be obeyed, and the man hadn't even seen Quentin's exchange with Sebastian, let alone told Sebastian how to respond to it. Therefore, for better or worse, Sebastian considered this action safe. If that was a lie, then at least Quentin truly knew where they stood.

He nodded to Laurence and followed Kane down the corridor. They passed the main living room and continued on toward an area Quentin never had cause to visit, tucked behind the garage, until they reached a door not unlike the others and Kane unlocked it with nothing more than a swipe of his fingertip over the handle.

Quentin blinked. There had been no key, and yet it was impossible to miss the sound of bolts as they withdrew.

"Fingerprint sensor on the handle," Sebastian muttered. "Keeps the youngsters out."

"Is that necessary?" Quentin murmured.

"Maybe not," Kane said. "But I file it under wise, not necessary. C'mon." He pushed on through and led down a narrow set of stairs that doubled back on themselves.

Quentin followed, with Laurence at his back. "Is this an original feature of the house?"

"Yeah. It's supposed to be a bomb shelter. That's why it's so deep." He unlocked the door at the bottom—which was far less ornate and considerably more dull and gray—with another press of his finger. The bolts on this door were quieter, and when Kane pulled the door outward the bloody thing was at least a foot thick with holes the girth of Quentin's forearm for the bolts to nestle into. "Plenty of people built them during the Cuban Missile Crisis, especially rich people. Wouldn't wanna die from fallout like the rest of us." Kane grimaced and disappeared into the room.

Light flickered from the open doorway, and then grew steady, as though it came from a long-disused fluorescent tube. Quentin entered with caution, but the room didn't seem to pose any immediate danger.

It *did* pose riddles.

The walls were lined with lockers and cabinets. The center of the room was home to a strip of benches. It was not unlike the changing room of a gymnasium in that regard, and it seemed a most peculiar thing to keep hidden behind so many locked doors in a basement which was gouged into the side of a hill.

Kane gestured to the walls. "Be my guest."

Laurence planted his hands on his hips and looked uncertain. "Why don't you open one?" he countered.

"Sure. Why not?" Kane reached for a locker and tugged the

door open, and then he continued along the wall, opening lockers and cabinets and leaving the doors wide in his wake.

Quentin blinked, but curiosity got the better of him, and he nosed into the first locker.

It was stuffed all the way to the top with shelves upon shelves of canned food.

He turned to Laurence and caught the florist peeking past him.

"Uh," Laurence said. "What the hell?"

Quentin checked the next and found more of the same. The third was full of empty backpacks, full first-aid kits, and a shelf of neatly arranged Swiss army knives. The fourth held what was most certainly a selection of ballistic vests, too bulky and hard to be mere tactical vests.

"What is all this stuff?" Laurence was at another cupboard, and held a coil of rope between his hands. "Build your own adventurer's kit?" He hefted the rope and added, "Are there ten-foot poles to go with this?"

Laurence may as well have been speaking in tongues so far as Quentin was concerned, but it made Kane bark a short laugh.

"Pretty much, yeah." Kane shrugged and sat on the bench. "You wanna know what's going on here? I thought we could do some good sometime. Go out into the world and help people." He held onto his knees and looked around the room. "We've got people with all kinds of abilities. People who can put out fires." He glanced to Sebastian. "People who can pass unnoticed, who can see events which are out of line of sight, who can talk to animals or read auras or—" he gestured to Quentin "—catch someone who's falling from a balcony. But we can do so much more than any of that!"

He sprang to his feet and circled the room, closing doors as he walked. "Once they're older, more organized, more practiced, do you know what they could do? They could solve crimes! They can put in anonymous tips to the cops. They can follow a criminal without him ever knowing, then just call the cops or feds and tell them where to find their guy. Wildfires? We can go in and help evacuate people, hold the fire back until they're safe." He stopped a foot away from Quentin and all but shone with enthusiasm. "C'mon. You know it makes sense."

Quentin pursed his lips and frowned. It *did* make sense. And Kane hadn't even touched on the sorts of threats people couldn't begin to defend themselves against.

Threats like Jack.

There was no way he and Laurence could have beaten the god without their gifts. Certainly there was a case to be made for the fact that he would not have been drawn to them to begin with had they been without psychic abilities, but Jack could not exist in a vacuum, just as Quentin and Laurence did not. There had to be others like him out there, and not all threats would be so gracious as to only target people able to protect themselves.

Fond as the Americans were of guns, there was very little that a rifle would do against a god. But a team such as Kane proposed? *They* stood a chance.

"Quen," Laurence said. "You can't seriously be considering this."

Quentin pursed his lips, and Laurence let out an exaggerated sigh.

"And you..." Laurence pointed at Kane. "You're crazy. How do you think you're gonna keep an operation like this secret once a bunch of superpowered kids starts leaping tall buildings and rescuing kittens out of trees? Goddess, you aren't gonna give them bright spandex uniforms too, are you?"

"The normals are going to find out about us sooner or later," Kane said levelly. "It might not be a bad idea to start the PR machine first. If we've got a track record of saving lives and absolutely zero vigilante actions, then people are going to have a hard time trying to paint us as dangerous freaks."

"No," Laurence insisted. "They're not. They'll see some bullshit on Fox News and start screaming on the internet that we all need to be killed. People will *die*, Kane!"

"That's why we have to have a spotless record before anyone finds out we exist," Kane insisted. "We're not gonna be chasing bad guys down the boardwalk. We'll only be doing what we can and nothing more. It's on us, guys. We have the chance to shape what future generations think of our kind, and we need to take that chance before it's taken for us." He looked between Laurence and Quentin, and stuffed his hands into his pockets. "So I guess it comes down to this. I'd be glad to have you. More adults, more level heads, stop the younger ones making any risky decisions and costly mistakes."

Quentin adjusted his weight a little and avoided eye contact with Laurence.

"C'mon," Kane said. "You want in?"

34

LAURENCE

LAURENCE SWORE HE COULD ALMOST *FEEL* QUENTIN'S "YES" working its way through the Englishman's brain. If Laurence didn't do something fast, Quentin would throw himself into the fray like some stupid comic book hero. Except this was the real world.

People stayed dead here.

"Why don't we talk it over," he said smoothly. He hooked his arm through Quentin's and patted his forearm. "This sounds like a big decision. I don't think we should rush in."

Quentin shut his mouth, thank the Goddess, and only gave a faint nod of his head in agreement.

"Sure." Kane shrugged like it was no big deal to him, but Laurence didn't miss the disappointment in his posture; the way his shoulders hunched forward and his head dipped to follow them. "Let me know what you decide, huh?"

"We will, I promise."

He steered Quentin out to the truck as fast as he could, and managed to get him to keep from making any rash statements until they were well clear.

"I DON'T THINK this is the best idea anyone's ever had," Laurence said.

Quentin settled on the couch to fuss over the dogs. Pepper slobbered on his hands, but the usually immaculate Brit didn't seem to care in the slightest. "I think Kane has a valid argument," he murmured.

Laurence ran his tongue along his teeth and then bit down on the tip. "I'm a florist, Quen. Yeah, okay, I can control plants. I can see through time. I heal pretty fast. I've got pretty sharp senses. But I'm not exactly a front line kinda guy, know what I mean? I'm not gonna be running into anything that's on fire, or getting into fights with bad guys, or whatever other crap Kane's planning on getting these kids into."

Did that make him a coward, or was it just common sense? And, hell, what was wrong with being a coward? Cowards stayed alive! It was a viable survival technique that worked overwhelmingly in favor of the people who chose to avoid dangerous situations. Maybe if he'd been more afraid when he was younger he'd never have let himself get into drugs.

The itch was there. It ran along his gums, trying to tempt him.

Forget all this.

Walk away.

You don't need it.

You don't need him.

Laurence gritted his teeth. "I need you," he said.

Quentin blinked and patted Pepper on the head. He looked to Laurence, and hesitated.

"I need you, too," he answered.

"I can't lose you." Laurence's voice sounded strained to his own ears. "Shit, Quen, I've been sober for *weeks* now. Because of you. I haven't even touched a joint. I'm in danger of actually earning a chip at NA. I used to laugh in their faces at the idea of chips, you know, because I always knew they were worthless, that I'd never keep them. But now I *want* one, and I want to keep it!" He sagged.

The words had rushed out of him and left him weak. He didn't expect to get so brutally honest. He thought he'd tell Quentin they shouldn't leap in to Kane's insane plan and then that'd be everything done, but instead one of his least favorite things happened: he'd been honest.

Honesty with Quentin wasn't so bad. It was the honesty with himself that hurt.

Quentin rose and came to his side. He enveloped Laurence in a tight embrace and held him against his slender chest as though Laurence were precious.

He wasn't, of course. Quentin was deluded.

"I'm here," Quentin murmured against his cheek. "Shh, darling. I'm not going anywhere!"

Laurence clung to him, arms around his waist, fingers digging at the back of his shirt. He struggled to put words together, but they ran from his grasp like rats fleeing a sinking ship.

Quentin kissed his cheek. It was a firm, lingering kiss, and after a few seconds of it Laurence turned his head so that it met his lips instead.

Quentin sank fingers into Laurence's hair and gripped his curls. They pulled on his hair, but Laurence didn't mind. It didn't hurt, but it did let him know Quentin had a good hold on him, and Laurence didn't have the words for how reassuring it was, how safe it made him feel.

He gasped into Quentin's mouth and parted his lips, and Quentin's tongue pushed into him, firm. Demanding. Possessive.

Laurence sucked on Quentin's tongue for all he was worth. His back arched and pressed his chest against Quentin's as his knees bent.

Despite the inch difference in their heights, Quentin towered over him now, holding him, kissing him, supporting his weight, dominating his world.

And all his fears sloughed away.

Laurence gasped with relief. Tears prickled his eyes, but he blinked rapidly to shoo them off.

Quentin broke the kiss. His cheeks were flushed. His hair had fallen forward, and strands dangled before his eyes. He gazed down at Laurence with ruddy, pink lips that gleamed with moisture.

"Better?" he breathed.

Laurence let out a light-headed laugh. "Goddess, Quen, how do you *do* that?"

"Ah, that would be telling," Quentin murmured. He smiled a little, and gazed into Laurence's eyes a moment before he straightened and helped Laurence do the same.

Laurence sighed and squeezed Quentin's hips. "Thanks, baby."

"You're welcome." Quentin's gray eyes danced with amusement. "It is not as though you alone benefit."

He bit his lip, then shook his head with a brief chuckle. "And you keep saying *I'm* terrible? Shame on you."

"Mm." Long fingers disengaged from Laurence's hair and stroked down the back of his neck, making him shiver. "Shame indeed. Now, what are we to do about this mess?"

Go have a bath together?

He cleared his throat and broke away. If he didn't put some distance between them he might do something idiotic. "We should talk it over with someone."

Quentin brushed hair back from his forehead. "What do you suggest?"

"Ethan. Freddy." Laurence shrugged at him. "We're not the right people to figure out whether Kane's idea is a good one. But they're regular people. They don't have any gifts. They'll have an outside perspective on this, and maybe together we can figure it out." He hesitated. "It'd mean telling Ethan about you, though."

"And Freddy about you." Quentin frowned at him. "I cannot say that I am wholly comfortable with this idea. I haven't spoken to Freddy in five years, and already he has seen what I'm capable of."

"So maybe bringing him in on this now will strengthen that bond," Laurence reasoned. "Make him feel connected. He came all the way over here from England to see you, Quen. He obviously cares."

"And Ethan?"

"Ethan was the only friend who stuck with me after I relapsed." Laurence shook his head. "Every time. He didn't judge me, didn't say I was useless, he just let me pick right back up from wherever we'd left and didn't lecture me or use me. You learn a lot about people once you're weak. People you thought were friends will kick you the moment you're down, but Ethan never did." He swallowed. "He's a good guy. I trust him."

Quentin pursed his lips and he crossed to the kitchen to wash his hands. His features drew down into concentration, and Laurence had learned there was no interrupting while Quentin was working something through in his head.

All he could do was wait, so he fussed the dogs and plucked their fluff off himself while he did so.

"Very well," Quentin eventually said. "Would you be so kind as to see whether Ethan is available?"

Laurence smiled to him. "Sure thing, baby."

Now all he had to do was pray that Freddy and Ethan could talk some sense into the earl.

35

QUENTIN

QUENTIN REMAINED UNCONVINCED THAT THEY HAD MADE A WISE decision.

Ethan agreed to meet them at Freddy's penthouse. Freddy was happy to let people congregate on his hotel suite, Laurence was pleased that Quentin had agreed to talk it over with others, but at the crux of it all it seemed as though this were merely delaying the inevitable.

The penthouse showed no signs of Quentin's previous visit. The walls were clean, and the broken lamps had been replaced. All was as it should be, although he suspected that Freddy's final bill would include the cost of Quentin's loss of control. There would be no point offering to pay it, either. Freddy wouldn't accept a penny, just as Quentin wouldn't should their positions be reversed.

Freddy had a small buffet laid out awaiting their arrival, from sushi to cold meats, and when Quentin eyed it Freddy snorted softly.

"Still a chore to get him to eat anything?" Freddy said to Laurence.

"Oh, man." Laurence groaned faintly. "Seriously."

"Icky, put some bloody meat on your bones." Freddy ushered him to the table and pushed a plate into his hands.

By the time Ethan arrived, Quentin had managed to drape salad across his plate enough to make it look full, and nestled a couple of pieces of sushi in there for good measure.

"Dude!" Ethan stared around the penthouse. "This is crazy! Hey, can you see the Coronado Bridge from up here?"

"Freddy, may I introduce Laurence's friend, Ethan," Quentin murmured as he retreated to a chair at the dining table. "Ethan, this is my brother, Frederick."

"'Freddy,' please," Freddy said as he offered Ethan his hand. "They're up to something. Likely trying to set us up for a date, but I'm afraid I must disappoint you. I'm not in town for much longer."

Ethan laughed as he pumped Freddy's hand. "It's cool. I've already got my forever dude anyway."

Quentin winced at the term *forever dude*. It sounded so... jovial.

Laurence sat by his side and eyed his plate, but said nothing. His own was piled high with what Quentin suspected may well be one of everything the buffet had to offer, and Laurence began to eat without waiting on the others.

"Right, you two." Freddy sat opposite and looked to Quentin. "I doubt this is a social gathering. What are we here for?"

Quentin picked at his salad while he waited for Ethan to sit, then he sighed faintly. "We have a dilemma."

"Spit it out, dear boy."

Quentin fiddled with his fork.

Freddy rolled his eyes and turned his attention to Laurence.

"Okay. You're both here," said Laurence, "because you both know one of us has psychic abilities. *We're* both here 'cause each one of you only knows that about one of us."

Ethan squinted as he chewed. "That was a fucking awful sentence, dude."

"Shut up." Laurence huffed. "Quentin and I are both psychic, okay? I can control plants, look at the past or the future, and I have pretty good senses. Quentin's got crazy good telekinetic skills and he heals as fast as I do. So there. Now you both know all of it."

Freddy exchanged a look with Ethan.

"Prove it," Ethan said.

"Man, not again!"

"It does seem redundant," Freddy agreed.

"But telekinesis is cool!"

Quentin cleared his throat. "There is rather more to this assembly than news alone. We have a situation we would like to solicit your opinions on."

He explained—with frequent interruptions from Laurence—the situation regarding Kane. He adhered only to the salient points, but Laurence insisted on fleshing it out with opinion or supposition until, in the end, both Ethan and Freddy looked aghast.

"I can't believe you're even thinking about this," Ethan began.

"I concur," said Freddy.

"I mean, you're gonna say yes, right?"

"I... *what?*" Freddy looked at him like he'd sprouted tentacles.

"What? That's what you do with superpowers, dude. You strap on your spandex and you go be a big damn hero." Ethan grinned. "And the world could use some heroics. So I say go for it! Join up, save the world, right? With great power comes great responsibility, all that shit?"

"How absurd," Freddy drawled. "You already know my opinion, Icky. This is a terrible notion which seems designed to reveal your existence to the world at large."

Ethan stuffed a rice ball into his mouth, and was too busy chewing it to answer quickly, so Quentin stepped in.

"But if we do not accept Kane's offer," he reasoned, "it will not stop his actions. If the revelation is inevitable, then it is so regardless of our presence."

"Mm." Freddy rose and wandered toward the kitchen. "White? Red?"

"We don't drink, remember?" Laurence said quickly. "Not anymore."

"I've gotta get to work after this," Ethan added.

Freddy shrugged and returned to the table with a bottle of

Napa Valley Cabernet Sauvignon which he offered to Quentin. "Can't find the corkscrew," he said.

Quentin sighed and tore the foil free, then eyed the cork. It would require care to ease it free of the bottle without damaging either the cork or the glass itself, and he took a moment to extend his gift around the cork and give it a gentle tug before he realized he'd have to hold the bottle in place too, or the pull would more likely wrench the bottle from his own hands.

The cork began to wriggle loose, one tiny step at a time, until it finally popped free, followed by the brief whiff of alcohol.

When was the last time he'd had a drink? Shortly after he and Laurence had got themselves completely blotto, wasn't it?

Ah, yes. When he'd set the whisky on fire.

He maintained a flat expression as he plucked the cork from the air with his fingers and passed the bottle back to Freddy. "Satisfied?"

"Okay, that was pretty neat." Ethan waved his knife at the cork. "You'd make a great waiter with those skills."

Quentin dropped the cork onto a napkin. He couldn't drink, not with Laurence present. The poor boy listed booze as one of his triggers. Which was a great shame, as the Napa Valley reds were among the best in the world.

Freddy set the bottle aside to breathe. "All right. What is it that Kane actually wants?"

"Well, to help people," Ethan answered.

"Don't be ridiculous. That's simply what he says that he wants."

Quentin raised an eyebrow. "You think it runs deeper?"

Freddy spread his hands and laid them on the table either side of his plate. "I haven't met the fellow, so all I am able to go on is your testimony, but I would view his actions as indicative of a wider vision." He tapped the table with an index finger. "Consider his behavior. He has chosen to take on waifs and strays and bring them all under one roof. I think we all know that it would be considerably more affordable to live in multiple smaller properties beyond city limits, but he chooses a premium location in one of the most expensive cities on this coastline. Why? Well, either delusions of grandeur, or because he has reason to want all his ducklings under one roof."

"It'd make them easier to control," Laurence mused.

"Correct. We do not know whether his gift works over the phone, and also he is clearly a control freak, so there's always the likelihood that he prefers to have his wards all together so that he knows where they are at all times. I say that he is a control freak," he added, "because he seems unable to stop himself from issuing imperatives within the first few seconds of meeting someone." He tutted faintly. "The man lacks subtlety. He is wholly used to getting his own way. He could readily have secured the funding to set these young people up in smaller homes. Houses on the outskirts of San Diego are preposterously cheap, especially for a man who can cobble together fifteen thousand dollars a month."

Laurence and Ethan looked about ready to protest Freddy's use of the word "cheap," then both grumbled in agreement.

"Therefore you suspect that he has an ulterior motive for selecting a mansion in La Jolla," Quentin nodded. "I understand. But it is hardly what one might call a central location."

"Correct. Thus centrality is not his primary requirement. Which is dubious at best for a man who wishes to create a team of superpowered emergency first-responders, don't you think? If I were to do such a thing I would want to be in the heart of a city so that I could dispatch the correct people to the most suitable emergency and have them arrive while they're still relevant." He reached for his knife and fork, and began to slice up some of the meats on his plate. "This returns us to the fact that prancing around rescuing people from burning buildings and the like will undoubtedly reveal you to the world sooner or later, and if Kane is indeed a control freak, then it is reasonable to conclude that doing so would not be a side effect. It is his goal."

Laurence popped a maki roll into his mouth and chewed on it before he spoke. "That can't be his endgame though, right? What would he gain from that?"

"Nothing," Freddy admitted. "Or rather, nothing that a control freak would enjoy. Chaos, anarchy, murder in the streets, his own life in danger…" He shook his head and reached for the wine to pour himself a glass. "You're quite right, Laurence. It's a stepping stone, not his end goal. He has himself a fortress, a retinue of superpowered bodyguards and spies, survival supplies, body armor, and we must assume that he also possesses weapons. One does not accumulate all of that and *not* gather a few weapons together at the same time."

"Sebastian is former military," Quentin offered. "He was in the US Army until recently. Honorable discharge."

"So Kane has access to the knowledge required to militarize a small base of operations." Freddy neatly set the bottle aside and returned to dissecting his dinner. "I dislike it intensely. It smells off."

Ethan nodded slowly. "But if Laur and Quentin both say no, he's gonna continue, right?"

"Unless we stop him. If one removes the head, the snake will die," Freddy murmured.

Laurence shifted in his seat and leaned forward. "Don't get me wrong. I don't like Kane at all. But we can't just straight-up murder the guy for being suspicious."

"Murder is such a harsh choice of words, Laurence." Freddy chuckled. "Goodness, whatever do you think of me?" He tucked a chunk of ham onto a cracker and popped both into his mouth.

Laurence watched, and then his shoulders relaxed. "You meant take him out of the picture," he said slowly. "Like, send him away. Frame him for a crime or something?"

Freddy shrugged. Once he swallowed, he said, "I cannot possibly suggest such a thing, dear boy. I am training to be a lawyer."

Quentin forced himself to eat at least some of his dinner as he listened. "Perhaps it would be best if we were to accept. That way we will have a front line view of whatever it is Kane intends to achieve."

"I can't," Laurence countered. "His gift works on me. I can lie until I'm blue in the face, but the moment he makes me tell him the truth we're blown."

"But it doesn't work on Icky," Freddy mused. "Honestly, do

you think you can infiltrate this organization, learn what they're playing at, and all without them noticing what it is you're up to?"

Quentin pressed his lips together as he met Freddy's gaze. "I don't know," he said softly. "But it seems to be our only option, does it not?"

"Just so long as you don't get hurt." Laurence pushed his plate away with a sullen stare.

Quentin reached for Laurence's hand and inclined his head. "I shall do my best, I assure you."

Laurence didn't look particularly comforted.

36

QUENTIN

His arrival at the mansion the following morning was far earlier than his usual time, and he was far from alone. He wasn't even properly dressed.

This was Laurence's suggestion. A show of vulnerability so as to make him seem trustworthy, which Quentin didn't feel all that comfortable with. He *was* trustworthy.

"Except Kane doesn't trust you," Laurence pointed out.

"But that is because he cannot control me. Arriving in a sorry state will not alter that."

"It's not Kane you need to convince." Laurence shrugged. *"It's Mia and Sebastian."*

Quentin didn't pretend to understand. This was Laurence's salesmanship in action, and it would work best if Quentin merely went along with it, so rather than head home after his morning run he went directly to Kane's with the girls in tow.

That was the part he disliked the most. Clifton's affinity with animals had never manifested with any meanness, but Quentin was still intensely uncomfortable taking them into a situation where they could be manipulated.

Laurence had insisted. Nothing showed that Quentin trusted Kane like taking his beloved dogs with him.

"I thought the point was that we don't *trust Kane?"*

Laurence sighed and rolled his eyes. "You trust me?"

"Of course."

"Then trust me on this. He won't hurt them. He can't afford to, because it'll alienate you, baby. He can't afford to have you as an enemy."

Quentin adjusted the strap of his bag across his chest and rang the doorbell.

It took longer than usual for the gate to open, and this time it was Soraya who came to do so. She cracked a wide smile at the sight of dogs. "Wow. They're adorable!"

"They are." He chuckled as he passed through into the courtyard. "Will it be all right to bring them into the house, do you think?"

She made a dismissive snort and turned for the front door. "They can't stay out here. It'll be way too hot."

"My thoughts exactly." He followed her inside and removed their harnesses, then rolled them into a single ball and stuffed them away in his bag. "Where is everyone?"

"Uh." Soraya looked aside, then shrugged. "Doing stuff."

"I see." He chuckled. "Is Kane home?"

"Oh, yeah. C'mon." She beckoned and led toward the back of the house.

"One moment."

She waited while he made a detour to the kitchen and found a pair of large breakfast bowls in a cupboard. He filled them with fresh water from the sink and set them down for the girls, then urged them to wait while he headed out.

"Quentin!" Kane rose from his seat by the pool. Scattered on the table by his drink were a selection of newspapers, and he dropped his phone onto them to stop them getting taken by the breeze. "You're looking... sweaty. Everything okay?"

"He's got dogs with him!" Soraya bounced on her toes.

"I came directly from the beach," Quentin chuckled. "Everything is quite all right, thank you. May I?" He gestured to a chair.

"Sure! Soraya, could you get Quentin a glass of something?"

"Water is perfectly sufficient, thank you." He smiled to the young girl, and she nodded as she hurried to the house, evidently eager to get back to the dogs.

"You can take the hoodie off if you want," Kane said as Quentin sat. "It's gotta be hot in there."

"Oh, no." Quentin shook his head. "It's fine." He eased the bag off over his head and set it on the ground by his feet. "I hadn't put you down as the sort of fellow to hold stock in the media." He nodded to the papers.

"You're kidding, right?" Kane laughed. "The media control our attitudes to everything around us. Gotta know what brainwashing they're feeding to the masses if we're ever going to survive." He eyed Quentin briefly. "You're lucky you caught me. I'm not often around this time of day. What's up?"

Quentin shrugged and looked toward the house. Soraya came bouncing from it, Pepper at her heels. And where Pepper went, Grace was never far behind, her chin bumping against Pepper's hip for guidance.

"Here you go." She put the water on the table.

"Thank you." He smiled to her. "No snacks for the dogs, all right?"

"Cross my heart!" She turned on her heel to run back inside, and Quentin dipped his head to Pepper.

She perked her ears, and he darted his gaze toward the retreating girl.

Pepper turned and did as she was told. She followed Soraya, and Grace followed her.

"I thought I would drop by and advise that while Laurence does not have the time nor inclination to take you up on your offer," he murmured, "I am here to do so."

Kane's gaze fell toward the pool, and Quentin caught a curl of his lip before the man smoothed it out. "He's not interested, huh?"

"He is uncomfortable in your presence."

"Stick with the truth whenever possible," Laurence said. *"Otherwise even the kids will see right through you."*

"Why?"

Quentin snorted softly. "Surely that much is obvious?"

Kane shrugged. "If he's got nothing to hide, then there's nothing to fear."

"Doesn't everyone have something to hide?"

"And what is it you're hiding?" Kane looked to him and raised his head.

Quentin pursed his lips. "I would like to say that I have nothing to hide," he admitted, "but we all have little things we worry about, which to others would seem utterly inconsequential."

"Like the fact that you can't swim?"

Quentin blinked.

It hadn't ever felt like a weakness before. He was hardly surrounded on all sides by the need to enter any water. He did not live on an island, he didn't ever find himself in swimming pools. Plenty of people, he supposed, were unable to swim. So why, when Kane said it, did it feel like a threat?

Because he said it like one.

Because it was something he had said offhand once in a moment of privacy. Bonding, even. And now Kane wielded it like a scalpel.

"Just so," he said stiffly.

Kane barked a laugh. "Well if you're gonna help out around here, we'll have to fix that. We're on the ocean. We can't afford to have one of our heaviest hitters unable to go save someone drowning on our doorstep."

Quentin reached for his water and sipped slowly. "I'm not especially fond of the idea of learning to swim," he finally breathed.

"Sounds like a good reason to do it." Kane shrugged at him. "But it's your call. Anyway, if you're in, maybe it's time to get you in on some training." He stood and gestured for Quentin to join him. "Bring a change of clothes tomorrow, though."

"Training?" Quentin echoed. "For what?"

"Ha!"

Kane set off for the house without another word, and all Quentin could do was tail after him.

For the first time ever, Quentin went upstairs.

It was strangely invasive. Despite there being no barrier, no security, floors beyond the first were distinctly off-limits. He had supposed that to be because the bedrooms were there.

The truth was considerably weirder.

Presumably up above them were still bedrooms, but the double doors Kane led him to screamed *ballroom* to his old-world sensibilities, and it was nonsensical to have a ballroom anywhere but the ground floor.

No. The doors didn't open into a ballroom at all. They led into some sort of gymnasium.

What equipment there was, was neatly lined against the wall to give the majority of space in the room to mats which were laid out in a vast square, easily thirty feet along each side. The mats interlocked like block paving and provided a soft surface for those who stood on them.

Sebastian, Mia, and—Quentin counted as quickly as he was able—eight of the house's teenagers. Clifton was here, which at least meant that he wouldn't be near the dogs. All wore loose-fitting clothing: T-shirts, sweatpants, some sort of martial arts clothing he didn't know the name for, and all were barefoot.

"All right," Sebastian barked. "The doors opened. Doesn't mean you stop what you were doing!"

The assembled kids eyed Quentin, but went back to wrestling with each other, and moments later bodies were thrown against the mats with light thuds.

Sebastian approached while Mia kept an eye on the students. "This is a surprise."

"Quentin's joining us," Kane said with a grin. "And I've got a busy morning planned, so I thought you could take the reins."

Sebastian's gaze roamed over Quentin's body in a way that felt almost intrusive, and Quentin squared his shoulders.

"We might break him," Sebastian snorted.

"Nonsense." Quentin eyed the students as they kicked one

another's legs out and fell about like lunatics. "This all looks…" He searched for the right word. "Tame."

"Right. Shoes and socks off, then." Sebastian pointed to a neat row of other people's footwear by the wall to Quentin's left. "And since that makes an odd number, you can partner up with Mia."

Kane laughed. "I'll let you get settled," he said as he patted Quentin's shoulder. "Have fun!"

"Thank you." Quentin eyed Mia as he crouched down to remove his sneakers. "This seems a little unfair," he added.

"Oh, you worried about getting into a fight with a girl?" Sebastian sniffed at him.

"Good heavens, no." He blinked up at the former soldier. "I'm considerably more concerned that she's about to hand me my own backside."

Sebastian had him warm up with some light jogging back and forth on the mat, as well as forward rolls, before Mia took over.

"You'd be more comfortable without the hoodie," she said.

"I don't doubt it," he replied.

She shrugged. "Okay. Have you done any self-defense work before?"

"Goodness, no."

She laughed. "Man, don't sound so shocked. It's fine. Let's just start with the basics. We're working with Aikido here, and it's not Yoshinkan, so you'll be fine."

That made little sense at all, but Quentin gave a soft nod.

"Don't worry. It gets easier."

He paid attention as she showed him a few different stances. Now and then Sebastian's words cut across the room, but she ignored them, and urged him to do the same.

"This group has been practicing for months," she said. "Don't do as they do. Just stick with me."

She showed him how the different stances affected his center of balance, along with the freedom of movement of his arms. She also spent a peculiar amount of time on the position of his hips, with cryptic explanations like "all the power comes from your hips," and "if the hips are wrong the rest is wrong."

He didn't argue. Perhaps it would become clear over time.

"What is the purpose of this?" he asked half an hour later. Shifting from one stance to the next was trying on his calf muscles, but he suspected that was only because he'd already been on a two-hour run.

"If you don't master the basic stances, we can't go any further," Mia answered.

"No, I mean this." He nodded toward the group.

Mia laughed briefly. "The purpose of Aikido is to escape close combat safely. You throw your opponent to give yourself breathing room. With harder forms like Yoshinkan you dislocate or break their limbs before you run to make sure they can't follow you. But the short of it is that these kids are vulnerable. I don't mean because of their powers. I mean because they're homeless, or they would be if it wasn't for Kane." She bounced on the balls of her feet as she talked. "And society always targets the vulnerable. So sooner or later one of them's going to need to be able to get out of a fight, whether they like it or not. Better if they know how." She flashed an almost feral grin. "Besides, I think it's something all kids should learn in school. This and first aid. Everyone should know how to get out of a fight and how to save a life."

"To be honest," Quentin panted as he shifted stance yet again, "I would rather learn first aid."

"Oh yeah, don't worry." She chuckled. "You're gonna."

He nodded as he tore his attention from the group and back to Mia, and had to wonder what the hell he was getting himself involved in here.

37

LAURENCE

Myriam brought a mug of tea to the counter and set it down by Laurence's hand.

"Thanks, Mom."

She smiled warmly and rested her own beside it. "You're welcome, dear."

He could feel her gaze drilling into the side of his head, so he turned to face her and waited.

Her hazel eyes shone with amusement. "I didn't say a thing." And before he could argue, she added, "but you do seem happy. Happier. I'm so glad to see it." She winked. "The sex is good, I take it?"

"Mom!" His heart pounded as his face burst into heat. "No! It's not... It's not like that!"

"Then tell me what it's like. Talk to me, Bambi."

He huffed and fiddled with a stack of gift cards next to the checkout. "He's, like... Urgh!" He threw his hands up and stalked away to pace the shop. "He's getting better," he had to admit. "More confident, you know?"

"I had noticed," she murmured.

"And I hate to say it, but since he told Kane a couple of weeks ago that he was on board for their superhero academy crap he's really doing good. He's reading! I'm not kidding. I went over there last night and he was reading a first-aid manual. I've never seen him read so much as a newspaper, let alone a book." He bit his lip. "They've been teaching him CPR and stuff. He's really into it."

"And?" she prompted.

He sighed as he returned to pick up his tea. "And, no, no sex," he grumbled.

Myriam smiled and reached across the counter to squeeze his arm. "You can't rush these things. I'm sure he'll get there."

All he could think of was Quentin's arms around him, his hands tenderly exploring Laurence's body, his teeth against Laurence's skin.

His fingers around Laurence's prick.

His cock digging into Laurence's back.

"Oh, yeah." Laurence cleared his throat into his mug. "Yeah, he'll get there."

"You've never been a patient one," Myriam chuckled.

She looked to the door before Laurence could answer, and he turned his head in time to see Freddy push it open. The heat returned to his cheeks.

No, I wasn't totally just thinking about boning your brother, man.

He gulped down some tea to give himself a second.

"It's Freddy, isn't it?" Myriam cooed. "Quentin's brother?"

"It is." Freddy gave her a warm and gracious smile as he offered his hand. "You must be Laurence's mother. Where else could he have gained his ridiculous good looks from?"

Myriam laughed as she took his hand. "Oh, aren't you terrible?"

"I do try my utmost." He dipped his head to kiss the back of her hand, then flashed the most dazzling of smiles. "I wondered if I might borrow him for a little while?"

"Of course, dear!" She tittered like a teenager. "Be sure to bring him back in one piece, won't you?"

"I shall try very hard not to break him!"

LAURENCE DITCHED his apron and followed Freddy out to a waiting car, which whisked them away in comfortable luxury. The vehicle cut out all sound from the outside world, and there wasn't even glass separating the rear from the driver's compartment; there was a padded wall with a television screen, and the only communication was by intercom.

Back here, with leather seats and darkened windows, it was almost as though the outside world had ceased to exist. Quentin didn't travel like this, but then Quentin couldn't afford to stay in a penthouse suite for weeks on end either.

Freddy hasn't been cut off.

And if Freddy hadn't been cut off, that meant he wasn't out of favor.

Laurence shifted in his seat and tried not to dwell on that too much. "What's up?"

"I thought it best to talk," Freddy murmured. "To touch base, as it were. It has been a quiet fortnight. Things are proceeding well?"

"Yeah, I guess. We aren't any closer to working out what Kane wants, but I don't think we expected it to be that easy."

"Indeed." Freddy chuckled. "A man who finds trust difficult is hardly about to open up so soon. How is Icky bearing up?"

"Yeah, good." Laurence nodded. "He seems to enjoy it. I don't think they suspect anything."

"Good." Freddy dipped his head. "Do be careful. Icky is an idealist. He's also a terrible pacifist. Wouldn't hurt a fly. If we leave him there too long they might fill his head with all sorts of nonsense."

Laurence narrowed his eyes and leaned forward to rest his elbows on his knees. He couldn't argue that Quentin wasn't one to do harm. Even in a fight to the death with a god, Quentin had acted defensively when it was well within his power to go on the attack.

"Okay," he said with care. "What're you suggesting?"

"While Icky is off being dreary and heroic," Freddy murmured, "we must get our hands dirty."

"How so?"

"We need to ascertain the reach of Wilson's organization. Who he interacts with, what influence he has, whether he mingles socially, where his interests lie, whether he has any history of violence or activism, that sort of thing. The more thorough a profile we are able to build of him, the more we will know of his thoughts and goals."

Laurence sat back and raised his chin as he regarded Freddy. "Is this why you want Quentin in Kane's house? To keep him out of the way of the actual investigation?"

Freddy laughed briefly. "Of course. He is hardly a subtle man, Laurence. He is a blunt instrument, but he is sufficiently flashy as a distraction. Now." He reached for a tablet tucked into a pocket by his side and ran his fingers across it.

The screen between the rear compartment and the driver came to life and displayed a web page which showed a news article. The publication date placed it at twelve years old.

FOOTBALL STAR PLUNGES TO DEATH FROM SCHOOL ROOF.

Laurence skim-read the article. "This is the kid Kane killed, isn't it?" he realized. "Quentin said he was really cut up about this."

"Mm," Freddy agreed. "I have done a little digging. I am by no means a private investigator, but by goodness reading law teaches you a great deal about performing research." His lips twitched in amusement. "Kane Wilson has been on the fringes of quite a few of these little mistakes over the years. Apparently he failed to learn after the first gaffe." His fingers darted across the tablet, and several more news articles scrolled across the larger screen.

Laurence skimmed them. Tragic suicides of popular people, the sort about whom all the other popular people only ever had good things to say.

The sort who were usually the worst kinds of bullies out there.

"You think he made all these people kill themselves?" Laurence breathed. "Goddess, just how many are there?"

"Eleven thus far." Freddy's nose crinkled. "He has rather a taste for it, don't you think? I would suggest that whatever path we take, we do so beyond his ken, and I'm sorry to say that means not discussing it with Icky. If Wilson gets even the faintest whiff of our digging into his personal affairs I have no doubt we'll be walking ourselves out in front of traffic in no time."

Laurence grimaced. "Holy shit." He gestured to the screen. "What makes you sure these were all Kane?"

"Largely the occasional eyewitness who distinctly recalls Wilson urging the victim to go kill themselves," Freddy said with distaste in his tone. "The man is about as subtle as Icky. Doesn't even have a third party do the dirty work on his behalf." He waved his hand toward the large screen. "This man is dangerous, make no mistake. He fears no consequence. He has a taste for bumping off his enemies. The only reason I do not urge that we pull Icky away from him is that, for whatever reason, my dear brother has proven immune to Wilson's power. You and I do not have that luxury. We shall have to take an inordinate amount of care if we are to proceed."

Laurence rubbed his jaw slowly.

There was a glimmer of excitement festering within him that he couldn't ignore. Wilson wasn't some mere do-gooder with a heart of gold. He wasn't the boring evangelist Laurence had initially written him off as. He was a predator, a killer. He was dangerous prey, and hunting him would prove a significant challenge.

And that challenge called to him like a siren.

You're a florist, not a hunter!

He scratched beneath his ear while he tried to keep his features neutral.

He'd felt this way before. Back when he thought Dan threatened Quentin, he was almost overcome with the urge to hunt the man down and tear into his flesh with his bare hands. And now that Wilson seemed to be a far greater threat, Laurence was itching to track him down and—

And *what?*

Rip his throat out? Feast on his entrails? Nail his head to the wall?

He lowered his hand and pretended to study the news article on the screen.

This dream he'd had. The dream of Herne and Sara, the past which had created Laurence's entire lineage. It taunted him with the knowledge that he was the descendant of a god and that his power came from a meeting of the human and other worlds perhaps two thousand years ago.

And it made it clear that he resembled Herne not only in gifts, but looks too.

Was his inheritance not only one of power, but also of personality? Did he have these urges to hunt because he was, without ever having acknowledged it before now, a hunter? Not some tame, modern-day creature who laid traps with salt licks and hid in the safety of a tree with a rifle, but a tracker, a stalker. A carnivore.

He bit the inside of his cheek.

"I can take care," he eventually answered.

"Good." Freddy smiled. "We also need to work out Wilson's weaknesses lest we are forced into a confrontation. It appears that he must issue his commands verbally, yes?"

Laurence nodded. "Yeah." Then he raised his eyebrows. "You're suggesting his victim needs to be able to hear them to obey?"

"You're rather bright, aren't you?" Freddy smiled at him. "Yes. Can he control someone who cannot hear his words?"

"How would we work that out?" Laurence cracked his knuckles.

"Well. You can see the future, can you not?" Freddy tilted his head. "Are you able to ascertain the outcomes of what-if scenarios?"

Laurence stared at him. "You want me to try and see a future that might not even happen?"

"Dear boy, I should hope that every future you witness has the potential to be averted, otherwise what is the purpose of such a gift?"

"I..." He swallowed. "I dunno if it can work that way." He paused.

Sideways.

He rocked his jaw, then nodded. "But I can sure as hell try."

38

QUENTIN

"You aren't gonna hurt me. Just do it."

Quentin eyed Sebastian. The man had at least a hundred pounds on him, and considerably more muscle power, but still the idea of intentionally tossing him at the ground seemed dangerous.

"I'm sorry," he murmured. "I cannot."

Sebastian had swapped Quentin into a less-experienced group, but they still knew more than he did, and so Quentin partnered with Sebastian until he could breakfall safely and use a variety of stances and basic joint control techniques, but now things seemed to have gone a little too far.

Sebastian sighed faintly. "Morote-Dori Kokyu-Ho is one of the three fundamental techniques of Aikido. All you're doing is breaking free from an attacker's hold on you."

"And throwing you to the ground." Quentin frowned at him.

"Unbalancing me," Sebastian corrected. "I'll fall, but only because you'll be putting me off-balance. And an attacker will be off-balance because they're relying on their hold on you to keep themselves upright. Trust me, you're better off not letting an assailant hang on to you if they do manage to get close."

Quentin pressed his lips together and crossed his arms.

Sebastian glanced to the students. "Have you ever been attacked? Like, properly, with intent to kill?"

"Yes."

"And how are you not dead?"

Quentin tightened his hold on his own arms and looked to the students himself. "Because Laurence stepped in," he said quietly.

"Okay." Sebastian nodded at him. "What happened?"

Quentin preferred not to think about it. It wasn't an easy thing to come to terms with, to know that he was alive because Laurence had killed to protect him. While Quentin's intent had been to allow Jack to exhaust himself, the tactic failed, and Laurence was forced to attack Jack directly.

Both Jack and his host, Dan, died.

Quentin didn't know whether Dan was already dead by then. There was no way to know; not now. And, of course, Quentin had blacked out during the fight. He couldn't know how far things went before Laurence's hand was forced.

He wasn't about to tell Sebastian that particular weakness. Not when his inability to swim was already in Kane's hands.

"We fought someone with powers similar to Laurence's," he murmured. "The plant they controlled was toxic, and one touch from it could have proved lethal, and I could not..." He took a breath as he worked out which words exactly to use. "I could not prevent each and every vine's approach. Laurence fought for control of the plant and directed it at our opponent, who died from the contact."

It wasn't wholly the truth, but it was true enough for this conversation, Quentin decided. There was no need to let Kane find out that gods existed.

Sebastian nodded as he listened. "Was your plan to just stand there and keep it away from you?"

"Yes."

"What was gonna make your opponent stop?"

"A lack of stamina."

Sebastian snorted. "Then what? They'd admit defeat and part ways, never to bother you again?"

Quentin tutted softly. "I do not believe so, no."

"Then ultimately it was going to be a lethal fight. Don't beat yourself up that Laurence killed to save you. That's not what's important here."

Quentin scowled up at him. "Is it not?"

"No." Sebastian gave a faint, sad smile. "What matters is that he intervened. What I'm trying to teach you here is a non-lethal method. If you can't learn it, then what're you going to do? You're gonna use your gift, and that carries all kinds of risks. You could out yourself. You could totally overwhelm your opponent instead of just dropping them to the floor. It's all about reasonable use of force. You don't want to respond to a street punk with a hurricane. The more tools you have in your kit, the more able you are to pull the right tool out when you need it." He adjusted his stance and indicated for Quentin to do the same. "You went into a fight with a guy who was ready and willing to use lethal force, and you weren't, so he overpowered you. Imagine what you're gonna do if you go into a situation that needs a light touch, and all you've got at your disposal is telekinesis. You're gonna break someone, Quentin. So stop whining and let me show you how to *not* break people."

He grimaced as he adjusted his footing and raised his hands. "Very well," he muttered. "But slowly."

Sebastian shook his head. "Jesus. Anyone'd think I'm asking you to murder a puppy. Okay. This is all about unbalancing your opponent without losing your own balance, so let's walk through it. Morote-Dori is for when you've been grabbed with both hands, like so."

Sebastian gripped his forearm, and the contact sharpened Quentin's attention. Another's hands on him felt wholly uncomfortable. Invasive, even.

Paying attention suddenly seemed far more appealing.

HE DID NOT SHOWER at Kane's mansion after studies. He disliked undressing anywhere but home at the best of times. The knowledge that he was well within range of Soraya's gift made it doubly impossible, and since he was already dressed for exercise it made more sense to jog home afterward.

Quentin collected his keys, wallet, and phone from the pile of pocket items by the door of the gymnasium and tucked each away where it belonged. As he zipped his wallet into his hoodie, he felt a presence at his elbow, and turned toward it.

Kimberly was there, her hair in disarray and her cheeks ruddy from the practice. One hand was stuffed into the pocket of her sweatpants.

"Kimberly." He smiled to her. "Can I help you?"

"You can call me Kim." She twirled a strand of hair around her fingers and then looped it past her ear. "Soraya told me what you did."

"What I... did?" He blinked in confusion.

"You know. Noticed I was gone. Asked her to find me." She shuffled on the spot and fidgeted with more of her hair. "Thanks."

Quentin inclined his head. All that had been some weeks ago now. Had Soraya waited this long to tell Kimberly, or did it take Kimberly a month to summon the courage to speak with him about it?

"You are welcome," he murmured. "I apologize for the intrusion. I thought it best to be certain you were safe."

Her fidgeting grew more intense. "It's okay." She looked around quickly before she withdrew the hand from her pocket and offered it to him. "I just wanted to say thank you properly," she squeaked.

He reached for her hand and took it, but there was something papery between their palms. At first he thought perhaps she was pressing a dollar bill into his hand.

Was she *tipping* him for looking out for her?

Her fingers closed tightly around his and she shook her head with urgency up at him. Her free hand pressed a finger against her own lips, only for a second. Then she pulled back, and he had to quickly grasp whatever paper she had passed him before it could fall to the ground.

"That's all," she added. The tension in her voice made it waver, and she ran from the room without another word.

Quentin blinked as he tucked the paper away. If she wanted it to be a secret, the least intelligent thing he could do this moment was even acknowledge that he received it, so he idly sneaked it away with his keys as he left the room and tried to ignore his own curiosity.

BY THE TIME he was home he had built up a sweat all over again, and he peeled his exercise clothes off on his way to the bedroom. He paused only to fuss the dogs as they mobbed him.

He divested himself of wallet and cellphone, and then took care to extricate his keys without loss of the little piece of paper curled around them. It had holes and torn fragments along one edge, so it had been ripped from some sort of notebook. That the lines on it were pink and it was bordered with cute little pink bears made it all the more likely that Kimberly had sourced the paper from a larger stationery item.

It was softened by damp and crumpled as though it had been stuffed in her pocket for quite some time. Indeed, if it had been there for the duration of the morning's lessons she had undoubtedly rolled over it and fallen on it countless times before she then clutched it in a sweaty palm.

She didn't want her message heard, or she would have whispered it to him. That suggested she did not care to have Estelita overhear her. And she did not want her passing it to him to be witnessed, or she would have handed it over without all the cloak and dagger.

The message, then, was important. She had planned how to get it to him, waited for the opportune moment, and carried it with her until she could seize that chance.

Quentin tossed his T-shirt into the laundry basket and then perched on the edge of his bed to pick apart the paper with care. It had become so balled up that it could tear with ease, and he didn't wish to damage what she had taken such great pains to pass to him. As he peeled the paper open, smudged ink was revealed, and he smoothed it across his thigh with the back of his hand to ease some of the creases from it.

The words were in an untidy hand, and sweat had made the ink run, but her words were perfectly legible.

I didn't choose to go.

He took a moment to figure out what she meant, but it seemed obvious once he added the note to her awkward thanks.

Kimberly hadn't gone to the gun show of her own free will.

Quentin set the note aside, and then decided to fold it again and slip it into his wallet rather than leave it out in the open for any nearby clairvoyant to read.

It was one thing for Kimberly to go and steal on behalf of the group, but another entirely for Kane to have forced her into it. Every instinct he had screamed at him to march back there and demand to know what Kane had been thinking. What gave him the right to force a teenage girl to do something against her will?

Absolutely nothing.

Common sense had until the end of his shower to change his mind. That was as long as he was willing to give it. If his brain hadn't come up with a bloody good reason in half an hour then to hell with the plan, and to hell with waiting for some sort of divine revelation to land in his lap.

39

LAURENCE

The back of a limo wasn't Laurence's preferred choice of venue for any attempt to see the future, but if he closed his eyes and pretended the vehicle didn't occasionally slow down or sway a bit then it was pretty cozy in here.

He could hear Freddy's breathing, soft and measured. Beyond that was the purr of the engine even after all the sound-dampening, which was probably enough to cut the noise completely for Freddy, but not for Laurence. He latched onto the engine noise as his meditative aid. It was a regular sound without any meaning, and would help distract him from the car's motion.

What if he approached Kane with earmuffs on? Could Kane control him, or was it doomed from the start? After all, if Kane knew his power wouldn't work, would he even try, or would he get one of his cronies to take the muffs off Laurence's head?

Even that was valuable information, though. If he went to Kane and Sebastian took the earmuffs away, there had to be a reason.

Unless it was—

He heard screams. So many screams.

There was no mistaking the location. Every high school looked the same. Corridors, lockers, glossy floors. They weren't usually this full of screaming kids, though.

The fashions looked early 2000s. Some of the girls had dyed the underside of their hair darker and wore hoop earrings. He saw a couple of guys in tartan fedoras and there were way too many faux hawks and popped collars going on.

Of course, there was also way too much screaming.

Laurence followed the flow to the main doors and outside, where the screams were a hellish din. He slipped past—and through—the kids who were here back then. It was easy. He wasn't here. Not really.

He smelled the blood before he saw it. It was almost overwhelming, like a tin roof that had baked in the midday sun. There was more, too, beyond the blood. The rancid stench of half-digested food and of bile. The gross odor of fecal matter.

He heard retching.

The children stopped in a wide circle around the thing which had drawn them all here. Some had thrown up already.

The blood was everywhere. Like a balloon filled with it had been dropped from above, it all radiated outward from a single point. Some had traveled up the school's outer wall and was drying fast in the California heat. The pool on the asphalt was too deep to dry so fast, though.

There were other things in the blood. A finger. A lump of meat. Goddess knew what else.

The body in the middle of the pool had ruptured with the impact. Laurence couldn't even make out a head in all the mess.

He convulsed. His stomach spasmed, and acid burned the back of his throat. It stung his eyes.

He pulled back from the scene, desperate to escape it.

Was he still in the vision? Where was he?

He coughed up fluid which tasted of vomit, and spat it out.

"Stay here, Wilson!"

"Yes, sir."

The man who hurried from the office was in his sixties. He wore a gray suit, nothing fancy. Probably the Principal.

The teen in the chair watched the adult leave, then rose from his seat and walked past Laurence to the window. He looked down.

A smirk touched his lips.

"Result!" *he breathed.*

His eyes lit up with a slow, almost disbelieving glee.

Laurence coughed again, and hurled so hard that it made his back hurt. Tears streamed from his eyes and fell forward. He spat as much as he could, but another wave of it came out of him.

The smell of blood seemed to linger.

"Laurence! Oh, God!" Freddy was scrabbling in a compartment, then he pressed something cold into Laurence's hands. "Here! Take this!"

Through the blur of tears, Laurence made out a bottle of water. The cap was already off.

He groaned and swigged from it, then swirled it around and spat it straight out. "Fuck," he croaked.

"Christ." Freddy hunted around and unearthed a box of tissues, then passed those over too. Laurence heard a click. "The hotel, fast as you can."

Laurence gulped a mouthful of water to take the edge off the burn in his throat.

"All right." Freddy sounded shaken. "No more of that, apparently! I'm sorry."

"It's—"

"You don't wanna do this." Wilson's eyes were bright with amusement.

He looked around sixteen, maybe seventeen. A scrawny little thing still; that hadn't changed. He had acne now, but not much—just a couple of zits on his chin.

The kid that loomed over him couldn't look more like a jock if he was in his football uniform. Short hair, ridiculous muscles, and a posse of clones with the popular girls at the back.

"Yeah?" The boy shoved Wilson hard in the chest. It made the far smaller boy slam against the corridor wall.

What was it with Wilson and high schools?

"Pretty sure I'm gonna enjoy smearing your pasty face all over this wall, Wilson."

Wilson wheezed for breath. The amusement left him, evaporating in an instant. Seething hatred twisted his features.

"Pretty sure," he gasped, "your buddies are gonna enjoy beating you to death."

Confused silence descended. A couple of the girls chattered among themselves.

"Huh?"

Wilson turned to the boy on his left. "Kick the crap out of him," *he hissed,* "until he stops breathing."

A nervous laugh rippled through the crowd, but before it came to a natural end the boy threw a punch at Wilson's assailant and it landed against the jock's nose with a sickening crunch.

Wilson turned to his right. "Help him."

Laughter turned to yells.

Yells became screams.

And Wilson slipped away.

Laurence's stomach had nothing more to give. "Oh, Goddess," he whimpered. "Stop. Make it stop!"

A stinging slap connected with his cheek.

Laurence howled and flailed at his attacker, and lost hold of his water bottle.

"Stop, Laurence!" Freddy barked.

Gray eyes swam into view. Firm fingers gripped Laurence's jaw.

"Are you with me now?"

Laurence hiccupped. "Where are we?"

"I have to get you inside and to the lift with minimal fuss. Are you about to yell again? Be sick again?"

Laurence crinkled his nose. The reek of vomit hung heavy in the air.

"Let's go."

Freddy's hands were under his arms. They dragged him from the back of the car and out into the glare of the sun, but then cool conditioned air gathered around him and the sun cut out. His sneakers squashed plush carpet underfoot, a whisper of rubber against pile the only sound they made as Freddy ushered him into an elevator and smacked his hand against a button. He pushed Laurence back against the elevator wall and held him there by his shoulder.

Laurence groaned. "I should've known." His body shivered with shock. "Fuck, I should've known."

"Known what?" Freddy gazed into his eyes, and worry creased his forehead.

Laurence let out a weak, humorless laugh. "I never see the good shit."

FREDDY LED him upstairs in the penthouse to an entire spare bedroom with its own en suite bathroom, and Laurence stripped down for a shower. There were toiletries in the bathroom, so he unwrapped a toothbrush and brushed his teeth while he showered to replace the vile taste in his mouth with mint.

His cheek was still a little pink from where Freddy had smacked him. He must've packed one hell of a wallop to leave that kind of a mark, but it had worked. Laurence was free from the visions which seemed so desperate to show him what a murderous shitweasel Wilson truly was.

Thank fuck.

He toweled himself off and wrapped the towel around his waist, then padded out into the bedroom.

His clothes were gone.

Every item from his pockets was lined neatly on the bed. Wallet, keys, phone, a business card holder, a stub of a pencil, and a small stash of rubber bands all woven together into a multicolored daisy chain. Without pockets to return it all to there didn't seem to be any point in collecting it, so he walked out of the bedroom.

Freddy emerged from another room, his hair damp, his body wrapped in a silk bathrobe. The deep burgundy of it looked breathtaking against his pale skin.

"I've ordered replacement clothing for you," Freddy explained as he wandered toward the stairs. "Shouldn't be too terribly long. I'm afraid you rather ruined your own."

"You did—" Laurence shook his head and tailed the Brit. He should be used to the d'Arcy way of things by now, and to be fair to Freddy, fresh clothing would get Laurence back on his feet faster than waiting for laundry. "Thanks, man. I really appreciate it."

"You're welcome." Freddy continued on past the sitting area and to the kitchen, where he fetched a glass of water and pressed it into Laurence's hands. "Here. You will be dehydrated. Little sips."

Laurence didn't argue. He nodded as he took the glass, and he sipped from it as instructed.

Freddy observed him for a couple of minutes, then inclined his head. "Now," he murmured. "If you can do so while retaining what remains in your stomach, would you care to let me know what it was that upset you so?"

Laurence gritted his teeth and set the glass down on a countertop, then rubbed his eyes. "We've gotta stop Wilson," he said. "I don't care what he's doing. I've seen what he's done already."

One of Freddy's fair eyebrows arched, and the gesture was so like Quentin that Laurence almost laughed.

"And what has Mr. Wilson done?" Freddy asked.

"All those articles you found. You're right." Laurence drew a breath. "Wilson's a murderer. He's killed over and over, and he's not gonna stop just because he's not a kid anymore."

Freddy licked his lips slowly. "Is Icky in danger?"

"No." Laurence shook his head. "No, not yet. But he will be if Wilson ever works out that Quentin's not on his side."

Freddy pressed his lips together tightly. "Then we had best ensure that he does not."

"Yeah," Laurence agreed.

They'd been so damn sure Quentin was safe because Wilson couldn't control him. Fucking idiots. Quentin was surrounded by children who would all do whatever Wilson ordered them to.

And Quentin wouldn't lift a finger to harm any of them.

40

QUENTIN

QUENTIN ARRIVED AT THE MANSION BY TAXI, HIS HAIR STILL DAMP. It was Mia who came to get him at the gate, and once he was indoors he was immediately assailed by a flurry of teens running past.

He and Mia stepped back out of the path of the stampede.

"What on Earth is that all about?"

She shrugged at him. "Who can say?"

"I suspect they of all people can." He set off after them, picking up into a light jog. "Kimberly?"

The young girl turned, and her eyes widened. The poor thing looked terrified and shook her head weakly.

"Where are you off to?"

"Oh." She relaxed and held a door open, beckoning quickly for him to follow. "Estelita was listening to a police scanner. Apparently there's a huge wildfire out near Scripps Ranch."

He caught up just in time to see Estelita and Soraya leaping into the back of a truck in the garage. Sebastian was already behind the wheel.

"And you're going?" He darted through the door and after her as she ran for the truck. "Are you sure this is wise?"

"We're just there to help Sebastian," Soraya called.

Quentin eyed Sebastian.

"Get in if you're coming," Sebastian grunted. "I'm not waiting around."

"Bloody hell." Quentin clambered up into the unclaimed passenger seat and buckled himself in. "This is reckless in the extreme!" He grabbed for the dashboard as Sebastian floored the accelerator before the garage door was fully open, and winced, fully expecting to hear the roof scrape against it.

They missed it, although he didn't dare guess at how much by, and the truck shot off along the road.

"Christ, Sebastian!" Quentin gritted his teeth and braced his feet against the floor to keep from sliding about in his seat. "We'll be no use to anyone if we're arrested before we even make it that far!"

"The problem's going to be getting in," Sebastian said. "Roads will be clogged with residents trying to escape and emergency services heading in to help them, so we're gonna have to go off-road at some point."

Quentin glanced to the back seat, where the girls seemed to be having a whale of a time in the back of a speeding truck. He eyed their seat belts, then looked to Sebastian.

Sebastian glanced at him, then shrugged. "Estelita can hear everything around us. She might pick up people in need, and help us avoid cops. Soraya can look ahead and tell us what we'll be facing. And Kim can sneak in and out of places without getting caught. It's a good team for this job."

"And you are here to do what?"

"Redirect fire, get people out of whatever sticky situation they're in." Sebastian shrugged. "Estelita and Soraya never even have to leave the car."

"But Kimberly does?"

"Only if absolutely necessary." Sebastian grunted. "I'm not putting these kids at risk, Quentin."

"No," Quentin agreed.

Kane is.

He pressed his lips together and said nothing as they shot onto a wider road.

SEBASTIAN DROVE LIKE A DEMON, sometimes bumping off the edge of the road to circumvent traffic, other times slowing down on Estelita's warnings to avoid drawing the ire of police. They weren't on the highway for terribly long, and soon Sebastian had the truck on a narrow road which was—as predicted—full to overflowing with traffic going the other way. In the end they were rattling over the brush-filled shoulder.

"Oh, wow!" Estelita stretched her arm between the front seats and pointed through the windshield. "Look!"

It wasn't long before Quentin could see what she'd pointed at: thick plumes of smoke which pulsed up into the sky.

When he was a child, there had been an outbreak of foot-and-mouth disease. It tore through livestock in Oxfordshire, as well as much of the rest of the country, and entire herds of animals were culled to try and contain the virus. Farmers piled the carcasses on the usually beautiful hillsides and set fire to the lot. For days, the horror raged on. Healthy animals had to be destroyed so that they did not provide a bridge for the illness to spread, and the countryside burned.

The smoke up ahead brought back grotesque memories, and Quentin felt sick to his stomach.

"It's so weird!" Soraya breathed.

"It's pretty," Estelita said.

Kim remained quiet.

The closer they came to it the more Quentin was able to catch glimpses of flame through the trees. The smoke passed above them, blown by the wind.

"Left," Estelita called out.

Sebastian didn't argue. He wrenched the wheel until they were cutting a swath through undergrowth and between trees. "The wind will drive the fire toward us," he grunted.

"Then you cannot leave the children in the car," Quentin argued.

"I'm seventeen!" Soraya insisted.

"Thus only proving my point."

"Then you stay with them," Sebastian said. "If the fire comes too close, get them out of here. Don't worry about me."

"Don't be ridiculous." Quentin huffed at him. "I can't bloody drive!"

Sebastian stared at him.

"I can!" Soraya said.

"No!" Quentin and Sebastian both chimed at once.

SEBASTIAN STOPPED ONCE the trees were too dense to drive through, and he looked to Quentin. "Are you sure about this?"

Quentin gave a curt nod as he unfastened his seat belt. "One older lady, three horses, two dogs. Half a mile in that direction." He gestured to his right.

"Nothing fancy. Just get the old lady and run."

Quentin snorted at him. "I shall do whatever I am able to."

He leaped out of the truck and into what felt like a furnace. The heat which surrounded the car went beyond a hot, dry afternoon in Southern California and well into punishing heat. Quentin shed his jacket and tossed it onto the passenger seat, then closed the door and bolted off through the trees.

All in all this afternoon was not going at all how he had envisioned.

THE CLOSER HE came to the ranch, the worse the situation became. The heat was intense, and the smoke overhead almost blotted out the sun itself, transforming the area into some hellish nightmare.

He heard the screams of panicked horses and ran on toward them.

Quentin broke free of the edge of the forest and sprinted across a rocky and uneven dirt track. There was the fence of a pasture ahead, and he saw three mares gallop along it, trapped by the metal fence and desperate to escape. The dogs were nowhere in sight, and nor was the ranch's sole human occupant, but if he could get the horses under control they had a means of escape.

Presuming that the horses were trained to be ridden, of course.

He scanned the fence for a gate and found one closer to the ranch, so he turned and followed the dirt track up toward it.

The far end of the pasture was a wall of fire.

Christ, Laurence would have a fit if he found out about this.

There was a big, sand-colored truck outside the ranch house. Two dogs were in the back. Both were black Labradors, and both were panting heavily.

Where, then, was the owner?

He took a breath to yell, and it seared his lungs.

"Hello? Is anyone here?"

There was no answer.

Quentin looked to the fire. It was a beautiful thing, transforming trees into black smoke and spitting them up into the sky. It turned the air into a wavering haze that made it difficult to judge distance, but Quentin couldn't see any fence at that end of the pasture.

Could the fire traverse the pasture itself, or was there not enough fuel for it? How *did* a wildfire spread?

Beyond the heat and the way everything was bathed in orange was the roar of the flames. The noise from them was stupendous, and it seemed to carry across the pasture in waves as though the air itself was sometimes too thick to let the sound pass.

"Who the hell are you?"

The voice jolted him back to the immediate, and he swiveled on his heel.

"I've come to help," he said.

"Then stop standing there and help me get this into the truck!"

The woman was hardly what he would call "elderly." If anything she was barely into her early fifties, and her hair was only gray at the temples. She had the deeply ingrained tan of someone who worked outdoors year-round, and as she spoke she gestured behind her to the most hideous armchair Quentin had seen in his life.

"Got it this far," she grunted as she stalked back to it. "Forgot how heavy it was, though. C'mon, kid, make yourself useful. What's your name?"

"Quentin." He tore his attention from the conflagration and darted to the chair. "Really, you should leave this—"

"Boy, this was my husband's favorite chair. He only got to sit in it half an hour a day, and when he died of a heart attack two years ago it was in this damn thing. It's coming with me, so either put your back into it or get outta my hair."

"Get water for the dogs," he countered. "I'll take care of it."

She eyed him, but disappeared back into the house without complaint, and Quentin raised the ugly, chewed old armchair into the back of the truck before she could catch him in the act. He jumped up after it to push it into a corner in the hope that it wouldn't slide around once the truck was on the move.

"All right." She came out with a gallon of water in a milk container, and she dropped it onto the back seat of the truck with the dogs. "Get in."

Quentin hopped down from the back and thumbed toward the horses. "You go," he said. "I'll get them."

"You're crazy. They're panicked. They won't listen to me, let alone you. Just open the gate and hope they make it, that's all we can do."

"Go," he yelled.

"You can't—"

He lost the rest of her words in a roar from the fire, and he looked toward it as he fought with the gate.

Apparently a pasture could burn just fine.

He shoved the gate open and strode into the enclosure as the truck began to drive away. He left the gate wide open so that if he failed the horses could at least bolt, but for now all he could do was hope to high heaven that Laurence was right, and that his affinity with animals was more than body language and empathy.

The mares galloped toward him. Their eyes were so wide that he could see the whites, and their tongues lolled from open mouths.

In this state, they could trample him to death and never even realize he was there.

Quentin drew himself up to his full height and kept his arms loose by his sides. He had to get their attention off the fire, so he remained in their path and watched them come closer.

"You must calm yourselves," he said. It didn't really matter what words he used, he supposed. The tone was what mattered, so he spoke with soft, measured words. "Calm down. Calm down, and we'll all be safe."

The horses' ears pricked forward.

They were barely fifty yards from him now.

"Calm down," he repeated. "Look at me. Calm down."

Tails rose a little, and the ears relaxed. As one, the horses slowed into a canter, and then to a trot. They huffed and snorted, but he could no longer see the whites around their irises.

Quentin tamped down on his shock. He wasn't sure whether he had expected this to work. His body was primed to leap aside at the last moment, and now that he didn't need to, his muscles ached.

He wasn't dead yet.

"There," he murmured. He lifted his hands slowly, palms toward the horses, and allowed them to investigate him. "We can't stay here."

The oldest of the mares sighed in agreement, and her ears twitched, so he gave her neck a firm pat of reassurance.

"I suppose that now is as good at time as any to see whether you have any objections to a bareback rider," he muttered.

He'd been forced to use a little telekinetic help to vault up onto the mare's back. She was a tall beast, easily seventeen hands, and he didn't dare risk getting it wrong.

He found his seat quickly enough, even though it was over six years since he'd ridden. He relaxed and allowed his balance to do all the work.

"All right," he said softly. "Let's go."

He steered with the lightest of touches, and the mare set off down the dirt track at a walk. Once he had the other two following, he urged her into a trot. It would help ease their jittery energy to move faster, and he'd have a better feel for her than at a walk.

They set off after the lady in the truck, and it was only then that it occurred to him that he hadn't even asked her name.

Riding without a saddle was every bit as difficult as he remembered. It relied on core muscle strength and an overdeveloped sense of balance, and while both his stamina and equilibrium were excellent, he was out of practice. The horse would likely outlast him.

Quentin risked a look to his left.

The entire pasture was alight now. The flames licked at the fence.

He glanced right, where there was nothing but trees.

It didn't take a degree in physics to see where this was headed.

41

LAURENCE

Laurence hopped out of the cab while Freddy paid, and by the time Freddy joined him he had the gate open.

Although it only took half an hour for fresh clothes to arrive, the limo had to go away to be cleaned. Freddy had the hotel's concierge arrange a cab as a replacement for the day. The taxi driver parked on the driveway, and Laurence let them into the apartment.

Freddy blinked as he walked through into the hallway. "This is ridiculous," he groused. "What on earth is Icky doing in a place like this?"

"What?" Laurence huffed as he took the stairs two at a time. "This is huge!"

"It's an insult." Freddy came up after him at a more leisurely pace. "Half of a house? Preposterous!"

"Yeah, well. Your dad didn't leave Quen with much money, you know?" Laurence slid his key into the door at the top and pushed it open. "Quen? Why aren't you answering your phone? Baby?"

Pepper scrambled from her bed in the kitchen and bounded over to head-butt his thigh, and Laurence patted the top of her head. "Quen?" he called again.

"Not here," Freddy surmised. His gaze fell to the piano and his expression turned wistful for a brief moment, then he shook his head. "Where else is he likely to be at this hour? Getting blotto, I assume?"

"Blotto?" It took Laurence a second to translate that. "Oh, drunk? No." He shook his head with a grimace. "We don't drink."

"Ah, yes. You did say as much." Freddy stepped around the dogs, since Grace now joined Pepper in greeting Laurence, and made his way to the kitchen, where he began to search through cupboards and drawers. "Wilson's, then?"

"Most likely." Laurence clenched his jaw and petted Grace as he watched Freddy. "What're you doing?"

"Looking for clues, dear boy." Freddy's nose crinkled briefly. "Although at the moment all I can surmise is that the dogs eat better than he does, so nothing new there. You really should get yourself a grounding in basic investigative techniques. Stop relying on your gifts quite so much."

"Relying?" Laurence huffed as he sprang to his feet. "If anything I don't use them anywhere near as much as I could!"

"Really." Freddy moved from the kitchen to the living room, prying into every corner, poking his nose into a vase of flowers here or a small stack of books there. "Then find him, Laurence."

Laurence scowled and poked his nose into the bedroom, which was neat thanks to the near-invisible hand of Quentin's maid. He had no idea what he might find in there, but it wasn't Quentin, so he backed out again and tried Quentin's cellphone.

It rang and rang, and then went to voicemail.

"We have to go to Wilson's," Laurence growled.

Freddy picked up a stack of envelopes from a side table and flicked through them. "To what end?"

"If Quentin's there—"

"Wouldn't he answer his phone?" Freddy sat at the dining table and began to open the envelopes. He plucked out cards of all colors and sizes and lay each one atop its envelope. "Yes, he would. Unless he were already dead, in which case there is little hurry." He opened and read each of the cards. "Hmm."

"You're not helping!" Laurence stalked to the table and looked down at the array of cards. Each and every one looked like an event invitation: parties, gallery openings, charity galas. The sort of thing Quentin would have leaped at a few months ago, yet now sat around unopened.

But not thrown in the trash.

Laurence frowned and reached for one of the cards. It was plain white with gold embossed text inside.

You are cordially invited...

He didn't recognize the name, which likely meant some banker or movie producer, rather than a rock star or actor. The location was the Skybox in the East Village, so the party was probably going to be stuffed to the gills with San Diego's richest. No wonder Quentin got an invite.

"Does he attend any of these?" Freddy continued to nose through the cards, and had his cellphone out to Google the occasional name.

"Not anymore." Laurence returned his card to the table.

"Hmm." Freddy consulted his phone. "God, what a dreary selection of people. No wonder he doesn't go. Christ, even politicians have hold of his address. Kill me now."

"What's looking at all these even telling us?" Laurence scowled.

"It tells us the sort of company my brother keeps. Or, rather, the sort of company who wishes to keep him. It's all very B-list." Freddy sighed and looked to the windows. "Really, Laurence, what's he doing here? A dismal little apartment, a slew of subpar invitations. It's not like him."

Laurence shrugged. "He's happy."

"For now."

"What's that supposed to mean?"

Freddy glanced up to him, his gray eyes glassy in the afternoon light. "The boy has ants in his pants, Laurence. Can't sit still for five minutes. But he's also used to far more than—" he waved a hand at the apartment "—this."

"Yeah, well, your dad cut him off, so he's gotta watch the pennies."

Freddy tutted a little. "Regardless, it's safe to say that he isn't here, and we cannot visit Wilson."

"So we gotta wait?" Frustration gnawed at Laurence's gut. "I can't just sit here and do nothing!"

"No, we don't have to wait. Now, I think, is time to switch from my skills to yours."

Laurence eyed him. "Oh, now the gifts are good enough?"

"We shall see."

Quentin hung back as a stream of children ran by, and looked to a young Hispanic woman at his side. Mia Torres, Laurence presumed.

"What on Earth is that all about?"

She shrugged at him. "Who can say?"

"I suspect they of all people can." Quentin jogged after the children and called, "Kimberly?"

The red-headed young girl at the back of the stream turned. She looked terrified. Her eyes were wide, and her mouth opened as she shook her head.

"Where are you off to?" Quentin caught up to her.

"Oh." Kimberly's look of fear faded, and Laurence had to wonder what it was she'd been scared of in the first place. "Estelita was listening to a police scanner. Apparently there's a huge wildfire out near Scripps Ranch."

They passed from corridor to garage, where the other girls were in the back of a truck already, and Sebastian was at the wheel.

"And you're going?" Quentin's voice pitched higher in disbelief.

"We're just there to help Sebastian," Soraya yelled from the truck.

Kimberly scrambled in and Sebastian rolled his window down to eye Quentin.

"Get in if you're coming," the older man grunted. "I'm not waiting around."

Laurence screamed in frustration, and it broke him out of the vision. "No! Goddess, Quentin, don't be so... Augh!"

Pepper nosed at his hand. Her ears were flat, and her tail thudded against the ground.

"It's all right, Pepper. Shh." Freddy gently eased the big dog back from Laurence with a light press of his hand to her shoulder, and her ears slowly came forward.

"No. It's not!" Laurence sprang from the couch to search for a television remote, and it took precious seconds to remember that Quentin didn't *have* a damn TV, so he grabbed his phone and jabbed at it to bring up a local news site.

"What is it?" Freddy stood slowly. "What did you see?"

"I think he's gone to fight a fucking wildfire." He couldn't keep the panic from edging into his voice.

Freddy blinked, and looked toward the window as though somehow the ocean might be ablaze. "Where?"

"Scripps Ranch. It's like a half hour east of here, maybe less."

He found a map of the fires.

Scripps Ranch didn't look good.

"Well, how bad can a fire be?" Freddy turned to him.

"You're kidding, right?" Laurence groaned. "No, I guess it always rains in England. SoCal's been in a drought for *years*. There's always a fire, even in winter, but with the summer and the heat waves they just come in all the time. They don't reach Downtown, but they've come in as far as Chula Vista before."

Freddy stared at him. "That's madness," he breathed. "A fire that size... it becomes a firestorm, surely?"

"Yeah." Laurence nodded. "Sucks in all the air at ground level, spews out smoke and embers at the top, gets so hot it can melt metal. It's crazy dangerous and they're heading straight for it."

"They?"

Laurence stuffed his phone away and strode to the door. "Yeah. Sebastian's going. He can control fire."

"Can he control this much fire?"

"I doubt it." Laurence wrenched the door open and sprinted down the stairs.

"Laurence, wait!" The door behind him slammed, and he heard Freddy trot down the steps. "We can't run off after them!"

"Quentin's in there!"

Freddy's hand closed around his arm, and spun Laurence with such force that he ended up facing the Englishman. "And Icky can manage. We cannot!"

"How the fuck do you suppose he can 'manage'?" Laurence screamed in his face.

"Because fire requires three things!" Freddy didn't let go of his arm. His grip was surprisingly painful. "Heat, oxygen, and fuel."

Laurence bared his teeth and fought to wrench his arm free of Freddy's grasp. "So?"

"He's telekinetic," Freddy snapped. "He can deprive fire of fuel."

"You think he can uproot trees?" Laurence spat.

"Can't he?"

Laurence's chest heaved for breath. He didn't know whether he was angry at Quentin for charging into a wildfire, or upset that he might lose the man he loved over something so stupid.

"Think, Laurence." Freddy's voice was gentler, and he slowly released Laurence's arm. "We don't have the luxury of running toward danger, and if you get yourself killed Icky will never forgive me."

"You?"

Freddy snorted. "You don't think he'd ever blame you for your death, do you? No. It'd be my fault. So let's go back upstairs and apply some intelligence to the problem, yes?"

Laurence's fear and anger coalesced into rage in his gut, and he slammed a fist against the wall as he roared his fury. The impact shot pain up his arm, and it hit his impotent anger like a pin to a balloon.

His shoulders sagged as he exhaled in a weak sob.

"Fine," he whispered. "But I swear to the Goddess that if he dies—"

"Yes, yes," Freddy muttered. "Vengeance on all, et cetera."

On you first. But Laurence didn't say it, and from the reaction on Freddy's face he didn't need to.

42

QUENTIN

Wind tore at his shirt and pulled it free from his trousers. Quentin had to grab the mare's mane to keep from falling off as she broke into a gallop.

Debris flew overhead. It made little sense. The wind blew toward the fire, yet far over his head it seemed to go the other way, throwing burning material at the forest.

That's how it spreads, you bloody idiot.

The heat down his left side was intense, and the fire crackled and spat as it ate everything in the pasture. He glanced up in time to see a flurry of bright embers blow toward the trees.

With no time to think, he reached for them and flung them back into the fire, but the concentration it took stole the focus he needed to stay on a horse bareback.

He slid from her back and fell.

The breath was punched from his lungs, and they burned. He felt as though he'd broken his spine.

All he saw overhead was smoke and flame. No sky.

No horses.

He struggled to breathe. Getting winded was nothing new, but that didn't make it any less terrifying when it happened. It was as if he'd been paralyzed, and his brain replayed the familiar panic: *Maybe you have. Maybe this time you really are paralyzed.*

In the middle of a wildfire.

He forced himself onto his side, and pushed away from the ground as he held his breath. He couldn't get air anyway, so he might as well stop trying.

There was fire in the trees.

Quentin lifted his head and looked up. Some of the canopy had caught, and already twigs engulfed in flame began to rain down on the dry undergrowth.

He must only have been flat on his back for thirty seconds at most, but that was all it took for the fire to leap the dirt track.

His lungs strained. His body ached. As the catalog of stresses and pains could finally be felt above the panic in his chest, wetness trickled down the back of his neck.

There was nothing it could be but blood, yet his hand went to it all the same, and came back to him sticky and red.

Head wounds bleed excessively. He'd learned that much. But if he did have one, it could prove problematic. He felt through his hair and found the injury itself at the back of his head, but his skull thankfully didn't feel spongy.

There was nothing he could do about it, so he shifted it down his list of priorities. Below the fire.

The dirt track was no longer viable. Once heat came from both sides of it he'd be cooked if he ran along it. His only chance was to outrun the fire through the forest and hope that Sebastian hadn't driven off yet, so he turned to the right and allowed himself to breathe as he began to shove his way through the dry vegetation.

Dizzy and light-headed, he pressed on while his chest began to recover and blood seeped down the back of his shirt.

It was far easier to use his telekinesis to tear the ground cover out of his way than to forge a path through it. The heat behind him had dried the blood and stuck his shirt to his back, and no matter how deeply he breathed it seemed as though there just wasn't enough air. Whatever he did manage to inhale made him cough, which exacerbated his headache and the dizziness which was growing worse with every passing minute.

You are going to die.

The thought emerged with such clarity that it made him stop. He leaned against a tree for support as his head swam.

Continuing forward as his situation worsened would resolve nothing. Turning back was fatal.

You are going to die!

"Shut up!" he hissed. "Think! *Think!*"

It was hard to fight through the wave of drowsiness which swept through him. Had he lost a few seconds there, or had the flames leaped three feet closer in an instant?

Concussion, his brain helpfully offered.

He'd really begun to regret taking Mia's first aid course now. All it seemed to have done was inform him of exactly what was about to kill him.

God, Laurence didn't even know where he was.

He swallowed tightly and reached for his phone. His hands skimmed across his shirt for precious seconds before he remembered that he'd left his jacket in the truck.

The chagrin at not even being able to say goodbye to Laurence was the final straw. Quentin leaned against the tree and turned to stare directly into the fire.

"All right, then," he croaked. "Let's see what can be done here."

It wasn't a candle. God, it wasn't even twenty candles. No, this was a monster. A giant which would consume all in its path and care little for the lives it took. He had to be insane to try to control it, but if he didn't—if he couldn't—he'd be dead, and the state of his mental health wouldn't be a problem anymore.

He pushed away from the tree and spread his arms to steady himself. For one giddy moment he felt like an orchestra conductor, his hands raised before the unstoppable force of a wildfire, and he laughed at the preposterous image.

The fire didn't stop.

Concentrate, you bloody fool.

With a roar which was drowned out by the hellish clamor of the fire, he snapped trees and rained splintered wood down on the ruined undergrowth. One by one the desiccated husks long starved of water were torn apart and flung into the flames, followed by fallen branches, scraps of underbrush, anything around him which could be flammable. He turned on the spot and threw one tree after another into the encroaching flames.

The sound was horrendous. Dry wood cracked like gunshots, and when it caught fire it crackled and screeched.

Quentin turned back to the fire and gritted his teeth, then swept his arms back to his sides.

The fire parted.

Sweat soaked his shirt. It stung his eyes and blurred his sight. He blinked and shook his head, but that just made his head pound all the more.

Fire swept toward the edge of his newly-forged perimeter.

"No!" he snarled. "No you bloody well don't!"

He tore the fire apart again, and directed it to either side of him. It gobbled tree after tree, greedy and unstoppable, until he stood surrounded by it in his own self-made clearing.

His lungs were on fire. He coughed. Tears streamed down his cheeks.

Hold.

All he needed to do was outlast the fire. It would pass him by and leave smoldering in its wake, and then he could sleep. Just for a few minutes. Just until his head didn't hurt anymore.

Where fire weakened trees, he knocked them down. Where fire threatened to step into his perimeter, he shoved it aside. The closer the fire came to him the more he was able to use it to widen the circle of bare earth around him until the space was so wide that he felt a faint flutter of cool air against his cheek.

He fought with every last glimmer of strength left in him until the flames left him alone and the only red in the sky above came from the setting sun.

Only then did he fall.

43

LAURENCE

Laurence prowled while Freddy continued to "research." How the man could sit here and play with his phone while Quentin was out there somewhere was something Laurence couldn't wrap his head around.

Unless Freddy was hoping that if they sat here long enough Quentin would die.

He hated the thought the moment it occurred to him, but the more he stewed on it the more it made sense. While twins, Freddy was the younger of the two, and if Quentin were dead Freddy stood to inherit everything. The castle, the titles, the money, all of it.

Freddy couldn't have traveled to San Diego and waited all that time in his swanky penthouse on the off-chance that Quentin would die while he was here though, right? That made no sense.

Freddy glanced his way and quirked an eyebrow. "I can't tell which you will wear a hole through first," he murmured. "That carpet, or the back of my head."

"I don't know what research is supposed to achieve," Laurence growled at him.

"Nor do I, or it would take considerably less time to research. Look." He laid his cellphone on the dining table. "Wilson has been attending some rather swish events these past few months."

"So?"

"So he is hardly the sort of fellow one would invite to those events," Freddy said dryly.

"He's using his gift to get in. I don't see—"

Freddy cut him off with a raised hand. "Or he's being invited," he said. "Either way he is hobnobbing far above his reach. Why?"

Laurence's hands curled into fists at his side, and he snarled. "Money."

"Don't be silly. Nobody carries cash to these events."

"Jewelry."

"Perhaps." Freddy pursed his lips. "We should speak with some of the other guests about these things, find out what they remember of them, whether they lost any precious earrings, whether he solicited them for anything else."

"Okay. Sure." Laurence bobbed his head sharply. "You go do that. Take the cab. It's probably still waiting."

"It had better be." Freddy gathered up his phone and eyed Laurence. "Are you sure you won't rush off to do anything foolish?"

"Maybe!"

"Well, don't. Icky will never forgive me."

Laurence bit back his response and gave another nod. "I'll stay here."

He managed to stay for ten minutes. That was pretty good as far as he was concerned.

Laurence fed the dogs and left them plenty of water, then slipped away down the stairs and out into the late afternoon heat.

There wasn't a single sign of anything wrong in the skies above. No smoke, not even a dark cloud. If he didn't have access to the news he wouldn't know a damn thing about the wildfires.

That was how Quentin lived, wasn't it? Utterly oblivious to the world around him?

Laurence snorted and closed the front door behind him.

He made it all the way to the gate before his cell rang. Probably Mom wondering why he'd been gone all day when Freddy had only intended to borrow him for a quick chat.

With a huff, he grabbed the phone, then his heart thudded as he saw the caller ID.

Quen.

He thumbed the screen and almost yelled into it. "Quentin?"

"No. But we have eyes on him. Where are you?"

"Who the fuck are you? Where's Quentin? I swear if you've hurt him—"

"Laurence, it's me!" The voice grunted. "Sebastian Wagner. Quentin left his jacket with us. There are five missed calls from you on his phone."

Laurence took a breath and tried to get a grip. If he blurted out what he knew, he'd be handing over a secret he'd guarded ever since he met Wilson. He had a tactical advantage right now, whether or not it ever came into play, and one wrong word could blow that advantage away.

"What's going on?" He gripped the gate to redirect his frustration into something physical.

Sebastian sighed. "We were headed out on a training run. Quentin invited himself along."

"Who's 'we'?"

"Myself, Soraya, Estelita, and Kimberly."

Into a wildfire? You call that a training run?

Laurence bit his tongue. "Okay. What happened?"

"There's a wildfire out at Scripps Ranch—"

"What?" Laurence cut in. If he *didn't* sound surprised at this point it'd be suspicious.

"The plan was clear," Sebastian snapped. "We found a way in, Estelita and Soraya were looking out for anyone in trouble, I was to go in and aid whoever we could and then get out fast."

Laurence scowled and paced back toward the front door. His feet crunched on gravel. "What went wrong?"

"The wind was against us. Quentin wouldn't allow the kids to be left alone in the car, and he can't drive, so I had to stay with the truck."

"Of course he wouldn't—" Laurence almost screamed into the

phone. "So you let him go alone."

"It was the only way to proceed. Soraya kept tabs on him. He got the target out, as well as her dogs and horses."

Laurence could hear it. The three letter word that Sebastian hadn't said. So he said it instead.

"But?"

Sebastian huffed. "The fire spread across the pasture too fast. The horses bolted. Quentin got thrown. The way Soraya's describing things he's got a concussion, but nothing's broken. He's—" Sebastian hesitated.

"Don't fucking hold out on me, man." Laurence paced to the gate again. "What is it?"

"He's directing the fire, Laurence."

Laurence stopped in his tracks. His mouth was dry.

"He what?"

"I don't know how. Soraya says it's like Moses parting the Red Sea. The fire's going around him. Did you know he could do this?"

Laurence shook his head numbly. "He's telekinetic," he breathed. "Maybe he's... Maybe he's moving whatever's on fire? Soraya could be mistaken..."

"I don't think she is." Sebastian sounded grim. "Laurence, even I'm not capable of standing in the middle of a wildfire and controlling it like that. What is it you two aren't telling us?"

"He's telekinetic!" Laurence shouted it into the phone. "He can't control fire!"

"Yes," Sebastian said. "He can. Where are you? I'll come pick you up and hopefully by the time we get there the fire will have passed and we can get to him."

Laurence narrowed his eyes. No way was he going to hand over Quentin's address, so instead he said, "La Jolla. Prospect. The Starbucks there."

"Got it. I'll be ten minutes."

Laurence hung up without another word. He had ten minutes to run to Prospect Street in the middle of a heat wave.

He let himself out through the gate and set off north as fast as he could go.

44

LAURENCE

Laurence made it to the Starbucks with a minute to spare, so he darted into the washroom and rinsed the sweat from his face and hair with cold water. The cool drips down the back of his neck helped, and he squeezed his curls to get the excess water out.

He checked his reflection. His skin was still pink, but not the bright red from a cross-town run, and he took deep breaths to bring his heart rate under control.

There. That was as close as he could get to matching the lie he'd told. It'd have to do.

He breezed out of the coffee shop and lingered by the curb, checking his phone for any messages or missed calls, but there weren't any.

A huge black Dodge pulled up and Sebastian leaned out of the window. "Laurence!"

Laurence pocketed his phone and circled the truck, climbing into the passenger seat. "Go," he said as he buckled up.

Sebastian didn't argue. He pulled out into traffic and flipped off the woman who honked at him, then rolled his window back up. "Soraya's still got him," he said.

Laurence twisted in his seat and looked to the back. Estelita gave him a small smile, while Kim stared fixedly at her own knees. Soraya's gaze was unfocused.

"But Scripps Ranch is like twenty miles away," Laurence breathed.

"Yeah. Looks like when she cares for the person she's looking for she can go a whole lot farther." Sebastian grimaced.

Laurence eyed the expression, but didn't ask. He imagined Sebastian wasn't too pleased that Soraya had found Kim at the gun show, and now that she could see Quentin from several towns away it suggested she was a lot stronger than Wilson had thought.

It also meant Quentin wasn't safe from Wilson's prying, if he set Soraya on Quentin at any point. The apartment wasn't safe from her gift anymore. If Soraya cared enough, maybe there was no limit to how far she could see.

Soraya cared about Quentin.

Laurence rubbed his jaw as he looked forward through the windshield. "How are we gonna get to him?"

"I'm hoping we can overshoot and double back. If we follow the path the fire took we should reach him without it coming at us."

"And if we can't do that?"

Sebastian shook his head. "I don't know. I don't have a Plan B."

Laurence snarled softly. "Then Plan A better work."

Sebastian did some ambulance-chasing to cut through traffic, then peeled off the road before cops could pull him over for it.

From the back seat, Estelita gave a steady stream of updates.

"Cops, half a mile ahead. Fire department, couple hundred yards, left. Ambulance, half a mile behind, coming up on us."

Sebastian said nothing as he drove, and he drove like he had a lot of experience evading other vehicles and zooming over rough terrain.

"Soraya?" Laurence muttered.

"He's still standing," was all she said.

Laurence ground his teeth. He hated this, hated relying on virtual strangers to save Quentin's life.

He should have been there.

How *dare* Quentin go into a wildfire without him?

Sebastian veered off the road and up an embankment, and an ambulance shot past where he'd been moments before, so he swung the truck back down and floored the gas after it.

Laurence cursed as he was thrown around in his seat and banged his head against the padded roof.

The ambulance got them another couple of miles, then Sebastian pulled off the road again and onto a dirt track.

The farther they were from the road, the more of the devastation Laurence could see. Entire pastures to his right were nothing more than flat, brown earth which smoldered and glowed. Beyond them, the skeletons of trees still burned, little flames licking up them and dancing around the trunks.

It was a wasteland.

To his left, the fire raged in patches. Dead trunks were caked in soot and jabbed into the evening sky like bones. Charred remains hung from them, ruined. Beyond the tree carcasses were patches of orange, which belched out black into the sky.

The reek of smoke slowly permeated the car, brought in by the AC and robbed of any heat. It was bitter and cloying.

Nothing could have survived this, right?

Soraya's head turned. "He's down," she squeaked.

Laurence swallowed down his panic. "What do you mean?"

"I mean he's collapsed. He's—" She tilted her head. "He's breathing. Just. But I don't think he's conscious."

"The fire?"

"He's clear." Her arm shot forward, between the seats. "That way."

Sebastian's fingers tightened around the wheel and he shook his head numbly. "This is insane. The whole place is a mess. Are you sure this is the right way?"

"Of course!"

The truck bounced along the dirt road a few more minutes.

Swirls of ash danced ahead of them, and the wipers disposed of a thin layer of the stuff every once in a while.

"Stop!" Soraya yelled.

Sebastian slammed on the brakes and the truck skidded to a stop.

Laurence unbuckled and kicked his door open. "Where?" he shouted.

Soraya pointed at the trees.

"Laurence!" Sebastian yelled.

He ignored the pyrokinetic and threw himself out into the brittle, hot air. He hit the ground at a run and took off towards the trees.

The area was utterly devastated. There wasn't as much underfoot as he might have expected, yet to either side were the ruined wrecks of bushes and grasses, as though a path had been torn from the ground.

Laurence followed it. He ran until the blood pounded in his ears and his breath stung. He ran until the trees fell away and there was nothing but torn trees and ash-covered ground.

He shot out into the clearing. It was vast. Absolutely huge. Easily two or three hundred feet in diameter. Around the outermost edge was the most ash, and it faded toward the center, where a still form lay unmoving and dark in the fading evening light.

Blood assaulted his nostrils. He stumbled over a stray tree root.

Quentin was white against the ground, with smears of ash and soot across his forehead, his shirt.

Laurence slid to his knees by Quentin's side and felt for a pulse at his throat.

"C'mon, baby," he whispered hoarsely. "C'mon. Don't leave me."

The skin beneath his fingers thrummed with a slow, steady pulse, and Laurence choked with relief. He scooped the body into his arms and clutched it to his chest as he stood.

Quentin's head lolled against Laurence's shoulder. The stink of blood grew stronger. Not the bright scent of a fresh wound, but the metal aftertaste of a long-dried one.

Laurence turned and began the long walk back to the truck. He held Quentin to him as though he carried the world's most precious cargo, careful not to bump or jolt him as they moved.

"I've got you, baby," he breathed as he kissed Quentin's forehead. "Stay with me. I've got you."

45

QUENTIN

HE WAS AWARE THAT HE WAS LYING IN A HOSPITAL BED BEFORE HE had fully woken. His familiarity with the process was so deeply ingrained that everything from the faintly antiseptic smell to the distant sounds of chatter were completely normal, and the only question was one of cause.

He flexed his hands and found the pull of tape across the back of one, which indicated the presence of a cannula, and the light pinch of a pulse monitor on his index finger. But he wasn't intubated, which was always a plus to any hospital awakening.

God, his head hurt.

With a slow wince, he cracked open one eye, but thankfully the lights were off. It wasn't wholly dark, but nor was it blinding, and he was able to open his other eye.

This wasn't an English hospital. He had his own room, rather than a curtained-off corner of a larger ward. And there was a shape to his right which spilled across the bed at his thighs.

Quentin blinked a few times and raised his unburdened hand to wipe his eyes, but the fact remained that he just couldn't see properly, as though everything had a faintly out-of-focus blur around the edges.

The dark shape had curly hair.

He squinted and reached for it.

The curls were thick, weighty. The rest of the shape was a body, slumped in a chair with one arm thrown across Quentin's thighs, head resting on the sheets.

Laurence.

Had Laurence been with him when... whatever it was had happened?

He didn't know, and it hurt too much to try to remember, so he laid his hand to rest across Laurence's shoulders and closed his eyes.

"Quen?"

Quentin stirred to life. He stifled a yawn, and was rewarded by a stab of pain to the back of his head, so he stopped that at once and opened his eyes.

"Oh, thank the Goddess, you're awake." Laurence squeezed his hand and pressed his lips to it.

The poor boy looked terrified.

"I'm all right." Quentin crinkled his nose at how rough and sluggish his voice sounded.

"You've got a concussion." Laurence wiped his eyes. "They say you can go home this afternoon, but you've gotta rest up for a couple of weeks. They say cognitive rest, too. Like, no reading. No piano. I've talked to Mom; I'm taking the time off 'cause you need someone with you, okay?"

Quentin began a nod, then decided against it.

"Why am I here?" he wheezed.

"Nuh-uh." Laurence's jaw set, and his eyes blazed with anger. "Cognitive rest. I'm not getting into it, baby. It can wait."

Quentin frowned as a sense of disquiet slowly enveloped him.

He'd upset Laurence.

Whatever it was that he did, however he ended up here, damage had been done.

"All right," he breathed.

Laurence gripped his hand, and he squeezed it as hard as he could.

HE LISTENED as the doctor ran through a list of do's and don'ts, but his head hurt to try and remember it all.

"It's okay, baby," Laurence murmured. "I've got this."

"The bandages can come off after a couple of days," the doctor was saying. "They're only there to protect the stitches. If there's a bleed, of course, he needs to come back immediately."

Quentin frowned and raised his hand to his head. Much of his hair was hidden beneath bandages, and when he took his hand away he had the oddest sense of deja vu, as though he'd done this before, but last time there was blood on his fingers.

He blinked at the disorienting difference between reality and expectation. His hand was clean.

"No Advil. Tylenol only. Absolutely no drugs or alcohol. No unattended bathing. If there are any residual side effects after ten days he needs to come back in."

"Got it," Laurence said.

"Good. How are you feeling, Mr. d'Arcy?"

Quentin blinked. "It isn't *mister*," he muttered.

Laurence rolled his eyes. "That means he's fine."

A WEEK of bed rest was dull at the best of times, but cognitive rest was a whole new level of hell. Laurence refused to engage in anything other than small-talk, and certainly didn't allow him to sit at the piano for any length of time. Myriam sent flowers, Laurence walked the dogs every morning, and all Quentin could do was lie in bed or—if he felt particularly bored of that—lie on a sofa and watch the ocean.

His vision righted itself after a couple of days, thank goodness. He hadn't been ready to incorporate glasses into his aesthetic.

Little by little, patches of memory would uncover themselves, like a flower opening in the morning sun. Some parts didn't come back, but he could extrapolate those. He was used to doing that.

He remembered freeing horses from a pasture.

He remembered realizing that he'd injured his head.

Logically, then, there had been a fall. Most likely he had tried to ride the horses to safety and fallen off in doing so.

He remembered the frantic fight to save his own life.

He knew the flames had engulfed trees several times his own height, and yet he'd directed them away from himself and stripped enough vegetation to keep the worst of the heat away.

Again, some logical extrapolation was required. He wasn't dead, and Laurence was here. Sebastian must have found him and taken him to the hospital and then let Laurence know where to find him, which was jolly decent of him.

Visitors came and went. Freddy. Sebastian. Ethan. Myriam. Even some of the children stopped by, especially Kimberly and Soraya, who came to visit every other day.

But it was impossible to shake the knowledge that Laurence was deeply upset with him.

"It's been almost a fortnight," Quentin groused. "I'm quite certain that I can at least step outside for some fresh air."

"Sure." Laurence fussed with Quentin's hair from behind. He parted it with his fingers and peered at the stitches.

Quentin scowled at their reflections in the bathroom mirror. Despite the fact that they both had significantly improved recovery rates, Laurence insisted on making him rest the entire prescribed period and then some more.

It was punishment, of that he was convinced.

"If you promise not to run off without me and nearly get yourself killed."

Quentin caught Laurence's reflected stare and froze at the intensity of it.

"I see," he said softly.

"No, I don't think you do!" Laurence blinked swiftly and stepped out of the bathroom, stalking like a caged tiger.

Quentin took a moment to smooth his locks back into place.

Thank goodness he had inherited a spectacularly dense head of hair. It would cover the scar.

Another scar.

He sighed and turned out the light as he followed. He paused in the bedroom only to slide his feet into slippers, and then continued out into the living room.

Laurence paced as he wiped at his eyes.

Quentin lowered himself into an armchair and curled his feet up by his side. He adjusted the hem of his bathrobe to ensure that he remained decent.

"I could have lost you!" Laurence's voice shook. His skin was pale, yet his cheeks were dotted with pink. His hands wrung together as he wore a trench into the carpet. "And you didn't even tell me where you'd gone. Don't you understand?" Laurence hiccupped. "Don't you even *care?*"

Quentin dipped his head forward.

Here it came. The argument which had been brewing for two weeks, lurking beneath the surface of every strained word and chaste kiss as it waited to strike.

God, he loathed arguments. Raised voices, anger, all of it. It made him feel small. Weak.

Out of control.

This was worse. Infinitely so, because Laurence was right, and because Laurence had made sure to wait until Quentin was recovered enough before he breathed a word of it.

"I'm sorry," he whispered.

"Sorry?" Laurence's back and forth came to an abrupt halt. "Sorry! You ran off into a fucking wildfire! You nearly died! You went away and you didn't even think to text me, let alone pick up the fucking phone and do me the simple fucking courtesy of telling me what you were going to do!" Tears ran in rivulets down his cheeks, and he'd given up chasing them away with his hands. They dripped onto his T-shirt and left dark dots there. His face was reddened now, all traces of paleness gone. "I wouldn't ever have known, you know. I would have had to look back on it and watch you burn to death to find out what happened to you. You did that,

Quentin! You made me watch you fall off a horse, you made me watch you drag yourself into a forest, and you made me watch you fight a wildfire until you damn well collapsed from the heat and the smoke inhalation and the strain." His hiccupping grew worse and he collapsed onto the couch. "When were you going to tell me?" he sobbed. "When were you ever going to tell me?"

It hurt. Laurence's tears, the pain in his voice, the hiccups, it stabbed Quentin straight through the heart and made his eyes sting.

He had done this to Laurence, and it was unbearable. The poor boy had clung to this anguish so that Quentin could recover from his injuries. He had refused to let go of this burning stone and held it to his chest this whole time, and the agony it had caused him was palpable.

He'd done it for Quentin. So that Quentin could get well again, even though Quentin was the one to inflict this torment on him to begin with.

Quentin felt utterly wretched. He loved only one person in his life, and he had caused misery to him.

"I was wrong." He struggled to raise his voice above a mumble. "You deserve considerably better. I am an idiot, Laurence. I didn't think. I..." He ran out of words, and all he could do was shake his head as tears fell down his own cheeks.

He had to stop. He had to regain his composure or he would hurt Laurence more, so he wiped his cheeks and drew a deep breath.

"Do you care what would have happened to me if you'd died?" Laurence hissed. "I'd never be sober again. How can you be so... so selfish!"

Quentin closed his eyes briefly. "I am unused to..." He tailed off.

"To giving a shit about anyone but yourself," Laurence finished. "This has to change, Quen. I can't go through this again. I can't!"

"I understand." His throat constricted around the words, and he struggled to push down his panic.

Laurence would leave him.

Guilt and terror crashed through him. They swirled together to break down the barrier he'd loosely erected around his panic, and it broke free with a vengeance.

Wind tore through the apartment. It scattered envelopes and flowers. Pepper barked and ran to hide in the kitchen, and Grace hurried after her.

"No." Laurence leaped from the sofa and closed the distance between them until he leaned over Quentin, and his fingers dug into Quentin's arms. "You do not get to do this. You calm down right fucking now, Quen. Do it! Look at me!"

He couldn't meet Laurence's eyes.

"Damn it, Quen, I'm not fucking leaving you! Not unless you pull another stupid-ass stunt like this one! Listen to me!" Laurence's grip tightened. "Get a grip!"

Quentin's head lolled back against the armchair and he found himself only inches from Laurence's tear-stained face.

"I'm asking you to *change*," Laurence snarled. "That's all. You've gotta grow up, Quen. You're not alone now, and if you want it to stay that way you have *got* to remember that I exist!"

"You do," Quentin said. "God, Laurence, I'm so sorry."

"Yeah, well you're gonna be sorry you lost your security deposit if you don't sort your shit out, hon." Laurence grimaced.

Quentin forced himself to look away. There was nothing in Laurence's expression that could help him regain control, so he fixed on the door as he took every scrap of trepidation and folded it away until the winds settled.

Laurence's hands left his arms, but they moved to his legs and pulled them from the seat cushion. Laurence repositioned Quentin like a mannequin, sitting him squarely in the center of the armchair, and then he straddled Quentin's lap, his knees on either side of Quentin's thighs.

Laurence's hands cradled his cheeks and turned Quentin's head back to face him.

"When were you going to tell me," Laurence whispered, "that you could control fire?"

Quentin licked his lips and focused on Laurence's chin. "I don't know," he admitted.

"Baby..." Laurence sighed and leaned his forehead against Quentin's. "You know I don't like fire."

"That did factor into my decision," Quentin confessed.

Laurence closed his eyes, and his shoulders sagged. "I came over once, and it smelled of burning. I thought you'd tried to cook."

"I'm sorry."

Laurence moved awkwardly until he could sit across Quentin's lap and curl up against his chest. His fingers gripped the edge of Quentin's bathrobe, and he laid his cheek against Quentin's shoulder.

"Promise me," he choked out, "you won't ever risk your life without me again."

Quentin breathed slowly as he wrapped his arms around Laurence and held him tight. "I promise."

"This isn't over." Laurence slid an arm around Quentin's back, slipping it between him and the chair.

Quentin nodded a little. Laurence's anger would take time to subside. Worse, Quentin had to rebuild the damage he had done, and recovering Laurence's trust would take time.

"I understand," he murmured.

46

LAURENCE

Laurence had to get a cab all the way to the shop. All this time without one of the trucks, he'd almost forgotten that Quentin's apartment was sixty bucks away from his own home.

He winced as he paid. Sixty dollars was a week's groceries. It was two shirts and a pair of jeans. What it wasn't supposed to be was a damn cab fare.

The bell jangled overhead as he pushed his way into the shop. Entering via the front door was weird, too, but once everything was back to normal he'd be here on time, in the truck, using the back door and—

He stopped in the middle of the store.

There was a total stranger at the cash register.

Laurence looked back to the brass bell which hung over the door, then at the stranger. The guy was at least wearing a Jack in the Green apron, so either he was a great burglar or a lousy employee. Just when Laurence figured nobody could get more slack than Rodger, too.

"Hey," Laurence said. He started toward the counter again.

The lad started in surprise, then laughed nervously and waved his hand. "Oh my God, it *was* the bell! I'm so sorry! Can I help you?"

The pitch of his voice was slightly nasal, and there was a telltale flatness to his *s* sounds. Laurence's gaze flitted quickly to the younger man's ears and caught the clear tubes of hearing aid hooks which disappeared behind his ears.

His irritation deflated. Only an asshole snarked at a deaf guy for not hearing something.

"I'm Laurence." He offered his hand across the counter. "Myriam's son. Is she here?"

The young man slid slender fingers into his and shook enthusiastically. "Oh, hey! Yeah, she's out back. Good to meet you at last. Ethan's told me so much about you!"

Laurence's eyes narrowed. "You're Aiden?"

"Uh-huh!" Aiden grinned, and his bright blue eyes were alight with excitement. "He's out back too. Got more of a gift for heavy lifting than I have, that's for sure." His cheeks flushed.

"Right." Laurence blinked. "Mom hired *both* of you?"

Aiden's laugh was a light thing, like a bird. "Yes! Isn't it awesome?"

"Ha. Yeah. I'm, uh. I'm gonna go catch up. It's good meeting you. We should do a thing some time."

"We should!"

Laurence chuckled as he made his way through the bead curtain.

Myriam and Ethan were waiting.

"Bright blessings," he said, but then his attention was stolen away by the sight of the new, improved back room.

It had been completely reorganized. Pots were arranged by size and then color. Loose sundries were no longer in piles, but instead tucked away neatly in boxes with clip-lock lids. There were no more cardboard boxes to be found other than those which were flat-packed and ready to put customer orders in for delivery.

"Bright blessings. Ethan did it," Myriam chuckled as she bustled around the table and wrapped her arms around Laurence. She kissed his cheek. "Isn't it wonderful?"

Laurence hugged his mom and eyed Ethan over her shoulder. "Who knew you had a thing for interior decorating?"

Ethan gave a light shrug. "Dude, I've been tending bar for

years. If there's one thing I know it's that a tidy workplace is a way safer workplace. More efficient, too."

"Speaking of bartending, why *are* you working here now?" Laurence peeled back from his mom and eyed them both.

"Made sense. I know the things. So if shit goes down here, you aren't caught short and forced to out yourself to any staff who are here when it happens." Ethan tapped the side of his nose. "That's just smart."

"And Aiden?" Laurence gestured to the curtain.

"Well, I thought that you could tell him, dear." Myriam smiled faintly.

Laurence eyed her. "Okay. Spill. What do you know?"

"You're just going to have to trust me." She patted his hand.

He huffed, then thumbed to the shop again. "He can't hear the bell."

"Yeah, his tinnitus messes him around sometimes," Ethan said. "Especially with ringing sounds. Myriam's ordered a flashing alarm system."

"It'll be fitted later in the week." She smiled. "We have a greenhouse at last, too."

Laurence lowered himself onto a stool by the table.

Two weeks. Two damn weeks was all he'd been gone for, and everything had changed.

Myriam sat by him and reached for his hand. "How is Quentin?"

Laurence doubled forward until he could lightly bang his forehead against the table. "A pain in the ass."

She laughed gently. "I meant more recently."

"We can't even fight properly." He straightened up and pushed hair back from his eyes. "If he loses control everything blows up, and I—" His throat closed around the words and he swallowed.

"You wanna have an all-out, and because he has to keep a lid on his shit the air hasn't cleared," Ethan concluded.

"It's just *hanging* there." Laurence huffed. "He could have died, and I just... I need to know he's got it through his damn head what he did."

"I guess the only way to know that is if he doesn't do it again."

Ethan turned away to fill the kettle. "And hanging around waiting for something to *not* happen is... Yeah. Like hoping the earthquake doesn't come, I guess."

"I can't shake the feeling the earthquake's always gonna come." Laurence bit his lip. "I think I know why he did it, though."

"Because he's a reckless asshole who reckons he's a hero?" Ethan fished out four mugs and lined them up.

Myriam chuckled faintly.

"Yeah," Laurence admitted. "That too."

"Well, you can't say that you didn't know what you were getting into with that boy," Myriam said. "It was all right there at the Valentine's party."

Ethan glanced over to them. "What happened?"

Laurence gave him a black look. "Okay, yeah. He stood up to a god and got his ass handed to him for it."

"I'm gonna need to hear more of that story later." Ethan distributed tea bags. "So he's a stubborn idiot who bites off more than he can chew a lot, huh? Then I guess you can't change that. You can only mitigate it."

"Assuming I want to deal with that shit."

"Oh, c'mon. You love him." Ethan chuckled as he poured water into the mugs. "Either buckle up for the ride, or cut loose while you still can, but don't sit around moaning about the way he is when that's the guy you fell for in the first place."

"Shut up, Obi-Wan."

"No, you. So what's this major insight into the thought process of a crazy guy you've found through all your peaceful meditation on the meaning of life?"

Laurence flipped Ethan the finger, but it was no use: the man's back was turned to him at the moment. He leaned to one side so he could dig his wallet out of his pocket, then he dug through it until he found a scrap of crumpled pink paper.

"When we got Quen to the hospital," he murmured, "I had to go through his wallet to get his health insurance, and I found this."

He unfolded the paper and smoothed it out flat against the table. The words written on it were scribbled there in a hurried hand and then smudged from some dampness the paper had gone through, but they were still legible.

I didn't choose to go.

He nudged the paper toward his mom and watched as she picked it up.

Her hazel eyes skimmed across it, and her eyebrows pinched together.

Ethan came around the table and looked over Myriam's shoulder. He frowned a while, and then his eyes widened. "Oh. You think whoever wrote this was... what? Forced to do something by this Wilson guy, and they've sneaked this note to Quentin to get help?"

"I think it's one of the kids." Laurence nodded. "And I think he figured that they were headed into this wildfire against their will too, so he went with them to protect them."

"Huh. Well. That takes us back to the Big Damn Hero theory, right?" Ethan went to the sink to begin fishing tea bags out of mugs. "And without Quentin there we've got no idea what else they've been up to in that house. Does that mean the spy mission's a bust?"

"I dunno. I'll have to catch up with Freddy and see what he's been working on. He wouldn't discuss it around Quen."

"In case of heroics, right?" Ethan brought the tea over and set it on the table.

"Thanks." Laurence shook his head. "I dunno, I think he's more concerned for Quentin's recovery and didn't want to risk it. He was super tight-lipped about stuff whenever he stopped by. I'll have to go see him and catch up."

"Well before you do that, dear," Myriam murmured, "you should speak with Aiden."

He eyed her. "Seriously? What if they split up? Ethan falls in love with every guy he ever meets. No offense, man."

"None taken."

"They don't have to be in love with each other to be good friends to you," Myriam stated. "Why don't I take the register for a while?" She took her mug with a smile and wandered to the curtain without leaving any space for Laurence to inject an argument.

Laurence sulked into his tea until the curtain clattered again, and Aiden appeared.

"I'm told there's tea!" he said with glee.

"Oh, yeah, there's tea." Laurence nodded to the mug and then sighed. "Why don't you take a seat? We, uh." He glanced to Ethan, who nodded. "We need to talk."

Aiden's delicate eyebrows rose in alarm, and he climbed up onto a stool across from Laurence.

Ethan sat by his side and wrapped an arm around Aiden's waist.

"Okay," said Laurence. "Shit. Where even to start?" He licked his lips, then shook his head. "The beginning, I guess."

47

QUENTIN

HE HAD TO GO BACK. NOW THAT LAURENCE WAS RETURNED TO work, Quentin had little to do but move forward, and there was still a plan to follow.

He watched the dogs as they slept together in the kitchen, and weighed up his options.

That he had to go was not in doubt. But something fundamental itched at him. It made him jittery and disconnected. It was more than the argument he had with Laurence yesterday, more than the dissatisfied feeling of things left unsaid and problems which lingered unsolved. There was an elementary part of himself that he had lost contact with, and it left him with a gnawing nothingness inside.

Quentin weighed his cellphone in his palm. If he were to go to the mansion, he must text Laurence first.

His eyes drew themselves toward the piano.

No practice for two weeks. He was sore from the lack of music. It distressed him on a most primitive level that he didn't try to understand.

He put the phone away and crossed to the piano. His frame eased onto the bench with the familiarity of muscle memory, and he raised the key cover.

The keys lay there. They waited for his touch.

One couldn't rush these things.

Quentin reached for his headphones, plugged them in, slipped them over his head, and made sure that they were comfortable. He began to stretch his hands, breathing calmly as he loosened his wrists and rolled his shoulders. He didn't rush. This wasn't something to hurry.

When he was ready, he laid his fingers against the keys and centered himself, and then eased himself into a series of warm-up triad scales. C Major. G Major. D Major.

It took time for his fingers to find their way, but as they did, the distress began to melt away, and left something else in its wake. An epiphany of sorts, he supposed.

Quentin had carted this piano across entire continents for six years. Music had been a formative part of his life since he was five years old. But it wasn't until he lost it that he truly understood how much it meant to him.

God. What a bloody fool he'd been.

HE TEXTED Laurence before even calling for a taxi.

Be careful, was Laurence's reply.

Quentin pursed his lips, and then tapped out, *I will*.

It was as though a weight had been lifted from him. For all that Laurence's request had felt like a dreadful limitation, he now saw it from Laurence's perspective.

From the point of view of a man who had almost lost his music.

This was no limitation Laurence had tethered him with. It ran deeper. It was a request for respect, and Laurence should never have been forced to ask in the first place.

He emerged from the taxi into the sweltering July heat. The sun thrashed down mercilessly without a shred of cloud to impede its assault, and he hurried for the shade of the mansion's tree-lined wall. His finger poked the intercom.

By the time the gate opened, his shirt was drenched.

Sebastian led him to Kane's office and fetched a glass of water for him en route.

"You sure you should be on your feet?"

"No lingering effects," Quentin assured him. "Other than a failure to acclimatize to this bloody awful weather."

Sebastian snorted at him. "What is it with the British and the weather?"

"We have quite a lot of it." Quentin chuckled and sipped his water. "Thank you," he added, shifting to a more serious tone.

Sebastian raised his chin. "For what?"

"For fetching Laurence. For letting him know what had happened."

Sebastian grunted at that. "It was the right thing to do. Don't sweat it."

"Thank you all the same."

He was buggered if he was going to take people for granted again.

He settled across the desk from Kane and placed his glass on a coaster as the door clicked softly closed behind him.

Kane sifted through a sheaf of envelopes and refused to acknowledge Quentin at first, but Quentin was well used to this treatment from his father. A crook would not make him break the silence first.

It took two full minutes before Kane set the envelopes down and cleared his throat. "You were just gonna keep that from us, huh?"

Quentin raised his eyebrow. Kane had chosen to begin with his power, it seemed, and not his well-being.

"I was unsure of it myself," he murmured. "I had not put it to any great test. In truth I think that had I not been in the situation we entered into with the wildfire I still would not know. There is a great difference between lighting a few candles and—" he waved a hand airily "—whatever I managed to do there."

"Two gifts," Kane hissed. He put the envelopes down and they scattered across the desk. "You and Laurence both. What are you?"

Quentin blinked at that. "I don't have an answer for you."

"Why not?"

"Why does it matter?" he countered. His gaze fell to the envelopes, which had a familiar air to them. Smaller than a letter, yet a little thicker.

Invitations.

"How can you be trusted if you aren't even a psychic?" Kane scowled and began gathering up the envelopes into a single pile.

"What else could I possibly be?" Quentin tutted and reached for his water, which allowed him one final glimpse of the envelopes before Kane swept them into a drawer. For the most part there were few postal marks that he could see, which elevated them to the hand-delivered sort, whether by courier or staff.

"How should I know? Maybe it's magic!"

Quentin's hand trembled, and the ice in his glass clinked against the edge.

"It is not magic," he snapped, far more forcefully than he had intended. He placed the glass down and withdrew his hands to his lap.

Kane eyed him as he sat back in his chair. "Wait," he said. "Are you saying magic is real?"

"Don't be absurd." Quentin narrowed his eyes. All his focus was on tamping down the flicker of fear which sprang to life at the suggestion of magic, and the last thing he wanted was a bloody philosophical debate on the stuff.

"You've seen it!" Kane leaned forward in earnest. "How does it work? What can it accomplish? Is it inherent, or can it be taught?"

You power-mad despot!

Quentin bit back those words. The struggle to keep his terror in check was not eased by Kane's sudden interest in knowledge he had convinced himself that Quentin possessed.

"I do not know," he spat. "I do not care to know. Magic is not to be trusted, and that is that. I did not come here to discuss it, and I will not be drawn on the subject."

"But—"

"No." Quentin stood and towered over Kane. He placed his hands on the table and loomed forward. It was a position his father had used whenever he wished to ensure a topic was never raised again, and it proved just as effective when he utilized it now if Kane's cowering was anything to go by. "There is nothing more to be said about it. Is that understood?"

Kane nodded quickly until it seemed his head might fall off. "Fine. Fine, okay. I'm sorry!"

Quentin ran his fingers down his sleeves to straighten his cuffs as he sat once more. He crossed his legs as he leaned back and raised his chin.

He was in control.

Everything was all right now.

"Now," he said smoothly, "I believe that we have work to catch up on."

Kane stared at him like he'd turned green. "We... what?" He blinked, then sat upright. "Hold on a minute. What kind of work?"

Quentin tilted his head. "The children's tuition, their practice."

"Christ. You just expect—"

"You sent them into a wildfire," Quentin cut in. "Sebastian was no match for that situation. You and I both know that they could have died, and that would be on your hands, Kane. They need to improve."

"And you think I trust you with them?" It was Kane's turn to stand now, but he didn't try and loom. Instead he paced to the window and folded his arms across his chest. "You think I can trust you at *all*?"

"You're a fool if you think that you cannot." Quentin watched the American. "When have I ever done anything to harm any of these children? I am incapable of doing so. We want the same thing. We want them to be safe. Protected. And if I can help them gain more control over their gifts, then that is better for all of us."

Kane sneered as he kicked at the baseboard beneath the window, then his shoulders sank. "You're gonna have to earn my trust back before I let you anywhere near them again."

Quentin pursed his lips. "Yours is not the only trust I must regain," he said softly.

"Yeah. I heard." Kane sighed and returned to his chair, and sat so heavily that the air made a faint rushing sound as it was squeezed from the cushion. "Laurence was pissed as all hell, so I'm told."

"He had good reason to be."

Kane tapped his palms against the desk's surface while he stared off into space, and then his hands stilled. "Okay. You do this one thing, then we're golden. Deal?"

"That would entirely depend," Quentin murmured, "on what it is."

Kane let out a soft breath before he began to outline what he wanted.

48

LAURENCE

Laurence entered Freddy's penthouse with a brief smile.

"Tea?" Freddy offered as he led Laurence through to the living area. "Coffee?"

"No thanks. I'm okay." Laurence's eye was drawn to the piles of folders neatly stacked along one edge of the dining table. "Thanks for stopping by and visiting Quen. He was bored as hell. I think the visits did him good."

"Cognitive rest must be insufferable. Whatever I could contribute to break that monotony, I did so gladly." Freddy paused midway to the dining table and turned to face Laurence. "If you're here now, I presume he's firing on all cylinders?"

"Yeah." Laurence gave a short nod. "He's gone over to Wilson's to get back into the swing of it. I'm kinda hoping you've made some progress in the past couple of weeks, though?"

"Ah, yes." Freddy's lip twitched. "Progress. Please, take a seat." He moved on to the table and sat on the side with all the folders.

Laurence settled opposite and regarded them. They were all brown, and mostly plain. They weren't all that thick, holding only a handful of sheaves of paper or whatever else might be between the covers. The tabs had writing on them, but in mostly squirrelly hands.

"I shan't waste your time," Freddy declared. "Nor will I be

drawn into an argument on ethics. I have, over this past fortnight, hired an assortment of private investigators to take note of the comings and goings out of Kane's mansion." His gray eyes gleamed. "Or should I say *my* mansion."

Laurence stared at him. "Since when?"

"Since last week. It has taken me quite some time to track down the previous owner. Russian oligarchs are ten a penny, and identifying the correct one in spite of data protection laws was rather trying, but I finally got ahold of him and convinced him to sell me this squatter-infested mess to save him the trouble of dealing with it himself." Freddy waved his hands a moment, palms up. "I may or may not have shown him photographs of the variety of indigents using his very expensive waterfront property as their home and wafted a sum of money under his nose to make the problem go away."

"You—" Laurence choked off his own words. "How much did it cost?" he said, his voice faint to his own ears.

"Eighteen million dollars." Freddy sniffed. "Which is only just a little over thirteen million pounds. Not an inconsequential amount, but I would suggest that it is a bargain. The purpose, of course, is twofold."

"Right," Laurence's mouth said. He wasn't sure he had any control over it at the moment, so he let it go ahead on its own.

"Firstly it gives us the ability to force Kane's hand. When we wish him to mobilize, we will allow him to discover the change of ownership. In doing so, he may act without thinking and show his plans more overtly. And secondly, I am not willing to leave this city knowing that Icky is living in a dovecote. Once this is dealt with he will have a home which befits him considerably better than the hovel he is currently in. I cannot allow my brother to go on as he is."

"You're—" Laurence stopped himself this time. Too many sentences tried to cram themselves out all at once, and if he let it go on it'd be a hot mess. He had to select one of them and prioritize it. "You're just gonna give him a place that cost eighteen million dollars?"

Freddy snorted. "Heavens, no. I'm not a fool. But he can at

least live in it. It's an investment, dear boy, both toward my own portfolio and toward my brother's reintegration to the real bloody world. But that was your intention also, when you bought him those dogs, wasn't it? To nail him down, make him stay put for more than six months?"

Laurence's cheeks heated, and he wriggled in his chair. "I wouldn't say nail him down, exactly."

"No. But it was an excellent idea, and I think he will do better with a decent home to keep them in. Of course, I insist that you both sell all the god-awful furniture to fund a redecoration. From what I've seen it looks like a chintzy nightmare."

"It's pretty fucking hideous, yeah." Laurence grimaced, and then leaned forward. "Wait. How'd you get inside?"

"I didn't." Freddy chuckled. "There were archived images from the previous sale available online. Really, the things one can find on the internet are ridiculous these days."

Laurence laughed. Goddess, Freddy was so like Quentin sometimes, and then at others they were so different that Laurence couldn't figure out how they came from the same parents. He was so used to Quentin barely knowing what Google even was that it was easy to forget that Freddy used it on a daily basis. "Man, you guys are like apples and oranges." He nodded to the folders. "Is this all the stuff from the investigators?"

"Indeed. I had to instruct the various freelancers to keep a significant distance, and I swapped them over frequently so that none tailed the same target twice. I also kept them away from Wagner, since he is a trained combatant and therefore far more likely to be attentive in a public space." Freddy flipped open files and passed a series of photographs in front of Laurence. "As we can see, Miss Torres visits cash machines many times a day, all across the San Diego area. She has not attended the same machine twice, but this was only a two-week observation period. Mr. Wilson himself pops out to rob people early in the morning, and then uses his evenings for socializing. Quite heavily political socializing, I might add. He likes to mingle with the nouveau riches. The up-and-comers, people in relatively early stages of their political careers. I would suggest that he is forging alliances."

Freddy's lips flickered into a fleeting smirk. "It's a good long-term strategy, and suggests that his goal is not one which will be achieved overnight."

Laurence skimmed the photos. Most were taken, he assumed, from a distance despite being reasonably tight crops. All were outside. Kane seemed to go rob people in pretty well-off areas, but he also wore fancy suits in the evenings, and hung out in the sort of spaces politicians loved to fundraise in: museums, art galleries, hotels.

"What the hell is it he wants?" Laurence muttered as he passed photos back to Freddy.

"Most of all he seems to hobnob with those whose policies and alignments are to the left." Freddy neatly arranged the images back into their respective folders. "Now, were I in his shoes and with his particular gift—and suspecting as we do that his goal is to reveal the existence of such gifts—then I would spend my time cementing my influence among those who already show a permissive and accepting outlook in their politics. Those who lobby for LGBT rights, for example, or who fight for universal health care. I would also spend a great deal of time then ensuring that those people got to positions of power so that, when I pull back the curtain, every single political structure already in place is ready to support me."

Laurence puffed his cheeks out and pushed his chair back from the table. "You think he's trying to shape the political landscape of an entire city?"

"An entire county. He isn't restricting his movements to San Diego. He's based himself in La Jolla." Freddy tapped a folder with his index finger. "He's chosen Southern California, already famed for its tolerance and gun control. He has picked a location where the odds of getting shot at are markedly below those in other areas of the country, and where people are fairly liberal. The only trouble that I foresee is that he's also selected a city which is home to major military installations, but then there would be an uproar if the US Military operated on domestic soil, so maybe that is already a factor." He hesitated. "There is a rather more troubling side to this."

"*More* troubling?" Laurence rubbed his jaw. "Like, just how more troubling can this even get?"

"Well. I for one would never stoop to getting my own hands dirty. It is not where the head of any organization should be. If this is indeed Wilson's plan, then he must put himself out there, or the power would reside within another. I suspect this is why he attends so many functions; to ingratiate himself with all and sundry." Freddy selected another folder and flipped it open before he passed the entire thing to Laurence. "But it does mean that the eyes are not on his hands while they follow the head."

Laurence dragged his chair forward and leaned against the table as he grabbed the folder. The very top sheet was little more than an outline of a human shape that had areas marked over it in pen, but when he lifted that sheet aside he found photographs of a body which was alternately black and red, with scraps of clothing stuck to it. It lay in a blackened and broken ruin.

The skin was charred, and teeth shone out from a face which was utterly beyond recognition. Where the skin had split, some of the corpse's insides were clearly visible.

Laurence pushed it away and swallowed air. "Oh, Goddess," he groaned.

Freddy crinkled his nose. "It is rather, isn't it?" He closed the folder. "That unfortunate fellow was Ignacio Perez, a public relations representative for Glen Lansky." At Laurence's bemused shake of the head, he added, "Lansky is a local Republican who has campaigned for voter restrictions. In a circumspect manner, Mr. Perez would only like rich people to have the right to vote around here, and wishes to limit the types of photo identification one can use. Perez was Lansky's most valued spin doctor, as he was rather good at being that one person of color every racist needs on hand to claim that they aren't at all racist."

Horror crawled up Laurence's spine and pricked at the back of his neck. It made the hairs rise there, and his scalp tingled in response. "You think Perez was murdered."

"Indubitably. The wildfires conveniently missed just about every other home in his neighborhood, yet consumed his before they died out in that area. Forensic investigation has found no accelerants at the scene, no fragments of any device which could tie the event to arson. The fire simply seems to have gone off-course and consumed a house all of its own accord."

"Sebastian." Laurence winced as he said it.

"That is the conclusion I would also draw."

"They killed a guy just to... to what?"

"Resource-stripping." Freddy shrugged. "A valid tactic in war. Target your opponent's resources while accumulating your own. When Wilson makes his move, his enemies will be weak and his own power will be strong. He is engineering an easy win. This raises a pressing concern."

"Ya think?" Laurence struggled to grasp the enormity of Freddy's findings. It all seemed so huge.

Kane Wilson was playing chess with everything south of Encinitas.

"Wilson is willing to kill his enemies." One of Freddy's pale eyebrows arched. "And that places us all in grave danger should he discover that we are hardly his allies."

Laurence trapped the tip of his tongue between his teeth, then pulled his wallet from his jeans. "Unless we're worth more as puppets," he muttered.

Freddy watched him as he fished out the note he'd found in Quentin's wallet, and his other eyebrow rose once he read it.

"Interesting," he mused. "His control is not total?"

Laurence shook his head. "No, I think you literally have to do exactly what he tells you to, but your mind's still your own." He rubbed at his eyes. "That's what I saw in my vision, when I looked back at... at the kids he killed." He swallowed. "Goddess, these kids, they just... they beat their own friend to death and they were crying and begging and they couldn't stop themselves..."

Freddy grimaced at that and returned the note to him. "You cannot tell Icky any of this."

Laurence nodded weakly. "I know. Soraya can see him. Her range doesn't seem to stop her when it's people she cares about."

"And we must assume that she cannot keep secrets from Wilson." Freddy pursed his lips. "My concern is that he is rather... obtuse."

Laurence snorted. "Worse than that. I think he's capable of rewriting his own experiences." He bit his cheek briefly and glanced at the view through the windows. "I know I asked before. About his childhood…"

Freddy shrugged. "Dear boy, it appears to me that if you truly want to know a single thing about Icky's upbringing, you are uniquely placed to find out for yourself."

Laurence's gaze returned to Freddy, and found the Englishman looking pensively toward the windows himself.

"You have a gift," Freddy mused. "And none of us can prevent you from using it." His gray eyes flitted toward Laurence, and he met his gaze.

"Would you want to prevent me?" Laurence murmured.

Freddy shrugged. "You are a smart young man. You have inferred what you believe the truth to be. On the basis of your evidence I… would be a fool if I did not consider your deductions to be a plausible explanation." He took a deep breath. "I suppose, then, that your question is one of will. If you are correct, do you have the stomach for what you will see should you look?"

Laurence pushed himself to his feet and paced away from Freddy.

He hadn't even considered using his gift to nose into Quentin's past, and he sure as hell hadn't thought through what would happen if his guesses were right. Shit, he'd thrown up after watching Wilson kill some kids, and it gave him nightmares for a week.

Could he watch—

His legs weakened at the thought of it, and he collapsed onto a couch.

"Mm," Freddy said. "Perhaps some stones are best left unturned."

Before Laurence could begin to work through any appropriate response, his cell rang, and he stood so he could get it out of his pocket.

The caller ID read *Quen*.

Laurence glanced to Freddy, then rubbed his cheeks and pushed his disquiet aside so that he could answer. He put the call on speaker, then tried to sound cheerful. "Hey, baby! What's up? Everything go okay with Kane?"

"Moderately," Quentin answered. "However, he is requesting that I undertake a task to prove my loyalty."

"Oh," cooed Freddy. "A quest! How exciting! What is it, Icky?"

As Freddy was still over at the dining table, Laurence doubted the microphone had picked up his words, so he said, "What does he want?"

"Ah," said Quentin. "Therein lies the rub, darling."

Laurence listened.

"You can't," he breathed.

Freddy shrugged. "He has to."

49

QUENTIN

THE TAXI DEPOSITED QUENTIN OUTSIDE THE ADDRESS KANE HAD provided. He hadn't heard of National City at all, but it didn't appear to be too terribly far south of where Laurence lived. The taxi had driven past some rather pretty houses on the way here. Small, of course, but with the colonial Spanish architecture endemic of the region, combined with the desert flora which was everywhere. All in all he had been grateful that at least he was headed to do dirty work in a pleasant area.

Naturally by the time the taxi arrived at his destination things had taken a rather dismal turn. They drove past a tall gate which was lined along the top with razor wire. Houses had fences all around them. There seemed to be a mixture of residences and warehouse properties side by side. And as Quentin paid for his fare and left the safety of the cab, the house he faced was dingy and unkempt, with an overgrown little yard in front of it, and a collection of broken plastic furniture piled up against the fence.

This would not go well.

Not that it could go any better if this were a palace, truth be told.

He gritted his teeth and pushed the gate open. It creaked and slammed shut after he passed through into the yard. The paving was crooked. He had to pick his way to the front door with care to avoid tripping. Thankfully there wasn't far to go.

There was no doorbell that he could find, so he rapped against the door with his knuckles and waited.

Only then did it occur to him that he could perhaps work out ahead of time what exactly he was supposed to say to the owner.

Excuse me, sir. I am here to kidnap your daughter.

Of course, that wasn't the word Kane used to describe it, no. Kane preferred "liberate," but that made it no better.

How many of the children at the mansion had Kane "liberated"?

How many of them had homes to go to, if only they could?

Quentin swallowed and focused on the matter at hand as the door opened. He looked down, since there was nobody at eye level, and found a young teen there with ratty hair and a rather unflattering yellow bruise on her cheek. Her cut lip was in the process of healing, but wasn't there yet.

She didn't look up at him. Instead she turned to face the dark corridor behind her and yelled, "It's a man."

"Which man?" bellowed a deep voice from inside.

"I don't know."

Quentin frowned faintly and crouched down to her level. "Are you Lisa?"

She flinched, and yelled, "He knows my name!"

"Lisa," Quentin breathed quickly. "I'm here to help. Did he—" he pointed into the house "—do this—" he gestured to her cheek "—to you?"

Lisa finally spared a look in Quentin's direction, though she avoided eye contact. She wiped her nose with the back of her hand, then nodded briefly.

"Well then." Quentin rose to his feet.

Darkness crowded the edges of his vision. It could have been the setting of the sun, or perhaps an increase in his focus. Certainly everything in the center seemed sharpened by it, so the cause was irrelevant.

A breeze snagged his hair and blew past him into the house.

"Tell him to fuck off!" The shout was accompanied by a thud, and then the slam of a door, and a shape formed itself into the corridor.

Lisa cringed and shrank back against the wall.

"I think you might like to hear what I have to say." The words didn't feel as though Quentin had spoken them, and he heard them only distantly. No. His attention was on the creature which stalked toward him.

It was a beast, that was certain. Tall and broad, in good physical condition. It wore some sleeveless shirt which displayed its muscles and hair in equal measure. There was some measure of creativity to the way it wore its facial hair, with long sideburns and an unkempt mustache without accompanying beard, but the hair on its head was ragged and dirty.

Most awful, Quentin supposed, was the stench of it. It reeked of cigarettes and alcohol, along with the distinctly pungent aroma of marijuana, all mingled with the sweat of a day or three.

The creature stopped on his side of the threshold and its dark eyes flitted up and down Quentin's form. "It better be good, son," the thing snarled.

"Perhaps we could step inside." Quentin fixed a smile. It wasn't honest, but he didn't care. "I have a proposition for you."

"You look rich." It spat onto the doorstep and narrowly missed Quentin's shoes. "Unless you're here to share the wealth, get lost."

"If that is what it will take."

The monster stepped back from the door and waved for Quentin to enter. "What is it you want?"

Quentin took two steps forward and pressed a fingertip to the door to push it closed. He had no desire to touch it any more than absolutely required. "I am here," he said softly, "for Lisa."

"Huh." It eyed him again. "Lookin' fancier than the kind we usually get." There was a pause, and then some slow realization crept across its piggy features. "Wait. There's no address on the site, just the cell number. How'd you know where to find her?"

That didn't make a whole lot of sense to Quentin, but then things rarely did. "I was given the address by an associate."

"Jesus fucking Christ." It paused. "You're not a cop?"

Quentin blinked owlishly. "Of course not."

"Okay. Your associate give you the price list, too?"

Quentin grappled with the question a moment, but there was no logical conclusion to be drawn, so he simply said, "No." He glanced down to Lisa, lest she shed some light on the situation, but she had remained against the wall, her head down.

"Well it's a hundred to watch her strip. Two hundred if you want to touch her. Five hundred if you want her to touch you. A thousand if you wanna fuck her, and an extra hundred bucks per mark you leave on her."

The world paused.

Quentin did his best to process the words which the monster had spoken, but no matter which way he parsed them, it all seemed to suggest that Quentin had come here to interfere with a teenager.

"When you say 'site,'" he said with care, "do you mean website?"

"Yeah, but a personal referral—"

"You advertise this," he turned to face the only other adult in the corridor, "on the internet?"

It shrugged. "Hey, if you want exclusivity you're gonna have to buy her outright."

The dark turned completely black. It flooded inward, washing away the walls, the floor, the filthy ceiling overhead. It chased toward the beast in the center of Quentin's line of sight.

Wind screamed down the corridor, trapped within the flimsy walls which shook in its wake.

Calm. You must—

He ignored the advice. Calm was for other days. Other places. Calm was to prevent others from getting hurt.

Lisa!

His lungs dragged in a fistful of the fetid air, and he turned back to look at her.

She had hunkered down a little. Her ratty hair was blown by the wind, and tears dripped from her chin.

Quentin struggled to push the black away. There was a child here. For God's sake, a *child*.

He crouched again and looked up to her. "Do you wish to

leave here?" he murmured. "And I do not mean for—" his brain skipped a beat, and his words faltered. "I mean to go to a better place," he whispered. "Where you never have to... to... do anything he wants you to ever again."

Lisa peered at him through strands of hair, then looked past him.

Quentin nodded to himself and pushed to his feet.

He had to admire the brilliance of Kane's move. Wilson must have known. He couldn't possibly be aware that Lisa had some sort of gift *and* not know that her father was using her as a source of income. He must also have realized what would happen when Quentin got to the bottom of things.

Quentin had allowed himself to be placed in a situation where using his powers in front of a witness was almost entirely guaranteed, whether through deliberate action or accident, and Kane was well aware that Quentin wouldn't kill.

This was more than Kane had asked for. More than any mere show of loyalty. It was forcing Quentin to reveal himself to a complete stranger.

He fought to draw the winds down, but there was a core of rage inside him which had ratcheted up several notches and refused to be unwound.

"Okay, you know what? This is too fucking weird. How 'bout you just leave and lose this address, huh?"

Quentin glowered at the creature whose one job on Earth was to protect the little girl he'd fathered.

"She's coming with me." Words came out of him now without any conscious involvement on his part.

"Then that's a hundred thousand dollars."

"No."

The filth flinched as plaster shook free from the walls and swept into the air-like puffs of smoke. It turned and disappeared through a side door.

Quentin turned and offered Lisa his hand. "Let's go."

She shook her head. "Gun," she squeaked. "He gone to get his—"

Quentin heard the distinctive sound of metal grating against metal, the *chk chk* which only ever matched a pump-action shotgun. There was nothing else like it. The first *chk* ejected a spent shell were one present, and perhaps more importantly at this precise moment, also cocked the weapon. The second *chk* was the sound of a shell as it loaded from magazine tube to chamber.

He turned toward it in time to see the owner step back into the corridor and level it at him.

There was no way to know whether it was birdshot or solid slug in there. He could only make an educated guess at the gauge of the weapon. He was forced to assume that a shot could be lethal.

Quentin watched the trigger finger. It rested alongside the guard for now while the owner yelled at him. Whatever the words were, Quentin didn't hear them.

"You should step outside, Lisa," he said.

The finger moved.

50

LAURENCE

"He can't just go steal someone's kid!" Laurence drummed his fingers on his thigh.

Freddy waved a hand. "Really, Laurence, if all Icky must do is encourage a gifted child to run off with him to a land of magical superpowers, then where's the harm?"

"Well how about Quentin getting arrested and thrown in jail?"

"Nonsense." Freddy sniffed. "I think you underestimate the efficacy of a judicious application of cash, dear boy."

Laurence stared. "Bribery?"

"You do use such vivid terminology."

"I think the word you're looking for is 'accurate.'" Laurence stood and crossed to the dining table.

Freddy glanced up from his piles of folders. He had neatened them into little stacks now. "Do you have any way to know where he is headed?"

Laurence shook his head. "No."

"Then I suggest we—"

Laurence's phone rang, cutting across Freddy's words, and Laurence grabbed it in case it was Quentin. The caller ID, though, read *Jack*.

His heart hammered. It was shorthand for the shop, but seeing that word on its own made his pulse race.

"Goddess, I really gotta fucking change that," he muttered as he answered it. "Hello?"

"Ah, Bambi!" Myriam's voice sounded troubled. "Could you come back here, please?"

"Mom?" Laurence gripped the phone. "Is everything okay?"

"I'm not sure. There's a young lady here. She says that she would like to speak to you."

Laurence pinched the bridge of his nose. "Can it wait?"

"No, dear. I don't believe it can."

"Shit." He sagged against a chair. "Okay. I'll be there in a minute."

Freddy raised an eyebrow at him as he hung up. "Trouble?"

"Probably. I've gotta go to the shop." Laurence sighed and began to tap at his phone for an Uber.

Freddy stood and tucked his chair neatly against the table. "Very well. As I am no use elsewhere, I might as well accompany you."

THE SHOP WAS CLOSED by the time they arrived, so Laurence had the Uber driver drop them nearer to the service street and led Freddy down the alley to the back door. He could see a cluster of people within, and before he could open the door Myriam did so.

"Bambi," she greeted warmly as she reached for him.

Laurence returned her hug. A waft of pizza smells came out the door after her. "Mom. What's going on?"

She ushered them inside. "Freddy. Good to see you again."

"Likewise, Mrs. Riley," the Brit murmured.

"Oh, please. Myriam!" She chuckled.

Ethan and Aiden were seated at the table, shoulder to shoulder. Beside them sat a red-headed girl who looked to be in her mid-teens. And on the table, two pizzas occupied much of the space, with a few slices already gone.

The girl was vaguely familiar, but Laurence had trouble placing her, so he offered his hand. "Hey. I'm Laurence."

"I know," she mumbled as she squeezed his hand. "I'm Kim."

"Oh!" Laurence smiled. "Right, you're Kimberly! Wow, you're a long way south, aren't you? What's up?" He slid onto a stool and reached for a slice.

Freddy sat beside Myriam and ignored the pizza. He winced briefly and glanced around the room.

Kim sighed. "I went to Quentin's, but he wasn't home, and I don't know his cell number and I don't have a cellphone anyway and I thought you might know how to find him." She fidgeted with the hem of her T-shirt as she spoke.

"He's, uh." Laurence glanced between Freddy and Kim, then shook his head. "He's not around at the moment. Can we help? I mean, I figure Mom's kept everyone after hours for a reason?" He eyed his mother.

Myriam smiled briefly. "I did."

"Okay, then we can definitely—" Laurence broke off. Freddy still seemed to be scouring the room, eyes flitting here and there while he maintained that calm demeanor he was so good at. "Freddy?"

"Yes?"

"Something wrong?"

"No, I..." Freddy cleared his throat and shook his head. "My apologies. I thought I heard something. Do continue."

Laurence eyed him, then nodded to Kim. "We can definitely help. What's the problem?"

Kim reached for the pizza and drew a slice toward herself, but left it on the box lid while she spoke. "I don't know. I'm scared." She hesitated and looked toward the ceiling. "Soraya, if you're watching, please don't. Not this. I'm going to say things you don't want him to make you repeat."

Laurence chewed on his own slice, and eyed the ceiling before he could stop himself. What was the point of that? If Soraya was eavesdropping on Kim, he wouldn't be able to see her.

Kim wriggled on her seat. "I gave Quentin a note. I don't... I don't know why. I thought he might help, but then I worked out he couldn't tell me whether or not he would because of Soraya."

Laurence frowned and set his pizza down. He grabbed a paper napkin from a pile between the boxes and wiped his fingers clean, then pulled the note out of his wallet and pushed it toward her. "This one?"

She eyed it, then her head bobbed. "He told you?"

"I found it in his wallet at the hospital, but it's tricky discussing anything when you never know who's listening in." He shook his head grimly. "But I guess we're past that now, huh? What happened?"

"He makes me do things." She swallowed. "Like the gun show. Like stealing stuff. I can get in and out of places and nobody notices me and mostly I just steal stuff for him because we need the money, right?"

Laurence nodded. "Go on."

She fidgeted on her seat and ate some more before she spoke again. "This morning he made me place something, not take it. It was a case. A plastic one, with a handle. It was like a tiny purse or something. He made me take it onto this huge fancy boat and hide it in one of the rooms, and I thought I'd seen boxes like that before." She licked her lips. "At the gun show. And he didn't tell me not to open it, so I had a quick look inside."

"And it was a gun?"

"Yeah." She bit her lip and glanced up at him. "A pistol, all in foam and there were some bullets and a silencer in with it."

Ethan and Myriam gasped. Aiden blinked and leaned back from the table.

Freddy frowned. "What was the name of the boat? Do you remember?"

"Um." She squinted. "Theo... something. Ass."

"Theophrastus?"

"Yes!" Her eyes widened.

"You've heard of it?" Laurence looked to Freddy.

"I've seen the name recently, although I couldn't put my finger on where, exactly." He pulled out his cellphone. "Do you recall where it was berthed?"

"Shelter Island."

Laurence grimaced and finished his slice of pizza. "It's a big fancy one then, huh?"

"Urgh, it's huge," she agreed with a nod. "I put it in a bathroom in one of the bedrooms, a VIP suite on the main deck. I hid it under the sink. That's where he told me to put it."

"You mean Kane," Laurence clarified.

Kim nodded. "I didn't know what else to do. I don't want anyone to get hurt." Her features creased and she blinked. "Especially because of me. You have to help. I don't know if Quentin had a plan or anything, but I'm tired of being used, you know? At least when I was just taking things it was to help everyone at the house, but this?" She gnawed on her lip. "I don't see how it can help anyone."

"Yeah, me either." He frowned at her. "Why don't you stay here tonight? There's an apartment upstairs, you can watch TV or whatever, and we'll figure out what to do."

She nodded. "Okay. Thanks. I don't..." She took a breath. "I don't wanna go back there."

"Then we'll work that out, too."

Laurence showed Kim around his apartment and made sure she had phone numbers for both him and his mom before he headed back down the stairs to the sound of chatter.

"So it's like a party yacht?" Aiden asked.

"It seems that way," Freddy agreed. "Alas as one might expect they do not list their upcoming events on their website."

"So there's no way of guessing why the gun's even there," Ethan said.

Laurence stepped into the room and found the three guys huddled around Freddy's cellphone while Myriam made tea.

"Why even make Kim get the gun on board in the first place?" Laurence sat and reached for a second slice.

"Ah, that would seem obvious." Freddy smiled to him. "During an event, attending guests are likely screened for weapons."

Laurence grimaced. "But if a weapon's already on board, a guest can go get it."

"Which implies Kane isn't going to use a crew member." Aiden tilted his head. "Why not?"

"Because that doesn't fit his narrative," Freddy answered. "Kane wishes to frame the gifted as the benefactors and saviors of mankind, not the perpetrators of crime or as any sort of threat. If he commands a regular crewmember to take a gun onto a yacht and shoot someone with it, that person will give evidence to that effect: that he was ordered, and he could not resist. But if Kane has a guest attend an event, sneak off, pick up the gun, kill a target, and then toss the weapon overboard, there is no evidence of a psychic's presence whatsoever. Particularly as he has taken the time to include a suppressor, which will ensure that the sound will likely not be heard over the noise of a crowd." He propped his elbow on the table and rubbed his forehead. "I wish I could remember where I've seen the yacht's name before."

"Theophrastus," Laurence mused. The name *did* ring a bell.

"Well if it's a party boat," Ethan reasoned, "then maybe you saw it advertised, or on an invitation or something?"

Laurence caught his breath and stared at Freddy, who stared at him at exactly the same moment.

"Invitations," they both said as one.

Laurence leaped to his feet just as Myriam set tea down in front of him. "Mom, can you look after Kim? I've gotta run."

"Of course, dear." She frowned at him softly. "Be careful."

"What?" Ethan waved his hand. "Wait, what? What's going on?"

"Invitations," Laurence breathed as he grabbed the keys to a van. "Quentin has an invitation to something on the *Theophrastus*. He gets like a dozen invitations a week, rarely looks at them anymore, but Freddy and I went through them and that's where we've seen the name."

"You think Quentin will have an invitation to the right party?" Ethan lifted his chin. "What're the odds?"

"I would say high," Laurence muttered, "if Kane's played his cards right."

Freddy hurried after him as he strode out into the alley. "You believe Wilson held a stronger hand than we imagined?"

Laurence nodded grimly. He used the remote to work out

which van he had the keys for, then dropped into the driver's seat. "Worse," he grunted.

"How can it possibly be worse?"

Laurence started the engine and glanced to Freddy as he eased into the passenger seat. "I think he's sent Quentin off to get him out of the way."

Freddy buckled up. He didn't respond, but the worry in his eyes was unmissable.

Laurence nodded. They didn't need to speak. They both knew what that meant.

Kane's plan was already well underway.

51

QUENTIN

There was no time to count down from ten, no time to ensure he retained what little control he had. All Quentin could do was take action and hope that he grasped some sliver of awareness throughout, or it would be over. If he slid into one of his episodes, he would be a sitting duck.

The trigger moved, and Quentin batted the barrel aside as the weapon discharged.

It was deafening. A shotgun blast in such a confined space left his ears ringing.

Heat burned his arm, and the wall to his right was all but obliterated.

Birdshot.

The gun had moved. The monster was no longer braced for the recoil when it fired the weapon. It howled in pain and tried to take aim.

Quentin swept forward and batted the gun aside once more. The beast's grip on it was strong, but Quentin was far stronger, and he tore it from hands twice the size of his own.

"No," he said.

He tossed the shotgun onto the floor behind him, and the moment's attention he spent on ensuring it didn't point toward Lisa cost him dearly.

A fist slammed into his cheek like a freight train.

His head snapped back from the hit so hard that it left him reeling. He stumbled against the wall, but the creature stayed with him and another fist landed in his gut.

Christ, how was he supposed to deal with this? A handful of weeks of Aikido training wasn't enough to take on such savagery. He barely had space to maneuver, trapped against the wall and gasping for air as a third hit slammed between his legs.

He swallowed bile and stared at his attacker in horror. This *thing*, this abhorrent bastard, had *touched* him.

Quentin pushed, and he pushed hard. He threw the pig against the far wall so hard that the massive body punched straight through it.

Then it began.

God, it began.

Excruciating pain ripped through his abdomen and stole every last ounce of breath from his body. He crumpled around his groin in a desperate attempt to protect it, but it was too late. The pain grew. It layered over and over on itself until he thought it might drive him insane, all while he struggled for air in a world which no longer seemed to have any. A wave of nausea followed, a sickness which crippled in its wake, rendering his limbs useless.

His balls were like lava, and that white-hot heat spread through him in no particular hurry, consuming all in its wake.

Adrenaline surged in the wake of the agony. It chased away the darkness at the edges of his vision. It screamed at him to get up, to run, but he couldn't move.

Lisa's father dragged himself back through the hole in the wall. There were jagged edges of wood and drywall lining it, and he tore more of them away as he heaved himself into the corridor with white dust in his hair and across his broad shoulders.

"Fucking come into *my* house," the man snarled, "and start shit with me? Cops aren't even gonna look at this twice, you fucking asshole." He strode past Quentin's head.

Quentin tried to watch him, but it was impossible. Everything was on fire, and not in any way that he could control.

He caught sight of blood on the carpet. Not much. It oozed

slowly from his arm, though he no longer felt that particular pain. No, that was a tickle compared to what he endured now.

"Just defending my little girl," his assailant snapped.

Quentin fought to move. He struggled against the agony, and managed to roll forward, but that stabbed a fresh wave of agony through his balls, and he grunted.

"Give me the gun, Lisa!"

"Leave him alone!" Her scream was filled with anguish and rage.

"I said give me the gun, you little bitch!"

"Don't." Quentin tried to call out, but it barely left him as a whisper. Christ, a girl her size shooting what was most likely a twelve-gauge shotgun without proper training or technique? The recoil would kick the gun's stock out of her control and she could break her bloody shoulder or jaw.

He rolled again and managed to push himself onto all fours. Nausea clenched his gut and sent bile to the back of his throat.

Oh God. Don't be sick. Don't!

Tears stung his eyes. He began to dry heave, and the convulsions sent him to the floor once more while the world spiraled around him.

A shot billowed through the corridor.

At first he thought it might be the ringing in his head, but no. The stench of propellant powder was acrid and it flowed down the corridor long before he heard the *whump* of a body as it hit the ground.

He heard a scream.

Get up. Get UP!

Quentin snarled and forced himself to his knees. He pushed away from the floor and slid up the wall to his feet, hands spread across it to keep from falling as his legs trembled.

Smoke wisped through the air.

Lisa's father was face-down. His blood was a black stain which crept sluggishly around the outline of his torso.

The shotgun lay abandoned by his outstretched arm.

Lisa had fallen to her knees. She cradled her right arm with her left, and sobbed wretchedly.

"Lisa," he wheezed, but she didn't answer.

God, this was an unmitigated bloody disaster. He closed his eyes and concentrated solely on trying to breathe until he felt better prepared to try and speak, and then he gave it another go.

"Lisa."

"I didn't mean it!" she bawled. "It just went off!"

"Lisa, are you hurt?"

Her only answer was another sob, so he forced his eyes open and began to stumble his way toward her, using the wall to hold himself upright.

The man on the floor twitched.

Quentin leaned on the wall and dug his phone out of his pocket. He dialed 911 and requested an ambulance. By the time he hung up he could just about stand without the wall's assistance.

"I can't stay here." Lisa's voice trembled. "I can't. They'll arrest me. I don't want to go to jail."

"Then we should leave." Quentin offered a hand to her. "Take your time. We'll go somewhere safe and then I can look at that shoulder for you."

"Why did you even come here?" She let him take her elbow, and it took two yelps and another scream to get her to her feet.

Quentin had no doubt that something was broken. Her collarbone, perhaps, or a rib. The way she protected her right arm suggested it could even be the arm itself. But he couldn't evaluate the injury here. Not with her father slowly dying behind him, if the man wasn't already dead. Quentin had no intention whatsoever of sparing that monster the effort of first aid.

"To get you away from him," he rasped.

"And go where?" She was like a wild animal, cornered and in pain.

Quentin glanced to the body and shook his head. "Anywhere is better than here," he breathed. "Come along. Let's go."

52

LAURENCE

The van ground to a halt in a crunch of gravel and Laurence sped to the apartment without bothering to lock the vehicle. He jammed his keys in the door and ran up the stairs, Freddy hot at his heels.

"Is he likely to have thrown them out by now?"

Laurence unlocked the door to the apartment and shouldered it open, almost tripping over the dogs in the process. "Goddess, I hope not!" The dogs clustered around his thighs. Pepper wagged up a breeze as she rasped her tongue over his hand, and Grace's nose pressed into the back of his calf.

"They need the loo," Freddy explained as he darted around the roadblock.

"Is that a d'Arcy thing?"

"Hmm?"

"Understanding animals?"

"Oh." Freddy shook his head slightly and grabbed the stack of envelopes from the dining table. "We had a lot of dogs around as we grew up. You get used to the way they communicate."

"Yeah." Laurence snorted. "That used to be Quentin's explanation, too."

Freddy paused and frowned at him. "What do you mean?"

"I dunno, man. What if Quentin's gifts run in the family like mine and Mom's? What if it's more than just a familiarity with dogs?"

"Don't be ridiculous." Freddy sifted through envelopes and tossed aside one after another.

"Yeah." Laurence nodded. "He said that, too. C'mon, girls. Let's go to the bathroom, huh?"

He led them down the stairs and out to the grass which lined the gravel drive, silently urging them to do their business as fast as they could and then, once they had, he glanced around to ensure nobody watched as he coaxed a Heuchera Obsidian to grow over the mess and obscure it from view. With the red-black foliage in the way, he herded the dogs back up to the apartment.

Freddy was on his phone again. The difference in the twins couldn't be more pronounced. Freddy used his cellphone the way most people used their own limbs. It was near instinct to him, never far from hand, and yet Quentin had barely worked out how to respond to text messages.

"You got it?" Laurence asked as he shut the door.

"I have." Freddy nudged an invitation toward him. "The *Theophrastus*."

Laurence swept it from the table and flipped it open.

Mr. Glen Lansky extends a most cordial invitation to Lord Banbury and guest for an evening of charitable fund-raising aboard the Theophrastus.

His gaze fell to the date.

"This is today," he breathed.

"It is," Freddy muttered, tapping furiously at his phone.

"Wait." Alarm rippled through Laurence's chest. "Lansky?"

"Correct."

The politician. The one whose PR guy was already dead.

"Fuck," Laurence breathed. "You think Kane's going after Lansky himself?"

"It could be any guest there." Freddy slid his phone away and launched to his feet. "Come along. Bring the invitation."

And for all that the twins differed, there were some unmissable similarities. When it came down to it, Freddy could bark orders every bit as confidently as Quentin.

Laurence ran after him. "Where are we going?"

"The Palomar. We have to change."

"Now?" He dug out the van keys as they ran downstairs.

"Dear boy, they will hardly allow us aboard dressed as we are."

Laurence looked to the invitation in his hand, then stared at Freddy.

"Shit," he breathed. "You're as crazy as he is!"

BY THE TIME they made it to the penthouse, a fresh tuxedo was waiting for Laurence.

"How the hell do you get this shit done?" Laurence held it up and eyed it. It was a deep forest green, so dark that the color only showed under direct light.

"That's what a good concierge service is for, Laurence." Freddy hurried up the stairs. "It may not be a precise fit, but it should suit our purpose."

"You can't think they're gonna mistake you for Quentin," Laurence called after him. He dragged his T-shirt off over his head and tossed it onto the couch.

"Possession is nine-tenths," Freddy called back.

Laurence snorted. "I take it back. You'll be a lousy lawyer." He hurried into the tux. "You're almost twice his size, man."

"We don't need to convince the attendees. We must only convince the doorman, and I will have both the invitation and you. Once inside our only job is to get rid of that gun before it can fall into the wrong hands, and we will be able to leave without ever setting foot anywhere risky. It can sink to the bottom of the marina as we saunter off into the sunset like heroes. Nobody is harmed, then we catch up with Icky and work out what to do about Wilson."

It was a ballsy plan. But more importantly, unlike one of Quentin's harebrained schemes, it was a *safe* plan, and Laurence had to admit he liked it. He could wrap his arms around Freddy long enough convince a doorman that the wrong twin was the right one. That was well within his ability. He'd faked things way longer than that in the past.

This was going to work.

He tucked his shirt in as he buttoned the tuxedo's pants, and slid his feet into the shoes which were set aside. They pinched, and if he walked around in them too long he'd get blisters for sure, but for now he paced slowly in them to try and get them to ease up on him, and checked his phone as he did so.

Nothing. No missed calls, no text messages.

He bit his lip and sent Quentin a text.

Going to the Theophrastus. *It's a yacht. Won't be long. We took your invitation.*

Laurence nodded to himself as he sent it, impressed that his phone even recognized the word without complaint.

That was fair, right? After chewing Quentin out for not warning him before he rushed off into a wildfire, he'd be a total asshole to not at least let Quentin know where he was going.

"Right." Freddy hurried down the stairs and grabbed the invitation. "Ready?"

"Sure." Laurence pocketed his phone, and his throat dried as he watched Freddy tuck the invitation into his jacket.

The figure Freddy obscured with casual clothes and loose fits was cast in sharp relief through exquisite tailoring. His broad shoulders tapered to a perfectly proportioned waist, and the mid-toned gray of his tuxedo flattered his pale coloring while matching the shade of his eyes.

"Hell," Laurence muttered. "That runs in the family too, huh?"

"Hmm?"

Laurence shook his head to clear it. Hotness was obviously a feature of d'Arcy genetics, but Freddy was the wrong brother, and they had work to do.

"Nothing," he said thickly.

A LIMOUSINE WAITED at the hotel's entrance, and the doorman swept them into it without a word.

"Concierge service?" Laurence snorted.

"Mine, although I'm sure they liaise with the hotel's." Freddy waved a hand. "So long as a task is achieved, I really don't care how they go about it."

Laurence shook his head and looked down at his own tuxedo. These miracle workers had it selected, purchased, and delivered in half an hour. During the day that must be difficult enough, but the evening? How was it even possible?

How much did that kind of service cost?

This was Freddy's world. A text, an email, and whatever he wanted was delivered to his door as and when he requested it. If Laurence had thought dating Quentin was hard enough, how must it be for Quentin to be reduced to a lifestyle where his apartment was rented and he couldn't afford the level of service he had been born into?

No wonder Quentin expected people to ask how high whenever he said jump.

"Penny for them?" Freddy murmured.

Laurence looked out the window at the familiar stretch of palm trees and yacht supply stores. "Quentin brought me this way once. A few months ago, before we were dating. We went to a party on a yacht." He smiled wistfully. "It was the first time we danced."

Of course, it was also the first time Quentin had fallen asleep in Laurence's arms—so drunk he couldn't stay awake—but it was a more romantic memory if Laurence skipped that part.

"I imagine that was quite the sight." Freddy chuckled.

"Yeah." Laurence grinned. "He was."

Freddy laughed softly. "You're hardly the back end of a horse yourself, dear boy."

"Pfft. I know." Laurence flicked hair back from his eyes. "I'm gorgeous."

Freddy groaned, and Laurence laughed in return. It made the worry subside a little, and allowed a ray of confidence to peek through the clouds.

The plan was so simple that it couldn't fail. All Laurence had to do was convince one doorman that Freddy was Quentin.

Piece of cake.

"Lord Banbury," Freddy drawled as he handed over his invitation. "Plus one, of course."

Laurence flashed his most dazzling smile as he clung to Freddy's arm. "Laurence Riley," he purred.

The doorman at the base of the gangplank eyed the invitation and then handed it back to Freddy. "Welcome, sirs. If you could proceed one at a time, please?"

"Of course. Darling?" Freddy gestured for Laurence to go ahead. "You first. That way I can watch your arse."

Heat rose in Laurence's cheeks, but he dropped the contents of his pockets into a tray and then walked through the arch of the metal detector.

"Thank you, sir." The security guard on the other side of the detector handed Laurence his tray, and Laurence stuffed everything back where it came from.

"Wonderful," Freddy cooed as he stepped through. "Thank you so much."

Laurence took Freddy's arm and they strode up the gangplank side by side.

"Goddess," Laurence whispered as he leaned in toward Freddy's ear. "That was easy, don't you think?"

"I believe they call it a confidence trick for a reason," Freddy answered with a smile. "Those who appear to belong are rarely questioned. It's when people dart around furtively that they draw unwanted attention. That and Icky is hardly an A-list celebrity. Not everyone in this city would recognize his face."

"I guess." Laurence continued to smile as he eyed the yacht.

It wasn't the size of the one Quentin had taken him to earlier in the year, but it was still massive by anyone's definition. He counted five decks, though he didn't doubt that there was more going on below his feet than he cared to know about. There were very few people out on the deck, and those who were seemed more interested in hushed conversation than looking to the new arrivals.

"Which is the main deck?" he breathed.

"This one," Freddy murmured. He strolled toward a walkway which led past the yacht's interior. "That way—" he gestured to stairs leading down "—is the lower deck, which is a mainly crew-only area. Above us, the upper deck, and above that the bridge deck. The top is the flying bridge."

"I get it." Laurence peered into windows as they passed, and through the darkened glass he could make out dim movement. "What's in there?"

"That would be the event itself. I doubt I'll be able to pass myself off as Icky inside. Much more likely to be the occasional bugger who'd see right through us. Best to circumvent the lot and head straight for the cabins."

"Okay." Laurence stopped trying to see inside. If the windows were a one-way tint he'd look like a complete idiot to anyone who caught him at it. "I'm glad you know your way around a boat. I wouldn't have a clue where to start."

"We're a good team," Freddy chuckled. "It's a shame you're already taken, or I'd snap you up."

"Huh." Laurence's blush returned in full force. "I thought you were straight."

"Oh, please." Freddy snorted. "I apologize if I gave you that impression." He pushed a door open and held it for Laurence.

The interior was a welcome relief from the summer heat. They passed into the cool embrace of an air-conditioned corridor, and Laurence heard the chatter of the party from his right. The corridor extended left and lights flicked on as they made their way down it.

Yet again Laurence prowled the interior of a fancy yacht while a party went on elsewhere, but the fact that this party *was* still in full swing reassured him that they'd arrived in time. Nobody had been shot. There were no cop cars out on the street, nor ambulances, and the noise didn't have that subdued tone to it which would suggest a tragedy.

So far, so good.

"Which one, do you think?" Freddy dropped his voice to a whisper as they moved further down the corridor.

There were two doors on either side, spaced so far apart that Laurence's entire apartment could have fit between them twice over.

"I guess we check 'em all." Laurence nodded. "C'mon."

He tried the first door on the left and it opened with a soft click. Freddy glanced back toward the party while Laurence peered through the gap and found only darkness inside.

"It's empty," he whispered.

They darted into the room and closed the door. Laurence felt around the door frame for a light switch, and when his fingers found one he tapped every switch along the row. He squinted briefly as the lights popped on, and he looked into it to find a door which could feasibly belong to a bathroom.

A shape registered as unusual, deeper into the suite, and his eyes were drawn to it just as he realized it was a man, seated on one of the suite's couches.

"Come in," Kane said. "Both of you." He smirked and pointed to another couch. "Sit."

Laurence's heart pounded. His body primed itself to run.

But he had orders.

53

QUENTIN

The best Quentin could do to mask their departure was destroy bulbs in the street lamps before they passed beneath.

They walked in silence for three blocks, neither capable of moving all that quickly. By the time they reached their fourth block together, Quentin's guts were less a sickening mess and more a throbbing ache, and he could straighten up as he walked.

As the pain in his abdomen lessened, the burn in his arm returned, and he examined it quietly.

The sleeve of his jacket had a light peppering of holes torn through it, and blood congealed around the entry points. He counted five holes in total, all within a six-inch area.

He'd been bloody lucky. The majority of the spread had missed him and destroyed the wall instead. His arm still worked. Hopefully the pellets were close to the surface and would pop out on their own after a little while.

Satisfied, he turned his attention to Lisa. The poor girl walked a couple of feet away from him, no doubt still half-convinced that he may be some godawful pervert, and cradled her arm against her chest.

Quentin cleared his throat and then asked, "Is it your shoulder?"

Lisa sniffed and her head bobbed briefly, only for her to cry out in pain a second later.

"All right. We can't walk forever. I shall have to call for a lift." He pulled out his phone.

"But the cops—"

"You may well have a broken bone. And I certainly have the injuries to prove self-defense should they ever put two and two together." Quentin thumbed the screen of his phone, only to find a text message waiting for him.

Going to the Theophrastus. *It's a yacht. Won't be long. We took your invitation.*

He blinked at the sheer incongruity of it. Who on Earth had Laurence taken with him, and why?

So much for Laurence picking them up. He would have to call for a taxi instead. But before he could, the phone in his hand rang, and *The Jack in the Green* showed on the screen.

"Laurence?" It was a foolish question, and he could kick himself for asking it into the phone. Of course it wasn't Laurence. He was on a bloody yacht.

"It's me, dear," Myriam said. "Bambi has gone off with your brother. They rushed out a little while ago. Are you available to come to the shop?"

Quentin glanced to Lisa and frowned faintly. "I have a... guest."

"What a pleasant coincidence. So do I. Young Kimberly came searching for you."

His lips pressed together a moment, then he murmured, "Is everything all right?"

"I would say no."

Quentin listened with growing concern as Myriam outlined events at the shop. Laurence's text message began to make more sense, and he rubbed his forehead. "I am in National City," he murmured, "and the young lady I'm with is injured. I think she may have a fracture. We're quite some way from any form of public transport."

"I'll send Ethan down to get you. What intersection are you nearest to, dear?"

Quentin squinted up at the green street signs just ahead. "West 15th and, er—" he hurried up to get a little closer "—National City Boulevard."

"All right, dear. That's ten minutes if he drives with lead feet. Stick to National City Boulevard, it will be easier for him to find you there."

He sighed with relief. "Thank you so much, Myriam. If he could bring a first aid kit, I would appreciate it immensely."

"Of course. You just sit tight and we'll get this taken care of."

By Quentin's estimation it took a little over ten minutes for Ethan to arrive. There was no public seating along National City Boulevard that they could find, and so he and Lisa wandered along it until a Jack in the Green truck screeched to a halt a couple of feet ahead of them.

He and Lisa hadn't traveled especially far in the intervening time. Sirens announced the arrival of an ambulance somewhere behind them and Lisa had become agitated by the sound.

"What if they save him?"

He blinked at her. It seemed such an awful thing to say, but the poor girl was in shock. "I don't understand."

"He'll tell them it was me."

"It was self-defense," he murmured.

It didn't seem to reassure her, but that was entirely reasonable in his estimation. The only adult in her life had not been a trustworthy figure, and now she was out of her home with a man she had never met before. Who would believe a single word anyone said in her place?

Ethan hopped from the truck and waved. "Hey! Over here! I got the first aid kit, dude."

His swift movements seemed to have even further impact on Lisa, who began to backtrack. "Who's this?"

"This is Ethan." Quentin turned to face her, but didn't follow. That wasn't the way to gain the confidence of a wounded animal, so he very much doubted that it would work any better for a teenage girl. "He'll take us somewhere safe. But I would like to pop that arm of yours in a sling so that you don't have to keep holding it, if that's all right? Then once we arrive we'll be able to look it over properly." He paused briefly, then added, "You're gifted, aren't you?"

She snorted at him. "I'm what?"

"Gifted. Psychic. Whatever term you wish to use." He tilted his head slightly. "You have an ability that no one else does."

"How—" She shook her head and took another step back. "How do you know?"

"I was told." Well, more that it was inferred, otherwise Kane would not have sent him here, but he saw little reason to go into that right now. "I am, also. As is the person who told me."

She eyed him, then looked back to the row of broken street lamps in their wake. "You're a mutant," she breathed.

"Er..." He winced and looked to Ethan, who gave him a thumbs up, so he looked to her and answered, "Yes."

"Good guys or bad guys?" She squinted at him.

"I'm not wholly convinced that anything is ever that simple—"

"Good guys," Ethan cut in. "C'mon, we've gotta get back to the shop."

"Are they mutants?" Lisa nodded to the van.

They?

Quentin looked. He saw only Ethan on the sidewalk, but there was another behind the wheel. A complete stranger. He blinked.

"Naw, we're just regular dudes. I'm Ethan." Ethan pointed to the cab. "That's Aiden, my boyfriend."

The young man at the steering wheel waved cheerily through the windshield.

"You're gay?"

"Gay as the day is long!" Ethan beamed.

Lisa stepped forward, then nodded. "Okay," she muttered.

Quentin offered a brief smile and took the kit from Ethan, then set to work on checking Lisa for injuries.

Lisa sat up front with Aiden, and Quentin shared the back with Ethan, so it wasn't until they arrived at the shop that Quentin noticed Aiden wore hearing aids.

He quirked an eyebrow in surprise. Laurence hadn't—to his knowledge, at least—mentioned that Aiden was deaf, and the last thing Quentin wanted was to cause any offense by behaving like a fool. He would have to ask Laurence whether there were any particular etiquette involved.

"Quentin, dear!" Myriam bustled down the back steps to sweep him into a tight hug, which avoided his bloodied arm. "Thank goodness you're here. Oh, you poor thing!" She swept on past him to Lisa and began to fuss over her. "Come on in, let's get you something to eat. You look like you've had a terrible time."

Myriam worked her magic quickly, that was certain. She had Lisa indoors and with a hot chocolate in her hands in no time, all while checking Lisa's shoulder and re-doing the sling to make it fit better across the back of her neck.

"You must stay the night," she insisted. "You and Kimberly would get along wonderfully, I'm sure, and I doubt she will mind letting you have the bed. And I'll stay, of course."

Quentin eased his jacket off while she took care of Lisa, and fiddled with the tattered sleeve of his shirt. It had adhered to the blood on his skin now, and he was hardly about to strip in front of all and sundry to wash his wounds. He sighed and pulled the jacket back on.

"Did Laurence give any indication as to when he and Freddy might return from their yacht excursion?" he murmured.

"Nope," Ethan said. "But I figure it won't be long, right? They're just gonna go get the gun and come back."

"Hmm." Quentin nodded. "Then if it is quite all right, I shall wait here for Laurence to give me a lift ho—"

He was interrupted by a soft clearing of the throat from the stairs. Kimberly stood there, her fingers entwined together.

"Kimberly!" He smiled broadly, but the smile didn't last. Her shoulders were hunched, and her head was bowed. "What's wrong?"

"I can't—" She shook her head and sat on the bottom step.

Quentin frowned and eased past Ethan and Aiden to crouch before her. "It's all right," he murmured. "You're quite safe here."

She shook her head with urgency and peered through her bangs at him. "The note," she whispered. "I gave it to you."

He nodded. "I understand. Kane made you steal from the gun show—"

She let out a groan of frustration and jabbed a finger at her watch. "Today!"

"Is this the note Laurence had earlier?" Ethan asked.

Kimberly nodded frantically.

"What did it say?" Aiden's voice was unfamiliar, and it made Quentin look toward him.

"I didn't choose to go," Quentin said. "Today." He looked back to Kimberly. "You didn't choose to go today, either. Of course not. It's all right—"

She stared at him wild-eyed and pointed at the floor.

Quentin shook his head slowly. She wasn't making any sense.

Myriam gasped. "Oh. Oh, I think that she means she didn't choose to come here today, either."

Kimberly threw her hands up.

"Kane." Quentin blinked quickly. "Kane made you come here."

She stared at him, desperation in her eyes.

"But why…" His breath caught, and he rose to his feet.

"It's a trap?" Ethan shook his head. "I don't get it."

"What marina is the *Theophrastus* moored at?" Quentin spoke faintly.

"Shelter Island," Kimberly said.

Quentin inclined his head, and turned toward Aiden. "Would you be so kind as to take me to Shelter Island as quickly as you can, please?"

Aiden already had the van's keys in hand, and he nodded grimly. "Let's go."

All Quentin had to do was stay calm for the duration of a twenty-minute drive.

And then all hell could break loose.

54

LAURENCE

Laurence sat.

He didn't want to, but his body did it, and Freddy sat beside him with an expression far more neutral than Laurence's own felt.

"There." Kane smirked. "Neither of you so much as move without my say-so. You're going to sit right here and allow me to tell you both what to do this evening."

Laurence snarled. The spike of fear, denied the ability to run, was transforming into something darker. With his option for flight removed, fight was desperate to rear its head. "You sent her to us," he growled. "You used a kid to get us here, didn't you?"

"Well, you seemed so reluctant to meet with me yourself." Kane chuckled at him. "And this is the elusive Frederick d'Arcy. What a pleasure to meet you at last. Tell me—" he licked his lips and leaned forward. "Why did you buy my house?"

Freddy gritted his teeth and narrowed his eyes. "To force your hand." His expression shifted slowly, from resistance to alarm.

"Yeah. How's that working out for you?" Kane barked a short laugh and eyed Laurence. "We're just waiting for Mia and Sebastian to return. They're off wrecking the yacht's electronics as we speak. Communications, security, fire suppressors, navigation.

You know, all those things a yacht tends to need when it has the city's richest and most powerful politicians on board."

"How did you do it?" Laurence tried to flex his fingers, to test the extent of Kane's orders, but they wouldn't budge. "How did you get her to make sure it was just the two of us?"

"It takes more pawns than one to win a game," Kane scoffed. "I chose this event because you'd need Frederick's help to get into it. You need an invitation, and you don't have one, but I made sure that one was sent to Quentin. It would have overplayed my hand to have one sent directly to the Viscount here."

Laurence swiveled his eyes toward Freddy. "You're a Viscount?"

"It's only a courtesy title," Freddy drawled.

"Nobody cares." Kane patted his palms against his thighs. "I don't have to use my power on every word I utter, you see. I can hide commands in plain sight, where people don't expect to find them. I can bury them beneath layers of conversation, planting them like seeds until they bear fruit further down the line." He grinned. "Kimberly has no idea that she's betrayed you. She thinks I've specifically told her *not* to go to you, *not* to tell you about the gun."

"Except you simply didn't use your gift on the word *not*," Freddy murmured. "How infantile."

Laurence bit his lip. Apparently goading bad guys ran through the d'Arcy gene pool, too.

Kane's smile transformed into an ugly sneer. "Laurence, get up."

Laurence jerked to his feet. "Kane—"

"Shut up. Go into the bathroom." Kane gestured toward a door. "You know where the gun is. Go fetch it and bring it here, then sit again."

Laurence fought every step of the way, but it didn't make a damn bit of difference. He did as ordered. The bathroom had a square ceramic sink embedded in a wooden pedestal, and beneath it was a cupboard which spanned between the wall and the shower enclosure. He crouched and opened the cupboard, and found the gun case tucked against the left-hand side.

"Honestly, whatever your intentions, I think you will find Icky far less likely to kill you if we are both alive by morning," Freddy said. "Particularly Laurence. I fear he might pop your head off if you harm Laurence in any way."

"Quentin," Kane rasped, "is dead by now. He won't give a damn what happens to either of you."

All Laurence could do was pick up the case and carry it back to the living room. He sat on the couch and rested the case across his knees, utterly unable to give voice to the rage which seethed on the tip of his tongue.

He can't be dead.

He can't be!

The fury in his heart began to coalesce. It hardened and condensed until it became pure and clear.

I will kill you.

Freddy eyed him, then smirked at Kane. "I see. Then apparently I'm an Earl now. If you could bump off my father too, that would be ideal. That way I shall be a Duke, and you can keep your silly little house by the sea. Call it a gift, if you will."

"You think I'm fucking joking here?"

Freddy laughed. "Well, really. Do you not watch *any* films at all? Do you honestly believe someone else has taken care of Icky for you when a bloody *wildfire* didn't do it?" He rolled his eyes then looked to Laurence. "Would you believe the stupidity of this blithering fool?"

Are you insane?

He was a d'Arcy. Of course he was insane. But Laurence couldn't figure out what the fuck Freddy intended other than to rile Kane even more.

The door clicked behind him. Laurence couldn't turn. All he could do was listen as footsteps approached.

"Done," Sebastian grunted. "Mia's just setting the charges. She'll be done in a few minutes."

Charges? The word wouldn't come out of him. No words would.

"Finally." Kane clapped his hands together. "Laurence, open the case."

Laurence's hands went to the clasps on either side of the handle on the little plastic case. He thumbed them until they popped open, and pushed the lid back.

Inside, fitted snugly into black foam, was a pistol and a silencer, just like Kim had said. There was a small plastic ammo case embedded in the foam to the left of the gun. Laurence had no idea about make or model. Guns totally weren't his thing, but if he could point it at Kane for so much as a split second he wouldn't hesitate to pull the trigger.

"Load it."

His hands pulled the gun from the foam, and then he turned the cold, silken metal in his fingers as he tried to work out how to get the damned magazine out. In movies the things just kind of fell out whenever necessary, but now that it was in his hands he wasn't sure how it actually worked.

Kane sighed. "Fine. You can speak now. Do you even know how to use a fucking gun?"

"No," Laurence growled. "Of course I don't. I'm a florist!"

Sebastian leaned over his shoulder and pointed to a small button near the trigger. "Press that," he said softly.

The magazine slid neatly out into Laurence's palm.

"Now press each round in, one at a time, facing forward. Don't rush it." Sebastian's instruction was calm and measured.

"Do it," Kane hissed.

Laurence ground his teeth. Every bullet scraped against the metal of the magazine as he forced it in. The resistance was surprisingly strong, like the bottom of the magazine was pushing back against him, and the more bullets he got in there the more difficult it became until the last one clicked into place. "Why? Why not just get your people to do this?" He snarled and pushed the magazine back into the gun. "You want my fingerprints all over it, don't you?"

"Very clever. Now, cock the gun, Laurence."

This bit he was pretty sure he could work out. He grabbed the top of the gun and snapped it back, and it rocked forward under its own steam with a horrible click.

"Aim it at Frederick."

"No—" Laurence's arm snapped out to his right, and the gun almost brushed against Freddy's arm.

Freddy narrowed his eyes.

"Here is what you are going to do, Laurence." Kane stood slowly and tucked his shirt into his waistband. "You are going to leave this room in a moment and enter the party, where you will seek out Glen Lansky and, with a great deal of showmanship, you are going to shoot him. You are going to scream about the inequality of distribution of wealth. Think of something juicy. You will aim to kill, and if you do not kill on the first try you will continue shooting him until he is dead. Then, and only then, you will turn the gun on yourself. And as with our friend Glen, if you fail to kill yourself on the first try, go again until you get it right." He raised his chin. "You won't mention my name. You won't mention any of us, in fact. Put the suppressor on."

"Why?" Laurence spat. He dug the silencer out of the case and screwed it into the barrel. "Why are you doing any of this?"

"Because one day," Kane answered calmly, "I will run this city. And both you and your beloved are a threat to every psychic in town. Two birds, one stone, all that."

"And the charges?" Laurence stared at him. "What's that? Is that a bomb? Why? With Lansky dead, why do you need that?"

Kane smirked. "Because the media loves a good lone terrorist. Think of it." He spread his hand out in front of him as though painting a headline. "Mentally unstable young man, poor family, struggling to make ends meet, targets wealthy politicians who fiddle while Rome burns. Assassinates his target in cold blood, sets bomb to take out the rest of the one-percenters after he kills himself. All good mentally ill gunmen shoot themselves. It immediately tells the audience that they'll never understand your brand of crazy, and they can move on to the next story without giving a shit." He beckoned Freddy to stand. "Frederick, you're with me. Can't leave the purse strings lying around, can we?"

Freddy stood, his motions mechanical. He looked toward Laurence, gray eyes calm and his chin raised.

"Go, Laurence," Kane said. "Win an election for me."

"By killing the opposition?" Laurence's feet jerked him toward the door.

"Hey. Politics is a cutthroat business." Kane waved farewell. "Knock 'em dead."

55

QUENTIN

Aiden skewed the truck against the curb and parked.

"Thank you." Quentin threw the door open and launched himself from the passenger seat before Aiden could respond. He ran toward the row of yachts moored with their sterns to the dock. Most were mega-yachts at this end of the marina, and he had to read the names emblazoned on the hulls until he picked out the *Theophrastus*.

Of course it had to be the yacht with the metal detector and security staff at the entrance.

The *Theophrastus's* gangway was fully extended and sloped down from the main deck to the dockside, passing over the lower deck's swim platform and terminating a couple of feet from the metal detector. It would be simplicity itself to circumvent the detector—or even run straight through it—and leap on board, but the trouble was that security would be on his tail.

His decision was made by the time he reached the staff.

"Sir, I need to see—"

Quentin ignored them as he sprinted past and leaped from the dock to the swim platform.

Shouts erupted at his back. He took the stairs up to the main deck three at a time and charged at the saloon doors.

"Icky!"

The shout came not from the saloon. It was open air, to Quentin's left, and he veered toward it without hesitation. He rounded the outer corner of the main saloon in time to catch sight of Sebastian hauling Freddy backward toward the cabin doors.

Blood trickled down from Freddy's nose in a dark splash against his pale skin, and Sebastian's forearm was coiled around his throat like a python.

Between them, Kane.

"You—" Quentin began.

Freddy jabbed a finger frantically at the saloon as Sebastian dragged him backward.

"What'll it be," Kane spat. "Are you going to save the brother, or the lover?"

Quentin paused. He looked past Kane to Freddy, and caught him mouthing *Go* before Sebastian dragged him through a set of doors.

Kane tapped his watch. "Tick. Tock."

Footsteps charged up the deck behind Quentin. He glanced toward the rail, then raised his chin and with little more than a thought sent Kane flying over the side.

The psychic screamed in shock as he was thrown past the safety rail, but the scream ended when he hit the water below with a splash.

"Man overboard," Quentin snarled. He turned to the saloon window to his right and tore it from its fittings, sending it over the side after Kane. With any luck the two would collide.

He vaulted the ruined window ledge and landed on a table of petits fours, which gave him a vantage point above the heads of the noisy crowd within, many of whom turned to gawp at him.

There.

He picked out Laurence's curls with the ease of familiarity and leaped from the table. Those who didn't move out of his way swiftly enough were pushed aside.

Laurence had a gun. It was held discreetly down by his side, but it was a gun nonetheless. Quentin was less familiar with handguns than he was with shotguns, but it didn't require an expert to recognize a semi-automatic pistol.

"Laurence!" Quentin grabbed his arm.

Laurence's eyes were dark with terror. "I don't know what Lansky looks like," he hissed. "I can't shoot him if I don't know which one he is, and I can't shoot myself if I haven't killed him."

"You aren't bloody shooting anyone." Quentin ripped the gun from Laurence's grasp.

Laurence howled and tried to grapple him for it.

Kane had done this. He'd given Laurence a gun and a target.

Are you going to save the brother, or the lover?

Both.

Quentin stripped the gun swiftly as he darted away from Laurence. He shed parts. First the suppressor, then the slide. He threw them carelessly as he dismantled the weapon.

Laurence caught his arm and dug fingers into the shot-spattered skin.

Pain stabbed through and into Quentin's chest. He thumbed the magazine eject and flung the recoil spring underfoot before Laurence bore him to the ground.

They landed heavily among a widening circle of partygoers.

"Give me the gun," Laurence snarled.

"I can't," Quentin whispered. He offered the grip, all that remained of the pistol.

Laurence snatched it from his hands and stared at it, and then a slow grin began to curl his lips. "You're a genius, baby."

"There!" The yell interrupted what Quentin had been about to say, and the guests parted to allow security through.

"Freddy," Quentin said.

"Where's Kane?"

"Overboard."

Laurence nodded. "Go."

Quentin rolled to his feet as Laurence began yelling at the security guards, and as he darted toward the cabins he could hear Laurence's tirade begin.

"What the hell is wrong with you people? There's a man overboard, and you're in here trying to do what exactly? Find a fucking life preserver?"

He couldn't stay. Laurence would be magnificent, he had no doubt, but Sebastian had Freddy, and if Kane reached them before Quentin did, it'd be over.

He shouldered the doors and barged through.

SEBASTIAN HELD a gun to the back of Freddy's head, but Freddy looked more concerned by the fistful of fire inches from his nose. Sweat trickled down his face, and he was taking quick, shallow breaths.

Quentin slid to a halt.

It was just the three of them. The corridor extended beyond Freddy and Sebastian to cabins and likely a more private saloon, but here in the modernist hallway with its Lalique glass inserts and Philippe Starck furniture they had come to an impasse.

"Let him go, Sebastian." Quentin spread his hands slowly. "It's over."

"You know none of us have any choice," Sebastian spat. "I don't even know whether we'll be free of him once he's dead. It runs deep. He's had us for *years*!"

"Icky—"

Quentin heard a light footfall just as Freddy spoke, and he turned in time to see Mia's hands dart toward his midriff.

No. He'd learned this lesson the hard way today. Allowing anyone into close combat was asking for trouble.

He pushed her away, hard enough to send her back several feet, but not to slam her into anything.

Sebastian and Mia were innocents. Living, breathing pawns Kane had sunk his claws into and held prisoner within their own bodies. None of this was their fault. They weren't monsters—not like Kane, not like Lisa's father.

Not like his own father.

The fire which surrounded Sebastian's fist flared, and Quentin pulled Freddy forward. He dragged his twin across the carpet and interspersed himself between Freddy and the jet of fire which shot toward them both, then batted the fire aside with the back of his hand. It hit a sheet of glass with a *shhh* and evaporated.

"Bloody hell," Freddy gasped. "Go easy, Icky. They've wrecked the yacht's electronics. I think they mean to scuttle it."

"Head ashore," Quentin muttered. "Take as many with you as you can."

Freddy didn't answer, but Quentin heard his retreat and the brief burst of noise as the doors to the saloon opened for a moment.

"Where's Kane?" Mia snapped.

"Quentin threw him overboard," Sebastian answered. Fire sprang to life around his hand to replace the one he'd thrown moments before.

Mia checked her watch, then swore. "Too fucking late."

A dull *whump* came from somewhere below deck. Quentin felt it vibrate the floor beneath his feet.

As if a switch had been flicked, Mia and Sebastian both launched themselves at him. Neither looked pleased about their actions. Mia ran with her hands outstretched. Sebastian was at her heels shooting fire at Quentin as he raised his gun to aim.

Quentin continued to flick the fire aside, and threw Mia against the wall. He was about to wrench Sebastian's gun from his grip when the yacht slowly tilted to the right, and the shot whizzed past his ear as the motion threw Sebastian off-kilter.

He could hear screams from behind him. His ears rang from the gunshot. He wrenched the gun away before Sebastian could fire it again and caught the incoming bolt of fire in his left hand, then threw it back and fed it until it was three times the size Sebastian had mustered. There was no time for him to marvel at how drastically his control of fire had improved.

Sebastian yelped and ducked below the gulf of flame. It seared over his head and impacted against the far wall, but he already had another in hand to throw before it got there, and Quentin strode toward him, ready to deflect it.

Mia jabbed at his outstretched hand and managed to glance her fingers across his. The electric shock numbed his hand, and he pushed her back with his gifts before she could do any more damage with hers.

The yacht was listing more forcefully now. The footing grew unsteady as the weight to the stern shifted around, presumably while people evacuated onto the dock in a panic.

"We have to go," he shouted. Without functioning systems, without its pumps and counterweights and all other sorts of safety measures designed to keep the yacht afloat in spite of an emergency, the *Theophrastus* wouldn't take long to go under, and Quentin had no idea how deep the marina's waters were.

"Damn it, Quentin!" Sebastian threw a sheet of fire which blocked Quentin's view for a second. "You don't stand a chance here! It's just a matter of time!"

Quentin swept the fire aside, but Sebastian was no longer where he'd been a moment ago, and it took another second for Quentin to realize that the ex-soldier had rolled for—and grabbed—his gun. "I outmatch you both. Easily." He punched the gun toward the ceiling as Sebastian fired again. "I'm not sure that I'm the one who stands no chance."

He tore a panel from the wall and placed it in front of him as an impromptu shield. The sheet of crystal must have cost tens of thousands of dollars. Its satin finish and decorative leaves were all classically Lalique in design and manufacture, and here he was using it to ward off Sebastian's flames.

It was utterly criminal.

"You fucking idiot!" Mia came for him, only to be swept back until she landed hard in a chair. "We know your weakness."

He nodded grimly. "We're not in the water, though."

She barked a laugh. "Your *real* weakness."

Sebastian snapped off a couple of hand signals, then they both charged at him. Sebastian aimed a gout of flame directly at his eyes, and when it hit the glass it blossomed across the surface, turning the crystal into a translucent fiery glow which Quentin had to throw aside if he were to see. By the time he did, both psychics were considerably closer, and he was forced to shove them back without finesse.

"Really," he gasped. "Do tell."

Mia fell into a breakfall and rolled backward. Sebastian aimed at the ceiling and shot out a light.

"Trouble is," Sebastian shouted, "you won't kill. You won't even hurt us." He shot out another of the lights.

"But we're willing to kill you," Mia said. "Hell, we have no choice. So we'll just keep coming—" She sprinted at him.

"—And sooner or later, we'll get through." Sebastian snapped off another shot which punched out a third light.

The corridor was half in darkness now. Light jumped from Sebastian's fire and made shadows leap across the walls, and Sebastian turned to ignite a five-thousand-dollar chair behind him. The fire took hold and added another set of shadows to the already-dancing horde.

Quentin managed to push Mia back, but she was little more than a silhouette now. One more shadow among many.

Damn it, though. They were right. He couldn't hurt them during Aikido practice. He hadn't raised a finger against Lisa's father, who arguably deserved everything he'd ended up getting, and now here he was having a shoving match with two people who were set on killing him.

This wouldn't last. The yacht was going down, and he couldn't bloody swim. He didn't dare stay here until they were under water, and yet he couldn't end this fight without harming his opponents, neither of whom warranted it.

They came again. And again. The fire grew until it consumed the far end of the corridor and began to billow smoke overhead, and still Sebastian and Mia threw themselves at him until Sebastian was out of bullets and Quentin had backtracked almost to the saloon doors.

And still they came. Sebastian used the leaping shadows and more fire to mask their movements, and Quentin fell silent in a grim fight for his own survival while his brain raced as he tried to work out how to stop this without doing either of them harm.

That was the kind of thinking which allowed Lisa's father to spray him with bird shot, and to punch him in the jaw. It was the sort of nonsense which earned him a fist to the balls, which still ached an hour later. If Lisa hadn't saved his life he'd be dead now, all through his dogged refusal to hurt anything living.

Sebastian and Mia were well aware of their advantage. They ran at him without fear. More hand signals between them, and Sebastian drew on the fire at his back, then flung all of it over his head and straight at Quentin's face. As the light source shifted, so too did the shadows, which ran away like rats deserting the very real sinking ship.

Quentin had nowhere to send the fire but back to where it had been drawn from, but in the glare of light and the jump of shadows, something brushed against his chest.

There was a crack of electricity, and a jolt ran through him from sternum to spine.

Then everything went black.

56

LAURENCE

THE PARTY HAD RAPIDLY BECOME A CLUSTERFUCK. HALF A DOZEN people tried to become the center of attention, which Laurence figured was the natural result of a room full of politicians, and the security guards struggled to make themselves heard over the din.

Laurence slipped away. He wove through the crowd and toward the window Quentin had destroyed, then clambered over the table. His hands batted plates and cake stands away until he found a small knife, and he plucked it from the tablecloth on his way out.

There were two guards there, holding the rope of a life preserver they'd thrown overboard.

Kane gripped it, and he clung to the orange float for dear life.

Laurence darted back out of Kane's line of sight and stripped his tuxedo jacket off. He dropped it to the floor and peeled out of his dress pants and shoes. Every piece of cloth which took on water would drag him down, and he wasn't willing to hand Kane any advantages.

He dragged his shirt off over his head and ditched it.

"Don't worry. I'm a trained lifeguard."

He wasn't, of course. But as he put the knife between his teeth, leaped over the railing, and dived over the edge, it was probably best not to tell them that.

Laurence stretched his arms forward together and his hands pierced the surface of the water a second before his head went under.

Goddess, it was cold! Not the bitter chill of the ocean in winter, but even in the middle of summer San Diego's waters were hardly ever above seventy degrees. He had to concentrate to hold onto his breath before the sudden shock in temperature could force it from his body, and he twisted in the water to right himself.

He opened his eyes slowly, blinking a few times while he adjusted, and then he scoured the water above for Kane.

There.

Legs kicked desperately at the water. The bastard was trying to get away.

No.

You're mine now.

A cruel smirk twisted his lips, and he powered through the water toward those legs. He wouldn't be able to punch Kane; the water's resistance would rob any such blow of most of its strength. But all a knife had to do was puncture, and the damage would be done.

He took the knife from between his teeth and slowed his approach, coming at Kane from the side to avoid his kicking legs.

He was the hunter, and his prey was within reach.

Laurence kicked forward and coiled his arm around Kane's waist, and without hesitation he jammed the knife into the older man's gut.

A little puff of blood clouded the water, and slowly grew into a miniature mushroom cloud. Kane's body jerked in Laurence's arm and began to sink.

Laurence coiled his legs around Kane's and clung to him as Kane slipped free of the life preserver until they were both below the surface.

Kane's eyes were wide. He opened his mouth, but all that came out were bubbles and indistinguishable noises.

Laurence grinned in triumph.

Kane had wasted his air on a command which Laurence couldn't decipher, and that mistake would cost him his life.

Laurence remained wrapped around the writhing psychic like a constrictor. All he had to do was wait. Kane's flailing and panic ensured that they weren't buoyant enough to make it to the surface. His prey was dying, and now Laurence's only choice was whether to wait for him to drown, or to give him a swift death.

A dull *whump* vibrated through the water, and everything shifted. There was a sudden undertow, and it sucked Laurence and Kane toward the hull of the *Theophrastus* until they collided against the yacht's thick metal skin.

The impact broke them apart, and Laurence lost his hold on the knife. It gleamed a second, then sank into the darkness.

He snarled in impotent fury as churning water spat him away from the yacht, only to pull him in again. He couldn't see Kane, and his own lungs had begun to burn. He must have lost some air when he hit the hull.

He twisted and propelled himself toward the surface. The life preserver should still be there. All he had to do was reach it, so he swam with all his might and fought the sucking current which threatened to drag him down with every passing second.

Thank fuck I ditched the tux.

Laurence fought like a demon as his lungs burned. He had no choice but to exhale, but before his body could betray him he broke the surface, took frantic breaths, and trod water.

There were screams and shouts from far above. Either he was imagining things or the yacht was at a weird angle now.

The life preserver bobbed past, and he kicked himself toward it until he managed to hook an arm over the hard plastic. He gasped for precious air.

With a splash, Kane's head popped out of the water ten feet away. Laurence heard his desperate, labored breaths.

Their eyes met, and Kane opened his mouth.

Fuck.

Laurence released the life preserver and ducked under the water before Kane could form a sentence.

His only hope was to get to Kane before he was forced to

surface, so he pushed through the choppy water and kept his head down. And without a weapon, all he had was his own body. His limbs, his hands, his teeth.

He didn't think of himself as a killer, but instinct had guided his hand when he stabbed Jack, and it did so now. He pierced through the water and snaked around Kane's body.

No mercy, this time. No wait. There would be no second chance for Wilson to escape.

Laurence dragged him down and curled his legs around Kane's waist. He hooked an arm under one of Kane's while the other man beat a fist against his chest.

Then he jammed his hand under Kane's jaw, took a firm hold, and twisted everything from his hand down to his toes.

Kane's neck snapped, and the crack sent a sharp sensation through his hand that was immediately followed by a rush of air from Wilson's mouth.

The body went limp, and Laurence kicked off against it before it could drag him down. By the time he surfaced, he'd lost sight of Kane completely.

He was triumphant. His prey was dead.

Laurence didn't even try to hold back the satisfaction that swelled within him.

He propelled himself from the water and up onto the dock, where hands helped him to his feet.

"Nothing?"

Laurence wiped water from his face and focused on the man who'd asked him the question. He was in a security uniform, and his features were only vaguely familiar. Laurence recognized him as one of the people who had been trying to rescue Kane.

Laurence allowed his shoulders to hunch, and he shook his head, injecting faux desperation into his voice. "Nothing," he agreed. "I'm sorry. I tried."

The security guard gave an abrupt, sympathetic nod.

Laurence looked to the *Theophrastus*. It listed to the right, and the back of it had raised a couple of feet from where it sat when Laurence first boarded. People scurried down the gangplank in a panic and then clustered at the bottom, which was causing chaos as more partygoers attempted to evacuate into what had effectively become a gridlock.

He forced his way through the milling bodies and grabbed the gangplank's railings, then hung on as he made his way back on board, going hand over hand, foot over foot, on the wrong side of the rails. Shouts went up behind him, briefly, and he ignored them.

He had to find Quentin.

At the top of the gangplank he leaped another railing and landed on a seat cushion. It looked easier to run over all the furniture than through the crowd, so he did that until he made it to the deck alongside the main saloon. His clothes were still piled there, abandoned, but there was no time to worry about them, and he sprinted past.

Heat radiated from the doors, which gave way as he shot through them, and the sight which greeted him made him stumble to a halt.

Quentin was dead.

It was unmistakable. His skin was gray. The swirl of energy Laurence always felt in his presence was little more than an eddy. The body lay on its back and eyes stared sightlessly at the ceiling, pupils wide and black.

Sebastian and Mia crowded the corpse. Mia had her hands on Quentin's chest, while Sebastian seemed to be trying to keep a raging inferno at bay.

Laurence screamed. He roared. He swore a thousand curses all without names as he launched forward.

If he couldn't have Quentin, he would at least have vengeance.

"Whoa. No." Sebastian leaped up and blocked Laurence's path. "Stop. Give her a second."

Laurence lashed out at the bigger man, his fingers curved like claws, but Sebastian caught his wrists and held them in mid-air.

And then the energy swelled. It sucked on Laurence's own like a black hole consuming matter, and he gasped as the familiar pull re-instated itself. A pull which was usually little more than a background sensation.

Until it was gone.

"All right," Mia said. "His heart's going properly again. It might take a few minutes for him to come around."

Sebastian released Laurence and stepped aside. The fire had leaped closer without him to act as a bulwark to it, and he cursed. "Mia, go get the crew to safety!"

Laurence slipped around the bigger man and dropped to Quentin's side.

Quentin was breathing.

He wasn't gray.

Laurence scooped Quentin into his arms and clutched him tight. Mia looked ready to say something to him, but he bared his teeth at her, and she turned to sprint out the door.

Fire.

Everything was on fire. Laurence's voice was hoarse from screaming and smoke inhalation.

The yacht was going to burn down, with them still in it.

Shit, he hated fire. Too dangerous. Too unpredictable. Too goddamn pretty.

Just like Quentin.

But Laurence couldn't leave him here. Not like this.

"Quen!" he screamed. "Quentin! Wake up! You have to wake up!"

"There's no time!" Sebastian yelled. "I can't hold this off much longer. We've gotta go!"

Laurence pushed himself to his feet, the featherlight body cradled in his arms, and together they ran from the flames before the fire could swallow them whole.

57

QUENTIN

His chest felt as though he'd been kicked square in the center by an angry horse.

Quentin fought to open his eyes. He was in bed, certainly, but without any of the chemical smells or anodyne noise of a hospital. The room was unfamiliar, with the inoffensive decor endemic to hotels. The floor-to-ceiling windows that overlooked skyline and water alike told him which one. This had to be Freddy's suite at the Palomar.

Thirst stuck his tongue to the roof of his mouth. He felt clean, not a trace of smoke in the air or on his person, so he must have been bathed at some point.

He sat up slowly as he assessed himself. Most things appeared to be in order: he could wriggle extremities and move limbs without pain, and the motion didn't cause him any dizziness or nausea, so he looked down at his bare chest to work out why it hurt so much.

There were no marks. Well, none which hadn't been there before. Perhaps all the bruising was inside, below the skin.

Quentin grimaced. Had Mia shocked him so badly that it had interfered with his heart? If so, how was he still alive?

And where was Laurence?

"Laurence?" His voice cracked, so he swallowed and tried again. "Laurence!"

"Right here, baby! One second!"

Quentin sighed and fell back against his pillows.

Laurence was safe.

The florist hurried into the bedroom like a vision, an angel of mercy descending from the heavens. The sun shone in through the windows and gilded his curls. He was glorious.

And Quentin wanted him.

He couldn't define how or why, couldn't put a word to this need which clawed at his insides. Without Laurence at his side life was hollow and meaningless, but *with* him there was music and color and heart and soul.

"Hey." Laurence grinned as he sank down on the edge of the bed. "You okay?"

"I am now that you are here." Quentin reached for Laurence's hand and held it tight. "What happened? Why are we here?"

Laurence puffed out his cheeks and looked down to their hands. "Oh, man. Where to even start?" He licked his lips. "Kane's dead."

"How?" His skin felt suddenly cold. He hadn't intended to kill Kane by tossing him overboard, but what if the man couldn't swim?

Had Quentin killed him?

"It wasn't you, hon." Laurence shook his head. "It was me."

"You killed him?" he breathed.

"Once he was dead, everyone he ever controlled was free." Laurence's fingers squeezed, but he didn't look up. "Mia saved your life. Kim was able to tell us everything Kane wouldn't let her say before. Some of the kids have even gone home to their families, Quen. That means Kane was keeping them against their will. They were prisoners. He took kids from their parents, their brothers and sisters, their schools, just because they were gifted." He sighed. "Hate me if you have to, but Kane was a monster, and I don't…" He hesitated, then shook his head. "I don't regret what I did."

"You do. You must." Quentin frowned softly and raised his hand to cup Laurence's cheek. "You are not a killer, Laurence."

"No, *you* aren't a killer," Laurence countered. His head pressed against Quentin's palm, and he let out a soft breath. "Goddess, Quen, you've gotta learn. Sebastian says they beat you because you refused to protect yourself."

"I refused to hurt them. They were innocent."

"But you can still look after yourself!" Laurence jerked back and to his feet, wrenching his fingers free. "Self-defense is an option, Quen! What if Mia did something to you she couldn't fix? You'd be dead!"

Quentin pinched the bridge of his nose. His head began to ache.

He loathed arguments. Raised voices, uncertain outcomes. They seemed tolerable enough when it was with an enemy, but with Laurence?

And when Laurence was right?

"I will do better," he said faintly.

Laurence blinked at him. "You... You mean that?"

"You deserve better." Quentin tilted his head back so that he could meet Laurence's gaze. "Considerably better. I have treated you abominably, and yet for some reason you remain by my side, where I need you the most. I cannot count on that forever. I must do better to be worthy of you."

Laurence's cheeks pinked. His shoulders slumped. The fight left him, and he sat down. "It's hard," he said quietly.

Quentin bit his tongue. The words which wanted to escape were lewd. Uncouth. Nothing at all like the sort of thing which anyone should say. They surprised him.

But maybe they would help.

"Perhaps I could help with that," he mumbled.

"I don't know how. There's so much I-" Laurence broke off, eyeing him.

Quentin's cheeks were hotter than hell, and he bit his lip.

"Oh Goddess!" Laurence straightened up. "Did you just make a sex joke?"

Quentin coughed. "I, er. Maybe. I don't know. Was it too far?"

"You're dirty!" Laurence's dark eyes were alight. It was as though clouds had parted. "You can help me with that any time you want, baby. Like, seriously. Any time. Maybe even several times."

"But not right now." Freddy's voice drawled from the doorway. "Urgh, it's sickening. Put it away, children; you have guests. Go on, in you go."

Quentin grabbed the sheets and pulled them up to cover himself. He stared in horror at Freddy. How could the man allow anyone to see him in this state?

Pepper and Grace thundered into the room, their tails cycling like helicopter rotors. Pepper leaped up onto the bed and stuck her tongue in his face, while Grace leaned against Laurence's leg and whimpered with excitement.

Freddy chuckled. "Fear not. It's a dog-friendly hotel." He gestured toward Quentin, but looked at Laurence. "Have you shared the news?"

"Give me a chance!" Laurence rubbed his jaw.

"That wasn't the news?" Quentin blinked up at him as he used the sheets to pat his face dry, then he ruffled Pepper's ears. "Settle down, sweetie," he murmured to her.

"Useless!" Freddy sauntered into the room and dropped languidly into an armchair by the window. "I bought Wilson's house out from under him, Icky. Laurence has a copy of the keys. It's yours to live in, should you so wish, but if you do you must promise me to do away with that ghastly decor." He waved a hand. "Sell it off, use the proceeds to redecorate. I won't have all that chintz in my portfolio."

Quentin managed to get Pepper to jump down off the bed, and frowned at Freddy. "I can't possibly."

"You must. I insist. I can't bear the thought of you living in that matchbox any longer. Besides, Laurence tells me his apartment is even smaller." Freddy shuddered. "Absolutely appalling. And at least this way should any of these youngsters still require a roof over their heads, they have a responsible adult looking out for them. I am, of course, referring to Laurence." Freddy grinned.

He glanced between Freddy and Laurence, and it was clear

from their expressions - Freddy's smug, Laurence's sheepish - that they had already agreed on this before Quentin regained wakefulness.

"Why don't you stay and take care of it yourself?" he grumbled.

"Because unlike you I have a career to get back to." Freddy sighed softly. "And one of us has to be there for Nicky."

There would be no back and forth with Freddy on this, Quentin could tell. They were both equally stubborn, and Freddy had already paid for the property. To leave it empty was senseless, and it was unfair to expect Mia or Sebastian to remain.

"Very well." Quentin inclined his head. "Where is Lisa?"

"She's out on the farm with Mom," Laurence answered. "I don't think it'll be long term. She just wanted to get away from everything for a while." He flexed his jaw. "And I think being around so many men was making her uncomfortable."

Quentin pushed his anger down before it could manifest. He quashed it until it was a cold thing, heavy and dense, but incapable of breaking anything in the penthouse. "Thank you. Both."

Freddy's lip twitched. "Come along, girls," he cooed as he rose from his seat. "Let's go for walkies and leave these two alone for, oh—" he checked his phone "—I would say two hours."

The dogs bounced out of the room after Freddy, tails held high, and neither Quentin nor Laurence spoke until the click of a door downstairs.

"I can do a lot in two hours." Laurence flashed his teeth, and his eyes gleamed. "Tell me what you want, baby."

Quentin licked his lips slowly. He settled the sheets down across his lap, careful to show nothing untoward. His anger thawed and began to melt while he considered his options.

Laurence waited patiently. Just as he had done for months now, and that wasn't fair. That wasn't fair on Laurence, and it did nothing to help Quentin with his own difficulties.

He inclined his head and cleared his throat. "Would you fetch me a glass of water please, darling?"

Laurence blinked. "That's... it? I mean... Sure."

He watched as Laurence padded from the room. He listened to

the light footfalls as they descended the penthouse's stairs. The headache would begin to abate once he drank something; he was dehydrated, that was all. He could have explained that to Laurence, but it seemed so inconsequential.

Besides. Laurence did so like being told what to do.

Quentin adjusted his pillows so that they were more comfortable to sit back against. Goodness knew where they might go within the time given, but it did sharpen the mind, and he knew where to begin.

The key would be to remain calm throughout.

LAURENCE HANDED him the glass and stepped back. He had a slightly grumpy frown which Quentin found most adorable.

Was that mean of him?

He took a slow sip. "No, don't sit," he murmured as Laurence began to do so.

Laurence bounced to his feet again, then blinked.

"Close the door, darling."

"Sure." Laurence span on the balls of his feet and crossed the room in long strides. He almost slammed the door, and caught it at the last moment to press gently into the frame. "Anything else?"

The tension in his voice was exquisite.

Quentin swallowed more water. The cold seeped up into his head and began to numb the ache. He focused on that sensation, and it helped him say the words which he had decided on.

"Remove your clothes, please."

He was impressed. His voice didn't betray him. He kept it level, at a normal volume, and it sounded even to his own ears as though he had everything perfectly under control. He focused on sipping more water, but glanced to Laurence across the top of the glass.

Laurence's lips were parted. His cheeks were rosy. There was a hard look in his eyes, a sort of desperation mingled with his lust.

"Today," Quentin prompted.

Laurence groaned helplessly and wrenched his T-shirt off over his head. His muscles were taut, limned in sunlight and dusted with hair, and his whole body flexed as he threw the top aside.

Quentin swallowed a mouthful of water. "Are you in a rush?" he gasped.

Laurence stared at him. His mouth hung open, and his chest heaved for air. He shook his head, then rolled his shoulders and straightened up.

Quentin clutched the glass in both hands while he did his damndest to keep a level head. It wouldn't do to fling a table lamp at Laurence while the man unzipped his trousers.

Which he was doing very slowly.

His thumbs dipped into the waistband and his stomach rippled like a wave while his hands began to push down.

Quentin had to count down from ten, but he couldn't close his eyes. He *would not* close them.

He could do this.

Laurence turned away as his trousers dropped low enough to reveal two inches of his boxer shorts. He bent double to slide the material down his legs, displaying taut hamstrings before firm calves.

He's showing off!

Quentin's eyebrows climbed, and he did nothing to stop them. Laurence's position as he peeled off his socks and stepped out of his now-discarded trousers made a very prominent bulge in his underpants really rather impossible to ignore. The boxers were loose enough that there were gaps between material and skin, though thankfully they were shadowed and Quentin couldn't see anything beyond them.

Though he'd better bloody acclimatize himself quickly, because Laurence wasn't about to stop.

Keep counting. He'd faltered, and couldn't even remember where, so he started over.

Laurence straightened like he had all the time in the world. He laced his fingers together, stretched his arms overhead, and arched his back. Muscles shifted and created a dip along his entire spine. When he turned, it was almost balletic. His arms remained high, and he twisted on tiptoes. With his back curved, his chest was raised, and his stomach muscles were clearly defined.

Christ. He really was the most beautiful creature Quentin had ever laid eyes on.

His nipples were hardened little balls of flesh. The downy hair which lightly smattered across his chest gathered together below his belly button and drew a line to the waist of his boxers. There was a lightly-defined pair of ridges above his hips which both delved toward his groin and disappeared either side of that line of fluff, as though to form a V. Everything moved smoothly, like a machine, when he finally dropped his hands to his underwear and began to ease the waistband down.

The hair grew more dense, but also curlier. The blond showed through as curls sprang free.

And then something entirely different sprang free.

It was gone again.

The after-image of it seemed seared onto Quentin's retinas. Big, and long, and reddened, and glistening, and—

Laurence bent over, though, to push the boxers down, and it was hidden.

Quentin bit the inside of his cheek. He counted over and over, but he felt like he was teetering on the edge of a precipice, and the slightest of breezes would shove him over.

As if he knew, as if he sensed the tenuous grip Quentin held on the here and now, Laurence turned away again as he straightened. He displayed a firm arse whose cheeks dipped in delightfully at the sides, and he stood with his legs together so that Quentin couldn't see anything between them.

Ice clattered against the glass and Quentin looked down to it, then closed his eyes.

He had no idea how much time passed. Now and then he risked a peek at Laurence, and found the man waiting patiently, back turned to him.

"Christ," he said thickly. "I love you, Laurence."

"I love you too, baby." Laurence spoke gently.

Quentin set the glass aside. He spread his legs and patted the sheet down between them, and then he took a breath. "Come and sit here."

He gazed at the spot as Laurence approached. At first there was only sheet, but then there was warm skin and that familiar musk, and he was safe.

Laurence wriggled back against him until they fit together. He rested his back to Quentin's chest, and lay his hands atop Quentin's thighs, separated only by thin cotton.

Quentin slid his hands around Laurence's waist. He rested his chin on the other man's shoulder.

He could do this.

There was no bath, no water to hide anything from him, but with Laurence's body there it meant that Quentin would have to look if he wished to see *that*, and it put exposure firmly under his control.

He *would* do this.

His fingers brushed delicately through soft hair, and Laurence sighed as his shoulders lowered.

"I've dreamed about this," Laurence whispered. "Not like a vision. I don't mean I've seen this before, but I've wanted it for so long. For you to touch me like this. The way you play the piano. Like I'm important to you, like you want to hold me."

Quentin tilted his head until his cheek rested against Laurence's jaw. He gazed to the edge of the bed, beyond Laurence's toes. There was a thing at the lower edge of his vision, past Laurence's chest, which could not be ignored, but he stared at a fixed point in the hope that he would grow accustomed to it.

"You are important to me," he whispered. "You mean everything to me."

"Words," Laurence said, strained.

Quentin nodded faintly. He understood.

Laurence was a being of touch, of sensation and instinct. Quentin could shower him with poetry, but what Laurence understood was *this*, and Quentin had starved him of it.

"Then let me show you," he murmured.

Quentin spread his fingers and drew his hands slowly up

Laurence's chest. His attention turned from the end of the bed to the rise and fall of Laurence's ribs, which quickened with some of Quentin's movements and evened out with others.

It was like learning to play all over again. Laurence's body was an instrument which Quentin had little knowledge of, and his only tutor was the man who owned it. If Quentin wished to master this skill he would need to focus on every little clue, every ounce of feedback he elicited.

But he *would* master it.

Laurence bucked in his arms. He moaned and cried out. His fingers dug into Quentin's thighs and his breath was hard and ragged.

Quentin drove him toward a crescendo. His touch alternated between airy and firm. Sometimes he did little more than brush at the hair across Laurence's skin, and at other times he slicked his palms across those hard nipples. No musical piece worth its salt launched in at the apex; there was always a rise, and the more one teased with that rise then the more gratifying the zenith. And so he played. He teased and he drove. His fingers would lighten after Laurence's back arched, then push harder once the man's reaction began to subside.

"Quen," Laurence whined. "Quentin, oh Goddess, Quentin, please!"

Laurence had responded well to Quentin's teeth during their shared bath, and now seemed the right moment to add that, so Quentin shifted his head and pressed his teeth to Laurence's shoulder.

Then he bit.

Gently at first. As with all else thus far it made sense to introduce this element with care.

Laurence bucked and howled. His hands jerked free from Quentin's thighs and delved down between his own legs.

Quentin snarled softly in satisfaction. His teeth and hands applied pressure while Laurence thrashed in his hold.

Laurence sagged. His whole body became limp and helpless. His head fell back against Quentin's shoulder, and his sweat stuck them together. Little quivers rippled through him, and Quentin felt them through his chest, his arms, his palms, and his fingertips. There was a new scent in the room, unfamiliar but not unpleasant.

Quentin stilled his hands and lay them to rest across Laurence's stomach. He kissed where he had bitten, and then rested his chin a little to the right of that reddened spot to avoid placing pressure on it.

Success.

Not a lamp or chair out of place in the room. No broken glass. No panic.

And - if the weak little laugh which escaped Laurence was anything to go by - one *very* happy ending.

Oh, there would be aspects he would have to work on. He knew that. Not only with Laurence, but in other areas of his life too. He couldn't afford another mistake like the error he'd made with Mia.

He had too much to lose now.

"Mm?" Laurence moved just a touch.

Quentin blinked sluggishly. He hadn't spoken, had he? No. Not that he could recall. So he bounced the question back. "Mm?"

Laurence broke into a slow, lazy grin. "No words."

Quentin chuckled. "I'm learning."

He held Laurence tight, and the world was nothing more than the two of them entwined. There was a word for it, somewhere deep in Quentin's heart. A word which percolated idly toward the surface the longer they sat together. The word took all of his confusion and his worry and set it aside, replaced by something pure and simple, and when that word finally broke free he smiled.

Mine.

EPILOGUE

FREDERICK

He ensured that Icky was settled into the La Jolla house before he departed San Diego. If he hadn't, the flight risk would be significantly higher.

For all that Laurence had done in tying Quentin down, it didn't go nearly far enough for Frederick's liking. Dogs were a good start. Making Icky fall in love with him was a better one. But putting a roof over Icky's head *and* a slew of children to care for was a gift which Frederick did not dare pass up on. He had even arranged for the removals company to take Icky's bloody piano to the house to make absolutely certain.

From here on out, every step would have to be a delicate one. Even more delicate than handling that fool Wilson.

Frederick glowered out of the tinted windows at the familiar rolling green countryside. The ignominy he had been forced to endure while feigning obedience to Wilson's gift chafed against his nerves. He was glad Laurence had the balls to kill the bastard.

There was a cunning intellect to the American. He was not to be underestimated. Where Wilson's words had power over him, he had thought to strike in the water, where they would be nullified. Incredibly smart.

And Icky.

Whatever was to be done with Icky?

The man wasn't even prepared to defend himself against his enemies, let alone kill them, and if Icky wasn't about to save himself then he wasn't anywhere near ready for Frederick's needs.

Of course, if Icky weren't as immune to Frederick's powers as Father and Nicholas were, this would be considerably easier. But then perhaps that was a blessing in disguise, for if Laurence's deductions were correct, those were *not* minds Frederick wished to see into.

Well, Frederick had done as much as he could without showing his hand. He had made suggestions and fed ideas as subtly as he could. If Laurence did as Frederick believed that he would, that should have the desired effect on Icky's willingness to do harm.

He smoothed his composure as the car passed the gates. It would be another five minutes before it reached the house itself, but every second of calm counted now.

Frederick watched as the vast house hove into view. Trees gave way to sculpted landscape and centuries-old lakes, and in the center of it all sprawled Castle Cavendish, named for the ancient fortification which had once sat upon the site. All gone now, of course. Long fallen to dirt before the land was given to the newly-created Duke of Oxford in the 17th century.

The walls were cream, made from stone mined in Yorkshire and brought all the way down to Oxfordshire by canal boat over the course of a century. The undertaking took four dukes to oversee before the house was finally completed.

This was how things were done. Not for immediate gain, but for the lineage. For the future generations of the d'Arcy family who were yet to be conceived. Centuries of sacrifice and endeavor in exchange for status and power. Marriages of strategic importance, not of love. Select breeding, not idle dalliances.

Father would be livid.

But Frederick had performed his task, distasteful and confusing though it may be. And once he reported back, he would be free to head off to London and forget all about this nonsense for a while.

The car arrived before the ostentatious stone steps of the north entrance, and Frederick pushed the door open before the chauffeur could even stop the engine.

The sooner this was done with, the better.

HE TOOK the ziplocked bag from his suitcase and examined it. There was no sign that the TSA had interfered with his luggage, but he still preferred to be sure before he presented it to Father.

The crumpled shirt within looked intact. Well, as intact as one might expect after all that it had been through. The bloodstains on it were brown and dull and it was riddled with holes.

Frederick had taken it after Laurence stripped Icky and put him to bed.

"Well, this is ruined. I shall dispose of it."

Whatever Father could want a sample of Icky's blood for, Frederick couldn't imagine. All he knew was that Father didn't care whether or not the sample was fresh.

He rolled the bag so that the brown stains were hidden from the eyes of any staff he might pass by, and then headed swiftly for Father's office.

THE DUKE HADN'T DIED in Frederick's Summer-long absence, more was the pity. Indeed, the old buzzard seemed fit as a fiddle.

"You failed to bring him home," was his only greeting.

Frederick placed the bag on his father's desk. It unfurled the moment he released it. "He was resistant," he agreed.

"Mm." The duke reached for the bag and drew it across his blotter pad.

Frederick watched as those gray eyes creased in satisfaction. Whatever thoughts fed that expression were beyond Frederick's reach.

"This will do," his father murmured. "Are you off to London now?"

"This afternoon, yes." Frederick stifled a small yawn which wasn't entirely feigned. "The jet lag is abominable."

"Very good." The duke nodded.

That was it. No praise for success, no well-wishes for Frederick's career.

Just dismissal.

Frederick inclined his head and turned toward the door.

"One thing," his father said.

"Yes?" Frederick turned back to face him, but didn't approach the desk.

"Were you witness to anything... unusual?"

Frederick raised an eyebrow with measured care. Too high and it would come off as comical. Too low and it would seem as though he had understood his father's meaning. "How so?"

The duke shrugged his broad shoulders. "Peculiar weather conditions? Unusual shifts in temperature? You recall Margaret's funeral, surely?"

"Oh." Frederick made a show of mulling the question over. He had been gone the best part of three months, after all. He had to look like he was parsing each week in the light of that question. "Perhaps once or twice?" he finally offered. "I cannot say that it occurred to me at the time, but now that you mention it..." He nodded slowly. "It did get rather blowy once or twice, yes."

The duke gave a curt nod. "You may leave."

Frederick turned on his heel and strode from the office, and he didn't so much as begin to relax until five hours later, once he was settled into his London home.

It was all down to Icky now.

~ *Inheritance* continues in *Lord of Ravens* ~

ACKNOWLEDGMENTS

Big thanks to Jen for being the best alpha-reader any author could want. Without their constant help (and yes, sometimes nagging, because I work best when nagged apparently,) this book wouldn't be here now. Particular thanks for giving me a stern look and making me rewrite an entire chapter because it was naff first time around. I'm sorry I whinged about it.

Huge thanks to Ed. I don't have first-hand knowledge of being punched in the balls, among other things, so as you can imagine having an expert on hand (har har) was tremendously beneficial.

Thanks to Helen for believing in me before even knowing me. What kind of a weirdo does that? From reader to friend to basically a sister in the space of a couple of years.

Thanks to John for painstakingly constructing the series timeline from picking through each and every book because for some reason I actually thought I could hold this entire universe inside my head. Master of Continuity, and emergency spare brother!

My writing companions (without their knowing it) for Knight of Flames were largely Hurts, John Paesano, and Pet Shop Boys. I once had a dream that I was in Burger King with Neil Tennant and Chris Lowe and Chris' fries were cold. Clearly we're BFF's now. Also I haven't actually eaten in a BK for over twenty years. Thanks, brain.

Thanks, Mum! I dunno what you did, but you obviously did it right! That doesn't mean I know how to use the dishwasher all of a sudden, though.

ABOUT THE AUTHOR

AK Faulkner is the author of the *Inheritance* series of contemporary fantasy books, which begins with *Jack of Thorns*. The latest volume, *Sigils of Spring*, will be released in November 2019.

AK lives just outside of London, England, with a charismatic Corgi. Together they fight crime and try not to light too many fires on the way.

Find out more at akfaulkner.com

Sign up for the *Inheritance* newsletter at discoverinheritance.com/signup

INHERITANCE

Season One:
Jack of Thorns
Knight of Flames
Lord of Ravens
Reeve of Veils
Page of Tricks
Season Two:
Rites of Winter
Sigils of Spring

Visit discoverinheritance.com to learn more about the characters and world of Inheritance, and sign up to the newsletter.